For Virginia,

My best friend,

To say that I love you, is the greatest understatement of all.

"Time is an illusion."

ALBERT EINSTEIN

"Better three hours too soon than a minute late."

WILLIAM SHAKESPEARE

"We're all so clock wise thinking we control our time yet the sand slips through our fingers and muddles up our wine."

DICKY DOETSCH

PROLOGUE

SOMEWHERE BETWEEN DREAMS AND MEMORIES

*N*ick skimmed across the cool, blue water, the kiteboard strapped to his feet cutting deep into the Atlantic. He held tight to the bar as he glanced ahead at his neon-green kite that caught the thirty-knot wind and pulled him through the waves and into morning.

With a flick of his wrist, Nick angled the kite straight up and launched into the air. Ten feet up. Twenty feet. Thirty feet, still climbing... As he floated through the sky, he glanced down at the waves breaking on the shore before looking to the horizon, where the rising sun painted the day. The view, the sound of waves and wind and seagulls, and the briny tang of the sea enveloped him in an adrenaline-fueled serenity. "Perfection of moment," he called it, when all his senses filled to overflowing and every worry and concern fled from his mind. For the six seconds he flew, everything felt right in the world...no troubles, fears, or nightmares.

What many considered an adrenaline addiction had become a salve for Nick's soul, the only escape that brought equilibrium to his mind. Given the stresses of work, family, and life, everyone needed relief. Some found it through golf, some through alcohol, some through other forms of entertainment. Ordinary exercise wasn't enough for Nick; he needed something slightly more intense.

Since childhood, Nick had sought escapes that felt proportional to his troubles: skydiving for work, speed-skiing for life, and kitesurfing for nightmares. The faster he went, the better he felt; the higher he jumped, the farther he left his troubles behind.

It had been three years. Three years since Nick had saved his wife Julia from bullets, crooked cops, and the plane crash...all of which had never happened.

Nick still had a tough time wrapping his mind around that.

For twelve hours, he had tried desperately to save Julia. To stop the world from falling apart. To find that singular moment that would undo disaster and set the planet back on its axis. Yet, in the end, after Nick had finally succeeded, in the minds of everyone but him, those events had never occurred.

Saving Julia and the others would have been impossible, a task beyond even his imagination, if not for the watch that Shamus Hennicot had given him. The ancient, gold-and-silver pocket watch had sent him on an impossible journey to undo the horrors of those twelve terrible hours.

Shamus Hennicot, a ninety-three-year-old billionaire who still drove around in his rust-dotted '68 Buick Electra, was more than Nick's friend. More than Julia's law client and pseudo-grandfather. He was their savior.

Only Shamus knew what Nick had gone through...and what had caused his trauma-induced nightmares after. Shamus knew not from memory—because to Shamus and the rest of the world, the tragedies of that day had never happened. Shamus knew because he was the only person Nick had dared explain it all to. The only one who would believe Nick because, after all, it was Shamus's pocket watch.

"Wake up."

The voice seemed to come from the far distance. Nick looked down at the open ocean but saw nothing. It was as if the voice came from one of his dreams, echoing impossibly in the open air.

As he listened for the voice, he couldn't be sure whether it was yesterday, three years ago, or tomorrow. But one thing was clear—the voice was real, and it was calling to him.

"Wake up...."

AUTHOR'S NOTE

You will not be mistaken when you turn the next page and see Chapter 12.

The chapter numbers in this novel run in reverse order and are meant to be read that way for reasons that will become evident during your journey.

CHAPTER 12

5:00 PM

The enormous wall climbed to heaven and stretched a quarter-mile wide, like a barrier constructed to keep out the barbarian hordes. Made of five-ton granite-and-concrete blocks, the dam loomed over the green valley, its growing shadow marking time like an oversized sunDial.

Nick stood on a balcony, staring up at the 410-foot-tall marvel of engineering, constructed in 1917 to hold back the billions of gallons of the Killian Reservoir.

The blue sky and crisp, clean air of the summer day helped clear his mind and calm his nerves. He had slipped through a lower-level door onto the teak porch, hoping Julia wouldn't mind his momentary disappearance from helping prepare for the reception.

The building that loomed behind Nick was as magnificent as the dam and far more beautiful. The large castle looked like something plucked from the Middle Ages, though it had never housed a king, queen, or any other royalty. Built on a whim by the eccentric industrialist James Francis Dorchester, it had been donated to the town of Byram Hills when Dorchester left for Hawaii shortly after meeting the fourth future-former Mrs. Dorchester.

Constructed of granite, the English-style castle was adorned with corner towers, high keeps, parapets, decorative merlons, and scattered turrets, with half the structure carved into the steep, rocky hillside. While the walls and battlements were stone, the architects had softened its medieval appearance with several levels of ornamented teak porches that wrapped three sides, overlooking the carved marble statuary and ornate garden of perennials below. The interior gained warmth and character from cherry-paneled walls, thick Turkish rugs, and enormous windows that provided panoramic views of both the valley below and the adjacent dam.

The warlike fortification, created out of nostalgia rather than for defense, had served as the designated fallout shelter for the local officials and their families during the 1950s and '60s. Its thick granite blocks, fused with a cement-like mortar, would not only withstand a 1960s-era Soviet bomb but also outlast the pyramids of Giza.

Nick smiled as he looked at the thousand-strong crowd gathering in the enormous, grassy park 150 feet below and wished he were down there instead of up here, dreading the next hour of his life.

"Wake up," Julia gently stroked Nick's whiskered cheek as she kissed him awake. "Wake up, my hero. Busy evening ahead."

Nick stirred, his mind rising to the surface as he sat up straight in his office chair, twisting his kinked neck, which had stiffened during his too-short nap. His eyes locked with Julia's, the spouses each saying so much more than they could have with words. He smiled as the fog cleared and he took in his wife. Her blonde hair framed the face he had known since they were teenagers, her full lips smiling, her impish glee at waking him etched in her warm, blue eyes. He loved when she kissed him awake; there was no better way to be pulled from a dream.

He had slept for all of a half-hour, having worked all day crunching numbers on a prospective real-estate transaction and finishing his first book here in his dark-wood library office. This was after a minor incident with Marcus early this morning which had upended his normal daybreak routine.

He had picked up his best friend at 7:25 a.m., kites and boards loaded in the rear of the Jeep Wrangler, the jet ski hitched to the back in hopes of a couple of hours of kitesurfing before work. But that all went to hell when Murphy's Law stepped in on the back of fate, ending his chance of getting anywhere near the water that morning.

"How's it feel to be a hero?" Julia asked playfully.

"Not a hero," Nick groaned, clearing his sleepy voice.

"They're saying you and Marcus didn't want your names mentioned."

"It's not like we did it for recognition."

"Surely, you can at least share the details with your wife."

"Well, the flames—"

"Tell me later. It's already after three. We've got to be at the castle by four." Julia leaned in and kissed him again. "We both know you're incapable of telling a short story."

"Four? Guests aren't supposed to arrive until 5:15."

"We're the hosts, remember? It's better to be early and prepared than—"

"Late and screwed." Nick finished her sentence for the thousandth time as an incessant ticking tickled his ears. "Where are you going?"

"I have to run some errands." Julia blew him a kiss and left his office before shouting back at him, "Do me a favor and take out the garbage."

"Of course," Nick called back.

"I'll be back at 3:45. Be ready. Don't make us late."

The ticking seemed to grow and echo as Julia exited through the foyer.

"I'm going to smash this thing," Julia shouted as she walked out the front door.

Nick already regretted having bought the mahogany, man-o-war-themed grandfather clock two days ago. It had been a foolish purchase. Like fireworks to a soldier suffering PTSD, the clock's ticking reminded Nick of what he had tried so hard to forget. To make matters worse, the beautiful antique wasn't only rattling his brain; it was also rattling his marriage.

Every hour, starting with a heavy mechanical click, the giant clock would ring out a brief, seafaring tune on its internal brass bells before intoning the hour with a rhythmic chime.

The chiming had lasted all of one night. Julia said it was worse than torture: not only the annoying clicks, but also the loud peal of the bell, which risked waking Katy every hour, on the hour. It took Nick forty-five minutes to figure out how to disable the bells, but the ticking of the brass pendulum continued. He had already listed the clock for sale online and promised Julia he'd move it out to the garage by nightfall.

It was 3:41 when Nick heard Julia's car roll into the driveway. He jumped up from his desk, raced upstairs, hit the bathroom, shaved, made himself presentable, and headed for his closet. Though he knew it would make her mad, he slipped on a pair of Levi's, a polo shirt, and his twenty-two-year-old cowboy boots. He also grabbed a pair of charcoal-gray Armani pants, a button-down shirt, a tie, and a sport coat; slipped them all on a hanger; grabbed a pair of dress shoes; and prepared to face Julia's wrath.

"You've got to be kidding me," she said as Nick hung the hanger in the back of her blue Audi, then climbed into the driver's seat. She eyed him up and down. "You had to wear the jeans? You're not going to have time to change."

Nick would have plenty of time to change, more than an hour, though he had no intention of arguing with her.

"Hi, Daddy," Katy said from her car seat in the back.

"Hey, honey." Nick turned and smiled at his daughter. "Don't you look like a princess."

And she did. With white-blonde hair, giant blue eyes that matched her party dress, and a broad, giggly smile, she could warm the heart of winter.

"Say hi to Abigail." Katy held out a stuffed giraffe.

"Hello, Abigail."

"She keeps the bad people out of my dreams."

"Well, that's a good giraffe," Nick told the toy as he kissed its head. "Thank you for protecting my little girl's dreams." He handed it back. "Hi, Bonnie," he said to the teenager sitting next to Katy as he started the car and pulled out of their driveway.

"Hi, Mr. Quinn." Bonnie Powers twirled her long brown hair around her index finger the way fifteen-year-olds do when they're shy and can't figure out what to do with their hands. Still, the teenage babysitter would keep three-year-old Katy entertained and occupied during the reception.

"Thanks for coming," he told Bonnie.

"Mommy said you're her hero," Katy whispered, struggling with the word *hero*.

"Well," Nick laughed, "I guess I am." He didn't turn to look at Julia, who clearly wasn't sharing his mirth.

"Did you remember to take out the garbage?" she asked without looking at him.

Nick knew that she knew he hadn't. Her question wasn't so much about the garbage as it was to point out that he'd forgotten to do what he'd promised. Again.

Three years earlier, Julia had asked Nick to take out the garbage, as per their custom, and then she'd taken it out five minutes later when he hadn't—also per their custom. It was out in the driveway, on her way back from emptying the garbage, that Julia's water had broken.

Nick had rushed her to Greenwich Hospital, but what they thought would be an easy labor process turned into a thirty-six-hour ordeal: slow to dilate, slow to efface. They grew frustrated, but it was when Julia finally began to push that Nick became scared. Without a drop of medication, without ever considering an epidural, Julia pushed as hard as she could to get that baby out, her face beet-red, her temples throbbing, her eyes swelling unnaturally.

As Katy finally emerged, healthy and screaming, Nick turned to his wife, beaming with pride, only to find her unconscious.

"Julia?" he'd said softly, knowing how exhausted she must be. "I'm so proud of you."

But Julia hadn't responded.

"Julia?" Nick rubbed her forehead. "Julia?"

And everything had slipped to hell.

Dr. Culverhart and the nurses rushed Nick out of the room as an oxygen mask was dropped over Julia's face. Nick could see through the circular door window as they desperately worked on her: mouth to mouth, pumping her chest, jabbing a needle in her arm. Dr. Culverhart's voice turned grave as he ordered the nurses about.

Nick thought he was going to lose her, certain she would die without ever getting to hold their daughter.

But finally, she'd opened her eyes with a gasp, looking around, confused at the commotion. Through the window, he saw her mouth form the word, "Nick?"

He burst through the door and raced to her side, bending to take her in his arms, holding her as tightly as he dared.

"I thought I lost you," he said through his tears.

In his ear, Julia had whispered, "I'll never leave you, silly."

Standing on the balcony of Byram Castle, Nick stared down into the valley at nearly a thousand people playing baseball, picnicking, and getting early seats on the enormous grassy mall for the best fireworks show in Westchester County. Festivities, from parades to awards ceremonies to school-band performances, had filled the afternoon and would continue into the night, all in celebration of the Fourth of July.

Nick looked at his iPhone to check the time: 5:05. Like so many, he had disposed of his wristwatch in favor of the multi-function device that was the modern-day equivalent of his Swiss Army knife. He had wandered about the castle for almost an hour after arriving, thinking it best to stay out of Julia's way and busying himself with phone calls, emails, and the internet.

The upper reaches of the fortress held modernized conference rooms and offices, while the bowels of the stone castle seemed to exist a century or two in the past, mimicking a European stronghold in every sense. Nick had never been in a dungeon but was pretty sure the castle's subbasement came close. It felt like the center of the earth there, the depths of a man-made cave cold and damp, the echo of life above blotted out.

He explored the lower recesses like a curious child, finding a host of rooms straight out of the past, each concealed behind doors of four-inch-wide planks strapped with thick iron bands, their heavy clasps rusted with age, all unlocked, empty and forgotten.

Tired of the dank and dark and the lack of cell reception, he moved back to the balcony and spent the last hour dialing, negotiating, and checking the live feed of the Yankees game.

As he watched the crowds below, Nick couldn't help but feel a bit of envy. He was stuck up here about to endure something only a notch or two more pleasant than a root canal.

He wasn't one for glad-handing and false smiles; he had a revulsion for politics and its facades and detested writing checks to the political elite—all of which he had done over the years in deference to Julia's work world. Today, his wife's law firm, Aitkens, Isles, and Lerner, was sponsoring the meet-and-greet with Byron Chase, the senior U.S. senator from New York, who was not only the head of the

Senate Intelligence Committee, but he also sat on Appropriations, the committee that held the all-important purse strings of federal funding: one of the sources of the lifeblood that made the consulting arm of Julia's firm viable.

Unlike most politicians, Byron Chase was a "friend." Hailing from Byram Hills, he embodied the hometown-boy-made-good, a politician who many believed actually possessed integrity and honesty. He had taught at Byram Hills High School twenty years earlier and served as Nick and Julia's swim coach. Despite not knowing any stroke beyond basic freestyle, Coach Chase had spent half his time yelling at Nick about how to swim better when Nick already held every school record, was all-county, and had been the team captain two years running. Chase had spent the other half of his time telling Julia she could do so much better than staying with young Mr. Quinn.

Chase had left teaching after getting his law degree at night and quickly found himself at Aitkens, Isles, and Lerner before becoming a state representative. Soon after, he became a U.S. congressman. And then he set his sights even higher.

He had been elected to the U.S. Senate on a platform of integrity and change with a large dose of voter sympathy over the loss of his son in the Akbiquestan War. Sadly, not much had changed since his election to the Senate: only the same politically-correct stances, abstained votes on controversial bills, and the hollow rhetoric of his predecessor.

At $1,000 per handshake and $2,500 per photo-op, Nick figured his former swim coach would be leaving the meet-and-greet with a take of more than $400,000, two tea sandwiches, and four martinis.

Nick wasn't sure if he still held a real grudge against Chase for trying to push Julia away from him when they were teenagers, or if he was being stubbornly childish due to his dislike of politics.

Nick turned and saw a Secret Service agent sweeping the castle grounds. News vans from the local stations parked in front with their reporters, hoping they could wangle a sound bite or interview with the man who many said was the apparent heir to the throne of the presidency.

Well, Nick hadn't voted for Chase before and wasn't about to change that now.

Another glance at his iPhone told him that he'd lost all track of time, forgetting to change out of his jeans and into his jacket and tie. He left the balcony, rounded the corner into the reception room, and ran headlong into Julia. It took a moment for her to digest the moment before she gave Nick *the look*—her expression telling him, *I can't believe you...not again.* Julia being Julia, however, she never verbalized it, not once in their nearly nineteen years together, although it was a phrase she could have easily uttered multiple times per week.

Nick stared back at her for a moment, not minding her anger. She wore an off-white linen dress, her hair brushed out, and looked like a model who had stepped off the catwalk. Her appearance was elegant and refined, projecting her professionalism while sprinkling it with a touch of glamor. She wore the simple gold necklace with a diamond at its center and the matching earrings that he had given her last Christmas; on her wrist was her mother's gold Rolex. Though never in need of makeup, she wore a touch of lipstick and eyeliner, which accentuated her beauty.

At thirty-six years of age, Julia looked ten years younger. Her skin flawless, her eyes filled with life and projecting her unending energy. It always amazed Nick that she could work out, grocery shop, get her nails done, and feed Katy, all before he even brushed his teeth in the morning. She would race into the bedroom in tight-fitting shorts and a t-shirt, her blonde hair pulled back in a ponytail, head straight for her bathroom and closet, and—within minutes—emerge sophisticated, alluring, and ready to take down the business world.

"What's going on?" he asked innocently.

"Seriously? Beyond the fact that people are due to arrive in ten minutes and you're not dressed? Or the fact you disappeared for the last hour? All eyes are on us today—the senator, his speech, this party, the news media—all on top of a crazy day of unfinished work and missed meetings."

She moved back into the reception room, rearranging flowers, moving chairs inches to the left or right, and ensuring that every wine bottle's label on the bar faced out.

"It's Coach Chase," Nick said.

"That's right. Senator Chase. Senator Byron Chase."

"Byron? He's no Byron. His name's Carl. Carl Byron Chase. Since when did he drop Carl from his name?"

"That was twenty years ago, Nick."

"Yeah, well, he's the same man, he just wears a fancy suit and sits in a bigger office that doesn't smell like sweat and Bengay."

"He's still a senator."

"He's still an ass." Nick regretted his words before they hit Julia's ears.

"Can you just let it go?" She turned and moved closer to Nick. "For me? This all reflects on me today. Do you understand that?"

He nodded. "Sorry. I'll shut my mouth."

Julia turned to adjust the podium, opening the curtains two inches more.

"It's an awful lot of security and hoopla for a senator," Nick said softly.

"Nick..."

"I'm just saying...."

"There're some crazy people out there, even some death threats, and Chase may announce he's throwing his hat in the presidential-election ring."

"Ha," Nick said with a laugh. "That explains the reporters. With his approach to—" At Julia's glare, he shut his mouth again. "Sorry. What can I do to help?"

"Just..." Julia bit her lip. "Go get changed, hurry back to greet people when they arrive, and use that faux happy-to-see-you smile you've got in your back pocket to pretend you're enjoying yourself."

Nick walked through the entrance lobby and down a long, sconce-lined hall to the bathrooms, only to find a Secret Service agent there. He headed back to the conference room, finding another agent on his phone, and opted instead to head back down into "the dungeon."

He found the kitchen, where caterers were busy filling trays with cheese puffs, stuffed mushrooms, and shrimp skewers. Nick smiled a guilty smile at a young hostess as he grabbed a handful of mini-hot-dogs and continued down into the dark recesses of the basement.

Once again, he found rooms within rooms, a forever maze that wound about the castle's foundation and deep into the cliffside. Finally, Nick stopped in an especially bare stone chamber. He figured here was as good a place as any to change. He quickly slipped into his dark slacks and Armani jacket, stuffed his other clothes in his bag, and found a door out onto a lower balcony.

"When you escape hell, you're supposed to bring your friends with you."

Nick turned as an oversized hand fell upon his shoulder.

"Right, Katy?" the voice continued.

"Daddy!"

Katy rode upon the shoulders of an enormous bear of man.

"Hey, kiddo," Nick said. "Did Uncle Marcus bring you down here or did you bring him?"

Marcus reached up and lowered Katy to the balcony, her tiny hand holding tight to his finger. "Fourth of July, cocktail hour...where else would I rather be than hearing a politician roar about his con-quest of the jungles of DC?"

"You know that the only one more upset about this than you is me, right?" Nick said, then added, "Thanks for coming."

Marcus Bennett stood 6'1" with 230 pounds of muscle, his bald, gleaming head shining in the late-day sun. Marcus was Nick's best friend, next-door neighbor, and partner in all things: hockey, kite-surfing, poker, and other brands of minor mischief.

"You'd think we'd get a pass after all we did this morning," said Marcus, as Katy pulled him toward the railing that looked over the valley.

As Katy's godfather, Marcus had gone from being a rough-and-tumble, ex-military businessman who couldn't keep his fists in his pockets, to a childlike uncle who didn't hesitate to roll on the floor and play with dolls. Katy was the David to his Goliath, slaying him with a smile, bending him to her will like no business adversary or bar-fight opponent ever could.

Nick marveled at the constant changes in Katy: her weekly growth, the teeth that seemed to suddenly fill her mouth, her ever-expanding vocabulary. She had a tender innocence to her voice, a Cindy Lou Who quality magnified by the words of toddlerhood: *finder* for finger, *vallilla* for vanilla, *peas* for please. He loved her mispronounced vocabulary and never corrected her, hoping she'd hold onto her innocence forever. He had never imagined the emotional depths of fatherhood—the joy, the worry, and how his heart burst with warmth every time he heard her voice.

When he'd first learned Julia was pregnant, he was secretly fearful. How would their lives change? What would come of their mornings lying in each other's arms, their lazy Sundays of breakfast and newspapers in bed? Would it all be lost and forgotten?

But as with most parents, what they gave up was replaced with something far more precious. Nick could no longer imagine life without Katy, without her laughter or tears as she explored and came to know her world; the swooshing sound of her legs against her diapers as she raced down the hallways of their home; the uncontrollable giggles and laughter when Theo, their six-month-old Bernese Mountain Dog puppy, licked her ears; or their simple game of peek-a-boo.

While raising Katy, Nick had rediscovered the wonders of childhood: the magic of Christmas, the spooky fun of trick-or-treat, manic

Easter egg hunts, and blowing out birthday candles. Life's priorities had come into sharp focus, and his had taken on a new sense of purpose and fulfillment.

Like most couples with a new child, Nick and Julia had experienced a paradigm shift with their friends, many falling away, those without children still spending Friday and Saturday nights out for dinner, movies, and dancing. Only their closest friends modified their lives to spend time with the happy trio, content to come over for take-out and share in Nick and Julia's parental joy.

"Where's Dreyfus?" Marcus asked Nick. "How did he get out of this?"

"I have no idea," Nick said. "But I'm sure he'll make it. He's never late for anything."

And he wasn't. Punctual was an understatement. You could set your watch by Paul Dreyfus's adherence to schedule. A security expert for Fortune 500 companies, as well as Shamus Hennicot and his wealthy associates, Paul Dreyfus was eminently successful, highly responsible, and always timely. He was also the third Stooge in Marcus and Nick's sandbox. He kept their reindeer games this side of legal, ensured their wounds were properly dressed, and served as a stand-in godfather to Katy whenever Marcus regressed into childhood.

"By the way," Marcus said, "Julia's looking for you."

"Mommy's looking for you," Katy echoed. "I tink she's mad."

"Why do you think that, honey?"

"Cause she said, 'Go find Fadder,' instead of Daddy." Katy giggled.

Nick looked to Marcus. "And you volunteered to leave the fun and find me?"

Marcus smiled and shrugged. "That's what friends do."

Nick and Julia stood at the large wooden entrance doors to Byram Castle, shaking hands, nodding, and endlessly engaging in questions of children, health, and the weather, while also wishing everyone a happy Fourth of July.

Among the guests was Marcus and his latest wife Anissa; Martin Rinab, another of Nick's kitesurfing buddies, and his wife Yolanda; their forever friends Kirstin and Rocco; John Bae, the rhythm guitarist from Nick's band; Michael Ponce, his skydiving compadre; the Clows, who actually enjoyed the politics of it all; the Mortimers, who would do anything for Julia; Donna Schreyer, Julia's close friend from the hospital; Sara Bitton, Katy's daycare teacher; and the Fitzgibbonses, the starstruck sort of people who jumped at a chance to meet their senator.

The castle now contained practically everyone on Nick and Julia Quinn's Christmas-party invitation list: at least forty couples, supplemented by partners from Julia's law firm, town officials, and political groupies. The only people not in attendance were the smart ones: the thousand-plus who filled the grassy mall and sports fields below the dam, enjoying their Fourth of July in the traditional way, with picnics and games while awaiting the evening's fireworks show.

Hors d'oeuvres and drinks were passed by college-aged interns of the senator as people broke into cliques of conversational comfort. Nick hated to admit it, but he was enjoying himself. As he looked around, he realized that these were the people he actually liked to be with—the people he cared about, who made him laugh, think, and smile.

"Where's Shamus?" Nick asked Julia in a quiet moment.

"I couldn't reach him all day."

"That's not like him."

"Well, he is ninety-three," she said.

"And he would never miss one of your parties, even if he had one foot in the grave."

"That's not right," she scolded.

Hailing from ancient English heritage, Shamus was the wealthiest ninety-three-year-old in the world—not that it mattered to Nick and Julia. To them, he was more than a friend or client. He was like a father or grandfather: stern but loving, filled with wisdom but never pushy with it. Shamus and his wife Katherine had no children and no other family, so they looked to each other to fill that void and chose their "family" with care.

"I didn't mean it that way." Nick rubbed her arm.

"I meant to go by his house, but work had me so tied up."

"We'll swing by his house on the way home. I'm sure he's fine."

At 5:37, twenty-two minutes late, the large entrance doors opened and the two Secret Service agents walked in, followed immediately by a tall Byron Chase, who smiled as he headed directly to Julia.

"I can't thank you enough for arranging all of this," Senator Chase said, looking properly regal in his dark-blue power suit and red, striped tie.

"It's our pleasure, Senator." Julia gave him a small hug.

"Julia," he chided her gently. "Formalities were for high school. Call me Byron." He turned to Nick and thrust out his hand.

"Coach Carl," Nick said, immediately feeling Julia's eye bore into him. He took the senator's hand and smiled the smile that Julia had asked him to pull from his back pocket.

"Julia said you just wrapped up two large real-estate acquisitions and finished your first book."

"She's always bragging about me."

"Good for you," Chase said. "You were the only high-school couple that I knew would get married and stay that way."

"Thank you." Nick held his false smile. "I'm hoping she keeps me for a few more years."

"If you'll excuse me," Chase said, "I just need to review my notes with one of my aides." Chase's focus had shifted even before he finished his sentence; now he moved with a young assistant to a far corner.

"Coach Carl?" Julia glared at Nick. "Really?"

Nick gave his wife the same smile that she'd requested as she turned away and marched into the reception room.

"This was supposed to be my moment," Senator Chase said through gritted teeth. "He was supposed to be here to introduce me."

"Things happen," the young aide said. "I'll introduce you."

"No offense, but you lack even the appearance of someone important. After all this effort I've gone through to help him, he screws me yet again? I want to know the real reason why he blew me off."

"I don't know if I can—"

"Just do it, or find a replacement who can."

"Ladies and gentlemen," Julia said from the podium, the crowd reacting by dropping their conversations to a murmur. "Please welcome Senator Byron Chase."

Chase climbed the eighteen-inch platform and stood at the podium, nodding to the applauding crowd, pointing at strangers as if they were friends. He was an imposing man, fit, with dark, grey-flecked hair, a disarming smile, and steely blue eyes.

He rested his hands upon the sides of the red, white, and blue podium and cleared his throat.

"Before we get it started," he said, raising his hands to quiet the room, "it's my great honor to announce something that has not even hit the press yet. President Matthew McManus, two hours ago, after a series of top-secret negotiations, signed not only a cease-fire but a far-reaching peace accord with Akbiquestan and Russia, resolving longstanding economic issues. As the head of the Senate Intelligence Committee, I am proud to have been involved with this process and

I applaud our Commander in Chief on a difficult job well done. The war in Akbiquestan is over."

The room erupted in genuine applause. The four-year war had dominated the press, water-cooler talk, and prayers of most Americans, who feared an escalation into World War III.

"Which is a perfect segue into why I am here today," Chase continued. "Peace through strength. Prosperity through charity. It's time to step back from war and focus on peace and prosperity for all Americans, while never letting our guard down against terrorism again."

Nick pulled out and glanced at his phone: 5:53. The two-minute political oration already felt like an hour. Julia turned toward him with a painted-on smile and gave him *the look*. He quickly tucked his phone away.

Katy charged through the room, her blonde hair floating behind her, and latched onto Nick's leg, pulling him toward the door as if he were being saved from hell by an angel.

Nick picked her up and carried her to the lobby, out through the enormous heavy glass doors, closing them carefully behind them, cutting off the droning speech in favor of far more important words.

"I want to go outside and play," Katy said.

"Honey," Julia said, following them into the lobby with Bonnie the babysitter at her side. She took Katy out of Nick's arms. "I need you to stay with Bonnie for fifteen minutes."

"Why don't I take her outside?" Nick offered.

"We need to be in there," Julia said with a forced smile. "We're the hosts."

"But Katy wants to play."

A side door opened, and a man stumbled through, looking barely coherent, and fell into Nick's arms. His clothes were wet, his salt-and-pepper hair damp. Shocked, Nick realized he knew the man and knew him well. It was his close friend Paul Dreyfus, who had been at the top of the guest list and uncharacteristically late.

Nick supported his friend's sagging weight and led him to a large couch on the far side of the lobby, where Dreyfus collapsed heavily.

"Are you okay?" Nick asked Paul. "What the hell happened?"

"Listen to me," Dreyfus whispered.

As Nick let go of his friend, he saw blood covering his hands. Quickly, Nick ripped open Dreyfus's shirt, revealing what looked like a bullet wound to the chest.

"Oh my God," Nick breathed. "Julia?"

Julia was immediately at his side.

"Bonnie," Julia turned to the babysitter, "could you take Katy to the bathroom in the back?"

Bonnie averted her eyes as she pulled Katy down through the back hall.

"What happened?" Nick asked his friend again.

Dreyfus pulled the strap of a dark leather satchel from about his neck and shoulder and looped it over Nick's. "Listen to me, Nick. Listen very carefully...." Dreyfus paused to breathe, struggling to get the words out. "Don't let that bag out of your sight.... He's coming for you. He's...coming for Julia."

"Who? What are you talking about?"

Dreyfus reached into the bag and withdrew a single picture that made Nick's blood run cold. It was an image of a man floating against the rocky shoreline of a lake, water lapping at his body, his face having lost all color, the skin white and curdled like rotted cheese, lips blue, cracked, and wet. There was no question that the man had died a painful death. In fact, he had almost surely drowned, his wet body and vacant stare leaving little doubt about the means of his demise.

Nick tried to catch his panicked breath. He knew the man, knew him well, better than anyone: he was looking into his own lifeless eyes.

"You all die...." Dreyfus whispered.

Julia turned to Nick, her skin flushing red as confusion filled her eyes. "Nick?" Her voice trembled.

Nick stared at Dreyfus, the impossibility of his words echoing in his head.

"You, Julia...." Dreyfus struggled to draw another breath. "Katy. Everyone."

Nick turned and looked through the glass doors at the gathered crowd, which listened in rapt attention to the senator's speech. Everyone Nick cared about was here, most listening to political rhetoric they couldn't care less about. They were all attending as a favor to Nick and Julia.

"When?" Nick whispered to his dying friend.

Dreyfus seized Nick's hand, locking eyes with him. "It's all in the bag."

"What's in the bag?"

"You have to find me...." Dreyfus's words sounded like a plea.

"I don't understand...find you where?"

"I'm so sorry—"

A sudden roar exploded from the room, cheers and applause, as if the senator had concluded the speech of his life. The rising voices of the now-standing audience only amplified Nick's dread.

And then a rumble shook the world, deep and foreboding.

Another rumble, an explosion, like a bomb, and then another and another and another....

The crowd fell silent, eyes darting about in confusion. New York was not the land of earthquakes, but the shaking earth said otherwise. Deep heavy rumblings seemed to roll the flagstone floor.

"Nick?" Julia looked around the lobby in fear as a hum began to grow. "What the hell is that?"

As the rumble grew in intensity, a collective panic took over the reception room, chaos filling the air as everyone tried to flee from the unknown with incoherent screams of fear, cramming through the doors to escape whatever danger was approaching.

The deep roar grew deafening, drowning out the screams, shaking the castle's foundations. And then, as if hell had been unleashed, the reception room's outer windows shattered; incomprehensibly, a wall of water drove through the space, rising toward the ceiling in seconds. Like a tidal wave, the barrage of water tore the room apart. Tables, chairs, fixtures, and carpets spun into a churning maelstrom. Men and woman were scooped up, helplessly tossed about, bodies hurled and twisted into dark whirlpools.

The light of day dimmed as the wall sconces winked out. Emergency lights reacted to the loss of power, their bright halogen rays flicking on, impervious to the water's assault within their clear plastic housings, their beams like shafts of lightning, piercing the murky, rising, roiling waters.

An enormous howl of wind groaned as air was driven from the building, its gusts sweeping the water's surface into blinding mist. Husbands and wives, friends and neighbors were quickly swept away, their screams doused as they were pulled under and sucked out through the narrow window openings like water through a drain.

From behind the thick glass doors, Nick and Julia watched in horror as their friends drowned, their twisted bodies becoming human flotsam and jetsam before being sucked out through the shattered picture windows on a violent tide into oblivion.

The lobby had already become a deep pool, the waters rising to Nick and Julia's shoulders. Then, as if a tornado had struck, the glass doors were torn from their moorings and thrown into the tidal flow. A rush of water quickly rose toward the ceiling, sweeping Dreyfus's body away.

Water filled the vestibule, its polished granite walls momentarily looking like an Italian pool. The couch where Dreyfus had lain, the tables and chairs splintered in the onslaught, all flushed through the main doors, carried on a raging current.

"Katy!" Julia screamed.

In the rising water, Nick swam for the bathroom where Katy and Bonnie had gone, the leather satchel looped about his body complicating the impossible task. The bathroom was at the far end of the vestibule, sequestered in a corner where the water's attack had been delayed by the turns of the hallway. But the small, high windows now exploded, water pouring through as if from the spigots of heaven.

Julia swam hard in the same direction, battling the raging waters that rose higher and higher. She fought with all her might, kicking and pulling against the current, but the suction created by the millions of gallons of flowing water took hold of her. Despite all her years of swimming, in spite of her natural strength, she was losing, drawn inch by inch toward the door where death awaited.

Nick caught hold of her hand, his other arm wrapped tightly around a chandelier overhead. They were pulled and tossed by the water as it rose, pushing them up against the ceiling. Holding on with all his strength, Nick pulled her to him, but the suction made her feel like a two-ton weight, straining his arms, his grip.

"Hold on!" Nick yelled as their heads banged the ceiling, the water continuing to rise around them.

"We have to get Katy!" Julia struggled to hold on as Nick fought with every fiber of his being to not let her slip away.

"Mommy!" Katy's cry pierced the cacophony of churning waters.

"Katy!" Julia screamed back. "Mommy's coming!"

As the water pulled at them, Nick and Julia's eyes locked in an unspoken understanding of what was happening. In order to get to Katy, to have any hope of saving her....

"Let me go," Julia pleaded. "Save Katy, please. Please save Katy."

Nick looked deep into his wife's eyes; he couldn't bear to do what she was asking. She was everything to him, his life, his heart. She was his soul.

"No," Nick said. "Hold on."

"It's okay," she said, holding his gaze. "Let me go."

With her free hand, she grasped Nick's fingers and gently pried them loose.

And with their eyes still locked, she released Nick's hand. Her body, caught in the suction, instantly disappeared.

Despite the agony in his heart, Nick turned his body toward the bathroom. He reached and caught hold of one of the brass wall sconces mounted on the granite wall as the water continued its rise, only an inch of breathable air remaining.

Nick plunged under, into the current. The brass sconces lined the wall leading to the bathroom like a horizontal ladder. Hand over hand he pulled himself along, fighting with all his might, his arms burning with the impossible effort.

He briefly surfaced. "Katy!" he screamed in the narrow airway as he gulped sweet oxygen. "I'm coming!"

But the force of the current, the draw of the millions of gallons of water flowing through the building, had grown tenfold. Sapped of strength, Nick dug deep within himself...he couldn't let her die, he wouldn't fail her.

"Peas, Daddy!" Katy cried from up ahead. "Peas...."

As the rising water squeezed away the last bit of air, Nick took a deep breath and dived under again.

He spotted the door, its giant brass handle gleaming with the refracted beams of the emergency lights. The thick mahogany portal opened outward, seated against a heavy metal frame, its design still withstanding the building pressure of the rising waters. But Nick knew it wouldn't hold for long, the waters were surely pouring under the door, through any and every crack as it sought the path of least resistance.

"Daddy!"

Even under the churning water, Nick could hear Katy's cry.

The violence of the current grew unbeatable. The weight of the satchel around his neck, like a bag of lead; his lungs burning, fighting the rush of water that pulled at him like a colossal magnet.

Nick reached for the handle of the door, his fingertips swiping the brass; straining for purchase, he planted his legs against the wall and used his last bit of strength to grasp the door.

The fire in his lungs pushed him to the brink, twinkling spots dancing before his eyes as his brain thirsted for oxygen.

And the suction caught hold of him, yanking him away, pulling him backwards toward the shattered windows.

With utter despair, his heart broken, having failed his wife and daughter, Nick knew he would join them in death.

Unable to resist, he gasped, and the water invaded his lungs....

And his world fell to darkness.

CHAPTER 11

4:00 PM

Nick's eyes flicked open, his head a tumble of confusion. A metallic, blood-like taste filled his mouth as a bitter chill coursed through him. He looked away from his prone position, realizing he was soaked to the bone, drenched, the water puddling from his clothes upon the stone floor of a darkened room.

Battered, bruised, and sore, he could barely move as he looked around the windowless space, a dim light seeping through an open door twenty feet away, a murmur of voices in the distance momentarily obscured by a rustling of heavy, moving objects.

Nick sat up, struggling to regain his senses and strength as he peered into the shadows.

As his mind sharpened, his focus returning, Nick tried to remember the day: arriving at the castle at 3:55, wandering the various levels of the old building while making a series of calls, some necessary, some not, most conducted as a matter of avoidance, a means of escaping preparations for the reception in honor of Senator Byron Chase.

Finally, Nick stood, his strength returning as the cobwebs swept from his memory.

A sharp pain exploded in his heart.

Everything he cared about, everyone he loved was gone.

Julia was dead, drowned, swept away on a raging torrent as the castle filled with water. Katy, helpless and all of three years old, trapped within a flooded bathroom, her father unable to save her or her babysitter.

Nick tried to remain on his feet, but despair crushed him, sending him back to the stone floor, waves of nausea consuming him as his body coiled into a fetal position. The guilt hurt worse than any pain he'd felt before. Guilt for failing to protect Katy, for waiting too long to honor Julia's final, sacrificial plea to save their daughter.

He couldn't make sense of what had happened—he'd never even considered it during the chaos and struggle—but he could only think of one explanation: the enormous Killian Dam had broken, unleashing a torrent into the castle and wiping out every life but his own. He cursed his fortune of survival, a cruel twist of fate that was already testing his sanity, for being left without those he loved left him little reason to live. And what of the others who lay in the wake of the dam break? The thousands gathered to celebrate the holiday, playing ball, picnicking, laughing.... Families, children...

As Nick wondered at the magnitude of it all, questioning how he'd escaped with his life, he felt the satchel strap about his neck. Paul Dreyfus's satchel.... *Don't let that bag out of your sight,* his friend had pleaded before dying.

Nick removed it from his aching body, laying it on the dimly lit floor. He realized its leather exterior was in fact a facade. He lifted the flap to find a heavy zipper and quickly undid it. There was no question as to the bag's design or purpose: it was waterproof, a dive sack, the kind used for SCUBA diving, constructed with a neoprene interior, watertight, including the zipper seal.

Peering in, unable to see its contents in the shadowed room, Nick dug his hand in and pulled out a video camera, a cell phone, a car key, and two envelopes.

He could barely read the writing on the first envelope in the room's lack of light, but he could see that it was addressed to him.

He tore it open and quickly read the letter as his eyes adjusted to the dimness:

Nick,

There's still time. To save Julia, to save us all. I don't have much time, which seems ironic. I have been....

Nick swiftly finished reading the letter and jammed his hand back into the satchel. His fingers scrambled about until his hand fell upon an object. He didn't need to see it to recognize it, to envision the cold disk of metal: round, small, compact, fitting perfectly in the palm of his hand. A mix of dread and of hope suffused Nick as he pulled out the ancient pocket watch. He pressed the familiar crown, popping open the cover and checking the time.

Despite the screaming of his logical mind, his eyes didn't lie. The hands of the antique watch read 4:04.

Nick leapt to his feet, suddenly understanding.

He tucked the watch in his wet pocket, stuffed everything else back in the satchel, zipped it up, and slung it over his shoulder and neck. He ran through the open door into the stone hallway, down the corridor, and tore open a dark wooden door, racing through and bursting out into the light of day, the sudden brightness assaulting his eyes. He stood upon a teak terrace at the foot of Byram Castle, looking down upon the valley below.

It was green, lush, the fields filled with families, bikers, softball teams, children on swings, teens playing Frisbee—a thousand people all enjoying the warm Fourth of July sun under a blue sky.

Nick turned and looked up the valley to the north. The enormous dam stood there in all its glory, casting a magnificent shadow. It appeared sound, showing no apparent breach or damage.

The same went for the castle behind him: dry as a bone, intact, nothing to indicate what he'd just experienced: not a hint of disaster, no dead bodies, not a drop of water. He scratched his head, momentarily wondering if he'd just experienced a new version of his old nightmares, but his drenched clothes told him otherwise.

Without further thought, he climbed over the deck railing and up the hillside in the enormous shadow of the castle. The completely dry and undamaged castle....

Trudging through the thicket into the trimmed topiary, he hoisted himself up and over a railing into the driveway proper of Byram Castle. The news vans and crews were there, plus a few private cars, including Julia's Audi, which they had arrived in.

Nick could barely catch his breath as his heart jumped with fresh hope.

"Honey?" The voice came from behind him.

Nick spun around to see Julia holding hands with Katy.

The moment hung in the air; Nick stared at them as if looking at ghosts. They were alive and smiling, unknowing and unharmed.

A mix of anger and bemusement seemed to keep Julia speechless for a moment. Then she asked, "What on earth happened to you?"

Without a word, Nick raced to her and kissed her hard on the lips, his hands wrapping her body pulling her in. She kissed him back, surprised by his sudden affection, but quickly stepped back.

"Your jacket! You're soaking wet," she protested. "What were you doing?"

Rather than respond, Nick crouched and pulled Katy into his arms, hugging her small body.

"Daddy!" she giggled. "Daddy's wet."

Nick leaned back and looked at her face as if for the first time, memorizing every freckle, every crease of her smile, her perfect skin unmarred by time, by life, her eyes filled with innocence and wonder.

"People will be arriving at five." Julia held out her wrist, pointing at her Rolex. "That's less than an hour from now,"

Nick took her wrist, looked at the ticking hands of her watch, and smiled.

"You need to go home and change," she said.

"Nope, actually, I need you to leave."

"What?" Julia squinted at him in confusion, then smiled at his foolishness. "What are you talking about?"

"I'm serious." Nick looked into her eyes asJulia stared back, trying to understand.

Nick scooped Katy up in his arms and hurried toward the Audi.

"Absolutely not," Julia called out from behind him. "This isn't funny!"

The crowd of reporters turned their way.

"Not trying to be funny," Nick said.

"You're funny, Daddy," Katy giggled as Nick opened the rear door and secured her in her car seat.

"The two of you are leaving here right now," he said. "Where's Bonnie?"

"Nick," Julia said as she caught up to him. "Are you insane?"

"Never been saner." Nick closed Katy's door and turned to his wife. "Though after what I just went through, most people *would* be crazy."

"What are you talking about?" Anger rose in Julia's voice.

"You need to trust me," Nick said. "Bad things are going to happen."

"Bad things?"

The reporters seemed to lean closer at the mention of "bad things."

"Stop it!" Julia raised her voice, trying to cut through the confusion. "How did you get wet?"

"Do this for me." Nick stepped back from the car and put his hands gently on Julia's shoulders, holding her at arm's length. He ignored her anger, still unable to shake the desperate look in her eyes that he'd witnessed an hour and fifty minutes in the future. A time that Julia had not yet experienced and could not foresee, when she'd slipped from Nick's grasp to her death.

"No," she said simply, opening the door to take Katy out of the car.

"Please, Julia. I'm dead serious. Indulge me."

Julia looked into his eyes once more, clearly weighing the day's obligation versus her husband's sudden, erratic behavior. Without a word, she turned and carried Katy back toward Byram Castle, glaring at the nosy reporters as she walked by.

An expanse of windows flooded the conference room of Byram Castle with sunlight, providing a view of the valley and sweeping vistas across Westchester County to the skyscraping towers of Manhattan in the far distance. The second-floor meeting room was large, a cherry table surrounded by fourteen large leather chairs its centerpiece. A makeshift stocked bar with a host of crystal glasses was set up in the corner next to an enormous fish tank. Inside the big aquarium, exotic fish swam about without a care for time, dams, or death. Against the far wall hung an enormous flat-screen TV, a pile of clickers in a basket beneath it.

Nick closed the door behind him, reached in his pocket, and pulled out the pocket watch, gold and silver, its casing's elegant etchings created in an era when craftsman spent months pursuing perfection.

With a shaky thumb, Nick pressed the crown once more, and the cover popped open. He looked at the time: 4:10.

Time had never moved so quickly.

He dug in the breast pocket of his wet jacket and pulled out his cell, waterlogged and dead.

He grabbed the phone in the center of the conference table and dialed.

Three rings and then voicemail.

Hello, this is Paul Dreyfus. Please leave a message.

Paul was the one person who would understand what was going on. After all, he was the one who had given Nick the watch and bag before dying in his arms.

"Where the hell are you?" Nick muttered aloud.

He had fifty minutes to stop the world and fix it. Fifty minutes to clear the castle and the fields and valleys below before he would be whisked out of this hour. He couldn't believe Paul would have given him Shamus Hennicot's unique pocket watch without any clue or hint about how to stop the looming disaster from happening.

Nick removed the bag from his shoulder, laid it upon the table, and unzipped it. Reaching in, he withdrew its contents: the video camera; a large, sealed envelope; a cell phone; a BMW smart key; and the smaller, second envelope containing the letter from Paul that he had already read.

Nick grabbed the video camera, quickly hooked it up to the large-screen TV, and hit play.

The screen instantly filled with a vision of chaos. A raging sea of large waves, filled with flotsam and jetsam swirling about as spray washed against the lens before cutting to—

A dark-haired news anchor spoke with a grim face. "The devastation is enormous, thousands dead. A warning: the images we are about to show are shocking."

The watery image returned and pulled back to reveal a churning channel of water, a roiling river crashing into a lake. The image pulled back farther, this time slowly panning back and forth, as if the establishing shot in some sort of nature documentary. Quickly, though, it morphed into a horror film.

A swath of bodies, hundreds of them, were caught within an eddy formed below a rock outcropping: men, woman, and children in everyday clothes, shorts and skirts, sweats, and baseball jerseys. Blankets and picnic baskets floated about while the tops of cars bobbed as they drifted by.

"A heinous act no doubt staged for maximum impact, not only to cause countless deaths on Independence Day, but as a direct shot at the U.S. government in the form of Senator Byron Chase, who at the moment of the dam's breach was giving a speech on the conflict in Ackbiquestan. A speech covered by our political correspondent, Margery Ross, who is presumed dead along with the rest of the media personnel attending the event.

"Fourth of July celebrations were in full swing in the shadow of the Killian Dam with thousands in attendance, when all were drowned by the sudden and deadly flood. Modest, working-class neighborhoods, large estates, and even forests now stand underwater in the southern section of the town of Byram Hills."

Horrible images continued to cycle, bodies broken, dead children afloat. Nick watched footage of the flooded valley, where neighborhoods had sprouted over the last ninety years around Byram Hills... and where nothing now remained.

"Numerous eyewitnesses reported hearing large explosions just prior to the bursting of the dam. Although yet to be confirmed, the incident is being classified as a terrorist attack."

The country had lived in fear of dirty bombs and weaponized viruses, chemical attacks and planes falling from the sky. But this had come as a complete surprise—the pent-up power of stored water more devastating than any ordinary assault.

On top of all the death and devastation, an even greater catastrophe loomed. The Killian Reservoir was the main holding body and junction for all of New York City's drinking water. Acting like a way-station, the reservoir served as a holding point for water from the five upstate New York reservoirs that had supplied fresh water without fail for more than a hundred years.

Eight million people would turn on their faucets to find nothing but air.

Not only showers and drinking water would be affected, but also fire hydrants, whose precious hookups were now rendered dry, and hospitals, now deprived of their most precious resource.

The repercussions would ripple through the economy of not only the city, but the country and the world, as the great metropolis transformed into a no-man's land for months, maybe years to come.

Suddenly the video image changed from formal and produced news coverage to haphazard, shaky, and amateur.

The footage cut to what was left of the dam. An enormous hole ran up the right side, millions of gallons per minute continuing to pour through in a devastating waterfall, its thunderous roar the only sound coming through the camera's speaker.

The camera swung around to reveal the castle that Nick now stood in, its uppermost towers and parapets barely protruding through the roiling waters.

As the camera cut back, it focused on a grouping of nearly a hundred bodies, all bobbing up and down, some face-down, others with dead eyes exposed to the world. As the camera zoomed in, Nick realized he knew many of them.

They were the bodies carried out of the castle by the massive current, their lifeless forms caught in a skein of boulders and trees beside the castle. Necks broken, arms twisted at odd angles, skin torn and pierced. The dead included Sharon and Bob Mortimer from down the street; Sabrina and Mitch Fitzgibbons; and young Sara Bitton, Katy's daycare teacher.

Marcus Bennett, Nick's best friend, had not been spared, his body bent at a grotesque angle, his bald head gashed and crushed on the left side.

Now the image spun around and focused on the face of a man floating against the rocky shoreline, his blonde hair matted, tinted red with blood, the blue lifeless eyes seeming to stare directly into the camera. There was no mistaking those blue irises: Nick was looking into his own eyes. It was the same image Dreyfus had shown him in the photo before dying.

But it was the body next to Nick's that took his breath away, the white linen dress obscenely bright, Julia's body strangely undamaged by the violence that had mutilated so many others. Her face appeared unmarred and peaceful, her eyes mercifully closed as she floated beside Nick in their watery grave.

Nick couldn't bear to see any more. If he glimpsed Katy's dead image, it would haunt him for all eternity. He pulled the camcorder's cable out of the TV and tucked the camera back in the bag.

Paul Dreyfus's point was clear. The footage was like looking through a crystal ball, peering into the future at a disaster of monstrous proportions. And it had clearly been no accident. Much like that nightmarish day three years ago, this disaster would begin in the future.

In less than two hours.

Nick clutched the antique pocket watch and said a silent thank-you to Shamus Hennicot and Paul Dreyfus. For despite the horror he had witnessed, the disaster had yet to happen.

It remained an event in the future.

And the future could be changed.

Detective Bill Shannon stood in the conference room next to Nick. His eyes locked on his friend, questioning his sanity. "How do you know?"

"You have to trust me," Nick said. "You need to not only evacuate this building but everyone downstream of the dam. There are explosives planted somewhere along the base on the right side. They'll go off at 5:56, killing thousands."

"You didn't answer my question." Shannon stood a little over six feet and was in better shape than when he had been a Golden Gloves Champion out of the Bronx at age twenty-two. Fifteen years on the force, six as Detective, three as Chief Detective—he was a hard-ass, though his friends knew that his gruff demeanor was only one side of the man.

Shannon had known Nick for more than three years now, having met him at the airport during a *situation*. They had saved each other's lives, a bonding experience neither had mentioned after that day, though their wives had become close friends, forcing dinners and parties at which Nick and Shannon endured their wives retelling the story of crooked cops, stolen artifacts, and mobsters.

The conference room door opened, and Marcus Bennett stepped in.

"Did he tell you this?" Shannon asked Marcus. "This thing with the dam?"

Nick stared at Marcus for a moment, startled, despite himself, to see his friend alive.

"I don't know what he told you," said Marcus, "but we both know he's not the lying type."

"If you're wrong about this," said Shannon, "this is going to pull in the feds and a mobilization of emergency personnel like this town has never seen. If you're wrong, losing my job will be the least of my problems."

"We have to evacuate. If we don't..." He shook his head, unable to describe properly what he'd seen.

"You gotta give me *something*." Shannon paced nervously as he spoke. "Even if you're right, even if they find your so-called explosives, they're going to want to know how you knew. Did you overhear someone? Did someone tell you about it? Do you have any idea who's involved?"

Nick stared at Shannon, wondering how far to take this.

"Give me something to hang my hat on, and I'll call in the world." Shannon paused. "But friends or not, I can't evacuate a senator, let alone thousands of people, based on a hunch. There's twenty-four-hour security on that dam. No one gets close without being detected."

Nick hooked the camera back up to the television. "I'm going to show you something too incredible to explain." He looked straight into Shannon's eyes. "What you're about to see will happen in a little more than an hour and a half."

Nick hit play.

The room fell into silence as the news coverage revealed the disaster, the anchor impassively narrating the details of the terrorist attack. Footage played over her words, overhead shots of the roiling water, the POV of a dead cameraman, the bodies floating away in the current. The debris, which at first looked like tree branches, was revealed to be human remains.

It was chaos like nothing Shannon or Marcus had ever seen. And as the footage continued, Nick couldn't look any longer, but he knew that the video's roar of rushing water led to the close-up image of the bodies caught in the culvert. Marcus would now see himself floating there. When the image showed Julia and Nick floating dead in the water, he hit pause.

In unison, Shannon and Marcus turned from the TV screen to look out the window at the reveler-filled park and the neighborhoods in the near distance.

"What the hell *is* this?" Shannon whispered, his gaze switching between the scene outside the window and the frozen TV image of mass death.

"Nick?" Marcus seconded Shannon's question.

"My house is down there, my family." Shannon's voice reached a higher pitch. "What kind of bullshit—"

"I know," Nick said.

"This is impossible," said Shannon.

For a moment, confusion hung in the air. Then Marcus spoke. "Evacuate now," he told Shannon, then turned to Nick. "You, explain later."

The evacuation was massive. A mobilization of emergency personnel, National Guard, and police raced door-to-door through the neighborhoods that sat in the path of destruction. Trucks blared evacuation announcements as they slowly rolled through the streets. And while many might have expected panic to have taken over, most simply got in their cars and left without a word. They had been conditioned to run for their lives after bearing witness to those who had not heeded warnings: the devastated cities in the path of tsunamis; the dead who'd thought they could ride out hurricanes; stubborn homeowners waiting out the latest volcanic eruption.

Concurrently, a team of Navy divers arrived by helicopter over the reservoir. The roar of the Huey's blades echoed across the water as the underwater demolition experts leapt into the water and disappeared beneath the surface.

They found the first line of explosives at the hundred-foot mark, the second line at 200, and a third at 300. The shaped Semtex charges were buried within the dam, wired together, and placed to direct the force of the blast along the seams, the most vulnerable parts of the enormous structure. The design was intended not to blow the dam apart, but rather weaken it, allowing natural forces to do the heavy lifting. The weight of 30 billion gallons of water, more than 250 billion pounds, would shatter the weakened barrier like glass.

The dive team leader opted not to remove the charges until they could be fully examined, instead removing the blasting caps and primers; without a fuse, the Semtex would remain as inert as mud.

"You're scaring me." Julia looked into Nick's eyes as they stood beside the Audi.

"I'll explain later."

"You and Marcus save a guy this morning and now you think you can save a thousand this afternoon? What the hell?"

Bonnie, Katy's babysitter, emerged from the castle and, without a word of protest, got in the other side of the car and sat next to Katy.

"You're sure about this?" Julia said. "There hasn't been an attack on American soil in years. I mean...come on, a bomb in the dam? Violence like this in our town?"

Behind them, three military men ran by a sea of army and emergency trucks, while a host of FBI agents held staccato discussions on their phones.

Nick opened the driver's side door and motioned Julia in.

"I'm not leaving without you," Julia said.

"Believe me," Nick said as he leaned in and kissed her, "I have no intent of hanging around. I just need to speak to the authorities. Shannon'll give me a ride home. I'll meet you there."

Nick watched as Julia drove out of the long driveway; he could finally breathe again, knowing that she and Katy were out of harm's way. It was as if a steel band wrapped around his heart had finally been released.

As Julia left and the evacuation continued apace, Nick reached into his pocket and pulled out the watch, flipping open its cover: 4:35.

He wondered at the successful evacuation effort. He had never seen anything so efficient. They would all live.

Nick hurried back into the conference room, pulled out Paul Dreyfus's hastily written letter, and re-read it.

Nick,

There's still time. To save Julia, to save us all. I don't have much time, which seems ironic. I have been shot. I'm dying, and I hope to get this letter to you before I succumb.

My words are clumsy, rushed, and unconvincing, which is why I am paraphrasing the far more eloquent Shamus Hennicot, but before reading further, I urge you to watch the video on the camera, for as horrific as the footage may be, it is far more convincing than the written word.

I hope the fog has lifted from your mind, though I'm sure it's now being replaced by an even greater confusion as to what is going on and why I have pulled you into this madness.

You are now standing in the very place you stood during the four o'clock hour this afternoon. You are now living that hour once again. But this time you are free to turn left where before you turned right, say yes where before you said no; no one will know the difference, nor will anyone else experience this phenomenon. You are on your own to choose direction as you see fit, to alter the future that you've just experienced.

My daughter Alice was murdered before my eyes in our home at 6:30 this evening, shot by the man who also blew up the dam, killing you, Julia, Katy, and so many others. It is for these reasons that I have broken a promise.

You must pay very close attention, as time is short:

Every hour, as the minute hand of Shamus's pocket watch arrives at twelve, you will slip back two hours in time to relive that hour of your life again.

One step forward, two steps back.

This will occur exactly eleven times, no more, no less, taking you back, hour by hour, ultimately to seven this morning.

By stepping back into each prior hour of the day, you'll have the chance to save Julia and Katy, my Alice, and thousands more.

I will not bore you with explanations and technicalities—suffice to say that, as the hour strikes, you will be whisked back to the exact location where you were two hours earlier to live that hour anew.

But be aware, each choice, just like in life, has consequences that we may not realize in the moment of its choosing. You have the ability to save your family and put our world back in balance, but be warned: it is a precarious route. Your choices must be well thought-out so as not to unbalance the rest of your or anyone else's existence. The unintended consequences of a kind or charitable act can kill many.

Hold onto this letter and the timepiece and remember: the pocket watch must never leave you, for if it does—if it is destroyed, damaged, or you lose it—you'll be lost to the moment you are tied to, reintroduced to the forward-flowing existence that the rest of humanity experiences. Saving Julia and Katy will be become a lost cause.

But for this letter, the cell phone to replace your wet, shorted-out phone, the pocket watch, and the camcorder—the contents of this bag belong to the murderer I stole it from. Do not destroy the contents, as their value cannot be defined and may provide you and the authorities not only with evidence against him, but also the leverage you may need.

Lastly, and most importantly, in the coming upside-down hours, be careful who you trust. I fear there is far more going on here, far more than we've already seen.

Good luck and Godspeed.

Paul

Nick tucked the letter in his pocket and stared at the watch. Handcrafted gold and silver, intricate filigreed designs etched in its casing. He pressed the crown, the cover popping open to show it was 4:40.

His eyes were drawn to the engraving on the inside of the watch cover: *Fugit irreparabile tempus*. A Latin phrase he knew as well as the watch in his hand:

Irretrievable, time flies.

Nick had possessed this watch once before, had known it intimately, using it for twelve hours in the darkest moments of his life. Given to him by Shamus Hennicot's assistant Zachariah Nash, it had pulled him backward through the longest of days, allowing him to save Julia and much, much more. He hadn't understood how it worked then, and he didn't understand it now.

Only four people knew about the powerful, antique timepiece: Shamus Hennicot, its owner; his assistant Zachariah; Nick himself; and Paul Dreyfus, who was not only Nick's and Shamus's friend and a respected security consultant, but also the guardian and protector of Shamus Hennicot's many secrets.

Nick had kept Shamus's original letter of explanation from three years ago, the only proof he'd retained of those extra twelve hours in his life. He had a picture of the letter in his phone and read it from time to time to remind himself that the impossible was not always impossible.

But unlike three years ago, when Nick had set out to find and stop the killer of his wife, today's events posed no further mystery: Julia and Katy were alive; the shattering of the dam had not only not yet happened, but never would. He had seen to that.

He didn't need twelve hours to right his world; he'd only needed one.

Nick grabbed the camcorder, removed the memory card, and tucked it in the change pocket of his jeans. He opened the dive bag and pulled out the large envelope. There were four names scribbled in pencil on it: three scared him, while the fourth confused him. Opening it, he spread out the papers on the conference table, twenty sheets in all. There were diagrams of the dam, maps of the town, papers on the New York City water supply, and pages of notes, all annotated in a language he didn't understand. He pulled the iPhone from the bag and photographed each sheet, confirming that the fine print and illustrations were clear and in focus. He tucked the BMW smart key in the breast pocket of his still-damp Armani jacket, then he reached into the satchel and found nothing else. To be sure, he turned the bag over and shook it. A small black memory stick fell out; he tucked it in his pocket, then put the camera and the large envelope back in the bag and zipped it up.

That's when Nick realized that he'd find no better hiding place for the waterproof bag than the large aquarium in the rear of the conference room, quickly submerging the satchel behind the coral and sunken pirate ship in the back of the 500-gallon tank.

Nick dialed the new iPhone.

"Hello?" Paul answered.

"Hey, it's Nick."

"Nick? Whose number is this?" Paul sounded confused. "Wait... this is one of my employee's phones. How did you get it?"

"I'll tell you later. We need to talk, in person. Where are you?"

"Don't worry, I'll make it to Julia's fundraiser. I may just be a little late. We can talk then. Can I bring anything?"

"Where are you?" Nick asked again.

"In my car."

"Well, I've got a familiar pocket watch in my hand."

"Shit." After a long silence, Paul's tone turned urgent. "Where did you get it?"

"You gave it to me."

"Oh, God. Where are you?"

"Byram Castle."

Another silence.

"Listen," Nick said. "Someone is after you, they.... You get shot."

Paul said nothing.

"You gave me the watch just before you—"

"Shit. All right. What did I say?"

"You also gave me a dive bag, told me not to lose it or the watch. In it was a letter from you to me, this phone, a camcorder, and a bunch of stuff you stole from your killer."

"And the watch."

"And the watch."

"Where's the bag now?"

"Tucked it in the back of the fish tank in a conference room at Byram Castle."

"Okay, not a bad idea. Let me think for second." After a moment, Paul said calmly, "I can save myself."

"It's worse than that." Nick paused, finally forcing the words. "It happens at your house, at 6:30 p.m. Alice is murdered."

"Oh, God."

Nick could hear the pain in his friend's voice; he knew the feeling, having endured the same agony during the dam break.

"It's okay. Remember, she's alive here and now." Nick took a breath. "But there's more. Someone blows up the Killian Dam. Hundreds or thousands of people are killed. That's what you came to warn me about after you were shot."

"Holy shit. What's the matter with this world? Do you know who?"

"You didn't say, but I'm hoping that the contents of the bag will identify the killer and the people behind all of this. The whole place is being evacuated now."

"You need to hand that stuff over to the authorities."

"Not until after I've pulled out any reference to the non-occurring future and I'm sure who I can trust."

"Smart," Paul said.

"You go find Alice," Nick said. "I've got the dam."

"Oh, God," Paul said again. "This is insane."

"Don't worry." Nick smiled as if Paul could see it and feed off his confidence. "We got this. We have time, thanks to you. No searching, no mystery, a bagful of evidence. We just take care of this in the next half-hour and all will be right with the world."

"Okay, I'm gonna find Alice. Be careful, Nick."

"Of course."

"And after you're done? Go home. Just ride it out. Hold onto the watch and slip back hour after hour until it doesn't happen again. Go to sleep, stay out of trouble. Don't talk to or see anyone."

"That'll be hard, but it's my intention."

"If you need to talk to anyone, call me. Don't do anything else."

"Paul?"

"Yeah?"

"I thought you destroyed the watch," Nick said. "Three years ago."

"Yeah, well, we're supposed to do a lot of things in life." Dreyfus paused. "Go home. We'll talk later. I'll see you in a few hours."

"It'll be a lot more time than that for me."

"You know what I mean. Be safe."

Three black Town Cars rolled into the granite courtyard of the castle, circling and coming to a sudden halt. Senator Byron Chase emerged from the rear of the lead car, his face determined, ignoring the flurry of activity as he walked past the scores of people rushing in and out of the castle, and headed through the large doors. Behind him, an entourage of twelve poured from the vehicles: aids, advisors, two Secret Service agents, a cameraman, and a reporter. They followed their leader two steps behind as he made his way through the grand foyer, past the elegant great hall staged for his speech that wouldn't be happening in an hour, and out onto the teak balcony. He turned in a choreographed spin and faced the cameraman who framed him within the background of the green valley, the littered mall now vacant of Fourth of July revelers, and the enormous dam. There, he began his newly rewritten speech.

"The Unites States intelligence services have once again proven their ability to prevent terrorist attacks on our country. A coming together of the NSA, the CIA, Homeland Security, and the FBI...."

Nick emerged onto the deck in time to catch Chase's opening remarks. He couldn't believe his ears; if they were so good at what they were doing, then why did the dam blow an hour from now? Detective Shannon turned and regarded Nick with a poker face.

"How dare these cowards come to my town," Chase continued, anger welling up in his voice now, "with the evil intent to kill my people, my friends? If you want to target me, fine, target me, and we'll stop you in your tracks; but when you target my friends, my family, my constituents, you are crossing the line and will face the full wrath and retribution of the United States."

It could not have been a more potent speech. No doubt it would be pulled out time and time again, painting the senator as a fearless leader, as an enraged man of the people looking to strike back at those who would bring the war to his backyard. It sounded presidential, and no doubt had been written with that subtext in mind.

"You've got some serious explaining to do," Shannon said as he walked over to Nick.

"I know."

"I've left a trail of lies," Shannon whispered.

"Sorry."

"Yeah, well, the lies sound far better than the truth, not that I even know what that is."

"Do you want me to come forward and—"

"I've kept your name out of it. They'd toss you in an insane asylum or worse if they heard."

"But I was right," Nick said, keeping his eyes on Byron as dozens of FBI, state and local police, military, and National Guard moved in the background.

"Tonight," Shannon said. "Valhalla. Dinner, drinks, and the truth are on you."

"Yep, you, me, and Marcus." Nick squeezed the watch in his pocket. "You may need more than a few drinks."

"Can't wait."

"Mr. Quinn?" A man in a black suit and tie approached Nick. "Could you please come with me?"

"Uh, sure...." Nick said uncertainly.

"Who are you?" Shannon asked with a hint of challenge.

"Special Agent in Charge Janos Zane. Who are you?"

"Detective Shannon." Shannon pointed at Nick. "What's up with my friend?"

"We just have a few questions for Mr. Quinn."

Shannon and Nick exchanged a glance and walked out through the building to the driveway.

"Nothing serious." Zane smiled. "You're the eighth person we've interviewed and certainly not the last. We need to talk to everyone who was here today. We can go to the conference room or stay out here and chat in the back of my car, whichever you prefer."

"Back of your car's fine." Nick didn't want to be anywhere in range of the waterproof bag he'd hidden. He turned to Shannon. "Don't leave without me—you're my ride home."

"I won't forget you," Shannon said.

Zane opened the rear door of the black Lincoln Town Car and Nick climbed in. Zane didn't bother closing the door, allowing the sunshine to fill the dark leather interior. The youngish man was broad-shouldered, a hint of military in his bearing.

"Crazy day," Zane said with a disarming smile.

"Haven't really wrapped my mind around it yet," Nick said. "But yeah, one of the craziest days I've been through."

"Have you been through worse?"

"No, thank God," Nick lied automatically.

Zane pulled a small notebook and pen from the breast pocket of his black suit jacket. "So, Mr. Quinn...."

"Nick. No one calls me Mr. Quinn."

"Nick," Zane nodded. "I've got some questions."

"Go ahead."

"What time did you arrive here today?"

"About four. My wife was hosting. You know how it is when your wife throws a party." Nick smiled. "You're relegated to assistant, coat check, valet, greeter, arm-charm—anything she needs you to be."

"I'm not married," the agent said without humor.

"Okay." Nick's smile shifted from real to wary.

"Did you see anything out of the ordinary, anything suspicious?"

"Actually, I spent most of the time on my phone, wandering the castle."

"So, that would be a no?"

"No, I didn't see anything suspicious." Nick shook his head. "Nothing."

"And the staff that your wife hired?"

"All supplied by the catering company." The sun began to shine directly through the car door into Nick's face.

Zane listened but didn't jot a single note. "So, you haven't helped your wife at all since you arrived?"

"Guilty." Nick shrugged. "You only do what you're told to. You'll understand when you get married."

Zane pulled the door closed, cutting off the bright sunshine and plunging the car into momentary darkness. Nick now realized all the windows were tinted, including the privacy barrier between them and the front seat.

In his black suit, Zane practically disappeared, but for his pale face and acid-washed blue eyes. "We understand that you provided the tip regarding the explosives in the dam."

"Who'd you hear that from?" Nick tried to hide his alarm. Shannon said he'd kept Nick's name out of it.

"Classified."

Nick cocked his head. "What is this, some kind of game?"

"Is that what you think it is?" Zane's tone remained unchanged. "I assure you, this is no game."

"No." Nick grew angry as he recalled everything he'd witnessed. "This is definitely not a game. Lives are at stake."

"You were in possession of a bag."

Nick's expression froze while his heart pounded. "Not sure what you're talking about."

"Dark leather, wet, a dive bag."

"Sorry?"

"It was on the security video that I reviewed. It was on your shoulder not more than a half hour ago. It was dripping, soaking wet, as were you."

Nick stared at the man.

"How did you get so...wet?" Zane asked. He didn't wait for an answer. "That bag does not belong to you."

The door locks clicked, sounding like thunder in Nick's ears.

"It was stolen," Zane continued. "I know because it's my bag."

The driver started the car. Nick looked through the smoked glass and saw no one watching as they pulled out of the Byram Castle driveway.

"Paul Dreyfus stole that bag from me."

"Did you kill him?"

"Why do you ask?" Zane looked genuinely surprised. "Is he dead?"

The car fell silent. Nick realized he had slipped. Dreyfus had died in the future, so even if Janos Zane had murdered him, he hadn't done it yet.

Zane lifted a small bag from the floor.

"Where are we going?" Nick demanded.

"Care to see what's in this bag?" Zane asked instead of replying.

"Not that curious."

"Maybe you should be." Zane squeezed the bag. "You're lying to me. You're in possession of stolen property, and for some reason you continue to deny it. You see, I believe you *are* involved in what's happening here today, whether you know it or not."

Zane reached in the bag and pulled out an object, placing it in Nick's lap.

Nick stared at it, unable to contain his rage. "What have you done?"

"As of this moment? Nothing," Zane said. "But...."

"Where is she?" Nick demanded, clutching Katy's stuffed giraffe Abigail.

"Don't you mean 'they?' Where are *they*?"

Nick lunged across the seat but was greeted by a gun to the head.

"How did you get that bag that you claim you don't have?" Zane's voice had dropped to a whisper. "Why were you soaking wet? How is it that you knew about the explosives?"

Nick sat back and stared at the shadowed face. "Who the hell *are* you?"

The black car headed through a town full of people walking the sidewalks, smiling and enjoying the day, entirely unaware of the future they had avoided. The car headed up Wago Avenue, climbing the hill and navigating a few more roads until they arrived at Townsend Court and pulled into Nick's driveway.

"Nice house," Zane said as he opened the door of Nick's house and directed him to enter. The foyer echoed with the ticking of the grandfather clock. Nick glanced at the time: 4:55. Only five minutes until the pocket watch pulled him back two hours earlier in the day.

A fireplug of a man in a black suit stood outside the family room, a gun in his hand as he stood guard.

Nick stepped into his shadowed family room, the blinds drawn, a TV screen casting the only light.

"Daddy?" Katy sat at a small table, a crayon in her hand, a haphazard stick drawing of a dog lit by the TV playing *Finding Nemo*.

Julia sat in a chair beside her, her hands zip-tied in front, resting in her lap.

"What's going on?" Julia asked with a soft voice and forced smile so as not to upset Katy. "Who is this jerk?"

Zane raised a hand. "Careful."

"Daddy?" Katy looked up at Nick. "Can we turn on the lights now? I'm scared."

"Honey," Nick said, "there's no need to be scared. Everything's going to be okay."

Nick stepped into Zane's space, face-to-face, and whispered. "I don't know who you are, but let them go. You and I can deal with whatever your problem is without them."

"But you see, Nick, my problem is not just with you, but with Julia." Zane stepped back from him and walked across the room. "How well do you know your wife? I hear secrets are one of the main causes of broken relationships."

Nick glanced out the doorway at the grandfather clock in the hallway, its mechanical ticking seeming to count down their lives.

"Do you know about your wife?" Zane said. "What she was really doing today? Who she was secretly meeting with?"

Nick turned and looked at Julia; she answered his gaze with a blank stare.

"She's my wife, not my possession. She meets with people I don't know—clients, friends. What's your point?"

"This man, the one she met with...what she was doing with him would shock you." Zane walked around the family room. "Would it surprise you if I told you that she was involved with today's events?"

Nick had known Julia since they were teenagers, loved and trusted her without question. He didn't know what Zane was talking about, but Julia would never have been involved in such a plan.

"She has secrets, Nick. Many secrets, things that would shock you right out of your perfect marriage, snap you into a whole new reality."

Julia stood from the chair, despite her tied hands, and walked over to Zane. No fear showed in her eyes. "How dare you come into my home and threaten my family. You have no idea what you've done."

"I know exactly what I've done," Zane said. "And I know far more about you than your husband does."

Nick stepped between them.

"And how well do you really know Nick?" Zane said over Nick's shoulder to Julia. "After all these years, have you lulled yourself into thinking he's honest with you? Nick has a secret too."

Nick had no idea what Zane was talking about. Beyond surprise parties and gifts, he told Julia everything; they shared their days, their ups and downs, the troubles at work, their fears. He told her when women flirted with him, usually to her amusement. He literally had nothing to hide.

Zane stepped toward the door and extended his hand. The fireplug man handed him Julia's purse. Zane opened it and pulled out her flower-blinged iPhone. He moved to Julia and held it out. "Thumb, please."

Julia glared at him.

"Please put your thumb on the phone to unlock it."

"Not a chance."

"Fine." Zane grabbed a chair, pulled it over, and shoved Julia into it.

"Mommy?" Katy cried.

Nick reached for Zane but was met with the barrel of his gun.

"Mommy's fine, Katy," Julia said softly. "You go back to your show. We're just playing a game here."

"That's right," said Zane agreeably. He pointed the gun at Julia and handed her phone to Nick. "Please do the honors."

"Are you crazy?" Nick asked.

"Do you want to test me?"

Nick took Julia's thumb and placed it on the sensor of the phone, unlocking it. He passed it to Zane, who stepped back.

"Password please?"

Julia glared at Zane.

"Give it to him," Nick said softly.

"nickquinn," Julia said. "One word, no caps."

"Cute. Not so original, but cute." Zane quickly went into the phone's settings, disabled the login requirement, and tucked the device into the breast pocket of his jacket.

Nick glanced out the door at the grandfather clock: 4:59. He slid his hand in his pocket and clutched the watch.

As shocking and dire as their situation had become, he still had the ability to save them all, to change the future without anyone ever knowing about the fate they'd escaped. He simply needed to survive for one more minute. He began counting backwards in his mind along with the ticking of the grandfather clock.

Fifty seconds...

Forty-five...

"Nick," Zane said as he pointed the gun at Julia. "Where's my bag?"

"Please..."

"Where's my bag?" Zane whispered, raising the gun to her temple.

"I don't have it."

Thirty seconds...

Zane moved the barrel to Julia's forehead. "Where's my bag?" he whispered, more insistently now.

"I don't—"

"Where's my fucking bag?" Zane exploded, his rage shaking his face, the gun trembling in his hand. His finger tightened on the trigger.

"Mommy!" Katy cried.

"Close your eyes, baby," Julia said, and the room fell to chaos.

"No!" Nick shouted as he leapt at Zane.

"Mommy!"

Zane pulled the trigger and everything seemed to slow: Julia's head snapped back as the bullet pierced her skull above her left eye; the roar of the report thundered in the room; Katy's piercing scream drowned everything out as she ran to her mother and clutched her, burying her head in her mother's motionless chest.

As Nick reached Zane, he saw the killer training his pistol on Katy.

"You might think you can save her," Zane said. "You might think you can stop all this from happening. But..."

As Zane paused, Nick told himself that all was not lost. He could still save Julia, he could still save Katy, if only—

But then Zane reached in his pocket, pulled something out, and held it up, clenched tightly in his left fist. As he slowly opened his hand, Nick's heart sank in fear and despair.

Impossible. It couldn't be....

Zane held in his palm a pocket watch, polished and ornate, with elaborate etchings in its gold-and-silver case. An antique timepiece identical to Nick's.

A second *pocket watch*?

And as the first chime of the grandfather clock struck the hour, Nick's world fell to darkness.

CHAPTER 10

3:00 PM

"Wake up." Julia leaned in, gently kissing Nick's lips. "Wake up, my hero."

Nick's eyes flashed open as he bolted upright in his office chair where he had been asleep.

Julia recoiled in surprise. "I didn't mean to scare you." She touched his arm. "Bad dreams?"

Nick stood and grabbed her, looking into her eyes as if confirming reality. "Horrible," he said, unable to shake Yogi Berra's famous phrase, *Déjà vu all over again.*

"Maybe if you slept a bit more at night and cut back on the sugar...." She kissed him on the cheek and stepped back. "I've got errands to run." Julia pulled out her flower-blinged iPhone and checked her calendar. "I'll be back by 3:45. We can't be late."

Nick could barely catch his breath as he watched Julia walk out the door.

"This grandfather clock's got to go," she called from the hallway.

Nick looked about his office, trying to organize his thoughts; Julia had died twice in the future and he hadn't been able to save her either time. He sorted through the last hour: stopping the dam's destruction, bringing down an investigation like Byram Hills had never seen before, warning Paul Dreyfus of his and his daughter's death so he could prevent them...and Janos Zane.

Clearly, Zane was the man Paul had warned him about, the man who owned the bag, the bag that Julia had just died for.

Nick could barely wrap his mind about the last image he'd seen before falling back in time:

Somehow, some way, Zane possessed a pocket watch identical to Nick's. He had no idea how Zane had acquired it, but the very fact that he had one meant....

Nick jumped from his chair, ran through the hallway, and yanked open the front door.

Julia's car was gone.

Janos Zane lay on the floor, his body in shock. His third time-jump and it still was a jolt to the system. He looked up at the TV behind the counter and noted the time. 3:01. It seemed impossible, but—

"What's going on with you?" a voice said from the kitchen doorway. "You look like shit."

"I'm fine," Zane said as he got to his feet and looked around. He was in Brichetti's Market and Deli on the corner of Main Street, where he had originally been at 3:00 o'clock. He had been flashing his fake FBI badge at the town's stores and markets, asking questions, trying to figure out where he could find Paul Dreyfus.

"Did you have a seizure or something?" The young man put down his broom and helped steady him.

"I'm fine." Zane brushed off his clothing and pulled away from the clerk.

"Weren't you going to look for Paul Dreyfus?" The kid's buzz cut and three earrings stood in sharp contrast to the MIT insignia on his grey shirt.

"I found him," Zane said as he opened the beverage fridge, pulled out a water, and chugged it.

"Huh?" The clerk said in confusion. "I just told you about him two minutes ago."

Zane paused as he too tried to shake the confusion from his mind.

"Sounds like you've been drinking too much...or drinking too little." The clerk smiled.

Zane held tight to the timepiece in his hand. It was hard to keep things straight; he not only remembered what he had been doing for the last two days in Byram Hills, but he also recalled the future—a future that had yet to happen.

Though the dam had been destroyed—he'd seen it happen, witnessed the devastation—it hadn't happened *yet*. The contradiction was enough to make a man insane.

He tucked the watch back in his pocket. He could change time, change outcomes, change the world...and that was exactly what he was going to do.

Without another word, he left the confused clerk behind and walked into the afternoon sun.

Nick ran back into his office, where, on the corner of his desk, his iPhone lay. The same iPhone that had shorted out in the flooding of Byram Castle three hours from now. For a moment, he marveled at the paradox of it all.

He dialed Julia. "Pick up, pick up," he murmured, willing her to answer. The phone rang again and—

"Hi, Nick," a man's voice answered.

Nick's heart stuttered.

"Nice of you to call," Zane said. "How you feeling? I have to tell you, this whole time-jumping process is an ass-kicker."

"You son of a bitch. You killed my wife."

"But she's alive right now, isn't she? She just left your house—"

"How the hell do you know that?"

"You'll find I know many things. Like where your wife is, where she's going, the secrets she's keeping from you."

"You stay the hell away from her—"

"Give me my bag and maybe I will. Keep it from me and I'll simply go pick her up and kill her."

"You bast—"

"And you assume that you'll simply slip back an hour in time and save her, right?"

Nick didn't answer. Instead, he tried to absorb the implications of a second person possessing an identical pocket watch to Shamus's original—not any person but a madman bent on destroying him, his family, and everything he loved.

"You'll try," Zane said, "but I'll be right there, hour after hour, jumping back with you, and you'll have no idea where I'll turn up. But I'll know exactly where to find Julia. In fact, I know where she'll be all day." Zane let the harsh reality hang in the air. "You see, Nick, Julia will die again and again and again until there's no time left for you to save her. Then I'll kill her one last time, and she'll be dead for good."

Nick had never felt more powerless in his life. This man Zane was running through time *with* him.

Nick sat and spun in his chair. He pushed aside the cabinet door in his bookcase to reveal a small safe. He thumb-print opened it and pulled out a Sig Sauer pistol along with two magazines.

Nick hated guns—always had. This one had been a gift from Marcus, along with shooting lessons. Marcus said it was about defending oneself and loved ones, being prepared. But this situation went well beyond defense.

"I own you," Zane said. "I own your wife. Let's just get that clear."

Nick closed his eyes. "I will kill you."

"Meet me at 20 Byram Lake Road. Bring me my bag or I'll kill Julia...again."

The line went dead.

Nick tried desperately to clear the panic from his mind and formulate a way to save Julia once and for all.

He didn't have the bag, but he had its contents: the smart key, pictures of the papers, the memory stick. The items he'd removed from the bag had made the leap back in time with him. He had no idea what the items meant to Zane, exactly, but he knew their value: they were worth Julia's life.

Nick's phone rang, startling him from his thoughts. He looked at the screen. It was Julia, or rather Julia's phone. He debated answering it....

"Listen to me you, son of a bitch," Nick growled.

"Nick?" Julia said.

"Julia?" Nick was shocked. "Are you all right? Where are you?"

"What the hell?" Julia said. "Why so angry?"

"I thought you were someone else. Where are you?"

"The flower shop. Did you just call me?"

"Do you have your phone?" Nick asked, sounding foolish.

"What do you think I'm calling you with?"

"Are you alone?" Nick's gut churned with fear at the thought of Zane lurking near her, unseen.

"Yeah. Katy's with Bonnie—they're upstairs. I told them not to bother you. What's the matter?"

"You've had your phone the whole time?"

"What the hell are you talking about?"

"Listen to me: do not go out the front door. Stay in the shop." Nick was planning on the fly. "I'm on my way to pick you up."

"What? Why?"

"Just listen to me." Nick couldn't hide the desperation from his voice.

"Why?"

"Someone's after you—"

"What? Nick, what the hell is going on?"

"I can't explain. I'm on my way." Nick hung up.

He ran out the front door, tucking the Sig Sauer behind his back, then climbed in his Jeep Wrangler, plugged in his phone, and shot out of the driveway.

He hit auto-dial. The ringing was answered almost immediately.

"Shannon, it's Nick."

"Hey, what's up? Am I going to see you later?" the detective asked. "Is Julia gonna have those mini-hot dogs and some scotch tonight? I have a feeling I may need both to get through the senator's BS."

It was hard for Nick to keep his memory straight. Everything he remembered from the four and five o'clock hours had not occurred for anyone but him—and, apparently, Zane.

To the rest of the world, Julia hadn't died twice; Shannon hadn't helped stop a terrorist attack; and the dam had never burst. They knew nothing of the future two hours from now, which to Nick felt like the *past* two hours. It was an advantage and a crippling bewilderment at the same time.

"Look I need a huge favor."

"Sure." Shannon's voice turned serious.

"Can you send a car by 20 Byram Lake Road?"

"Why? What's up?"

"I'm not sure." Nick only knew that Zane had instructed him to bring his bag to that address. He didn't have time to explain or prove his point this time by showing Shannon the video on the chip in his pocket. "Just hearing some crazy rumors...."

"Rumors?" Shannon pressed.

"Please?"

"No problem. I'll knock on the door myself."

Time. It was a concept that no longer made sense to Janos Zane. It had taken him almost twelve hours to reach his goal and now he was traveling backward through the same twelve hours he'd just lived.

And while the world around him marched forward, he was on a one-way course for 7:00 a.m. The point where it all began.

Three hours ago, or three hours from now—the thought made Zane's head hurt—he had pulled into the long cobblestone driveway of a mini-mansion. It had been 6:15 this evening, the dam in the valley already blown, hundreds dead or dying, first responders working furiously to save lives in the raging floodwaters. Three hours ago, he'd driven onto the mansion's grounds, winding his way through pristine gardens, past vast lawns, a tennis court, and a large pool in the rear. He had visited earlier in the day but found no one home. At 6:15, however, he'd discovered a dinged-up, blue Honda parked by the side door. The crappy car seemed incongruous with the Tudor house, probably a visitor, as it wasn't parked in the four-car garage. Zane had hoped it belonged to someone who could lead him to Dreyfus.

Zane clutched two long, octagonal-faced keys, the narrow face of each side etched with unique patterns of dots and curves. One key was brass, the second copper. He had never seen anything like them before until he'd taken the brass key from the chain around the dead man's neck. The man who'd possessed the second key was still alive, though barely. Hopefully, getting the third key would be easier.

As he exited his car, he noticed the host of hidden cameras, tiny, expertly camouflaged; he had come across similar security measures before. Zane had read up on the background of the man who lived here, his businesses, his family, and his connection to billionaire Shamus Hennicot. Given the man's renowned expertise in security, Zane knew his defense measures would be hard to defeat. Zane decided to employ an atypical means of entry into the home of Paul Dreyfus.

He looped the strap of his leather satchel over his head and exited the car.

The sound of the far-off sirens cut through the summer evening air as dozens of rescue and news copters roared, danced, and hovered in the distant sky.

As Zane rounded the side of the house, he saw her and drew his gun. The girl was poolside in the smallest of bikinis, sipping a drink, earbuds filling her head with music, all of which masked his approach. Her wet blonde hair was pulled tight in a ponytail, her phone resting on a pile of fashion magazines discarded on the chair beside her. As he grew closer, he noted she was young, mid- to late-twenties, with an engagement ring on her left finger.

She seemed entirely unaware of what was happening in town, the distant sirens blotted out by the music in her ears.

Zane tucked his gun in his concealed shoulder holster and sat beside her.

He tapped her leg and she jumped.

Seeing Zane, she ripped out her headphones. "Who the hell are you?" she blurted. Instead of fear, anger shone in her eyes. "What do you want?"

"Friend of your dad's." Zane smiled. "Are you Alice or Annie?"

"Alice..."

"Is your dad here?"

"No, he's not due back for another hour."

Alice slowly turned her head as she heard the distant sirens, her eyes drifting skyward as she saw the circling helicopters.

"What's going on?" Alice stood and wrapped herself in the towel as fear crept into her eyes, then ran to the house, through the rear French door into a large family room. The TV was on, images of the shattered dam and roiling waters filling the screen.

"When did this happen?" Alice's eyes went wide with shock as she looked up at Zane, who stood in the doorway.

"About twenty minutes ago." He closed the door.

Alice stared at the TV. "Oh my god. My father—"

"I'm sure he's fine." Zane had no idea, but hadn't seen him arrive at the party, which was the main reason he'd decided to come back to the house for a second look.

He reached in his satchel, pulled out a small video camera, pointed at the TV, and began filming.

Alice's eyes fixed on the TV images, the tragedy unfolding in real time, the brunette news anchor unable to hide her tears. Images of the shattered dam filled the screen before cutting to the churning waters of the new lake and rivers that masked the horrors beneath their surfaces, the depths covering hundreds of homes and roads where thousands of people had been moments before.

Paul Dreyfus walked through the front door and stepped into the family room, a young blonde woman beside him, her face red and tearstained. "Who are you?" he asked.

Zane didn't answer. He tucked the video camera in the satchel.

Alice looked confused. "He said he was a friend of yours—"

Zane held up the two keys.

"Where did you get those?" Dreyfus asked, clearly shocked.

"I need the third. And I need that box."

"Girls," Dreyfus said softly. "Wait outside."

"Please stay here." Zane drew his gun and pointed it at Alice. "I'm running out of time and I will not waste it on pleas or begging. Just give me what I want."

"I don't have it."

"The box or the key?"

Dreyfus stared at Zane.

"I know you didn't destroy it," Zane said. "You were supposed to. You and Zachariah Nash were supposed to have dropped it in the Marianas Trench three years ago."

"I don't know what you're talking about."

Zane raised his gun and pointed at Alice. "Please lie down on the floor."

"What?" Alice snapped with a mix of fear and anger. "Why?"

"What's going on? What are you doing?" Annie, the blonde asked.

"Lie *down!*" Zane shouted, his tone startling both women.

Alice began trembling as she lay on the floor. "So easy to be tough when you have a gun."

"Bring me the box," Zane said to Dreyfus.

"Please," Dreyfus whispered. "Let them go—"

Without warning, Zane shot Alice in the back of the head.

"No!" Annie screamed as her knees buckled.

Instinctively, Dreyfus grabbed Annie and pulled her behind him.

"Lie on the ground," Zane said as he pointed the gun at Annie.

"Stop!" Dreyfus shouted.

"Lie on the ground!" Zane screamed at Annie.

Dreyfus threw up his hands and nodded. "Okay...okay, we're going."

Keeping Annie in front of him to shield her, Dreyfus led Zane through the hall and kitchen and opened a rear door into a large, high-tech workshop: immaculate tables with electronic instruments, tools neatly hung on the wall, three computers on a desk, strange devices in various states of construction and repair. The large desk in the corner was spotless and clear but for three small, skeletal, metal sculptures: an elephant, a lion, and a gorilla.

Dreyfus took Annie by the hand and pulled her to his side as he walked to the tool rack on the far wall. He pushed against the floor-to-ceiling organizer and it popped away from the wall—a hidden door that revealed another door, this one much sturdier and made of steel, with a keypad at its side.

He pressed his left thumb on a glass pad while punching in a code, and the vault door swung open to reveal a bunker-like room. Along the wall of the ten-by-ten room were metal shelves, various cardboard and metal boxes upon them. Zane also noted an air-filtration system, jugs of water, rows of food, inflatable mattresses, spare clothes, and a radio rig.

"Nice safe room," Zane said. "I'd say you're paranoid, but considering the circumstances...."

Dreyfus picked up a two-foot rectangular box made of mahogany. He carried it out of the saferoom and laid it upon his workbench.

"Open it," Zane said as he pointed the gun at Annie.

"I need your keys."

Zane handed Dreyfus the brass and copper keys. Pushing aside a small sliding panel on the front of the box, he revealed three slots. Dreyfus inserted the two keys on either side of the center hole.

"Where's the third key?" Zane asked.

Dreyfus stepped to his desk and picked up the small metal lion sculpture. He removed its spine: the third key.

"They each need to be turned to the right at the same time, one full rotation." Dreyfus inserted the third key in the center hole.

Holding his gun in his left hand, Zane grasped the copper key while Dreyfus gripped the other two. Dreyfus nodded and they turned the keys a full turn.

A subtle thud within the case could be heard as the latch released. Dreyfus lifted the lid to reveal a dark velvet interior.

In two recessed spaces lay a pair of gold-and-silver pocket watches.

"There're two?" Zane said in surprise.

"You have no idea what you're doing." Dreyfus stared at Zane.

Zane lifted out one of the watches; looking at the intricate etchings, he pressed the crown, flipped open the cover, and stared at the watch face and the engraving on the inside cover: *Fugit irreparabile tempus.*

Zane removed the satchel from his shoulder, placed it on the table, and unzipped the large pouch. He withdrew a big envelope, making room for the mahogany box. A list of names had been written on the manila envelope: Nicholas Quinn, Julia Quinn, Senator Byron Chase, and Charles Hadley.

Zane caught Dreyfus staring at the names. "Friends of yours?"

"Stay away from them."

"That would be a yes. Perhaps you can help me find Julia Quinn."

"Annie," Dreyfus said as he turned to his daughter. "There's a red box on the second shelf. Could you go in there and grab it?"

Without a word, Annie stepped into the safe room and emerged with a foot-long lacquered box.

"And the blue one on the same shelf?"

Annie went back into the safe room. Almost immediately, Dreyfus kicked the metal door closed, locking her in.

"No!" Annie screamed from inside. "Dad!"

"What did you do that for?" Zane looked up from the watch in his hand.

"You're not going to hurt her."

"Obviously not now." Zane kept his gun aimed at Dreyfus, who reached into the wooden box and picked up the second watch.

"How do they work?" Zane asked.

"Let me show you." Dreyfus flipped open the red lacquered box, pulled out a Glock 9mm pistol, and began firing before he even aimed.

Zane dived through the door into the kitchen, quickly returning fire. Dreyfus grabbed the satchel from the workbench, snatched up the envelope, stuffing it in as he raced out the rear door of the workshop, the door slamming behind him.

Zane scrambled up from the kitchen floor and charged through the workshop after Dreyfus. He hit the rear door; the handle turned, but the door wouldn't budge. He shook it violently before seeing the magnetic lock at the top of the doorjamb. As he turned to run, he saw drops of blood on the floor. Dreyfus had been hit.

Zane raced back through the kitchen and out the front door, only to see Dreyfus's Volvo tear down the street. Jumping in his car, Zane flew out of the driveway, drifting around the corner, tires spinning as they grabbed the road.

Zane caught sight of the Volvo a hundred yards ahead as they raced down into town; emergency vehicles were everywhere, the sidewalks vacant, cleared in the wake of the attack. The two cars weaved through the traffic, heading out of town.

The Volvo sped down Route 22. Zane glanced to his right to see the Killian Reservoir three quarters empty, the tips of ancient trees hidden for a century poking through the low water. Zane put the accelerator to the floor and caught up, only fifty yards back now. Going a hundred miles an hour through the winding turns, the Volvo disappeared for moments around each bend, only to be seen again as the road momentarily straightened. Dreyfus disappeared once more around a large turn. Zane pushed his car to one hundred and twenty. And—

Zane locked up the brakes, the tires screaming and smoking in protest as he came to a sudden, sliding halt. The Volvo was on the side of the road and Dreyfus was running into the woods.

Zane leapt from his car, cutting through the thick forest, his feet slipping on the underbrush. He caught intermittent sights of a lake through the trees: boats, kayaks, and divers dotting the surface, ambulances and fire trucks lining the water's edge.

Zane ran along the new shoreline, past the roof of the submerged Byram Castle, his eyes seeking his prey. But Dreyfus had disappeared.

He needed his bag; without it he would fail, everything would fail, and that wasn't an option.

He reached in his pocket and pulled out the watch. For nearly half a day, he had searched, he had killed, he had done everything in his power to get it, and now, without Dreyfus, he had no idea how it worked.

As he continued through the woods, he caught a glimpse of Dreyfus at the shoreline, filming, the camcorder in his right hand sweeping left to right, up toward the dam and the peak of the castle. He turned the camera to a tributary, an outcropping, hundreds of bodies floating within it, trapped within tree branches, limbs of all kinds intertwined. Dreyfus turned the camera off, his head nervously turning, looking for Zane. He laid his gun on a rock beside him and tucked the camera in the satchel on his shoulder. Then he pulled out his phone and began shooting pictures.

As he silently approached, Zane could see Dreyfus's chest was bleeding, his white shirt crimson-soaked.

"Give me my bag." Zane aimed his gun as he stopped ten feet away.

"All these people..." Dreyfus said as he stared out at the horror. "Why?"

"You don't understand," Zane said.

"Are you going to stop this from happening?" Dreyfus tucked his phone in the bag, zipping it closed as he turned and stared at him with pleading eyes.

"No," Zane shook his head. "Those deaths are inconsequential."

"They were my friends." Dreyfus eyed his gun, three feet away on the rock. "You killed my daughter."

Zane could see the tears in the man's eyes; he was broken, bleeding, and dying.

"Give me my bag."

Dreyfus reached in his pocket and pulled out the other watch. "You have no idea how dangerous this is." Dreyfus pointed at the shattered dam, at the new, rising shoreline a foot away. "That's nothing...a drop in the bucket of disaster compared to what *these* things can do."

"Desperate men do desperate things."

Dreyfus steadied himself against a tree. With a click, he lifted up the gold crown atop the pocket watch, twisted it twice to the left, pressed the crown post back down and, without a word, dived into the water.

Zane lunged for him, gun aimed, ready to shoot, but Dreyfus had disappeared.

At a loss, Zane had spun about, confused, looking for Paul Dreyfus before finally realizing what had happened. Then he'd looked at the watch—6:59 p.m.—quickly mimicking Dreyfus's gestures, he lifted and twisted the crown. He looked about, steeled himself, and pressed the crown back in place.

Zane sat in his car, staring at the watch. It was 3:40 now. Nearly three hours since he'd stolen the unique timepiece, a theft that had actually taken place three hours in the future.

So, three hours since he'd begun his backward journey.... Such a warping of the mind.... He avoided trying to parse the logic of it all and instead focused on his mission.

He'd had a mission going forward, and now he had a mission going backward. He was halfway done. And while the first half—obtaining the watch—had been difficult and nearly cost him his life, he knew this part would be much worse.

And if he didn't get that bag, not only would his mission be over, but the world would be irreparably changed.

Zane reached in his pocket and pulled out the iPhone in the flower case—Julia Quinn's iPhone—and smiled. He opened the calendar and studied it. It was more organized than anything he had ever seen: appointments by the hour, addresses, phone numbers, an itinerary, and a list of who she was meeting, not only today, but for the following month.

He marveled once more at the impossible—the existence of two copies of the same cell phone in the same time and place. He wondered what Einstein would have made of it.

Better than Julia's calendar was the locator app he found in this copy of Julia's phone. He watched the blinking dot and smiled.

Zane knew exactly where Julia Quinn was.

And it was time to pick her up.

Nick parked on Main Street. He turned off his Wrangler and looked at the photos of the files on his phone, but his mind kept going back to the four names on the envelope: his, Julia's, the senator's, and that of Charles Hadley, a man dead for more than 120 years.

No one knew the name Charles Hadley unless they'd grown up in Byram Hills thirty years ago—or a century and a score ago. Hadley, the town constable, had died in 1898 under mysterious circumstances.

Before social media, the internet, television, and even radio, news was carried on the tongues of the locals, passed from neighbor to neighbor, town to town and, if deemed worthy, by a local newspaper. Hadley's story had been passed down from generation to generation, and by the time it had reached ten-year-old Nick, it had become legend.

Charles Hadley, they said, was killed by the ghost of the Leatherman, a mountain man who hunted the woods of the county, dressed in the hides of his kills, who had been thrown in jail by Hadley for unsubstantiated crimes. It was said he escaped his cell one evening, disappearing into the woods after vowing revenge on the constable.

Six months later, Hadley had gone missing after his evening walk. He was found the following day in the middle of the woods, the lower half of his body missing as his dead hands clutched the branch from which his torso still hung. The town folk said one eye was missing and his mouth was locked open in a scream.

Legend said the Leatherman and Charles Hadley's ghost haunted what Nick and his young friends had called Hadley's Woods. Neither young Nick nor his friends ever went in there; no one in town had except Johnny Goodheart, and he'd been crazy, unafraid of anything. Johnny was the kid who'd catch snakes and carry them around in a burlap bag, then slip them through mail slots and toss them into local stores before getting chased by the police.

Johnny headed into Hadley's Woods on a dare one evening, a cigarette hanging out of his twelve-year old mouth, a bottle of Fanta in his hand.

He came running out twenty minutes later, pale, shaking, and scared, too terrified to tell anyone what had happened. A few years later, though, Goodheart finally fessed up. There were no ghosts or goblins, witches, or monsters. It was two guards raising their guns and taking aim that had spooked him. They told him to turn and walk out and, if he dared to look back, they'd shoot his balls off. He made it thirty feet before curiosity made him glance over his shoulder, only to see a guard raise his gun and splinter the tree next to his head. At that, Johnny had broken into a sprint, never looking back.

Nick's phone rang. "Hey."

"It's an empty house," Shannon said. "Been on the market three months. No one there."

"Okay," Nick said, but he was already focused on his next request. "Can you do me another favor?"

"Don't I already do you too many favors?"

"Yes. And I'll owe you for this one as well."

"You're going to make me a very rich man when I cash in on all these favors. "

"I hope so...." Nick paused. "Can you check out Hadley's Woods?"

"What do you mean? Like walk around?"

"Yeah." Nick pictured the name of Charles Hadley on the envelope, alongside the others. He had no idea how they were all connected, but Hadley's Woods—the place he'd once feared so much—seemed a good place to start.

"You think the Leatherman's back?"

"Very funny. No, but something's going on out there."

"You gonna share what that might be?"

"Honestly, I have no idea, but it scares me."

Bill Shannon pulled out of the driveway of 20 Byram Lake Road and headed into town. Cutting through the traffic headed for the holiday festivities at the dam, he drove across the village, leaving the streets and homes behind and coming to a stop a half-mile down one of the three remaining dirt roads in town. Lined with stone walls under the shadows of the summer canopy, a long driveway led a hundred yards in from the road, turned right, then disappeared. The grass along the unkempt drive was tall, uncut, as it had been for years. There were no visible utility lines going in. In-and-out traffic was minimal at best, as evidenced by the scattered weeds growing through cracks in the asphalt.

While the taxes were always paid on time, not much was known about the 200-acre parcel, but there had been rumors of late: a buzz around town about activity in those woods. Strange noises. Odd lights. Soon, rumors had blossomed into fact, then into legend: silent, hovering aircraft; UFOs; medical experiments; ghosts and apparitions.

Shannon had laughed at them all, but now he found himself driving up the cracked driveway, half as a favor to Nick and half due to his own curiosity. He rounded the corner a hundred yards in and saw that the driveway went on and on in a meandering path through dense forest.

Around a final corner, he came to a gate—a thick, iron fortified structure where two armed guards stood. Shannon pulled up, turned on the police lights in the grill of his unmarked car, and got out.

"Good afternoon," Shannon said, careful to keep his hands visible.

"May we help you?" The lead guard was polite, but the pistol and the rifle over his shoulder sent a different message.

"Detective Bill Shannon, Byram Hills Police." He handed over his badge for their inspection.

The guard took it and looked it over before handing it back.

"How may we assist you, detective?"

Shannon didn't know what to say, so he went with the rumor. "There's been talk in town about activity out here at night."

"What kind of activity?"

"Odd lights." Shannon shrugged. "Strange noises."

"Not from here." The guard shook his head.

"Don't suppose I can do a drive-through?"

"Sorry, sir." The guard was grim. "Not without a warrant or a really good reason."

"Who do you guys work for?"

"The homeowner."

"And is he home? May I speak to him?"

"Sorry, sir."

"And his name is...?"

"Sorry, sir."

Shannon nodded, slowly looking left into the woods, thick with summer greenery and a host of chirping birds.

"Happy Fourth, guys." Shannon nodded, got back in his car, and drove out to the end of the driveway.

A half-mile ahead, he caught a glimpse of the top of the Killian Dam. He planned to bring his wife, Sheila, and their two sons to the fireworks later tonight, taking advantage of police privilege for good seats.

He wasn't sure how he'd pulled the short straw to be commanding the day shift of a holiday. He was looking forward to escaping to Nick and Julia's fundraiser reception later. Sheila had called him three times to remind him not to be late, if he wanted those mini-hotdogs.

Looking back at the woods behind him, Shannon reined in his wandering mind. He opened his phone and pulled up Google Earth, punched in the address of the woods behind him, and zoomed in on the hundred-acre parcel.

It was not what he expected at all.

"Martha?" Shannon said into his car's police radio as he continued to stare at the image.

"Yes, darling?" The department dispatcher's voice was groggy and rough from a combination of vices.

"Is John in the office?"

"As a matter of fact, his lazy ass is sitting on the couch watching the Yankee game instead of whatever it is he's paid to do."

"Put him on."

A moment of mumbling arguments, then, "Hey, Bill, what's up?"

"The tax office is closed, as is building-and-planning and pretty much everything else, so I need to pick your brain."

"Not much to pick at," John said. "But be my guest."

"Who owns Hadley's Woods?"

"Well, the Hadleys held it for generations but sold it in the eighties to a corporation."

"Do you know which one?"

"Let me think." John Goodheart knew the town, its history and sordid past better than most. Following his wild childhood, he'd become a cop and stayed with the force for nearly twenty years.

"No problem," Shannon said. "I can get it on Mon—"

"Lord of the Valley," John belted out. "A foreign company."

"How the hell do you remember that?"

"Because when they were building in there, no one from planning was allowed in. Everyone tried to find out who the company was, but since it was foreign, it was too hard to trace. The owner's more mysterious than the damned Leatherman."

"So, there's a house in there?"

"Whatever it is, it took over two years to build. The town was kind of freaked out, but it died out over time since the owners paid the crazy tax assessment the town hit 'em with."

Shannon looked again at the Google Earth image; something didn't make sense.

The two heavily armed guards he'd encountered were protecting a hundred acres of nothing. According to the image he was looking at, there were trees, woods, stone walls, and a small pond and field in the center. The only habitable structure was a small, cabin-sized house. Hard to see in the poor resolution of the satellite photo, it couldn't have measured more than 500 square feet.

Shannon doubted it took two years to build.

Nick stood impatiently on the sidewalk in downtown Byram Hills, looking up and down the street. It had been five minutes and still no sign of Julia. And then it occurred to him.

He opened the locator app on his phone—something they'd agreed to use and share in case either lost their phone, a common occurrence over the years.

Nick saw the blip signal of Julia's phone a mile outside of town at an address he didn't recognize. He kicked himself for not doing this in the first place. He dialed Julia.

"Hey," Nick said. "Where are you?"

"Just grabbing some things from town. Where are you?" Julia asked.

"At the flower shop, where you told me you were. But you're not here; in fact, they say you were never here."

"I'll be home in fifteen minutes."

"From where?" Nick said, his voice turning angry.

"Don't start in on me."

Nick's phone beeped an incoming call. Bill Shannon.

"Hold on a second." Nick hit the call-waiting button. "Hey."

"Nick?" Shannon said. "Why'd you want me to check out Hadley's Woods?"

"What did you find?"

"I'm not sure, but I've got a lot of questions. You want to tell me what's going on?"

"I've got Julia on the other line. I'll call you back."

Not waiting for Shannon's response, Nick clicked back to his wife. "Julia—"

"Dammit, Nick. Now is not the time."

"You're in danger."

"*What*? Don't be so dramatic."

"I'm not being dramatic," Nick said. "Someone's after you."

"Who? What are you talking about?"

"Shut up and listen to me." Nick could barely control himself. "I can't explain it over the phone. Please, just stay where you are. I'll be there in two minutes."

"You said you didn't know where I was. How do you know where I am?" Julia asked. "Are you tracking me?"

"Well, you told me you were at the flower shop."

"I can't believe you're tracking me!"

"I can't believe you lied to me." It was true. Julia never lied to him.

"I'm getting in my car," she said.

"You don't understand—"

"I'll meet you at home. If you don't believe me, watch my every move on the app." Julia hung up.

As Nick laid the phone on the seat of his car, he saw a second blip on the locator app, less than a quarter mile from Julia. That didn't make sense. *Two* Julias? Nick couldn't be sure which signal was hers.

He looked at the first signal, stationary; the second signal was in motion...and moving toward the other Julia.

Moving fast.

Julia punched in the security code while turning the key, locking the door of the storage unit, and headed across the empty parking lot. Nick's anger scared her, his words a catalyst that ignited her already fomenting paranoia.

She doubted anyone was trying to kill her; instead, she figured Nick was onto her, onto her secrets, and had put the pieces together incorrectly. She dreaded seeing him, afraid of what he knew, what he'd found out.

She turned toward her Audi as a black Town Car raced into the small parking lot, screeching to a halt in front of her. A tall man leapt from the car and charged at her.

Instinct taking over, Julia ran to her car, fumbling her keys as she hit the door release, ripped open the door—

And was grabbed by the hair and violently pulled to her abductor's vehicle.

Nick cut down Maple Avenue, racing toward the two signals, which had converged, forming a single blip. Moments later, the pair of signals was on the move and driving fast; twice as fast as he was. There was no doubt in Nick's mind who it was and what was happening.

He quickly dialed Julia as he sped down the road.

"Hello, Nick," Zane answered.

"Let her go!"

"You sent the police. Why did you do that?"

"Just let—"

"Bring me my bag and we can talk about keeping Julia alive."

Nick glanced at the app. Zane's car was less than a quarter mile ahead of him, approaching the busiest intersection in town.

He tried to calm himself. "Where do I bring it?"

"Stay tuned. I'll let you know five minutes before the top of the hour. Don't want you sending the police again. Be ready and don't be late."

"If you harm her...."

"I need to chat with your wife about a few things, so we'll be disappearing for a while."

Nick hit the intersection and found not a car in sight; he looked down for the dual blips of Julia's phone, but they'd both vanished.

"Your husband has no idea, does he?"

Julia stared at Zane. She was tied to a chair in the middle of a concrete basement, the floor scattered with toys, boxes, and broken furniture.

"How many secrets do you have from one another?" Zane circled her as he spoke.

"Who the hell are you?" Julia glared at him. "Are you trying to scare me?"

"Scare you? This is so crazy." Zane shook his head. "You have no idea what I did to you an hour from now."

"What are you talking about?"

"It's difficult to explain," Zane smiled. "But I've already looked into your terrified eyes."

There was a calmness to this man, a confidence in the crazy words he spoke. Julia could feel the fear she was masking beginning to creep to the surface.

"How did you come to meet Colin Armor?"

"Who?"

"Colin Armor."

"I don't know who you're talking about."

"Come, now. I just need to know where he is."

"That's a death wish."

"Maybe for both of us," Zane nodded. "But you clearly know who I'm talking about."

Julia stared at Zane, engaging in a battle of wills.

Zane looked down at his copy of Julia's phone, turning it on.

"Is that my phone?" Julia's eyes darted to her zipped-up purse on the floor by the door. "How did...? How do you know my password?"

Zane quickly texted: *33 Whippoorwill Road. Be here by 3:55. No later or you won't like what you see.*

"You'd be surprised at what I know." Zane looked up at Julia. "I know that you're involved with Colin. I know that you're involved in the day's events. Where is he?"

"They'll kill you if you go near there," Julia said with a bit of hope in her voice.

"I'm sure that would make you happy."

"Who *are* you?" She struggled against her bonds.

"Who are *you*, Julia Quinn? Mother, lawyer, wife?" Zane paused. "Liar?"

Julia looked away from his gaze and his question, filled with regret. She never should have gotten involved. She wasn't sure why, but as she thought about it, she realized that it had been her ego.

Of all men to get involved with....

The thing that scared her almost as much as her situation was that it had been so easy to lie to Nick, to tell him to his face that she was going to a friend's house, that she had to work late, that every-thing was fine when he asked her about her day.

Her nerves and earlier bursts of anger had been not so much directed at him as at herself. The secrets were killing her. She felt like unseen eyes had been watching her the past few days. She had never been one for paranoia, but it had begun to consume her. She never kept secrets from Nick beyond Christmas gifts and the occasional pair of shoes she'd promised him she wouldn't buy. But this was no ordinary secret; this was something she could not speak of.

Nick had once been able to read her face like a letter. He knew her emotions from the curve of her lip, from the look in her eye. If she even dared try to deceive him over something silly, like throwing out his favorite shirt, he detected it instantly. Had she gotten better at deception or had he lost the ability to read her? Or worse, had he simply stopped looking? Caring?

There was no good answer.

Could it really be that, after all the years they'd been together, things had become commonplace, mundane, uninteresting? Was she trying to fill a void in her life? She couldn't help admitting that it made her feel emboldened, excited, as she snuck around. Is that why Colin Armor and everything about him thrilled her so much?

"Tell me where he is," Zane said.

"So you can kill him?"

"No, actually, I don't want to kill him. I'm going to help him."

"Why would he possibly need your help?"

Zane picked up a large gasoline container and began pouring the liquid around the perimeter of the room.

"What are you doing?" The odor assailed Julia's senses as her fear finally boiled into her voice. "Why are you *doing* this?"

Zane circled inward, moving around Julia, closer and closer.

"Oh my God." Julia realized what was about to happen. She thought frantically of Nick and Katy and her promises and lies. She wanted to live, desperately wanted to live; her family had only just begun, her daughter was everything to her and Nick. Katy had only started to notice the world around her, and Julia desperately didn't want to leave her.

And Nick...would he understand what had happened? Their last words spoken in anger, her hanging up on him, not listening to his words of warning?

"'Oh my God,' is right," Zane said, as he placed the now-empty jug beneath her chair. "You won't understand, but time is precious and it's running out for both of us. Now, tell me where I can find Colin."

"I can't."

"What you don't understand is, I will find a way to break you. The question is how many times will you die? It's a hard concept, though one Nick fully grasps." He shrugged. "Everyone has a breaking point. To some it's money: they'll sell their own mother for a buck. Others, it's power, happy to be elected even though a puppet master will forever pull their strings. To most, it's love, their boyfriends or girlfriends, husbands or wives, and most particularly, children."

"Don't you dare—"

"And of course," Zane cut her off, "the soldier's go-to method: pain. Is your breaking point pain, Julia?"

Nick raced up the steep Whippoorwill Road, pushing the Wrangler to its limits, climbing higher and higher. He knew the house. A nondescript colonial he'd driven past a million times. He glanced at the digital clock on his car radio: 3:57.

He was late and he lacked Zane's bag. It was lost to the future, but he still had its contents. He could trade them for Julia, for her life.

As Nick crested the hill, he saw billowing clouds of black smoke roiling into the sky. He rounded the corner, pulling straight into the driveway, only to find the white colonial fully engulfed in flames. Deep, jaw-rattling explosions blew out the windows as fiery tendrils writhed from holes in the roof.

Nick burst from the car, shielding his face from the searing heat of the fire.

It took him a moment to realize his phone was ringing; his heart leapt as he saw it was Julia.

He quickly answered. "Thank God. Are you okay?"

"Hello, Nick," Zane said. "You're always late, and this is what happens.... If only you were more punctual. I recorded her screams. Would you like to hear them?"

"I'm going to—"

"I'll tell you what you're going to do. You will do exactly what I say or this will happen every hour until you can stop it no more. Julia, Katy, you...you'll all burn."

CHAPTER 9

2:00 PM

Julia Quinn hustled into her office building in the business park on the outskirts of Byram Hills while Janos Zane watched from the far end of the nearly vacant parking lot. As Julia disappeared inside, he turned his attention to the blip on the phone in his lap, once again wondering at its impossible, duplicate existence.

Her calendar appointments for the last hour seemed to have fallen apart, but it didn't matter; he didn't need to know where she was scheduled to be, only where she was.

He watched as the dot floated about before stopping in the far corner office; at the same moment, from outside the building, he saw the room's interior lighting flash to life.

Julia was unaware of not only his presence, but also of his existence. She had no reason to look over her shoulder. She knew nothing of the destruction of her town that would happen later in the day, nothing about the ways she had already died.

Julia was tougher than Zane had expected, far more resilient than most of the people he had applied his skills to. He scolded himself for thinking of her as fragile, reminding himself that women were not only stronger in their resolve, but also in their constitution.

He didn't doubt that he could extract the information that he needed, but having experienced her resolute will, he feared it could take hours. Thanks to the pocket watch, any efforts he made would be lost after sixty minutes, leaving him to start anew an hour earlier in the day.

So, instead of physically prying what he needed from her about Colin Armor, he would simply watch her movements. At some point in the day, she would lead him where he needed to go. Sometimes you didn't need to go to extremes. Sometimes all you had to do was observe.

His copy of Julia's phone rang, startling Zane. He waited a moment, answered, and listened.

"Julia?" a woman's voice asked.

"Hey, Sara," Julia said as Zane held the phone to his ear and listened to their conversation. "Please don't tell me Nick's late to pick up Katy again...."

Nick couldn't help staring at Marcus, who had died only hours before...or later. Nick still struggled to keep the order of the day straight. Though he was beyond relieved to see his friend alive, the danger to Julia and Katy overwhelmed all positive emotions.

He had awakened five minutes ago, sitting in the high-back leather chair in his home office, the papers he'd been reviewing in the two o'clock hour scattered on the floor, having fallen out of his hands.

The house was empty as he took the video chip from his pocket, stuck it in his computer, and transferred the files to his phone. He spun around, got his gun from the safe, and ran across the long, green yard that separated his home from Marcus's large colonial.

Moments later, they sat on bar stools across from each other in his friend's kitchen.

"You okay?" Marcus asked.

Nick tried to smile. "Yeah, I'm fine. Say, do you still have that big casting net?"

"This about fishing?" Marcus shook his head in confusion. "You want my help catching fish?"

"I need your help to do something...bad."

"I'm real good at bad." Marcus waggled his eyebrows. "Just ask any of my ex-wives."

"This is worse," Nick said. "I'm in trouble."

"Again?" Marcus's face turned serious. "How much trouble?"

Nick fidgeted in his chair.

"With Julia?"

Nick sighed. "I wish it was that simple."

"What did you do this time?"

"This is hard to explain."

"Don't worry, I'm your greatest critic and skeptic, so give it a shot."

"Julia's in grave danger."

Marcus's eyes narrowed. "What are you talking about?"

"And so is Katy."

"From who?"

Nick knew that Marcus would do anything and everything to protect Julia and Katy—he loved them like they were his own family. Julia had served as Marcus's voice of reason through too many relationships and marriages. She'd even served as "best man" at Marcus's fourth and last wedding (Marcus blamed his prior failed unions on Nick's bad luck in the role). She was the friend that told Marcus when he was wrong, when he needed a haircut, and when he looked like shit...things his doe-eyed, newlywed wife wouldn't be telling him for a few more years. She knew his favorite foods, always stocked his favorite whisky, and bought him the best presents at Christmas—a surfboard, a drone, a waterproof camcorder—instead of what others thought Marcus *needed*, like socks, neckties, and golf balls.

"I need you to suspend logic and reason for a few minutes." Nick called up the video on his phone.

"Don't we do that every day?"

"Just watch the video."

The footage from the future dam break played. Teary news anchors stumbling through their words described the unraveling disaster; images of horror reflected on Marcus's face. Nick paused the video for a moment and allowed the initial minute of coverage to sink in.

"Are you shitting me? What the hell *is* this?" Marcus said. "The time on the bottom of the news ticker says 6:15 p.m. today."

"I know."

"What the hell's going on?" Marcus's voice rose in confusion and anger.

"Just bear with me. It's gets worse."

Nick hit play and the footage swapped over to that of a handheld camera. The image of the dead, of the bodies floating by in the churning waters. The camera focused on the culvert where the mass of bodies bobbed up and down against each other like logs in a flume.

And then Marcus's body appeared in the corner of the screen; a moment later, so did Julia's.

"Turn this shit off," Marcus said, turning away. "What the hell *is* this?" He began to pace the room. "What the fuck, Nick?"

Nick took back his phone and looked at the tracker, at Julia's location. She was on the move....

"It's going to take a leap of faith." Nick stood and glanced at his phone again. Now he saw the second dot, two miles away: Zane also moving, converging on the same location. And Nick knew what that location was.

"Nick!" Marcus shouted to get his attention.

"I'll explain while we drive."

For the second time today, Nick screwed up picking Katy up from daycare. The first time had been at 2:10—the original time he'd experienced 2:10 today. Now he arrived late again, at 2:13, but instead of feeling the fear that comes with dereliction of duty, he felt a much deeper and more visceral terror.

"Wait here," Nick told Marcus as he ran across the lot and through the front door of the single-story brick building. He raced down the long hall of Flynn's Daycare to Katy's room.

"Nick?"

Nick turned to see Julia marching toward him. "You're late."

"I know. I'm sorry. We need to talk...."

"You're always late." Julia walked right past him without making eye contact.

"I'm sorry." Nick caught up to her. "I'm here now."

"You have no idea how crazy my day is. I was on my way to one of the most important meetings of my life," she said. "Do you understand that? And on top of that, we have the reception at five, and *then* I get a call from daycare that Katy's dad didn't show up to get her."

"I'm sorry."

"You're always sorry." Julia stopped and turned to Nick. "Katy must be freaked out."

"I'm sure she's fine." Nick opened the hallway door and followed her down a second hall.

"No. You were late two days ago, and you know what she said this morning? 'Is Daddy going to forget me again?'"

Nick's head drooped.

They walked past the vacant classroom in silence and stepped out onto the playground, where two female aides chatted while Katy swung on the swings. A man was gently pushing her, laughing along with her as they talked.

"Hi, Daddy." Katy's smile spread across her face as she saw Nick.

"Sorry I'm late, kiddo."

"Dat's okay," Katy said. "My new friend is swinging me."

"Hey, Nick." Zane turned, his broad smile sending a chill through Nick.

"I'm sorry," Julia said. "I haven't had the pleasure."

"Janos Zane," he said. "A friend of your husband's."

"He never mentioned you." Julia turned to Nick. "You should have told me you at least sent someone to wait with her."

"Nick's always looking out for you guys. He didn't want Katy to be left alone." Zane offered his hand. "You're Julia."

Julia smiled as she shook his hand. "You work together?"

"We're working on a deal." Zane smiled. "You look so familiar to me."

"You too," Julia said. "Though I generally don't forget a face."

"Nick said he was going to be a little late and didn't want Katy to worry."

Julia looked at Nick with suspicion in her eyes. "Really?"

"Yeah," Nick nodded. "You got Katy from here?"

"Not really," she said. "I really need to get to a meeting, but—"

Nick gestured at Zane. "Thanks. Janos and I have to review some deal points." Together, they walked toward the playground exit.

"Wait. So, you came to pick her up, but now you *can't* pick her up?"

"Sorry," Nick called without turning back.

Zane paused and turned to face Julia. "You look stressed."

"It's always the unexpected, the things you don't plan for, that can ruin a day."

"I understand." Zane nodded. "The best laid plans...."

"Please stop by our fundraiser reception tonight: bland food, watered-down drinks." Julia pointed at Nick. "He'll give you the details if he hasn't forgotten them."

"Thank you," Zane said. "I'll try to make it, but if not, I'll be there in spirit."

"Don't be late, Nick. We need to leave no later than a quarter to four."

"I won't." Nick opened the gate for Zane.

"Famous last words," Julia said under her breath.

"Your wife is so organized." Zane said as he walked through the parking lot, holding up the duplicate of Julia's phone. "Her calendar is practically down to the minute."

Nick glared.

"And not just for her, but for Katy and you. I know where she is all day. Do you?"

Nick said nothing.

"No. You don't," Zane said. "Because if you did, if you knew what she was up to, what she wasn't telling you, you wouldn't be happy. She lies to you so easily."

"Fuck you."

"There's another man in her life. Did you know that?"

Nick grabbed Zane and slammed him against the side of his Jeep, his rage unleashed. "Stay the hell away from them! If I find you within ten feet of my daughter—"

"Nick," Zane said calmly as he looked him in the eye. "If you don't cooperate, if your wife doesn't cooperate...nothing is off-limits. I can be far worse than you've seen."

Nick released Zane.

"I'm glad you—"

"Glad about what?" Marcus said as he came up behind Zane, jamming a gun in his back.

Nick parked his Wrangler on the edge of a tree-lined, dirt road in an isolated section of Byram Hills. He got out, walked around and opened the door; he pulled his gun and aimed it at Zane, motioning for him to exit the passenger seat.

Marcus climbed out of the back, unfolding his body from its tight confines, never lowering his gun.

Nick pulled a large duffle bag from the back of his Jeep and threw it over his shoulder. He waved his gun at Zane, motioning him to head down the path into the thick forest. Nick and Marcus walked in silence several steps behind Zane until the reservoir came into view.

They were at a rocky outcropping with an artist's view of the Killian Dam a mile away; the granite ledge hung ten feet over the deep, dark water, not a soul in sight, the only sounds birds, bugs, and water lapping against the sheer drop.

"It's amazing how far we'll go to save the ones we care about, the ones we love," Zane said coldly.

"Give me Julia's phone," Nick demanded.

Zane reached in his pocket, pulled out the duplicate phone, and threw it on the ground.

Without a word, Nick stomped on it, crushing the device. "Stay the fuck away from my wife."

Marcus took the duffle from Nick and opened it at the edge of the rocky ledge. He reached in and pulled out a large mesh net, spreading it over the rock. The fifteen-foot circular net had large weights evenly spaced around its circumference.

"I need you to go back up to the car," Nick told Marcus.

"No way," Marcus said.

"I don't know who else he's working with; you need to watch my back from up there, not down here. Make sure no one wanders down to fish or fool around."

"Don't underestimate this guy." Marcus walked by Zane, pausing, then sucker-punching him in the temple. "I'd be happy to beat his ass before you kill him."

"I'll remember that," Zane said to Marcus as he recovered from the sudden blow.

"Sadly," Marcus said, "you've only got a few minutes of memory left."

"Go." Nick waved his gun. "I won't underestimate a thing. I'll call you down when I'm done."

Marcus headed up the path as Nick motioned Zane to toward the edge of the lake.

"You won't be able to explain a bit of this," Zane said.

"There will be nothing to explain." Nick pointed to Marcus's large casting net.

"Smart," Zane said. "Body at the bottom of the lake. I'll be fish food." He looked at the net and sighed. "Would you ever have thought of such a thing before?" Zane sounded proud. "Would you ever have contemplated murder or such a brilliant means of disposing of a body? I've brought out the best and worst in you all at once."

"Only you would think that."

"This is who you really are." Zane smiled. "Behind the facade of the upstanding husband, a killer lurks."

"Give me the watch," Nick said.

Zane pulled it from his pocket and threw it on the ground.

"Before you crush that and shoot me," Zane said, "you should know, it will happen when you are happiest."

"What's that?"

"When you can no longer change time, right wrongs, stop my murderous hand."

"What are you talking about?"

"You haven't saved the future, Nick. You're not the hero you think. The halting of the destruction of the Killian Dam is in the future. But those bombs in the dam are active now and can still be detonated. Surely you don't think I work alone." Zane tilted his head to the side. "You should know, blowing up the dam was never my end-game. There're others involved, bigger things that you can't see, that you couldn't possibly conceive." He gestured expansively with his hands. "My death will trigger a far worse catastrophe than you can imagine. And a far more personal consequence for you."

Zane pulled three pictures from his pocket and threw them to the ground next to the watch. Each was a small headshot of a different man, their only commonality being their averageness.

"My colleagues," he explained. "After the watch's twelve hours are up, when you least expect it, they'll look for your wife at her job, in your home, in your bed. Whichever one provides proof of her death gets one hundred thousand dollars. So, whether I'm dead or alive won't matter. My reach will be from the grave. Julia will be killed and there will be nothing you can do to stop it—no police to call, no pocket watch to rewrite her fate. Two of these men have a shade of morals and look at it as a contract. To one of them, though, it's not about the money; it's about the permission to be himself. He doesn't go for the simple bullet to the back of the head. He'll kill her in a terrible way, probably in front of your daughter. Then he'll kill Katy so there will be no witnesses.

"There's only one way to stop them," Zane said softly. "And that's if I give them the order to stand down. My survival means Julia's survival; my death means her death. Permanently."

Zane bent and picked up the three pictures, tucking them in his pocket.

Nick looked out at the reservoir in frustration. Despite his plans, despite what he perceived as having the upper hand, he was powerless. Even with the advantage of the watch in his pocket.... He slowly lowered his gun.

Zane bent down, picked up the watch, and held it tight.

Nick now realized he'd *never* had the upper hand. Zane had been toying with him the whole time.

"Now," Zane said as he leaned into Nick's space, "where's my bag?"

Nick barely heard Zane's words as anger rose within him.

"Where's my satchel?" Zane repeated.

"You want to know where your bag is?" Nick said evenly, his rage threatening to explode. He whispered, "It's in the future."

"Very funny."

"I'm serious. Your plans, your memory stick, your smart key, everything—tucked in the fish tank at Byram Castle at 4:45 this afternoon. It couldn't be farther or more impossibly out of your reach."

Zane slowly nodded, closing his eyes for a moment. When they opened—

His hand snapped out, snatching the gun from Nick and jamming the barrel under Nick's chin. "Then you're useless to me."

Julia and Katy sat on the front stoop outside their home, sipping from apple juice boxes.

"Why can't you stay?" Katy asked as she rubbed her mother's arm.

"Well, sometimes Mommy has to go to work."

"I want you to play with me."

"There's nothing I want to do more than play with you, honey, but sometimes Mommy and Daddy have to work now and save the play for later."

"How come Daddy gets to go play?"

Julia smiled. "Daddy works very hard, but sometimes Daddy needs to go find his smile."

"But Daddy's always smiling."

"He is, but sometimes happy on the outside hides the worry on the inside. So, Daddy goes out to play with Uncle Marcus to make that worry on the inside go away."

"What about you? Is that why you go to the gym? So you don't worry?"

"Yes and no. I go to the gym to be healthy and get exercise, but Mommy usually wears her worry on the outside."

"Like when you yell at Daddy?"

"Yes." Julia laughed despite herself. "Sometimes yelling at Daddy makes Mommy feel good. It's not right and you should never yell at anyone—"

"Until I get married?"

"Oh, dear. This conversation is really going to cost me."

"What's dat mean?"

"It means I love you, honey. And I have to go."

"Stay." Katy looked at her mother with large, watery eyes.

"I just have one more meeting. Then I'll be back and we'll go to a party."

"Whose party?"

"A big party." Julia gestured with outstretched arms. "Daddy will be there, and Uncle Marcus. Lots of food."

"Can I dress up?"

Julia leaned close and looked into her daughter's eyes. "That's what parties are for. Bonnie's going to give you a bath and wash your hair and maybe, when I get back, we'll put on a little makeup."

A smile bloomed across Katy's face as she jumped into her mom's arms and hugged her tight around the neck.

Julia looked up at Bonnie, who stood in the doorway. "You got this?"

"Of course," Bonnie said as she took Katy's hand and led her up the stairs. "Mommy loves you."

Katy turned back. "Katy loves you."

After a long moment, Zane pulled the gun away from Nick's chin and stepped back.

"Senator Chase."

"What about him?" Nick asked.

"You know him." It wasn't a question.

"So?"

Zane paused again. "There's a safe in his house."

"How do you know that?"

"Because I broke into his house today and saw it."

"What did you find?"

"Nothing, because I couldn't get it open. But you will."

"And why do you think I can open it?"

"Desperate men are innovative men." Zane smiled.

"Excuse me?"

Zane nodded. "You're going to break into the senator's home and bring me the contents of that safe."

"How the hell am I going to do that?"

"You figured out how to commit the almost-perfect murder." Zane waved the gun at the net on the ground. "This shouldn't be that hard. Don't waste time figuring it out. You've got less than forty minutes."

"And if I do happen to pull this off?" Nick asked.

"Bring whatever's in the safe to that house on Whippoorwill Road."

"Which house?"

"It's so easy to forget the future," said Zane. "The one that burned with Julia inside. I'll be waiting."

Nick stared at him. "What if someone else kills you? What if you die in a car accident or the dam breaks with you in front of it?"

"Well, then you'd better protect me a whole better than you've protected Julia," Zane said. "If I have a heart attack, find a crash cart and revive me; if I'm about to be shot by your friend Marcus, you'd better take the bullet." Zane held the gun to his own head, mocking Nick. "Remember, I die, she dies."

Byron Chase wrote his own speeches because he found that the words of others didn't flow from his lips in the same way. He wasn't as convincing with other people's prose. Over time, he'd learned that when he told a story, whether true or false, it had to be worded by him. It was easier to sell a lie when it was your own instead of someone else's.

He had gone over his speech five times in the last hour, rewriting at least half of it. Every word had to have a purpose, otherwise it was cut from the text. This was the most important speech of his life. It would set the stage for his career and propel him to his ultimate goal.

It was the perfect opportunity: Fourth of July in his hometown, in the community where he was once a teacher, a man of the people, shaping young lives. The press had been arranged for; his political party was on board. He had the endorsement of everyone relevant in power and the financial backing of the region's most powerful financial titans.

But what he enjoyed even more than amassing power was what he had accomplished in the last month.

He'd left the country without anyone knowing, traveling to Budapest under a false passport, flown in under the cover of darkness, and been whisked to an ancient manor house for a meeting that would set the world on fire if anyone learned about it.

His passport had read Brett Matting, a financial consultant. His silver hair had been dyed brown, the lifts in his shoes making him two inches taller. A restrictive brace on his right knee gave him a slight limp, and he dropped his shoulders the way the man who'd given him the new identity instructed. It wasn't only the change of color tones that created disguises; it was also the shape of the body, the way one carried oneself. Body language spoke louder than any word.

The Learjet had picked him up from Teterboro Airport just across the Hudson. He had a single pilot for the nine-hour flight, and not a word was spoken.

After he'd landed at Vaclav Havel Airport in Prague, a man boarded his plane, stamped Chase's false passport, and led him to a black Range Rover. He was whisked up into the mountains and through the rusted wrought-iron gates of a large estate. The stone manor house had a single light on.

Chase was greeted by a man whose facial scar had disfigured half his face and rendered one eye milky and sightless. He was led into a room where six armed men stood on either side in the shadows, each clutching a pistol as they guarded the single man who sat at the head of a long, black conference table. He was broad-shouldered and thick in a five-thousand-dollar suit, his palpable charisma filling the air with menace.

Byron Chase had never been more terrified.

The meeting lasted three hours. He was back on the jet before dawn.

He had survived and achieved his task and, in return, he would be rewarded.

They say spoils come to those who dare, and those who risk most win the greatest share.

"Senator?" asked Andrew, his aide.

Chase looked up from his speech.

"Another session in the park in fifteen minutes."

Chase nodded, smiling inwardly. This would be the last of the smalltime meet-and-greets. After this evening's reception, everything would change.

Julia drove out of her driveway and headed down Sunrise Drive. She glanced at her phone and saw two new messages from Nick. She had already listened to two others, his voice pleading with her to call him right away, that he needed to speak to her. Of course, when she needed his help, he'd run off with some new business partner, leaving Julia to get Katy home from daycare without any regard to her job, without any thought how it would impact her afternoon.

She had no intention of calling Nick back yet; while she felt more than a tinge of regret, it was the least of her worries today, which had literally turned into the craziest day of her life.

It had started like most days: spin class at 6:00 with a roomful of Wall Street bankers, moms, and early birds; grabbing her coffee and paper from Country Kitchen; a quick bit of shopping for breakfast; then back home and in the shower at 7:05. She was dressed and eating breakfast at 7:30 when she'd gotten the phone call from the police.

Heart pounding, she'd raced towards town. Katy, hastily tucked in her car seat in back, was still asleep.

For four minutes, Julia thought Nick was dead, her mind exploding in grief, tears pouring as she faced a reality that no one ever anticipates.

As she rounded the corner onto Banksville Road, she saw the black smoke billowing into the sky and screeched to a halt where Bill Shannon and John Goodheart were directing traffic around a tangled mess of crumpled vehicles. Her eyes finally fell on the two white sheets covering bodies on the ground. She could barely breathe as she leapt from her car and raced past the line of vehicles and across a sloping lawn toward the mayhem.

First, she took in a crushed landscaping truck and an accordioned Toyota, the injured walking around, holding their hurt limbs.

And then she saw Nick, leaning over an elderly man, giving CPR, while Marcus shot a fire extinguisher at a tipped-over, mangled Mercedes, dousing the roaring flames.

With newfound energy, she sprinted to Nick at the same time that paramedics arrived and took over.

She ran into Nick's arms, hugging him as if he had returned from heaven.

"Oh my God." Julia couldn't stop her tears of joy, grabbing Nick's face, kissing him all over, hugging him again as she finally caught her breath.

"My turn?" Marcus asked.

"Get over here." Julia turned and hugged him, enveloped in his enormous, bear-like embrace.

"What happened?" Julia asked as she watched the paramedics working on the unconscious man. "Who is he?"

"No idea."

"You saved his life," Detective Shannon told Nick as he approached them. "If you weren't here, we'd be loading him into the coroner's truck instead of the ambulance."

"Is he going to be okay?"

"Hard to tell. He's still unconscious, but he should survive. Thanks for knowing what to do," Shannon said, then returned to the ambulance.

"Unbelievable." Julia wrapped her arms around Nick again as he laughed at her overreaction.

"I'm perfectly fine. We weren't even *in* the accident," Nick said. "You okay?"

"I thought you were dead." Tears filled Julia's eyes again.

"Why would I be dead? I was never in danger."

With Julia's adrenaline slowing, the added efficiency, strength, and focus fell away. She began to shiver, pant, and gasp. Looking around her, she finally saw Nick's Wrangler with the Jet Ski hooked to the back. Now, she grew angry. "This needs to stop."

"What needs to stop?" Nick asked, genuinely confused.

"You being around when accidents happen."

"We were just on our way to go kitesurfing."

"Yeah," Marcus said. "Believe me, this wasn't part of our plan."

"Of all days for this to happen." Julia glared at Nick. "Please come home. I don't need you to get in some accident out on the water. This is enough stress for one day."

"We'll only be gone a couple of hours," Nick said as he kissed her forehead. "Wow, are you sweaty."

Julia stepped back. "I'm going home."

"Don't you want to hear what happened?"

"Later. I'm mad at you. And don't be late to pick Katy up at two. And don't forget, we need to leave by a quarter to four." Julia looked at Marcus. "And that goes for you too."

"What did I do?" Marcus asked.

"It was your idea to go kitesurfing today. The two of you are like children."

"Your husband saved a life," Marcus said. "Cut him a little slack."

"Really? Defending him?" Julia's anger rekindled. "You have no idea what went through my mind—it was four minutes of hell that aged me four years! Now I have to go home, take another shower, clean the kitchen, take out the garbage, make Katy breakfast, take her to daycare, and I'm going to miss my meeting—it was an important meeting, Nick—while you two go out and play."

Julia stormed back toward her car before turning back. "And don't be late to pick up Katy again."

"Wow." Marcus said. "She's pissed."

Nick smiled.

"Why are you so happy?"

"Because she still worries about me."

Julia had heard every word they said before getting in her car. Nick couldn't understand how important the meeting that she would miss was. Even more annoying, she'd hated having to lie to him about it.

In the end, she had indeed missed the meeting at eight a.m. and had gone back and forth between her office and home four times since, running too many errands prepping for tonight's big event. It had all been too much. Overwhelming, really.

Now, at 2:23, suddenly, she had a moment of free time. She drove through Byram Hills, immediately cursing her luck as she was detoured around a construction site in the middle of Main Street, a blue concealment tarp flapping in the breeze revealing a deep trench amid several concrete barriers on the roadway. Finally making it through the detour, she sped out of town.

"You should have just let me kill him," Marcus said as he paced back and forth. "Or at least let me throw his ass out of the moving car instead of setting him free in town."

"And then wait for his assassins to show up in the middle of the night to kill Julia and Katy?"

Nick had gone from triumph to enslavement in a matter of seconds. Zane was three steps ahead of Nick's every move.

"So now you're his errand boy, robbing houses to fetch god-knows-what so he can blow up the dam?"

Nick and Marcus stood on the corner of Bayberry Road, three houses down from Senator Chase's home.

Nick ignored Marcus's jab. "Dreyfus can get the safe open."

"Maybe," Marcus said. "But it goes against his professional ethics. Plus, you'd have to convince him of your pocket watch journey, and you said we don't have much time."

"How do we get it open, then?"

"I know a guy who can definitely get it open, but it'll cost us."

"And you can get him over here now?"

"Yeah, he's not far. What about Julia? Is she safe?" Marcus asked. "Where's she right now?"

"She's back in her office; that place is locked tight."

"Really?" Marcus said. "I doubt locked doors are a problem for Zane."

Nick pulled out his phone, opened the locator app, and looked at the blue dot as it moved along the screen, driving away from town. "Damn it."

"Not in her office, then?" Marcus shook his head. "What a surprise. Where's Zane?"

"At a house on Whippoorwill, waiting for me," Nick said. He couldn't get the image of the house burning out of his head. He looked at the blue blip again. "Where the hell is she going?"

Julia flipped her blinker, turned right, and headed down the dirt road; the tree-lined street was uneven and bumpy, potholes filled with puddles from last night's rain. She turned right into the unmarked driveway into Hadley's Woods and drove for a quarter mile until she came to a security house, an imposing large metal gate, and two well-armed guards.

"Good afternoon, Ms. Quinn." The lead guard nodded.

"Hey, Jimmy, sorry you're working the holiday."

"You too."

"Think you'll get a chance to watch the fireworks tonight?"

"Hoping." Jimmy smiled. "How can I help you?"

"I was hoping to get back down there. I missed this morning and got locked out. Just got some free time."

"Sorry, still on lockdown."

"Really?"

"The director's been up to the surface a few times. Said we just have to sit tight until he gives the all-clear."

"Is that normal?"

The guard shrugged. "There's nothing normal down there."

Senator Chase's house was large, a white, French colonial with a cobblestone driveway, manicured trees, and big white pillars. Nick had knocked on the door five times, his prayers fulfilled when no one answered.

Marcus's friend arrived in a Ford pickup. With a shock of brown hair over a face that looked like it had been through the world more than a few times, the man looked familiar, but Nick couldn't place him. Without a word, he went to the side door, slipped a small gun-like tool in the lock, and pulled the trigger until the door opened. The man walked into the house and followed a loud beeping to the security panel. He pulled out two alligator clips with wires leading to a small box, then removed the front of the alarm panel and attached the clips to two leads. A series of numbers flashed across the small box until the beeping stopped. He tucked the box in his bag and gestured for them to come in.

"His name's Tony Santo," Marcus whispered as they walked into the senator's house. "He lives on the other side of town, a former thief; he knows this stuff far better than Dreyfus does, but don't tell Dreyfus that. He's a competitor to Dreyfus, but they move in entirely different circles."

Nick and Marcus followed Santo through the house arriving in a beautiful, teak library where, behind a large partner's desk, sat a large, heavy safe. The floor around it was scratched, marring the dark polished wood.

Santo crouched and looked at the old-fashioned flywheel. He ran his hands along the corners of the three-by-three safe, as if massaging a woman.

"Do you consider safecracking an art or a science?" Marcus asked, but Santo ignored the question.

Pick up, Julia. Nick listened to three more rings and finally clicked off.

"After your run-in at Katy's daycare, I doubt she'll be answering your calls for a while," Marcus said. "Why don't I call her? Who knows if Zane isn't already looking for her?"

"Maybe, there's a way to keep Zane from chasing Julia...to keep him right where he is." Nick quickly dialed his phone. "Hey, Bill."

"What's up?" Shannon said.

"Listen, there's a guy, a very bad guy, named Janos Zane."

"Where are you?" Shannon asked.

"I'm in White Plains." Nick looked around Chase's library, wondering how many laws he was breaking as he lied to his friend again.

Zane sat at his computer in the basement of the house on Whippoorwill. He'd reformulated his plan for the coming hours down to the minute. Everything needed to be in place. Janos Christoph Zane was nothing if not meticulous.

He had spent his life in death. It was what he excelled at, a skill honed in war. He had never married, never loved, his needs satiated with one-night stands and fifty-dollar tricks.

While most assassins came from broken homes, dysfunctional nightmares, or misspent youths, Zane had grown up in the midst of normalcy, he and his brother the center of attention and close as siblings could be.

It was love that had created "Janos Zane." Love for his family. That and arriving two minutes late on a fateful night.

Since he was young, everyone had called him JC, a nickname his father had coined. Gerald was JC's older brother, and they were true Irish twins, born ten months apart, nearly identical: jet black hair, pale blue eyes, tall, lean, with a layer of sinewy muscle on a strong athletic frame. January and November birthdays put them in the same grade, so everyone in the town of Bedford assumed they were twins. While both were straight-A students, there were subtle differences between them: JC had street smarts, a sharper wit, and was slightly more confident, with a tendency to get in fights, while Gerald was the better negotiator, the calmer brother, able to talk himself into or out of any situation. He couldn't stomach bullies, always intervening to even the odds or right a wrong. He was more popular with the girls—the kinder boy—whereas JC was the fractionally better athlete with an extra dose of testosterone-fueled aggression, on and off the field.

They were both excellent fighters, skills honed from an early age of beating one another bloody; fists to jaws, blows to stomachs, alternating headlocks till someone cried uncle. Two years of Tae Kwon Do and Aikido introduced kicks, blocking, holds, and epic backyard battles. Their parents never broke them up, their father insisting they fight till someone lost or backed away.

After each brawl, no matter who was more bruised or bloodier, the boys would be laughing a minute later, forgetting what argument drove their tempers into battle. But the lessons learned were marginally different: Gerald realized that fighting was the last resort, while JC considered it the first weapon in his arsenal and a fear-based deterrent for everyone around them.

Their parent's marriage fell apart when they were in fifth grade. JC and his brother alternated between anger, tears, and shame, blaming themselves as so many of their friends had. They stayed with their mother, slowly drifting away from their father as the years passed. Their mother never remarried, hardly dated, dedicating herself to her boys. They saw the sadness in her eyes despite the mask of her smile. Both became the "man of the house," burying their grief to remain strong for her. It hardened the brothers, thrusting them into adulthood, wiping away the last bits of their innocent youth while laying bare the reality and unfairness of life.

In the spring of their senior year, they were meeting friends in the city—Gerald coming from his girlfriend's house, JC from the gym.

JC's train was two minutes late.

Gerald had gotten off the subway at 12:30 a.m. and stepped into the dark station at 14th Street, climbing the stairs into the crowded neon lights of the warm spring night. He headed down a series of streets that pedestrians avoided, and the night grew more vacant. He walked without fear, overconfident in his size and ability, enjoying the solitude with only two more blocks to walk.

A piercing scream caught his ear and sent his senses on high alert. Without thought, he raced into an alley to find a teenage girl amid four guys who were taunting her, pushing her, laughing as they tore at her shirt.

Gerald rushed to her side, his size causing the four teenaged punks back into the shadows. He was helping the tearful girl to her feet when a punch caught him in the side of the head.

He spun about, his leg flying up, sending his attacker to the ground with a single kick. The three others pounced. Gerald blocked, attacked, and fought them off, his countless fights with JC paying dividends. The three were unskilled, smaller, but they were also feral, wildly swinging, biting, and scratching.

A knife struck Gerald in the back, stunning him, searing pain racing through his core. It came again and again, the wild animal thrusting and slashing in a senseless rage, sending him to the ground. Smelling weakness, the other punks dived in, kicking and hitting the defenseless young man who'd interrupted their fun.

JC traveled the same footpath two minutes later and, hearing the commotion, spotted the wildlings upon their prey.

The punks immediately scattered, and the girl—who turned out to be bait—ran with them into the night.

Gerald was near death, his face swollen, his pierced and shattered body bleeding out. JC held him in his arms, cradling him to his chest, his brother's blood soaking them both. Gerald's desperate eyes looked up, pleading for help, but there was nothing JC could do. If he'd arrived on time, if they'd stood together against the thugs, it would be their assailants lying dead in the street.

Despite an intensive investigation by the NYPD, the wanted posters, and news stories, the killers were never found.

Gerald was buried on a Tuesday; their mother killed herself Thursday.

With nowhere to go, with no close family left and nothing but rage to drive him, JC joined the army. Over the years, he quickly rose through the ranks, his intelligence, fighting skills, and drive unique among teenage enlisted soldiers.

As JC's fighting skills became military grade, he learned the lessons of war: how to track, how to investigate, how to hunt, capture, and kill the enemy. He was an expert marksman, be it with rifle or pistol. For JC, each pull of the trigger was dedicated to Gerald.

When there was a mission to carry out, JC was the one to turn to. He would fight his way in and out of battle no matter how intense, how difficult, how impossible. He soon became the captain of a six-man unit. A constantly revolving, continually refreshed team that formed another tool in his arsenal, like a rifle, handgun, or grenade. JC was feared yet respected, an example to strive for, though never equaled.

He had spent many years at war: in Iraq, Afghanistan, and four years in Akbiquestan. Everything JC did, he did to make up for being two minutes late. But the truth was, he barely thought of Gerald anymore, and he never thought of his mother, or his father; he only thought about succeeding. In his rare, reflective moments, he realized he'd become more machine than soldier.

A noise in the driveway startled Zane. He scooped his gun off the table and walked up the basement stairs.

"You've gotta be kidding," Zane said aloud as he watched the police surround the house. "Fucking Nick Quinn. If I didn't need you, I'd kill you."

He pulled out the pocket watch and looked at the time. In thirty minutes, it wouldn't matter—they'd never find him.

He walked to the back of the house, opened the window, and fired a single shot in the air. Returning to the front, he saw that the police had scattered behind their cars, rocks, and trees. He counted to five.

Zane knew standoff protocols and procedures: no rushing, no risk, drag it out. He had to make sure they didn't come in before the top of the hour and take him down; more importantly, he couldn't allow them to separate him from the pocket watch.

That single gunshot bought him an hour, though he only needed half of it.

"Can't you just put your ear against it and hear the clicks?" Marcus asked.

Santo ignored him as he reached in his bag and pulled out a small drill press. He affixed it to the front of the safe, the bit placed slightly to the right of the flywheel. He started up the drill, its tip nosediving into the metal, the safe's steel screaming in protest as the titanium bit sliced it away like butter.

He pulled out the bit and slipped in a thin wire. The screen in his hands glowed as the fiber optic thread filled the interior of the safe's door with an orange glow. He turned and twisted until a large set of gears were magnified on screen.

"Tony," Marcus said, "time is of the essence."

Santo continued to ignore him. With his eyes glued to the image, he turned the flywheel slowly, watching the interior gears spin. A small, metal rod dropped into a small corresponding hole. He stopped and fingered the wheel in the other direction, slowly turning it until he saw another rod drop. Three more rotations, three more rods, and a subtle click sounded.

He turned the handle.

Shannon huddled behind his car, his gun drawn and aimed at the house. John Goodheart was twenty yards to his left, also behind his car, while three state police officers stood at the sides and rear of the house.

Why was it always on the holidays that the crazies decide to make themselves known? Being so shorthanded, Shannon had had to call in a favor from the state police. That was bad. Not only because he didn't like them, but also because he'd owe them, and Shannon hated owing anyone.

A black SUV pulled up and parked out on the street. A tall dark-haired man in a black suit exited while the SUV behind him poured out three uniformed marines.

The lead man pulled out his billfold and snapped it open, displaying his ID—Renzo Cabral.

"How the hell did you know what's going on so fast, Agent Cabral?" Shannon asked as he read the ID.

"We have folks listening to the police feeds, and Janos Zane is high on our list."

"For what?"

"Classified."

"Really?" Shannon said. "Don't bullshit me. You always travel with a marine contingent?"

"Why are *you* here?" Cabral turned the question around. "Why are you after him?"

"My town. My jurisdiction." Shannon wasn't about to reveal Nick tipping him off. "It's classified."

The silver-haired man dialed the phone on his desk.

"Hello?"

"How are you?" the man asked.

"I haven't gotten the satchel back yet," Zane said.

"What about the location?"

"I don't know where they are. There's got to be intel somewhere we can get our hands on."

"The woman knows. You're telling me you can't get her to talk? Focus on her. You need to find Colin Armor."

"Where are you?" Zane asked.

The man turned from his desk and muted the TV, sipping his scotch as he stared out the window at the snowcapped mountains. "I'm more concerned about where you are and what you're doing. There are people counting on you. Don't let me think I made a mistake in calling you."

Zane hung up and looked out the window at the police—and now military personnel—surrounding the house. He focused on the SUV and the newly arrived man talking to the police. He knew him, despised him, and wondered how Renzo Cabral had gotten here so quickly.

With so much uncertainty in the day, Zane was sure of one thing: Renzo had come with only one goal in mind. To kill him.

Nick stared into the safe as Santo stepped aside. Inside were two handguns, a diplomatic pouch, several loose pictures, a photo album, and three envelopes. Nick grabbed it all and put it in his duffle bag.

Without a word, the safecracker packed up his burglar tools and walked out the door.

"What do I owe him?" Nick asked.

"He didn't ask for payment," Marcus said. "He deals in favors; now, we both owe him."

"Story of my life." Nick started with the diplomatic pouch, which contained a stack of papers, some in Russian, some in English.

"I always knew Chase was an asshole."

"What is it?"

"Something about meetings, some loose pictures, a photo album, a fake passport." Nick looked at the passport with the name Brett Matting; the photo was of Chase, though his white hair had been colored brown. "With a bad dye job."

"Doesn't every politician get a fake passport when they're sworn in?" Marcus smiled. "You're not going to give all this to Zane, are you?"

"A gun's to my head."

Marcus nodded.

"But that's not to say I won't change things later."

Nick's cell phone rang. He quickly answered and listened

"How we doing with that safe?" Zane asked him.

"How'd you get my number?"

"I know everything about you. How's that safe?"

"Done."

"Impressive. You got the contents?"

"Yep."

"Good man, because we have a new issue," Zane said. "Remember what I said would happen if I die?"

"What's your point?"

"It was smart to send the police after me, keep me occupied for the hour, keep me away from your wife."

"Thank you, I guess. But you're not going to die. They're not there to kill you, just keep you busy and away from Julia."

"You obviously didn't think it through. See, the feds have shown up now, and they're not nearly as benign as your police friends. They *are* here to kill me."

"What are you talking about?"

"You've got maybe five minutes to save me. And remember, Nick, if I die, Julia dies."

Nick and Marcus jumped out of the Wrangler on Whippoorwill Road and ran up the driveway. The house was surrounded by police along with three marines and a dark-suited fed. The federal agent looked to be in good shape; he had dark hair but otherwise seemed nondescript, as most feds did. Nick thought he had seen him somewhere but couldn't recall where.

"I'm going in," Nick said as he walked toward Shannon.

"Are you crazy?" Shannon stepped in front of Nick.

"You don't understand."

"What's there to understand?"

Nick grabbed Shannon by the arm, pulling him away from the others.

"That guy in there?" Nick whispered. "He dies, Julia dies."

"What are you talking about?"

"This guy, the guy in the house...he's blackmailing me."

Shannon looked at Marcus, who nodded in agreement.

"He just had me break into Senator Chase's house and bust open his safe." Nick opened the duffle bag and showed him the contents.

Shannon couldn't hide his shock. "You can't be telling me this."

"Who the hell am I supposed to tell?"

Shannon shook his head. "Is Julia in there?"

"No, but he has set it up that if he dies, his colleagues kill her."

"Shit." Shannon turned away, thinking. He turned back and snatched the bag out of Nick's hands, rifling through it, and pulled out the two pistols. "What the hell, Nick?"

"Keep 'em," Nick said. "This is about the files and photos."

"From the senator's safe?" Shannon tucked the guns in his gun belt and threw the bag back at Nick. "This is all *kinds* of crazy. You're dripping in felonies right now."

"I don't care. Gotta go in."

"And you're giving that stuff to the guy inside?"

"You've got to get me in there," Nick pleaded.

"He'll use you as a hostage. You could die."

"I don't care," Nick repeated, his voice rising.

"It's not my show, Nick," Shannon said softly as he pointed to the armed marines. "Why are they so interested in him? You've got to help me out, help me understand so I can help you."

"Two minutes," Cabral called out.

"They're going to kill him," Nick said into Shannon's ear.

"How do you know that?"

"This guy is as bad as they come; they want him dead."

"Why, who is he?"

"I'm not sure."

"Nick, goddammit." Shannon leaned in. "I can't help you if you don't tell me something that's got weight."

"He's trying to blow up the Killian Dam."

"The *dam*? Are you sure?"

"One minute," Cabral said to the three marines.

"Come on, this is for Julia," Nick pleaded. "I promise I'll explain later."

"How do we know there'll *be* a later? Are you gonna help him escape?"

"No." Nick's lie was hard to mask.

"You're going to get yourself killed."

"I'm going to get Julia killed if I don't get in there," Nick said. "I have to talk to him face to face."

"You're fucking me, Nick." Shannon grabbed Nick by the arm and marched him across the lawn toward the front door.

"What are you doing?" Cabral shouted as he ran up to them.

"He's going in." Shannon pointed at Nick.

"Who the hell *is* this guy?" Cabral jumped in Shannon's way. "No way."

"Move," Shannon said.

"We have jurisdiction." Cabral stood ramrod straight.

"Not at the moment." Shannon pushed past him.

Cabral pulled his gun, aiming it at Shannon's face. "Stop."

Shannon pulled his gun and aimed back. Anger burned in both men's eyes.

The marines trained their rifles on Shannon; a second later, Goodheart drew down on the marines, the State Police following suit.

"Whoa," Cabral said, still aiming at Shannon but raising his other arm to hold everyone's fire.

Goodheart double fisted his gun as he circled the marines, who aimed back at him.

"Everyone calm down!" Cabral called out.

"Nick, go," Shannon said, keeping his eyes trained on Cabral.

Nick ran up the three steps and into the house, closing the door behind him.

"Well done. And with less than a minute to spare," Zane said as Nick walked down the stairs into the cold basement. "You've got a good friend there...you really took advantage of him."

"The only reason they haven't come in here and killed you is me."

"Well, part of your job is to keep me alive. "

Nick took a moment and finally said, "You taught me something."

"What's that?"

"You're not afraid of dying—you're afraid of not completing your mission, whatever that may be."

Zane stared at Nick.

"I think you fear failing your mission as much if not more than I fear losing my wife."

"Did you get me what I asked for?"

Nick threw the bag at him.

A rushing commotion came from upstairs with people racing about, shouting.

Zane thumbed through the contents of the bag: the passport, the diplomatic pouch, the photo album, and the plans. "Holy shit."

Nick saw an emotion he hadn't expected wash over Zane's face, as what began as shock turned quickly to fear.

"My God..."

The front door burst open. A flash-bang exploded and filled the air with thick smoke. Gunfire tore into the living room, rapid-fired slugs shredding the walls.

Having cleared the upstairs, Renzo Cabral entered the basement, gun held high, his marines steps behind him. He looked at four concrete walls, no doors, no windows.

The room was empty.

CHAPTER 8

1:00 PM

Renzo Cabral emerged from the depths of the earth. If the world knew what was occurring four stories beneath the ground, it would send a shock wave that would reverberate throughout history. He was the only one allowed to leave, the only one trusted to come and go.

He exited through the front door of a small white, Cape Cod–style house that appeared perfectly normal and unassuming atop the hidden world below.

Renzo looked at the helicopter to the right and the fleet of vehicles—SUVs, Humvees, tractor trailers, buses. Sixteen in all, they had arrived under the cloak of darkness three days ago. Now all were parked within a large open lawn beside a green tent that adjoined the small house.

Fifteen fatigue-dressed marines scattered the grounds, their eyes sharp and weapons gripped tight.

"Sir," Sergeant Walker said.

"Sergeant." Renzo nodded. "How's the day?"

"Good, thank you. Much nicer than the desert."

"That it is." Renzo looked around at the thick woods. "Definitely don't miss it."

"What's going on?"

"All clear," Renzo said. "We'll be leaving just after sundown."

"Good, sir. Thank you." The young, redheaded sergeant gestured to the scattered soldiers under his command, nodded, and walked away.

Renzo carried authority among these men. A former soldier, he understood war, he understood soldiers, and he always took time to speak to them. Also, he was the only person they'd seen going in or out of the facility over the last several hours.

The soldiers were experienced and equipped to handle almost any situation, though they had no idea what was going on below their feet; it was Renzo's job to make sure they never did.

What had happened in the last few hours had never been contemplated, and if it were to get out....

Sergeant Steve Walker was glad to be stateside after three years of fighting in Akbiquestan in what had been dubbed *The War with No End.*

Many said it was escalating into another world war. The press and capitalists said it was about resources, newly discovered oil fields and mineral-rich deposits in the mountains. The Marxists and isolationists said it was about expansionism, but most of the public was just plain confused. Much like how the assassination of Archduke Franz Ferdinand had sparked World War I, this conflict began with the killing of the Sultan of Kre, the self-proclaimed ruler of the Sebit tribe that had protected Akbiquestan's territory for centuries.

More than 10,000 US troops dead in thirty-four months, 15,000 Russians, and 25,000 Ackies. Thirty countries had thrown their support and resources behind one of the three nations: the EU behind the US, the former Eastern bloc and China behind Russia, and the Middle East behind Akbiquestan. Peace talks had started and stopped without progress. Leaders had retreated to their corners of the globe after weeks of discussions under the daily spotlight of the hourly news cycle and social media. All while the great industrial war machine raged on, fueled by the blood of the patriotic, who were convinced they fought for freedom but unwittingly had gone to war over money, confusion, and power-based egos.

Walker had fired upon Russians, wondering if they were fighting back with the same anger that he felt (and not quite understanding why). He had battled the nomadic Akbiquestans, who were simply fighting to protect land their ancestors had roamed for seven hundred years. He wondered how he would have felt if war came to his home state of Nebraska.

The twenty-three-year-old sergeant had seen too much death, had lost too many friends, and was surprised even to be alive. As he looked up at the thick summer trees, the blue sky of New York, he was thankful; he had never appreciated the little things, but, having seen the horrors and felt the uncertainties of life during war, he was simply glad to be breathing.

Walker gripped his gun, thankful he wouldn't be firing it today. The threat was minimal and, it being the Fourth of July, he doubted there would be any trouble in suburban Byram Hills, let alone here in the middle of the woods. After all, no one even knew they were here.

Zane's eyes snapped open. He was in his car parked outside the local police station. It took him a good minute to acclimate, to shake off the chill, and focus his thoughts. He was thankful that he hadn't been driving when he had jumped back; he had no idea what would happen if he landed in a moving car. It wouldn't be good.

He pulled the watch from his pocket and stared at its hands joining at one o'clock.

Nick's final words were the first words that had scared him since he was a teenager. He had figured out Zane's greatest fear: failure. Specifically, failing what he had set out to accomplish today. If he died, the world would be in greater peril than Nick or anyone realized.

For eighteen hours, he had been running at full speed. He had searched, tortured, and killed his way to now, and he still had not found Colin Armor.

He needed Julia Quinn. She knew the truth. She knew what was going on. She knew Colin Armor and where he was hiding. She was an amazing liar. Not even her husband suspected.

Zane should have tortured her straightaway, extracted what he needed, and been done with her. Now, without the copy of her phone, he no longer knew where she was, where she would be, or how to find her.

But he still had Nick...still held his emotions, controlled his fears. Love was the greatest weapon. It forced people to act against all logic, attempt and do the craziest things: sacrifice their future, spend their last dime, risk everything, commit acts against every moral code they hold dear.

Love wasn't only about roses and diamond rings, and it wasn't simply the glue that held families together. It was the reason for violence, for murder, for war.

Love destroyed reason, the two being polar opposites.

Love was entirely illogical.

Menelaus had launched a thousand ships to avenge the taking of his wife, while Shakespeare had practically invented the English language by writing plays about love gone wrong. People tended to forget that crimes of passion filled not only books, but prisons. Nick Quinn would break every law, both God's and man's, to protect his wife and child.

Zane dumped out the contents of the bag he'd taken from Nick. There was a file, pictures of the Russian ambassador and Senator Chase date-stamped three weeks ago, clearly an unauthorized meeting with the enemy.

There was an elaborate set of plans for the Killian Dam, a Swiss bank account number, a counterfeit passport, and a photo album.

Zane flipped through the album, studying the senator as a young man with a smiling wife and two young sons at the beach, playing ball, attending birthday parties.

He turned the page to a second woman and two more kids. The first family faded from the album as Chase smiled with a new happy family, which itself soon disappeared.

Over the course of the album, Chase morphed from a grey-hooded gym teacher to a suited, polished man of distinction; photos reflected a new career, a new arm charm, a marriage to his third and current wife, the woman the country knew from her blue-blood heritage. Chase's political achievements were laid out in photo ops, pictures with presidents and prime ministers, celebrities, and dignitaries. In this section, the album contained pictures of power, no need for family, for ex-wives and children. Zane shook his head. Chase had lived as three entirely different men. Three different wives, two sets of kids, and several careers with a single common denominator: himself.

There was a formal picture of a soldier in his ASU dress blues, unsmiling, staring into the lens with anger. There was an article with the same picture above a headline, "Congressman Chase Loses Son to War: The Sacrifices of a Father." The article spoke of the father and son, Jason Chase, dedicating themselves to their country. Zane nodded to himself. The sympathy vote had won Chase his senatorial seat.

He picked up the photo of Chase with the Russian, then the plans for the Killian Dam. Finally, he put it all aside. He couldn't help wanting to kill the treasonous bastard, but that would have to wait. It would be the final step of the day's events.

The phone rang, startling Nick from his barely-awakened state at his desk. He jumped out of his chair, trying to gather his thoughts as he ran into the kitchen and grabbed the house phone. "Hello?"

"You okay?" Julia mouthed as she walked through the kitchen, carrying a box into the garage.

"Hello...? Hello?" Nick repeated and hung up. He looked at the caller ID but didn't recognize the number.

"Who was that?" Julia asked as she came back through the kitchen, carrying another box to the garage and putting it in the trunk of her car.

"No one there...must have been a wrong number."

Julia came back in and kissed Nick on the cheek as she passed. "You okay?"

Nick stared at her a moment, still getting his bearings.

She put her cell phone and purse on the kitchen counter as she picked up and carried a box of vases through the kitchen and into the garage.

Nick looked at the house phone. He thought for a moment, his suspicion high: Zane was looking for her. He looked through the house phone's caller ID for the day and found the same number had called at 9:00, 10:00, and 11:00 a.m. Nick peered into the garage to see Julia arranging the boxes in the trunk of her Audi.

He ducked back in the kitchen and grabbed Julia's phone from the counter. He quickly punched in her password and looked at her call log. He saw the same number as a missed call, the only difference being Julia had called them and they evidently hadn't answered. He quickly scrolled through the log for the last week and saw that the same number had called Julia multiple times.

Julia walked back in. "Someone call my phone?"

"No." Nick clicked it off and handed it to her. "Didn't want to you to forget it. I know how you get that choking feeling when you're away from it for more than five minutes." He turned away so she couldn't read the lie on his face.

"Thanks." She took it and tucked it in her purse.

Nick held out the house phone, displaying the number of the missed call. "Do you recognize this number?"

Julia glanced at it and shook her head. "No, should I?" And she grabbed the last box off the floor.

"Probably just some telemarketer." Nick looked away, fearing again that she would detect his lie. "Listen, do me a favor. Don't go to your office."

"What?" Julia smiled as if she misheard him.

"Are you going to your office?" Nick asked. "Don't go to your office."

"And where *can* I go?" Julia's expression stood between a smile and annoyance. "What are you talking about?"

"Just go somewhere you usually don't go—do something different."

"Should I go play tennis, or maybe golf? How about tea with the ladies?"

Julia had a tendency to mock women who didn't work, who said being a mother was a full-time job. That made Julia smile because, if it were the case, she had two.

"Well, lucky for you I have an appointment." Julia grabbed her keys.

"With who?"

"A client," Julia said slowly, sensing Nick's suspicion.

"On the Fourth of July?"

"Really? I told you I would be consumed with work and getting everything right for the reception this evening for Senator Chase. And you said you had work to do, which is why Katy's in daycare. Or are you forgetting all of this?"

"No, I'm not forgetting."

"Well, it sounds like you are and that's not exactly shocking." Julia shook her head. "I've got to go."

"For how long?"

"A couple hours...that is unless you fail to pick up Katy."

"I guarantee I won't."

Julia nodded with pursed lips. "Yeah, well your antics this morning made me miss my meeting, and I *needed* to be at that meeting, Nick. And now, what a surprise, you're making me late again."

"Where's your meeting?"

"With someone who will actually listen to and understand me."

"Is it Colin Armor?"

"What?" Julia snapped. "How do you know that name?"

"Who is he?"

"Goodbye, Nick." Julia walked out the kitchen door.

Nick grabbed the house phone, read the missed number, and punched it into his cell phone.

"Hello?" a man answered.

"Who is this?" Nick said slowly.

"You called the number, who are you trying to reach?"

"Is this Colin?"

"Who?"

"Colin Armor?"

"Who the hell *is* this?"

Nick hung up. He didn't recognize the voice, but one thing was confirmed—it wasn't an office line, as there'd been no phone-answering protocol in place.

Nick quickly Googled Colin Armor on his phone, finding nothing but a few mundane nobodies in Michigan and Chicago. Despite what logic told him, Nick was suspicious. Julia had grown distant, wrapped up in work, wrapped up in Katy, wrapped up in her life. They had spent so much time together, so many years...had the magic worn off? *Was* Armor another man?

At first Nick had thought it was Zane messing with his head, but the more he thought about it.... He tried to quell his mind, still his thoughts. Julia had blatantly lied to him: she knew the number, had called it and received calls from it numerous times.

Despite his efforts, his temper flared, and he swiped everything off the kitchen counter, hurling it into the wall and shattering it to pieces.

"It's such a pleasure to see you again, Marie," Senator Chase said to the woman as he smiled down at her three kids.

"You were my favorite teacher." Marie Barris gave him a starstruck smile as she took her youngest by the hand and walked out of Womrath's Bookstore.

Chase had dissuaded his staff from accepting "donations" for photos with him today. This was his town, where he'd started out, where he'd taught, where he'd lived and had his greatest rapport, where the media would always be returning for sound bites about the schoolteacher who took on Washington. He couldn't risk the country seeing a disgruntled townie badmouthing him over a hundred dollars for a photo op.

Men have one of three aspirations in life: money, power, or love, with one of them often becoming the focus to the detriment of the other two. At the age of eighteen, Chase fixed his sights on power. In his mind, power would bring money, and money would bring love. But he never understood how love worked until it hit him.

Chase had been a dual major at Fordham, history and poli-sci, planning on law school and a career in politics. Connie Hart fell in love with his ambition and deep blue eyes. He fell in love with her laugh as much as with her body.

The plan for power was derailed in his sophomore year. The unplanned pregnancy, followed by a quickly planned wedding, forced his aspirations aside. He became a swim coach during the day and finished college at night. Byram Hills High School offered him a teaching position in their history department and he was suddenly locked into a life path of barely getting by as he clothed and fed what would become two kids.

After ten years, the love he felt for Connie long extinguished, he walked out on his young family without a word. He never missed an alimony payment, never missed a Saturday with his children...until he met Marissa. Beautiful, exotic, and filled with life, Marissa reignited his heart and reintroduced hope. They married nine months later.

Marissa's young son and daughter began to edge out Chase's first family to the point that, three years later, he saw his own children every other month, at most. As the coach of the swim team and a history teacher to fifteen-year-olds, Chase'd had his fill of kids.

Marissa forced him to go to law school, to chase that original dream; after all, she said, why *not* go back to school at thirty-five? So, for three years, day and night, she did everything for the family while he worked, went to school, and studied. It was a sacrifice for both of them, but also an investment in their future.

Once Chase graduated, though, he knew he needed a new relationship for his coming career. Carlina was a polished, pearl-wearing blonde from a wealthy family, the perfect accessory and pocketbook for his aspirations. He left Marissa, wed Carlina, and soon became partner at the law firm of Aitkens, Lerner, and Isles. Within a year, he launched his first political campaign. Carlina's $80-million trust backed his run for the state house, then Congress. Having a background as a schoolteacher played to the masses better than *Mr. Smith goes to Washington*, easily winning him three terms in the House of Representatives.

When his son died in the war, Chase had the perfect sympathy tale for his Senate campaign. Having a son killed in action worked out ideally: all of the public sympathy with only a touch of personal grief. He wrote a book, did the talk-show circuit, cried to Oprah. It won him the Senate.

The bookstore crowd was dwindling. Ten remained, and the store was fresh out of books.

"We need to go," his young aide Andrew said.

"Not until I'm through," Chase smiled as he turned to Rob Risken, owner of Risken's Deli. "It's so good to see you, Mr. Risken."

"Senator," Risken shook his hand. "It is such an honor to have you represent us."

Nick looked at all of the things he'd lied to Zane about spread upon his kitchen counter. While he technically hadn't lied about the bag being in the future, many of its contents and copies of the other contents had been with him the whole time: the BMW smart key, the memory stick, and photos of the files that he'd printed from his phone.

Nick knew now that he had been going about this all wrong: rash, impulsive, thinking he could simply kill Zane and dump him in a lake, thus saving Julia and the town. The man had managed to steal a watch protected by the ultra-sophisticated security system designed by Paul Dreyfus; he had blown the dam, killing thousands, and was three steps ahead of Nick's every move. Nick was foolish and entirely outmatched, and he knew it.

He needed to deal with the facts, not his emotions.

He needed to defeat this man without killing him, without endangering Julia or Katy. He had to win, once and for all, and not just now and in the future, but in the past.

He plugged in the memory stick and pulled up a single file, quickly realizing its contents were written in a language he didn't recognize. He wasn't sure if it was code, Russian, or Akbiquestani. It looked like pages and pages of what might as well have been ancient Greek until he saw four names, the names he'd seen on the envelope: Nick Quinn, Julia Quinn, Senator Chase, and Charles Hadley, along with an address he recognized.

17 Kavey Lane.

On the other side of town.

Marcus stood in his garage, staring at Nick, not a word said as he digested the video on Nick's phone.

"Are you shitting me?" Marcus shook his head. "And you told me this before? Or later? Or...?"

Nick nodded.

"Did I react the same?"

"Actually, you freaked out on me."

"I get that." Marcus took a breath. "I'll save that for later. Where's Julia?"

"She wouldn't tell me, but she's in a meeting outside her office. If I can't find her, at least this guy Zane won't either," Nick said. "Do you think she's been acting a little different lately?"

"What do you mean?"

"Secretive?"

"Julia? You have no idea what that word means." Marcus laughed. "You remember Dana, battle ax number two? Secretive was her middle name."

"She's just been—"

"I'm going to stop you right there." Marcus stared at Nick. "I don't know what you're thinking, I'm sure everything you've gone through today has twisted your mind, but the one thing you *don't* need to worry about is Julia."

"You know what? Wait for me outside."

Marcus threw his hands up. "You're an idiot."

Nick sat in his car in Marcus's driveway. He dialed the number from Julia's phone again. He couldn't contain his anger at her outright lie; she had never lied to him like this. Zane was right: she had secrets.

This time the number was answered on the first ring.

"Hello—"

"Listen to me you son of a bitch—" Nick began but was quickly cut off.

"How did you get this number?"

"You tell Colin Armor to stay the hell away from my wife. I'll find him, and when I do—"

Marcus opened Nick's door and ripped the phone out of his hand. "What the hell are you doing?" He ended the call. "I'm telling you, man, I highly doubt Julia is messing around on you."

Nick looked away.

"And if she is, that's not how you deal with it. But that doesn't matter, because she isn't." Marcus walked around and climbed into the Wrangler; he handed Nick back his phone. "You're such an idiot."

The grey house at 17 Kavey Lane needed a paint job, a lawn cutting, and someone to pick up the newspapers scattered around the mailbox. Nick saw a blue, four-door BMW in the driveway as he drove past. He turned around at the end of the street and slowly drove back. He pulled out the BMW smart key he kept from the satchel, hit the center button, and watched as the brake lights flashed with a chirp of the horn.

"Son of a bitch," Marcus said. "You think they're in the house?"

"No idea." Nick shook his head as he looked at the unkempt home. He drove another block before parking.

"What the hell are we going to do?" Marcus asked, as they got out of the car and walked up the street. "Ring the doorbell?"

Nick walked up the driveway to the BMW. "Looks like your car."

"Someone else has taste besides me," Marcus said as he pulled out his key and thumbed the button. "Hm. I guess they really do program these things individually."

Nick hit the button on the smart key and opened the driver's side door. "Pays to have the right key."

The interior was spotless; he checked the glove compartment and armrest, both empty.

"Something is definitely up," Marcus said from the passenger side as he spun the tree-shaped air freshener that hung from the mirror. "Don't usually see these fifty-cent things hanging in a six-ty-five-thousand-dollar car."

Nick hit the button and popped the trunk. Inside they found two duffel bags in an otherwise spotless space.

"Well," Nick said, "*your* trunk hasn't looked like this since the day you bought it." He always joked about the amount of stuff in Marcus's trunk: golf clubs, two baseball mitts, a bat, old maps, a defibrillator, empty paper bags, three-week-old laundry, and a spool of kitesurfing line. And that was only the surface...who knew what lay beneath.

Nick unzipped a duffle bag to find several sets of clothes. "Did your BMW come with these features?"

"Not this one." Marcus picked up three different license plates and looked at the tags on the BMW. "In case Mommy didn't pay her parking tickets?"

Nick turned his attention to the house and walked around the rear of the structure.

"Should we ring the doorbell?" Nick asked again as he peered through the small, dusty window of the back door.

A loud screech startled Nick. He ran back to the driveway to find Marcus lifting the garage door manually, its hinged wheels squealing along its rusty tracks. "Who needs a doorbell?"

Sunlight cut through the dust of the shadowy two-bay garage. A large white van took up nearly both bays, oddly shiny and clean for such a dirty place.

Nick tore open the rear door. Along the van's right wall was a stack of air tanks, masks, fins, and regulators; both wet and dry suits hung on a rack; and three footlockers marked *Semtex* were tucked in the corner. He pulled a dive light off a small shelf and flipped it on. The dive equipment was new, high-end. He also found a host of unfamiliar tools, torches, and electrical equipment.

Marcus grabbed a light, flicked it on, and shined it around the garage as he walked around the van.

"Uh, Nick...?"

Nick walked to the front of the van.

The four bodies lay on the concrete floor. Stacked like logs upon each other; each with a single bullet wound to the head. They were all fit, muscled, various tattoos painted on arms and shoulders.

"These aren't the type of men you easily kill," Marcus said as he crouched over the bodies, looking closer. "Dead a couple hours at most."

"And how would you know that?"

"No bugs yet. It's summertime-hot. They'd be all over this meal by now."

"Thanks, Sherlock."

Before working in finance and accumulating companies, Marcus Bennett had served ten years in the Army. He had joined as an alternative to a bleak future of flipping burgers and working intermittent construction in upstate NY in the town of Wintosh, where the economy had collapsed on the heels of the textile industry pulling up stakes and heading overseas. Marcus had quickly moved up the ranks of the country's oldest service on the merits of shooting abilities gained through years of hunting with his father in the Catskill Mountains.

Prone to fighting, Marcus found the Iraq war to be the perfect place to take out his aggression in service of his country. He had arrived in the desert as a captain, leading assaults in the city of Baghdad, the palace, and outlying areas.

He never spoke of what actually happened, of the horrors he had seen, the lives he had taken, the friends he had lost, but things leaked out over the years. When each of his marriages collapsed and Marcus got lost in an alcohol bath for a few months, stories of raids, blood, and death escaped from his mind to invade Nick's nightmares.

Nick held his best friend in the highest regard, knowing that his sacrifice for his country hadn't ended on the battlefield. That was merely where it had begun; it now rode silently with him for life.

Marcus walked back to the rear of the van and opened up the first case of Semtex, only to find it empty. Opening the second, he revealed two brick sized blocks wrapped in wax paper.

"Whoa."

"Plastic explosives, right?"

Marcus nodded.

"What could you do with that amount?"

"Rip the face off of Mother Nature, destroy a city building...but that's not what concerns me."

"What does concern you?"

"The location of the contents of the empty boxes."

"I think we know that full well."

"Do we?" Marcus asked. "You sure they haven't wired an additional place?"

Marcus picked up an FN SCAR assault rifle, removing the clip and eyeing the sight. He put it down and picked up a regulator, looked at an air tank, and came upon a Hollis rebreather. It captured every exhale and minimized the telltale sign of bubbles on the surface. "This is expensive stuff. High-tech. Our tattooed friends are well funded."

"Were." Nick scoured the front interior of the van. The keys were there, along with empty thermoses, bags of chips, and jerky.

Marcus returned to the bodies, knelt, and examined the tattoos that adorned the naked backs and arms of the dead: designs of horses, devils, and monsters with gaping mouths swallowing souls; an elaborate jaguar, its eyes seemingly alive. He leaned closer, over the back of an enormous, ponytailed body and read the lettering running from shoulder to shoulder, the image of a large ghost inked beneath it. "Kasper."

"What?"

"That's what it says on his back."

"Like the friendly ghost?"

"I don't think friendly was ever in this guy's vocabulary. And he's from Akbiquestan."

"How do you know?" Nick said as he searched the glove compartment.

"Because this isn't how you write 'I love Mom' in English." Marcus pointed at a small tattoo. He turned over the ponytailed man and stared into his vacant, blue eyes. There was a long, jagged scar running from brow to jaw, several circular white scars on his shoulders, and a concave patch of lumpy flesh on his neck. Injuries not incurred by falling down on the playground. The most glaring wound was the small bullet hole caked in blood at his temple.

Nick pulled a small black velvet bag from the van's glove compartment. He loosened the drawstring and dumped the contents in the palm of his hand.

Diamonds.

"Well, whoever killed 'em wasn't here to rob 'em."

"These guys had been through death more than a few times." Marcus waved a hand at the other bodies, all equally scarred, all dead from a single shot to the head. "They don't die without a fight. They were killed by a comrade, a friend, someone they trusted and allowed to get close."

"Zane," Nick said.

"Maybe, but these guys don't seem to be from his polished world. These aren't SEALS, Delta, or SAS types. These guys were hardened by the worst kind of military experience."

Nick examined a motorized submersible the size of a beer cooler, a large antenna sticking up in the front. "What's this?"

"An underwater tow sled. You punch in the exact coordinates and hold on and it'll pull you to your destination. That's why dam security never picked anything up. With this equipment, they could enter the reservoir a half-mile away, ride underwater to the base, and slip away with no one the wiser."

"Marcus," Nick called from beneath the van. "What the hell is this?"

Marcus lay beside Nick and looked at a large block of Semtex affixed under the van. He ran his fingers from the protruding wires to a small electronic device. "Shit. This is the detonator. Not sure if it's a timer or a trigger."

A noise came from outside. Nick slipped out from under the van and peered out the garage window as a rusted Ford Bronco drove into the driveway. "Who is *this*?"

They watched as the vehicle hesitated in the driveway before backing up.

"They're leaving," Nick said as the old SUV pulled away.

"Yeah, because they saw the open garage—"

The lights on the detonator lit up.

"Nick!"

In unison, they raced through the open garage door, cutting across the driveway into the rear yard—

And the house exploded. Like a matchstick structure, it blew apart into splinters as balls of fire rolled into the sky. Nick and Marcus were hurled from their feet by the concussive blast, landing and rolling on the ground, bruised and battered, ears ringing as they tried to reorient their minds.

Slowly, they sat up and stared at the missing house.

"This house didn't blow up the first time I experienced the one o'clock hour," Nick said as he rubbed the small abrasions on his arms.

"What are you talking about?"

"A house exploding? We would have heard about it; the whole town would have heard about it. Why did it blow up now?"

"Cause you're fucking with time," Marcus growled as he rubbed his head.

"Yeah, well, what's different now?"

"You were here, that's what's different. Are you forgetting, everything you touch changes the future? It's how life works." Marcus looked at the bombed-out house. "Actions have consequences."

"We've got to get out of here."

"You think?" Marcus shook his head as they moved to Nick's car.

They never saw the car down the block as Zane keyed the ignition and drove away.

"We could have died," Marcus said as he dabbed at his bleeding elbows.

"But we didn't." Nick drove through town, detouring around the construction site on Main Street and heading up Route 22 toward Dreyfus's house. He kept checking his mirror to see if anyone was following them.

"Have you stopped and thought about how dangerous all of this is?" Marcus asked.

"Nope," Nick said as he wiped dirt from one eye while trying to keep his other on the road. "If I do, I might hesitate. Julia's already died because of my mistakes. Because I didn't act quick enough."

"I get that, but that's not what I mean. I'm talking about the dangers you're *creating*."

"I don't follow."

"Everything is interconnected. Every life reverberates, no exceptions; we all influence the world around us without realizing how far those ripples of influence go. It can be through our actions or inactions. Blowing a bomb or blowing a kiss."

When Nick didn't respond, Marcus tried again.

"Let's say a woman in Manhattan texts a friend about dinner, the friend's phone rings while he's driving to New Jersey, he pulls out his cell phone on a bridge, and as he tries to read the text, he gets in an accident with three other cars, who now bring the bridge to a standstill; it affects not only the three other drivers, but the five hundred people in the three hundred cars now stuck in traffic behind him for at least fifteen minutes. But people don't realize that the traffic jam reverberates through those five hundred individuals to their families, children, jobs. Doctors late for surgery, fathers late for their kid's birthday party, a boyfriend late for a date, a daughter now too late to say goodbye to her dying mother. Now, if that woman didn't send the text, and if her friend didn't pick up his phone...." Marcus paused. "What I'm saying is, if you go back in time and make ripples, no one knows how far those ripples go or how many lives you're changing."

Nick nodded to let Marcus know he was listening.

"And when you're playing God, Nick, remember: God doesn't always make choices we think are fair. People die in God's world. When God saves one person, someone else may die, and that's what you're faced with. Save one, kill a thousand. Are you sure you can handle the power of God? Can anyone? Even the saintliest are fallible. Imagine if the watch was in the hands of someone truly evil, someone even worse than this Zane fella."

"Another watch is already in the hands of the devil," Nick said. "And before I see morning for the second time today, I'm going to send him back to hell."

"What the hell happened to you two?" Dreyfus said as Nick and Marcus stood in his doorway, clothes torn, hair singed, smelling of smoke.

"It wasn't a barbeque," Marcus said.

"Nick?"

Nick reached in his pocket and pulled out the watch, the afternoon sun bouncing off its gold-and-silver casing.

"Shit." Paul ushered them quickly into the house, his eyes darting about, scanning the grounds as if they were being watched.

"That's an understatement," Marcus said.

As they sat around Dreyfus's kitchen table, Nick brought him up to speed on the future, on everything that had happened: the blowing of the dam, Paul's death, his daughter Alice's murder, and everything he knew about and had experienced at the hands of Janos Zane.

"Do you know the name Colin Armor?" Nick asked at last.

"No, should I?"

"Well, he seems pretty important to Julia."

"You sound suspicious."

"Curious," Nick said, avoiding Marcus's stare. "She's been very secretive; out nights, not telling me much about her day the way she used to."

"Well..." Dreyfus sat back and tried to pose an answer.

"Don't listen to him," Marcus said to Dreyfus. "He's been talking stupid for a while now."

"What do you know about Hadley's Woods?" Nick asked.

Dreyfus nodded. "That's what it is."

"That's what *what* is?"

"Three weeks ago," Dreyfus said, "Shamus Hennicot called."

"Why?"

"He owns Hadley's Woods."

"What?"

"He's owned it for years through one of his companies."

"Since when?"

"Since before the eighties. There's a whole facility in there. I've done a lot of security work on it."

"Julia handles all of Shamus's legal work...." Nick said, thinking it through.

"And his trusts," Marcus added.

Nick found hope in this line of thinking: Julia *was* like a daughter to Shamus. The watch in Nick's pocket had first been given to him three years ago by Shamus as a means of saving Julia. "Well, some of the papers you give me a few hours from now mentioned Hadley's Woods."

Dreyfus raised his eyebrows at that. "Okay...not long ago, Shamus asked me to write up all of the security measures I built into the Hadley Woods site: charts, plans, et cetera. A couple of days later I met with three men."

"Who were they?"

"Didn't even get names. Shamus was there, so was Julia. They said I could trust them. I reviewed every single inch of the facility with them, all of the codes, security measures, utilities. Shamus sometimes rents out the facility to help organizations or causes. But this review was more thorough than any I'd done before."

"Was he selling it?" Marcus asked.

"That's what I thought. No idea. He may already have. You'll have to ask Julia."

"What's in there?"

"You mean, what's *under* there."

Nick stared at him in confusion.

"The whole facility is underground—a bunker built twenty-five years ago by Shamus. It was actually an update of an existing bomb shelter created back in the early sixties. It was updated again three years ago with the latest security protocols, amenities, and luxuries. Two levels, forty feet underground. There's a movie theater, game rooms, a pool, living rooms, and luxurious dining rooms. A restaurant-sized chef's kitchen. There's also a five-thousand-gallon freshwater holding tank, a storage facility with enough food for twenty people to last ten years, a water-treatment plant, geothermal heat, generators, and a ventilation system with air scrubbers and surface vents to seal the place off from the world if an incident were to occur."

"Incredible," said Marcus, looking to Nick.

"And I'm just getting started," said Dreyfus. "It has conference rooms, a full medical facility, including an operating room, drugs for everything from headaches to cancer. Plus, a full lab and a machinist's shop."

"All this for a fallout shelter?" Nick asked.

"Initially, yeah. But over the years it morphed into a place that could be used for research, meetings, or experiments that Shamus believed would better the world though needed to remain top secret.

"It's been used by Nobel Prize scientists, drug manufacturers, CEOs planning mergers out of the public eye, think tanks, and even a few black-op government branches looking to stay off the books. There are very strict nondisclosure agreements signed by anyone visiting the facility with an onerous financial penalty that would bankrupt even billionaires if enforced. Basically, it's a secret place for secret secrets."

Nick walked out to Dreyfus's pool. He dialed Julia's office, but it went straight to voicemail. He tried the house and her cell but couldn't reach her. He grew more and more anxious as his thoughts began to run away from him, his imagination filtering the horrors he had seen her experience today into a new, terror-filled scenario.

To avoid working himself up into a full-blown panic, he dialed the suspicious number again. No answer. He hung up. Dialed again. Again, no answer. He called it a third time, unable to control his anger.

"Hello?"

"Who is this?" Nick growled into the phone.

"You called me. Who is *this*?"

Nick debated what to say. Whoever this was, he was a key to the puzzle, to whatever was going on. Nick shifted gears, tempered his anger, and lied. "I know all about Colin Armor. I know all about your secrets. And I'm going to tell the world."

Julia pulled into the driveway of Washington House, the large colonial mansion on Bedford Road that dated to the time of the revolution. Of course, the home had had an addition or two tacked on over the years. What was once a two-bedroom, eight-hundred-square-foot home had grown to a mansion of more than ten thousand square feet. It was the first thing people noticed when they drove into Byram Hills; it was on the cover of the town brochure, setting the tone for the white-clapboard style of the village and surrounding neighborhoods.

Of the three houses that Shamus and Katherine Hennicot owned, this was their favorite and the one they called home.

To Julia, it was like a second home. She loved coming here, an experience akin to visiting her grandparents. The smell of cooking always filled the kitchen, fresh flowers abounded in every room, cigar smoke hung in the air of the library, warm blankets and bright fires welcomed her in winter. The day's newspaper was always on the kitchen counter while an old transistor radio played in the background, the elderly Hennicots preferring to receive their news the old-fashioned way. On occasion, Julia would arrive to find music pouring from the piano, Katherine's arthritis-ridden fingers playing Chopin, Joplin, or Rodgers and Hammerstein.

Katherine knew Julia's favorite foods and delighted in cooking for her. She was an elegant woman who not only possessed the manners of a lady, but also the brilliant mind of an intellectual. With a PhD in economics and agriculture, Katherine had quietly been at the forefront of creating self-sustaining agricultural models that successfully brought an abundance of crops and newfound prosperity to third-world nations. She was one of only three people ever to turn down a Nobel Prize, preferring anonymity and asking that the money and recognition go to the people who put her theories into action. But to Julia, all of Katherine's brilliance aside, it was her chicken and dumplings and fudge that truly made the world a better place.

For their part, Shamus and Katherine had embraced Julia as their own. Being childless, they saw her not only as the daughter they never had, but also the daughter they'd always wanted. Julia was always welcome, always comforted, and always loved, no matter her day, her outfit, or her mood. Shamus and Katherine were like parents, grandparents, and friends all in one. She could confide anything to Shamus, and he never hesitated to regale her with stories from his past, of the way history really had happened before it was homogenized and burnished for the books. He'd listen to her troubles, whether they be from work or home, and he had a clever way of telling her when she was wrong while still somehow lifting her spirits.

When Nick and Julia's daughter was born, they thought there was no more fitting name than Katherine. Katy had been named as a tribute to both Katherine and Shamus: there could be no better role models for their child.

Julia had served as Shamus's personal attorney for years, handling his estate, his business matters, and managing many of his secrets. Shamus's wealth was published in *Forbes* at six billion, though Julia knew it was twice that now and previously had been four times the amount. Starting with a sizable inheritance, Shamus amassed his fortune through shrewd investments and a keen management style. He was a confidant of kings, presidents, and inquisitive children, his advice sought out, his perspective enlightening, his mind always sharp. For the last two decades, he had done nothing but try to give his luck and success away. Donating paintings, establishing think tanks, creating nameless foundations that supported the needy, the advancement of science, medicine, and education, and the ceaseless effort for peace.

Julia got out of her car and walked to the back of the house, the front entrance being for guests. There was no need to knock as she climbed the three steps to the screen door and headed into the rear hall.

"Hello," she playfully called out. "I'm home."

Julia listened a moment, assuming they were upstairs, and went in the kitchen. She reached in the cupboard and grabbed a two-liter bottle of ginger ale, the only soda in the house, and poured herself a glass. She sat at the white marble island and thumbed through the *New York Times* and the *Post* as she sipped her drink. She smiled as she saw the fresh-baked brownies on the counter but restrained herself from stealing one of Shamus' favorite treats.

And that's when it struck her. The silence. No radio. She looked at the 1960s plastic rig and clicked it on. The small speaker filled the room with a nasal voice talking about the Yankees' latest win.

"Katherine?" Julia called out as she carried her drink through the dining room to the front hall. She listened a moment but didn't hear a sound. "Shamus?"

Her radar up, she peered in the living room, the sunroom, but saw nothing. She crept quietly, cautiously looking around her as she arrived at the closed pocket doors to the library.

"Shamus?" she said, softly as she pulled open the doors.

She saw the first body, Shamus's trusted assistant Zachariah Nash, his bloody shirt ripped open, a bullet hole in his chest. As she gasped for breath, time seemed to slow, and confusion poured in.

And then she saw Shamus.

He lay on the floor by the bookcases in his freshly pressed, three-piece suit, his legs at an odd angle. His tie ripped away, his shirt torn open, exposing his pale dead skin. She fell to her knees beside him and felt for a pulse. Seeing his hazel blue eyes dry and staring into nothing, she knew it was too late for CPR, too late for help, too late to save him.

She saw Katherine's legs protruding from behind the couch but froze where she knelt, unable to look. Pushing the panic from her mind, she pulled her phone from her purse and hit speed-dial on her phone.

"Julia?" Nick answered.

"Nick?" Julia cried. "He's dead."

"Who's dead?"

"Shamus is dead."

"Where are you?"

"And Zachariah and Katherine."

"In their house?"

"Yes," she sobbed.

"Get out of there as fast as you can."

"But—"

"Now!" Nick yelled.

Julia bolted up and, shocked into action by Nick's outburst, charged through the house and out the back door. She was running across the large driveway to her car when she saw a man coming up the driveway. She fumbled through her purse for her keys, trying to calm herself.

She looked up to see the man, twenty feet away, a gun held low and trained on her as he approached.

Without thought, she bolted back to the house.

Nick redlined the Wrangler, racing out of Dreyfus's driveway, Marcus riding shotgun and on the phone with the police.

"Washington House, now, Martha!" Marcus yelled into the phone. "They're going to kill Julia!"

Nick cursed himself for not thinking to go there...for being unable to protect her. He was five miles away. No matter how fast he drove, he knew he would be too late.

Julia ran through the kitchen to the back stairs; charging up three at a time, she ran down the hall to the master bedroom and slammed the door shut. She threw the lock and raced for the window.

She was fumbling with the window latch when gunshots struck the lock, the door kicked in, and her pursuer appeared, gun held high, aimed at her head.

"If you want to live, Julia," Zane said, "step away from the window."

Julia glared at the man as she took a step back.

"Listen to me—"

"Stay the hell away from me!"

"You're going to take me to Colin Armor."

"You son of a bitch," she said. "You killed them! You killed them all."

"You have no idea what's going on," Zane said.

"I swear to God—"

"Let's go." Zane waved her toward the door.

Julia didn't move, fighting back her mixture of fear, anger, and grief.

"You don't want me to make things worse, I promise."

Julia turned and walked out the door, tears welling in her eyes. "Why? How could you do such a thing?"

Zane didn't say a word as they arrived at the rear stairs.

And Julia leapt, vaulting down the twelve stairs in two steps, landing in a run, charging down the hall through the dining room as fast as she could. Zane sprinted behind her, then slowed as he raised his gun and took aim at her legs.

As Zane's pursuit stopped, Julia knew what was about to happen—

"Julia!" a voice yelled as the back door burst open. Shannon and Goodheart bolted into the house, guns raised.

"Here!" she screamed as she cut into the living room.

Shannon quickly came to her side, wrapping his arms around her, scanning the room with his gun up as Goodheart raced through the house, clearing rooms.

Julia turned back but saw no sign of her pursuer.

Zane was gone.

"Why would anyone want to kill him?" Julia held tight to Nick. "He was such a good man."

Washington House overflowed with emergency personnel. Shannon called in everyone who was off for the holiday; uniformed cops were at the door keeping the press out; detectives were dusting for prints while the coroner examined the bodies.

Nick kept hold of Julia, feeling her tears soaking through his shirt. "Powerful men have enemies."

Julia looked up into Nick's eyes. The pain he saw was crushing. Shamus and Katherine had been violently ripped from her world. Two people who were her stability, her rock, had been violated in the worst way.

"They were so good, so kind...."

Nick hugged her close and stroked her back. "Try not to think about it."

"How can I not?" Julia murmured. "How can I stop?"

On the surface, Nick acted calm for Julia and those around them—but inside, his mind was spinning. He knew who had done this, knew it was Zane, but there was nothing he could say. No one would believe a word. How could they? To steal the pocket watch, Zane had needed the keys that would open the mahogany box that held it. Two of those keys had been around the necks of the dead men in the other room.

"He had secrets, Nick." Julia looked up. "They're going to want to know about them."

"Who?" Nick couldn't mask his concern.

"The people investigating this."

"What kind of secrets?" Nick whispered.

"Some are dangerous, some unbelievable. I can't tell them." Panic rose in her voice. "I can't tell anyone. I promised."

Nick wondered if she had any idea about the watch but said nothing.

"Julia." An elderly man in horn-rimmed glasses stepped into the kitchen with Marcus. Dr. O'Reilly was a family friend, someone who many in the town turned to for their basic medical needs and advice.

"Hey, Doc," Julia said, sniffling to clear her throat.

"I thought I could check you out real quick, maybe get you something for the shock."

Nick looked at her and nodded.

"I need to grab my phone from the car," Nick said as he turned to Marcus. "Could you stay here a minute?"

Marcus nodded.

Nick walked outside and ran straight into Shannon, who was lighting up a cigarette.

"Since when did you start smoking?" Nick asked.

"I've got a house exploding up on the hill with four bodies inside, a triple-murder here in town.... What the hell's happening in Byram Hills on the Fourth of July?" Shannon shook his head as he took a long drag. "I need more than a cigarette."

Shannon took in Nick's disheveled, singed appearance. "And what the hell happened to you? Are those cuts on your arms? Burns?"

"Give me two minutes." The last thing Nick needed was an interrogation. "I need to get my phone from the car."

Nick walked down the driveway, the bright sun warming his face as he walked across the street past the cops, onlookers, and press. He jogged over to his car, reached in, and was grabbing his phone off the dash when a bee stung him on the back of his neck. His hand reflexively reached upward to swat it, but his limb fell limp as his knees buckled. The last thought running through his mind was: *It can't be anaphylactic shock—I'm not allergic to bees.*

"So, Mr. Quinn, why are you so desperate to find Colin Armor?"

Nick slowly awoke, rising up from a hazy darkness to look into the dark eyes of the man questioning him. His hair was short, his suit black without a wrinkle. Nick recognized the man but couldn't remember from where. Nick's head tilted left and right to see a small, cramped room, only two chairs and a door, nothing else except a single vent next to the bright light in the ceiling.

"Who?" Nick whispered as he realized his hands were cuffed behind his back.

"Six times you called this number that is unlisted, unknown, and never misdialed."

Nick remained silent as the fog washed from his mind. He'd been darted and drugged, not stung. Though he couldn't check with his hands, his pockets felt empty, which meant he no longer had his wallet, phone, keys, or the pocket watch.

"What time is it?"

"Tell me why you're interested in Colin and I'll tell you the time."

Nick knew that without the watch at the top of the hour, everything was over: he would continue in regular time, marching forward like everyone else, unable to figure out what was really going on, unable to stop Zane, who could control the past with no one to stand in his way, and, most importantly, unable to save Julia.

"I don't know anyone named Colin." As he said it, Nick realized that this was the same fed who tried to stop him from going in the house on Whippoorwill Road to save Zane an hour from now. The one Zane claimed had come to assassinate the assassin. Of course, this man couldn't remember the future the way Nick did.

"Yet you called this number and asked for Colin Armor—"

"Where's Julia?" Nick's voice grew stronger as he struggled upright in his chair.

"—six times."

"If you harm her—"

"Who's Julia?"

"My wife, damn it." Nick growled, "If you—"

"Mr. Quinn, we don't have your wife. Again, why were you looking for Colin—"

"Because my wife's been seeing him and I don't know what's going on. She's in grave danger and it's because of him."

The interrogator lowered his voice. "What do you suspect?"

"I'm not sure. I don't know if he's a client or...." Nick paused before finally voicing his fear. "I don't know if they're in a relationship."

"Julia Quinn?"

"Yeah." Nick looked up into the man's eyes and watched as they softened.

"They do have a relationship." The man nodded. "Why did you call him? What were you going to say to him?"

Nick thought it better not to answer that.

"You were suspicious?" the man asked.

"Wouldn't you be?" Nick was beginning to realize that much of his suspicion had been seeded by Zane and his many insinuations about Julia and her secrets.

"What do you know about Colin Armor?"

"I only know my wife is in danger." Nick was acutely aware of the minutes slipping away.

"From who?"

"A man named Janos Zane," Nick said. "He's going to torture and kill her to learn your Colin's whereabouts."

"Janos Zane...." the man repeated slowly, suspicion in his voice. "And where is your wife now?"

"Who *are* you?"

The man stood there a moment, then left the room without a word.

Nick sat in the confined space, panic seeping through him. He didn't know the time, he had no idea how long he had been unconscious, how long he'd been in this room. One step forward, two steps back. It wasn't just the way he was moving through the day, but how it felt trying to find a way to save his family and his town. He would discover one truth only to find it wrapped in more mystery.

And something else gnawed at Nick. He had seen this man before, but it wasn't just during the armed standoff with Shannon. Nick recognized him from somewhere else...he just couldn't place it.

There were too many mysteries.

Minutes later, the man stepped back in the room, walked behind Nick, and released Nick's handcuffs. He laid his business card on the table as Nick rubbed the ache from his shackle-bruised wrists.

Then, Renzo Cabral—or so claimed his business card—pulled from his pocket Nick's wallet, keys, phone, the BMW smart key, and

Shamus Hennicot's pocket watch and placed them next to his card on the table. "Nice watch, by the way."

"Thank you," Nick mumbled as he grabbed and opened the watch cover and breathed a sigh of relief.

1:58 p.m.

"We need you to help us find Janos Zane," Renzo said.

"Who is he?"

"He is behind a terrorist group planning an attack on US soil. And we're afraid we don't have much time to stop it."

"Secret Service?" Nick held up the business card. "I thought you guys protected presidents and the mint and went after counterfeiters...."

"We do a little more than that." Renzo let his annoyance hang in the air.

"It's the Killian Dam," Nick said. "He's going to blow it up later today."

"How do you know that?" Renzo spoke quietly, though his eyes couldn't hide his shock.

Nick paused a moment, thinking, choosing his words carefully. "I saw his satchel. It had various plans of the dam."

"Where did you see this satchel?"

"Zane had it." And so, Nick's lies began to pour out. The satchel was in the future, but its readable contents were in his house and the smart car key in his pocket right now. "I know where it is."

The excitement shone in Renzo's eyes. "If we can get that bag, we can stop him."

"How?"

"It belonged to the lead terrorist who was killed earlier today. Zane took it and escaped. That bag is the key to stopping this." Renzo rushed to the door.

"Hey! What about my wife?"

"We'll tuck her in one of the safest places on earth with a full security detail." Renzo turned back to him. "I assure you no harm will come to her."

"No offense, but how can you guarantee that?"

"Because," Renzo said, "the team that will protect her is under my direction, and nobody's better at it than us. Plus," he said with a wink, "Colin Armor will insist upon it."

CHAPTER 7

12:00 PM

Zane's eyes flashed open, his heart pounding as he sprang up from the floor. He was in Chase's house. It was where he'd begun this hour earlier in the day, trying to get the safe open. He stared at it now, knowing its contents full well because he possessed them. Nick had stolen them, yet they remained inside the safe now...it made Zane's head hurt, reminding him of Schrödinger's cat.

He pulled out the pocket watch and flipped it open: 12:01.

He raced outside, surprised to see his Town Car sitting in the driveway. He spent no time figuring it out, jumped in, and drove off.

Despite stepping back an hour so many times, Zane wasn't used to it—he would never get used to it. It was like being ripped from life, dragged through hell, to be reborn again, over and over. And every time, his head filled with nightmares: his brother's death, his mother's suicide, so much pain. This time was the worst.

And the centerpiece of those dreams was a memory that came straight from hell:

The missile hit the lead Night Ghost's right wing, exploding the jet in a fiery ball that lit the nighttime clouds in a halo of death. Its flaming tail section hurtled through the air towards Zane's plane as he shouted at his men to jump.

The team of six leapt from the open rear door as the burning debris hit their craft, setting it ablaze, exploding it into a rain of metal, shrapnel, and bodies.

The two jets had dropped from thirty thousand feet to fifteen thousand, knowing it put them in range of enemy defenses, but intel had told them this side of the mountain was clear, enabling the three teams of six to deploy without the high-altitude gear they didn't possess in this hastily thrown-together mission.

Zane rocketed toward the earth, arms and legs pulled in, pushing his terminal velocity past the usual 122 MPH, angling his body to rocket away from the tumbling, flaming wreckage. His five-man team spread in formation ahead of him as they dived toward the tree-covered mountain in central Akbiquestan.

They were ten miles short of their drop zone and falling into enemy territory. What was to have been an eighteen-man mission was now down to six.

Like shooting stars, the wreckage of the two planes filled the sky around them. Zane and his paratroopers tried to navigate around and away from pieces ranging in size from baseballs to cars.

At six thousand feet, the newest member of Zane's team never saw the flaming tire as it plummeted through the dark sky, hitting him in the head, knocking him out and sending him tumbling, his lifeless arms and legs cartwheeling earthward.

Twisting his body, Zane rocketed through the debris-filled sky toward the death-sentenced soldier. He had no idea if the wound would prove fatal or if the man was already dead, but he desperately needed him on this already tragically compromised mission.

Four thousand feet. Zane struggled through the sky to reach the young lieutenant; he had no propulsion, nothing but the air acting on his falling self to help guide him.

As Zane leveled out, he came in alongside the soldier, wind buffeting his face as he struggled in the dark of night. He reached out for the young soldier's spinning legs, grabbing one, stabilizing him.

Two thousand feet. With the moonlit trees and fields in perfect view, Zane crawled one hand toward the soldier's left shoulder and caught hold of the metal ring, yanking it hard, deploying his reserve chute. The canopy popped out, quickly catching the air, jerking the injured soldier skyward as Zane continued to plummet.

Nine hundred feet. Zane angled away, grabbed and threw out his pilot chute, its canopy ripping out of his pack, trying to grab air, finally fully deploying at two hundred feet above the trees. Deceleration gave him a bone-jarring yank, but Zane used the toggles to steer away from the rocks and approaching branches.

His team landed in a small field in the moon shadow of a rocky mountain. While Zane's team grabbed their guns and searched the area for the enemy, Zane ran to the lieutenant, who had landed gently beside a stand of trees. He patted down his body and carefully removed his helmet. He slapped the man's young face, the soldier's eyes snapping open as he woke. The man looked around, realizing what had happened as he caught breath.

"Can you move?" Zane asked.

The soldier nodded as he got to his feet.

"Can you fight?"

"Yes, sir," he nodded as he shucked off his parachute.

"Okay," Zane said." Let's go, then."

"JC?" the soldier said quietly. "You saved my life."

"No time for thanks, Renzo. We gotta go."

Nick shook off his disorientation and looked around his office to get his bearings. He took a deep breath before dialing the number on the card before him. After a quick conversation, he hung up his phone, tucked Renzo Cabral's business card in his pocket, and grabbed the stack of papers from the printer behind his desk. He threw them in the large envelope and headed out to his car. He looked at his phone, watching the blue dot hovering over Julia's office.

He jumped in his Wrangler and, three minutes later, drove into the parking lot behind Decicco's Supermarket. Agent Renzo Cabral stood impatiently beside his black Suburban. Nick parked next him and got out of his Jeep.

"Thanks for coming," Nick said.

"Who are you, and how did you get my number?"

Nick handed him the large envelope.

"What is this?" Renzo asked.

"This is hard to explain," Nick said. "But I know you're looking for this stuff."

"And *who* are you?" The twelve o'clock Renzo had yet to meet Nick.

"Nick Quinn."

"Julia Quinn's husband? I've been looking for her for a few hours; she missed a meeting this morning."

"That would be my fault. She's not very happy with me."

"I'm sure she'll forgive you," Renzo said as he opened the large envelope to find several files, the BMW smart key, and the memory stick. "Where did you get this?"

"It was in a satchel I took from a man who's after Julia." Nick wished he could tell Renzo everything, wished he could simply give him the pocket watch and walk away from all this, allowing the far better-equipped man to find Janos Zane and kill him for good.

"What do you mean, a man after Julia?" Renzo seemed concerned.

"This man, Janos Zane, is trying to get Julia to help him find someone named Colin Armor. He said he'd torture her to get the information...said he'd kill her."

"Okay." Renzo held up a hand as he dumped the contents of the envelope on the hood of his Suburban. He thumbed through the papers and examined the memory stick. "Do you know what this is? Any of this stuff?"

"No idea beyond the fact that it revolves around Zane trying to blow up the dam."

Shock shone in Renzo's eyes. Nick could see him working out his next question carefully.

"Blowing up what dam?"

"The Killian Dam, the one just outside of town."

Renzo's dark eyes bored into Nick. "How do you know this?"

Nick felt his web of lies wrapping around his neck like a noose. He tapped the papers with his finger, pointing at the dam's schematics. "Read these documents."

Renzo picked up the page, then another, and another, quickly looking at each, panic creeping into his eyes.

"I'm helping you," said Nick, "and I need you to help me."

Renzo turned around, looking out at the park while still absorbing what he'd seen.

"I need you to pick up my wife. I know you can protect her," Nick said.

"Where is she now?" Renzo asked as he turned around.

"In her office."

"Well," Renzo said in a softer voice. "I'll pick her up myself."

"You know where that is?"

"I've been there a few times. She's been working with us."

Nick nodded, wounded by another secret that his wife had never mentioned.

"No one's going to harm her," the agent assured him.

"Thank you."

"I'll bring her somewhere safe, somewhere Zane won't get within a hundred yards of her."

"You know who Zane is, right?"

"Yeah, I know who he is, and you're lucky to be alive. But we need to talk." Renzo pointed an accusing finger at Nick. "I need to know everything you know. How you know him, how you stole this satchel you're talking about, and where he is. I need you to help me find him."

"Happy to. Let's go."

"You can't come with me," Renzo shook his head. "The place I'll take Julia is restricted."

"That's fine." Nick put his hands up in deference. "And thank you."

Renzo nodded.

"Be aware, she's going to be pissed," Nick warned the agent with a smile.

"Tough shit. I've seen her temper. She knows I don't have time to screw around."

"So, you *know* her?"

Renzo nodded.

"How'd you come to work together?"

"I can't say."

"That sounds ominous."

"Not meant to be. I'll explain when we sit down. Where can I meet you?"

"How about Schrieffer's in town? It's a deli."

"No. What about Franzel's?" Renzo offered.

"How the hell do you know Franzel's?"

"Everyone knows about Franzel's."

"Fine," Nick said. "That works. What time?"

"Fifteen minutes." Renzo folded up the envelope and looked at Nick. "And you'd better show up."

"You'll have my wife as collateral." Nick said. "I'll be there."

Julia sat at her desk, staring out her office window as she tried to gather her thoughts. She was mad at Nick but knew it wasn't justified. It was just her default state when she grew frustrated.

She so wished she were in the midst of the action in the bunker in Hadley's Woods, but she had been late and, as a result, been locked out.

Being late was her greatest pet peeve. Julia was known for always being five minutes early; she always accounted for traffic, contingencies, the unknown, and the never-timely Nick. But she never thought she could have been so late this morning. It wasn't her husband's fault, per se; it was the domino effect of Nick's saving that man's life. Things like that always seemed to happen around him: car accidents, heart attacks, children nearly drowning in pools. And Nick coincidentally being there to CPR them back to life, pluck them from the water, pull them from their shattered vehicles. It became their running joke that he was somehow causing the events simply so he could save people. But despite all the joking, Julia loved him for it. Nick would do anything for anyone—give them his last dime, the shirt off his back. Even his life.

The fact that she couldn't tell him what was going on now weighed on her like a millstone. Not being able to tell the one you love the truth because you signed a non-disclosure agreement.... She shook her head. It was crushing. She wished she had never agreed to the secrets, the subterfuge, the silence. It was straining her marriage more than anything ever had. She now had *real* secrets, beyond the usual silly ones.

After missing the early-morning meeting and getting locked out of the facility, she had tried to get in touch with them, with anyone, but everyone had gone radio-silent. She had no idea why she couldn't get through, but the silence made her nervous. There was no one she could tell, no one she could reach out to, because of the non-disclosure.

Not Nick, not the police...

Julia looked up from her desk to see Renzo Cabral standing in the doorway.

"How did you get in?"

"According to your husband, you're in danger."

"Nick?" Julia said. "He contacted you?"

Renzo nodded.

"How does he even know who you are?" Julia said with a mix of anger and confusion.

"Not sure," Renzo said. "But that's a question for later."

"What do you mean danger?"

"I need to tuck you away somewhere safe. Right now."

"Oh, come on. That's ridiculous."

"Maybe, but ridiculous or not, we've got to go."

"I'm not in danger," Julia said. "And where have you been? I've been trying to get through for hours and no one's answering."

"Well, I've been looking for you too, and I found you, here in your office, working on a holiday."

"Not by choice. I'd prefer to be with my family." Julia was tiring of the banter.

"Someone's looking for Colin Armor," Renzo said. "And they think they can get to him through you, and we can't take that risk."

"You're joking," Julia said. "You sound like my husband."

"This is not a joking matter." Renzo held his arm out abruptly and motioned Julia to the door.

Julia shook her head, stood, grabbed her purse, and led Cabral out of her corner office. They marched down the hall, past the empty offices and cubicles, and headed down the stairs.

"Sorry you missed the meeting this morning," Renzo said.

"The one time I run late, I'm locked out of history."

"Who locked you out?"

"The men at the gate."

"Well, I'll get you past the men at the gate. Everyone's still there. I think we can write you back into history."

"Really?"

"Really," Renzo said.

Julia walked outside to her car and pointed to the Suburban next to her Audi. "Are we taking your car?"

"You'll follow me," Renzo said as he opened his SUV's door. "I don't know if I'll have time to drive you back later."

"Works for me. I've got the reception to host later on. God help me if I'm late for the second time in my life."

"Reception, huh? And you didn't invite me?"

"Come on," she said. "You know you're always invited to my parties."

"Who are you?" Zane whispered in the man's face.

The man stared back, defiant and silent. Zane turned to the woman, her eyes vacant as she looked ahead.

The concrete basement was cold and damp. But for the two chairs they sat upon, there was nothing down here, and nothing else at all in the vacant rental home.

It was an old trick his superior had taught him: find the homes for rent, which are usually vacant (as opposed to those for sale). Brokers paid less attention to rentals, as the commissions were far smaller than those of for-sale listings. The ones on the market for a while saw the least activity and made for the best places to hide.

At one o'clock this morning, Zane had driven to the small Adirondack town of North Creek, where the man and woman's home sat back from the road behind a stand of overgrown pines and a perfectly trimmed lawn. The target, a white saltbox-style house, was unlocked. Zane found it immaculate and simple. An ancient TV, a wood-burning stove in the corner, and wall phone made the house look like it was stuck in a 1970s time warp.

He crept to the second floor to find a middle-aged couple sound asleep, unaware as he compared their faces to the pictures in his hand.

The man's strength shocked him as he laid the chloroformed cloth over his mouth. Kicking and swinging, the man's left jab caught Zane in the head, making him see stars as he pressed the cloth harder into his face, his struggle finally abating as he fell limp.

When Zane turned to the woman, he found her on the floor in the corner, terrified. A single one-word mantra pouring from her lips as he approached, "Please, please, please..."

Once he had them securely bound and thoroughly unconscious, he worked them into the trunk of his car and drove them back to Byram Hills, tucking them in the basement of the vacant colonial on Harper Road at four o'clock this morning. He'd taken a picture of them as instructed and left them. He had no further orders as to their handling or what would happen to them.

He also had no idea who they were, what they had done, or why he had kidnapped them. His handler hadn't explained, and Zane hadn't questioned his orders. But now...

He took hold of the woman by her face. "Who are you?"

There was a fear in her eyes that went beyond Zane. He could see that she had a secret—a revelation worse than Zane's threat.

Zane pulled the watch from his pocket and glanced at it: he was running out of time.

The house was in the valley in the shadow of the dam. Were they here to die in the flood? If so, if they had to die, why not just a bullet? A fire? A noose? All far less effort. What did they have to do with today?

Zane got back in his car and drove out of the driveway. He had a sudden, terrible premonition about this day, which he was now moving backward through toward seven a.m. A feeling that he was marching toward his death, as if it had already happened, and he simply wasn't remembering it...as if it were inevitable. As if, despite his manipulation of the future, a part of Zane's past that he had somehow forgotten had become set in stone.

Julia followed Renzo across town and onto the dirt road leading into Hadley's Woods. Turning right into the rutted driveway, she followed him for a quarter of a mile until they arrived at the security gate. Renzo rolled down his window, said a few words, and the guards waved both cars through.

They continued up the dirt road and came to the small white house surrounded in military vehicles. Four marines stood guard, rifles at the ready.

Julia pulled out her phone and dialed Nick. She knew she'd be out of touch for a while and didn't need his paranoia kicked up another two notches. The phone rang three times before going to voicemail.

"Listen," Julia said. "It's me. Renzo just met me. You scared him with your ridiculous notions. I appreciate your love, but you're being silly. At any rate, I'm out of touch for at least the next hour, so don't freak out if you can't reach me. And more importantly, don't forget you have to pick Katy up at two. Love you."

Julia hung up her phone as Renzo approached. "You have to leave your phone or check it." He pointed at the device.

"I know." Julia tucked her phone in her purse and threw it on the seat as she got out of her car, closed the door, and locked it.

"Nice to see you again, Ms. Quinn." Sergeant Walker accompanied her toward the small house.

"I'm sorry I didn't bring you all a coffee, Sergeant."

"That's quite all right, ma'am."

Julia followed Renzo into the small house, leaving Walker behind. They walked through the sparsely decorated foyer, through a living room filled with dated, worn furniture from the '60s, the pale walls covered in dime-store paintings. They cut through the kitchen and stopped at a security checkpoint, where two well-armed marines nodded as Julia walked through the scanner, then waved her ahead.

"Good afternoon, Ms. Quinn." Private Michael Lowery wore his usual pressed camouflage uniform.

"Afternoon, Mike." Julia smiled. "Actually, happy Fourth of July."

"Same to you, ma'am." He turned to the other marine and nodded. "You're both good to go."

Renzo reached over and pulled open a set of white pocket doors to reveal a large elevator, its door opening to a modern, brushed-steel cab. They stepped in, the door closing behind them, and faced two buttons: *Surface* and *Sub*. Renzo hit *Sub* and they began their decent.

"Are things still on schedule?" Julia asked.

"Pretty much, just a couple minor complications."

"Serious?"

"Don't know," Renzo said. "Not really my area of expertise nor my position to judge. But, listen, I'm going to need your help with something."

"That's why I'm here." Julia smiled.

"It's of a rather serious nature, and I don't think anyone is as equipped as you are."

"Sounds ominous," Julia said. "You know I'm happy to help with anything you need."

The elevator stopped as the doors opened into a small vestibule; a large steel security door stood in front of them.

Renzo inserted a key into a slot and pressed a button beside it. A whoosh of air washed over them as the door in front of them opened. Stepping in, she felt the door close immediately behind them. They now stood sealed in a cold, stainless-steel box with another door ahead of them. Julia looked up at the twelve-foot ceiling, dotted with nozzles and vents.

Renzo inserted a second key, and this time placed his right hand upon a fingerprint reader. A series of mechanical sounds reverberated within the walls before the door opened to reveal another world.

They stepped into an elegant foyer. A fireplace stacked with wood sat in the corner, a Persian rug covered a polished oak floor, and two New England landscapes by Henniker Green hung on the walls on either side of an incongruous window. On the far side of the room stood a white, elegantly carved, wooden door.

"Where's Charlie?" Julia asked.

"Probably dealing with something."

She nodded.

"Charlie and Harry always follow protocol—the door's closed for a reason. Don't worry. They're probably off dealing with a request." Renzo looked around the space and its advanced security. "When your husband asked me to protect you, I don't think he realized how protected you'd be."

"He's going to be so mad when he finds out what I'm doing."

"He'll get over it."

"I don't know about that."

Renzo hit the red button beside the steel door, opening it, and walked back into the stainless-steel transition area.

"Where are you going?" Julia asked.

"I have to tell Sergeant Walker to inform his men that we may not be leaving 'til tonight."

"I don't envy you."

"I'll be back down in a few minutes. Wait for Charlie to come back and let you in." Renzo pointed at a tray of donuts, coffee urn, and bottles of water. "Have something to eat, relax. That's probably something you haven't done in weeks."

"Thank you, Renzo."

As the doors closed, Julia rode a wave of mixed emotions. She was angry at Nick for telling Renzo she was in danger, but happy she'd been dealt back into the game. She'd feared history would pass her by. But now...

Julia grabbed a bottle of water and the last jelly donut off the table, biting into the pastry with embarrassing relief. It was the first food she'd had since 5:00 a.m. She had thought about grabbing breakfast after her workout but opted only for coffee. With the day's crazy events—fearing that Nick had died in a car accident; getting Katy to daycare; missing the morning's meeting—the opportunity for food hadn't existed. While she might have forgotten to eat, her stomach hadn't; it was clearly glad for the sugar and carbs, healthy eating be damned.

She was truly amazed at Shamus's underground hideaway. It never felt as though you were so far underground. Across the room, the window shone bright with the light of a summer day.

The maroon curtains didn't actually frame a window, but a large, window-shaped, video screen with an outdoor image mimicking the movement of the heavens, keeping the underground staff's circadian rhythms intact.

Julia finished the donut and sipped her water as she paced the room, trying to burn off her nervous energy. Her dealings here today and over the past weeks as a liaison stemmed from a favor she'd agreed to do for Shamus. At ninety-three, he remained sharp as a tack, filling his days with trying to make the world a better place. He and his wife Katherine had both slowed in recent years and had brushed up against death more than once, only to emerge from the other side more determined not to waste a single moment. She never imagined that when he first asked her to get involved in his most recent escapade that it would involve a matter as earthshaking as this. Shamus was truly a miracle worker. She had actually called him twice this morning, simply to touch base, but hadn't reached him. She vowed to swing by his house later today if she had time before the reception.

She was a bit surprised by the lack of activity, the lack of anyone down here. There were usually at least thirty people working, but she reasoned they were fully engaged in the plan, focused on trying to make history. They weren't assigned to sit in the vestibule and wait to meet and greet her.

She glimpsed a splotch of something on the far wall, tiny, no bigger than a dot. Shamus wouldn't be happy. He took such pride in this facility, not only its usefulness, but its upkeep. There was never a mark or stain on the floor, dust in a corner, or a thing out of place.

As she got closer, she realized it was a series of dots—red dots—and as she moved closer...she saw it was blood.

Julia quickly spun around.

Fear filled her as she reached for her phone, forgetting its absence and the fact that it wouldn't work down here anyway. She ran to the white door, nearly tripping as she reached for the handle and ripped it open...

And saw Charlie.

Her heart ran cold as she spun about in fear, panic finally filling her mind, and she did the only she could do...

She screamed.

Nick sat in the small rear booth of Franzel's Beer Hall, the hundred-year-old restaurant not having changed much since its establishment except for a paint job in the '70s.

He looked out the window at the enormous Killian Park, already half full for the evening festivities, the early birds getting the best seats to see the fireworks, none aware what happened to them in the future—a future that had already been changed, a future that would never happen.

Nick pulled out his phone and listened to Julia's voicemail. He smiled, appreciating that Renzo was a man of his word. Nick laid his phone on the table and

pulled up the tracker.

She was smack in the middle of Hadley's Woods.

Nick looked out the window again, craning his neck to the right to catch a slim glimpse of the forest a mile away. He shook his head; he should have known.

The absurdity wasn't lost on him that the place that scared him when he was a kid still gave him a bit of a chill now. Yet it had somehow become her sanctuary, the refuge where she would be protected from Janos Zane and his ill intent.

"Hey, Nick," Suzy McGloughlin said.

"Hey, Suze," Nick said with a smile. They had known each other since he was five; she had babysat him every Friday night while his parents went out.

"Eating alone again?" Suzy smirked. "We really need to buy you some friends."

"Only if I get a money-back guarantee." Nick appreciated her always-cheerful disposition, especially since he knew that the bubbly facade concealed a broken heart since her husband's death two years ago. "And no, I'm waiting for someone."

"What are we eating today? Peanut butter and bacon, or chicken parm?"

"Just a Coke to start."

"You got it." She disappeared in back.

Nick could feel the weight of the watch in his pocket. He couldn't wait until 7:00 a.m., when this would all be over, when he could become a chronological conformist and start riding its hour hand forward, like everyone else. He actually—

The ground rumbled suddenly, deep and foreboding.

The hanging beer glasses chinged against one another as three bottles of whiskey fell and smashed on the floor behind the bar. The room fell silent as everyone looked around, hoping as a group for someone to tell them what had caused the unearthly disruption.

Nick bolted up from the booth and raced for the door; he knew exactly what it was. As impossible as it seemed, history was repeating itself.

"Everyone get to high ground!" Nick shouted.

But no one listened as he bolted out the door. He didn't bother with his car but headed straight for the sharp hill beside the restaurant. He didn't look at the dam that rose behind the restaurant. He didn't have time. Two hundred yards to the top of the rise.... Nick ran like he had never run before, the steep grade already setting his thighs on fire.

A second rumble shook the ground, nearly knocking him off his feet, but he didn't stop—only charged harder, ignoring the pain in his lungs and the fear in his mind. A third earthquake shook. Nick couldn't recall if there had been four or five explosions.

A sharp cracking filled the air, like breaking ice on a lake, only magnified a thousandfold. Stone ground against stone, screaming as the century-old Killian Dam began to crack and give way.

Nick finally crested the top of the hill and fell to his knees; he turned and looked back down on the field, watching a mass of people staring up in confusion, no one realizing what was about to happen... that these were the final moments of their lives.

The enormous dam split straight up the right side, the crack running from the base to the top like a lightning bolt in reverse; water began to spit through and within seconds the cracks radiated like those of a shattered windshield.

And then it happened: the massive four-hundred-foot wall gave way, the granite-and-concrete blocks exploding outward as the water pressure ended their purpose. Five-ton squares, launched by the pressure, hurtled thirty yards into the swarm of people below, as a wall of water blasted out like Niagara on adrenaline.

The human outcry was massive as a thousand voices screamed at once—but as suddenly as the collective cry began, it ended, smothered and washed away in the roar of the torrent, the onslaught wiping away the giant field, a three-hundred-foot tsunami scooping up and carrying everything into its wake.

And the water kept coming, shooting through the breached dam like a broken pipe draining the ocean.

Nick stared down at the devastation, the water quickly rising, the new sea dotted with bodies, cars, trees, and debris, all crushed by the unrelenting power of nature.

Franzel's was gone, splintered and wiped away, along with the neighboring houses. Byram Castle still stood, though water filled its interior, air and spray jetting out of its windows in a deafening howl.

Nick looked down the valley, the churning reservoir now stretching for as far as the eye could see: houses, streets, lampposts, neighborhoods, all gone. The water continued to rise and lapped against the new riverbanks formed by the surrounding hills.

Nick looked south, where Hadley's Woods had disappeared. He frantically dialed his phone, but Julia's number went straight to voicemail. She had warned him of this. He dialed a second number.

"Holy shit," Dreyfus said as he answered his phone. "Where are you?"

"Standing on Route 22. Where are Sandy and your girls?"

"All here in the backyard. Katy and Julia?"

"Katy's in daycare, high ground, far from danger."

"Julia?"

"I need your help."

Dreyfus's Ford pickup skidded to a stop and Nick jumped in. Dreyfus drove, cutting through the emergency vehicles racing toward the disaster, past cars and rubberneckers looking down over the shattered dam and the flooded aftermath.

"Julia's in Shamus's bunker."

"Are you sure?"

"I sent her there to be safe."

"How do you even know about Shamus's bunker?"

"I'll explain on the way, but you've got to get me in there."

"It should be airtight. She'll be okay."

"Really?" Nick didn't believe him.

"I know that place like the back of my hand—I upgraded all of the security, I did every lock, every light. It has surface vents but those are only opened once a week, and they have to be done by hand. There's a full air-scrubber system to seal the whole place off from the world in case of disaster. I promise it's safe."

"And if it's not?" Nick pressed him. "Can we get in there?"

Dreyfus thought a moment, his eyes drawn to the right, to the churning waters of the new body of water a half mile away. "Yeah. The air locks... If we're gonna get down there, we go through air locks; they're designed to keep the smallest of particles out. Problem is, I only have one set of SCUBA gear."

Nick thought a moment and turned to Dreyfus. "I know where we can get more, but let's get yours first."

Dreyfus drove back to his house and raced into his driveway, leapt from the truck, and ran into his workshop. He came out with a dive bag and air tank, throwing it in the flatbed; then he ran back inside and emerged with a duffle bag of tools.

"Waterproof?" Nick asked as he helped him lift it all into the pickup's bed.

"Of course, give me a little credit." Dreyfus dismissed the question. "More importantly, we need a boat...and I don't have a boat."

"I've got that covered too."

Nick jumped into the driver's seat of Dreyfus's truck.

"Can you explain to me what's going on?" Dreyfus got in on the passenger side.

Nick hit send on his email. "Just read the email."

Dreyfus opened up his phone and the email. "*I* wrote this?" Dreyfus said with confusion.

"Just read it."

Nick ran through Marcus's house, with Marcus and Dreyfus close behind him.

"I'll do whatever you need," Marcus said between breaths. "Though I'd kind of like to get a clue about what we're doing."

"I'll tell you on the way." Nick stopped in front of a large door. "But we need guns."

"Okay," Marcus said without hesitation. "This should be interesting."

Marcus punched a code into a security panel and the heavy door popped open. He pulled out three handguns and a handful of clips. "Enough?"

Nick nodded and they ran out.

Nick cut through the garage, jumped in Dreyfus's truck, and backed it up to the large trailer with the Jet Ski on it that had been sitting in the driveway since early this morning, when they had been diverted from kitesurfing by the car accident. Marcus and Dreyfus quickly hooked up the trailer, leapt in the truck, and they drove off.

It was a four-minute drive to Kavey Lane. Dreyfus did his best to explain to Marcus everything in his email, including the pocket watch, then showed him the videos from later that day.

"You're shitting me," Marcus said.

"You know you say the same thing every time you learn about this?" Nick said.

"This happened before?"

"Not this moment, but we did a little dance in the future."

"In the future...?" Marcus threw up his hands.

Nick nodded.

"Are you messing with my future?" Marcus was pissed.

"More the past..."

Marcus sank back in his seat.

"You okay?" Nick asked.

Marcus looked ahead, digesting. "When all this is over, and Julia's safe, and this disaster shit is put to right, you're going to owe a debt to me that will take years of alcohol, parties, and other irresponsible fun to pay off."

Nick parked on the road outside the grey house with the blue BMW in the driveway.

"Whose house is this?" Dreyfus asked.

"It's for sale," Nick said. "But the people using it are the ones who planted the bombs that blew the dam."

"I take it they're not the friendly type."

"No, they're killers...but last time you and I saw them, they were dead."

"I've been here before?" Marcus shook his head.

"In so many words."

"This is a mindfuck of epic proportions." Marcus's laugh held a tinge of madness.

"I'm sorry."

"No need to apologize," Marcus said, as he slammed home a clip into the butt of his pistol. "I'm going to love the payback."

The three slipped out of the Ford and hustled to the side of the house.They ducked under the windows and arrived at the garage door. Marcus and Dreyfus lined up on either side as Nick peered in.

"Well?" Marcus asked

"No bodies," Nick said.

"That's a good thing."

"Not really...they don't fight back as hard when they're dead."

"Good point."

"There were four...they could be anywhere."

"Comforting."

Nick gently lifted the garage door as Marcus and Dreyfus raised their guns, scanning both inside and out.

"Hurry," Marcus whispered.

Nick ran in, dropped to all-fours, and looked under the van. The block of Semtex was affixed there, fused and wired to the black box, ready to explode, but hopefully not for another hour.

"What the hell are you doing?" asked Marcus.

"Nothing. Doesn't matter." Nick jumped to his feet and opened the rear of the white van. He grabbed three dive masks, regulators, fins, BCVs, weight belts, three small dive bags, and underwater lights, then quickly trotted them out to the truck. He ran back, grabbed three air tanks, and set them in the pickup's bed.

"There's no one here," Marcus whispered.

"Well, let's not tempt fate," Dreyfus said as they ran back to and jumped in the truck.

"Not my point," Marcus said, as Nick drove away from the curb. "Where the hell *are* they?"

Nick drove down the tree-lined Maple Way on the edge of Byram Hills until the road ended in floodwaters. He spun the Ford pickup around and backed the trailer a couple of feet into the deluge until the Jet Ski touched the water.

"Can it hold three?"

"It can hold four," Marcus said as he untied the Jet Ski from the trailer and floated it on the floodwaters.

"Well, it can hold two people plus Marcus," Nick said with a smile.

They quickly donned the dive gear. Dreyfus plugged GPS coordinates into his phone and threw his bag of tools on the back of the Jet Ski. Nick pulled out the pocket watch and looked at the time: 12:28. He stuck the old watch and his phone in the dive bag, sealing it up, and tucked it in the pocket of his buoyancy control vest.

"So, what happens when we find Julia and whoever else is down there?" Marcus asked. "We're not equipped for a rescue."

"We're just confirming they're all alive," Nick said. "We'll figure out that part later."

"Can I ask you a question?" Marcus said quietly as he pulled Nick aside. "And please understand, I don't mean to be cold. God knows, I love Julia. But with such a narrow time window, why save Julia now? Why not investigate, gather intel, facts, figure out the end solution so you can end this? And then you just go back an hour or two earlier and save her once and for all?"

Nick stared at his friend a moment. "Could you let Anissa suffer? Could you live with yourself knowing you could have stopped your wife's agony? What you don't understand is, despite everything I prevent, despite going back an hour when Julia won't remember the pain and death she went through, *I* will. I'll remember every scream, every drop of her blood, the pain in her eyes, her lifeless body. I'll remember every death, even if no one else does."

"I get it," Marcus whispered in sympathy.

"But even worse than that," Nick continued, "what if I don't save her now and Zane kills me? It's game over and she's dead for good. What if I somehow lose the watch and Zane goes back an hour earlier and kills her? I have no way to prevent it."

Marcus nodded.

"No matter how illogical this all seems," Nick said, "I will always try to save her."

"I'm sorry."

"Yeah, well..." Nick jumped on the Jet Ski and started it up, the roar of the engine echoing out into the flooded forest. "Welcome to my nightmare."

Dreyfus took a seat while Marcus pushed off and climbed aboard. Nick piloted down the road and emerged from the forest, into what could only be described as epic chaos. The dam was still spilling out into a massive lake. The entire new body of water was dotted with bodies and cars. Emergency, police, and fishing boats puttered through the deep water, looking for survivors. Entire trees drifted by, as did two houses, mailboxes, planters, and the awning for Franzel's.

Nick navigated carefully through the turbid water, avoiding the dead, maneuvering the Jet Ski while Dreyfus looked at the GPS on his phone from within its clear dive bag.

He pointed and Nick steered.

A mile out in the middle of nowhere, the water rose above the treetops, a nearly placid surface masking the devastation below.

Dreyfus tapped Nick's shoulder. Nick cut the engine and drifted to a stop.

Dreyfus looked at his watch and set his timer. "Figuring the depth of the flood and the further depth of the bunker, plus decompression stops back up, we've got thirty-seven minutes."

"We'll barely make it," Nick said. "Why thirty-seven?"

"Twenty bottom-time, fifteen for stops, and only two for panic."

"Panic?" Marcus shook his head as he checked his regulator.

Dreyfus didn't hesitate. He pulled down his mask, stuck the regulator in his mouth, and rolled back into the water.

"Let's go find Julia and tell her how much you owe me." Marcus patted Nick on the back.

Nick nodded and they joined Dreyfus.

Simultaneously, they flipped on their lights, the intense beams illuminating a world of mud and debris that limited their vision to only five feet. Nick angled himself and kicked down, clearing his ears as he went, Dreyfus and Marcus close behind.

At fifteen feet, they arrived at the treetops, like something out of nightmare, wooden limbs reaching out for them like arms, leaves and needles waving in the undulating current.

Nick caught sight of a red-headed soldier trapped within an oak tree, his belt caught on a branch, his vacant eyes staring at nothing.

Continuing down, a small white house came into view, glowing in the wash of their lights. Half the roof was gone; there were no windows or doors. A green tent clung to its anchor drifting about like a flag in a breeze. A pile of Army vehicles and black limos were piled together on their sides, upside down, butting up against a large stand of trees. Beside them sat Julia's crumpled blue Audi.

Nick swam into the structure, the interior destroyed, looking like a hundred-year-old haunted house: entire walls missing, magazines floating up and out of the roofless home. He swam into what was left of the kitchen, past an incongruous security scanner.

The doors were missing, as were all of the walls around a protruding concrete shaft of an elevator. Dreyfus swam past Nick to a steel door. He inserted a special key, turned it, and pulled a crowbar from his tool bag. He wedged it into the door, planted his feet against the wall, and pulled open the door. An explosion of air bubbles jetted out to reveal the darkened elevator shaft.

Dreyfus shined his light into the depths and followed the beam, kicking down into the vertical shaft. Nick and Marcus trailed behind single file, another thirty-five feet, nearly eighty feet from the surface now.

Arriving atop the elevator cab, Dreyfus pulled out a small drill and made quick work of the hatch, throwing it aside and swimming down into the elevator car. There, he pried open the door to reveal the small, flooded elevator vestibule of the bunker.

Swimming to a large metal door, he inserted his key above the hand scanner, turned it, and grabbed his crowbar. He jammed it in and pulled hard, but it didn't budge. Marcus took hold; the two of them braced their feet against the wall and pulled.

The door cracked open and slowly slid aside.

The three swam into a ten-foot-square holding space, another door before them. Dreyfus spun around and forced the door behind them closed, sealing it tight. Nick looked up above the door line to see a large air pocket in the twelve-foot-high room.

Dreyfus cracked a glow stick, its green glow filling the space. He banged on the second door and listened. He banged again, harder. No response. He slipped another key in the slot beside the next door. He pulled out an oddly shaped tool, inserted it into the handprint panel that he himself had installed, cranked it through a series of notches, and grabbed his crowbar. He slipped it in and forced open the door.

The foyer was flooded to the ceiling, though everything was still in place, the couch, chairs, paintings on the wall, wood in the fireplace, as if the space had slowly flooded as opposed to suffering the violent torrent that had destroyed the world above.

Dreyfus cracked and dropped another glow stick and swam ahead, leading the way, their beams of light danced through the murky water like klieg lights at a show, dancing and reflecting off the artwork, tables, and chairs. He pulled open a white, hand-carved door to reveal a wide, stylish hallway, but there was no one there....

Until Marcus pointed up at two bodies floating against the ceiling, dressed in dark suits, earpieces dangling from their ears.

Nick swam down the hall, stopping at a large set of double doors. He placed his hand on the handle. While he hoped against hope that he'd find life, he prepared for the worse. He turned the handle and shined his light inside.

And it was worse than anything he could have ever imagined.

Ten people drifted amidst papers, pencils, and water bottles. There were two small flags, Russian and Akbiquestani, in the corner, dominated by a large American flag that floated proudly above them amid all the death.

Nick, Marcus, and Dreyfus swam in, reaching out to the bodies, looking at the dead faces. Seven men, three women, all dressed in business attire. Nick checked the two blonde women: neither was Julia.

He lifted up the head of a prone floating body, stared into the dead eyes, and a shock ran through him. Nick knew the man, knew his face; it took a moment before he realized what had happened. He was staring into the eyes of Matthew McManus, President of the United States.

But the president hadn't drowned.

A bullet above his right eye had taken his life before the flood.

As Nick looked around, shining his light on every face, he realized they had all been shot: Russians, Akbiquestanis, and Americans, all murdered before they had even gotten wet.

Nick pointed toward the door and they swam back out and down the green glow-stick-lit hall, through the lobby vestibule, and up into the air pocket above the security area. They treaded water there and spit out their regulators.

"What the hell?" Nick shouted.

"The peace accords," Dreyfus said, overcome with emotion. "That's what Shamus set up. That's why everything was so secretive."

"They're all dead," Marcus said as he ripped off his dive mask. "What the hell *is* this? You said the bunker was supposed to be air and watertight."

"The vents must have been left open." Dreyfus shook his head. "Had to have been intentional."

"That doesn't matter," Nick said. "They were all shot dead before a drop of water hit this place."

"Holy shit," Marcus said. "Byram Hills wasn't the only target today—so were these heads of state."

"Or they were always the target," Dreyfus said. "And the town is just collateral damage."

"But the water, the dam, that's going to destroy New York City." Marcus slammed his fist in the wall. "Think about it: they just crippled the most important city in the world. Who *did* this?"

The gravity of their situation sunk in.

"Julia," Nick whispered aloud. "What have I done?"

"You guys wait here," Dreyfus said.

"Where are you going?"

"I need to check something...just wait here."

Paul Dreyfus swam out of the room quickly, heading through the hallways. He came across a woman and two men, all three shot in the face and now floating placidly. He kicked gently by, trying not to disturb them, respecting them in death as they had not been respected in life. He cut to the back of the large facility, past living rooms, bedrooms, and the medical facilities, shielding himself from more floating bodies.

While Dreyfus had SCUBA-dived since he his twenties, it had been mostly for thrills and pleasure. He always felt as though he were in another world, silent, dark, and cold, never knowing what lay above, below, or behind you. It felt almost as if a blanket had been thrown over your most basic senses, creating a constant feeling of dread. As he came across two more bodies, each riddled with bloodless bullet holes, Dreyfus's fear cracked his mind; he could barely contain his pounding heart and deep, rasping breaths.

He continued to a doorway, opening it and swimming down a set of stairs. In a labyrinth of halls, he shined his light ahead and watched it reflect back in an explosive glow. He floated forward and stopped at a flat steel panel, a red plunger button beside it; he ran his hands along the edges, inspecting it. He finally looked up and saw a small green LED glowing above the door.

Dreyfus pounded on the door. He waited a moment and pounded again.

After a moment, someone pounded back.

A shadow shimmered below Nick and Marcus, large and dark, skimming past the room's door...and then another.

"What the hell was that?" Marcus pointed at the green light pouring through the door below their air pocket.

"Someone's alive," Nick said.

"Another air pocket?" Marcus said. "There could be a lot of them."

"Maybe it's Julia."

Nick pulled down his mask, bit down on his regulator, and swam out of the room with Marcus behind him.

Was all of this Zane? Nick wondered. *Did he kill all these people?* Zane wasn't working alone, there was no question of that. And that was exactly the point...this place is what Zane had been looking for; this is where he'd needed Julia to lead him. Yet Julia hadn't led him here. And even if Zane had made it down here, past the guards at the gate, past the military contingent above, past the Secret Service agents—which seemed impossible—he couldn't have done all this in the last hour.

Not without help.

Somehow, Nick thought, he had to stop all of this. But then he realized that *this*—dead presidents, a shattered dam, a town's worth of people drowned—was far beyond his capabilities. It didn't matter that he had an inexplicable pocket watch that he could use to change the past to fix the future: saving Julia was now only the tip of an iceberg.

Nick signaled for Marcus to split away and search elsewhere while he continued forward through the hall, past the two dead Secret Service men floating against the ceiling. He turned left, swimming through a large great room, cookies, coffee cups, and plates drifting about. He cut through a theater and gym and arrived at the dining room, always looking up, but unable to spot any other air pocket. He pulled a glow stick, cracked it, and dropped it, a breadcrumb to lead him back.

With his ear to the door, Dreyfus pounded again. The response was instantaneous this time. This was the safe room. He'd built it and he knew it better than anyone; he'd built an almost identical replica in his home. It was a bunker within the bunker, a last-ditch location to retreat to if all else failed. It was stocked with survival gear and food, independent of the facilities' systems, and, most importantly in this case, air- and water-tight. Dreyfus didn't know how many people were in there, but there was at least one person.

He prayed it was Julia.

He banged on the door once as a shadow caught his eye. It had been to his right, but by the time his light flashed in that direction, it was gone.

He shined his light in a circle, feeling surrounded by ghosts. And then he saw him. The man was swimming toward him, kicking hard. Dreyfus could see his tattooed neck. Dreyfus whirled about and swam away as fast as he could. He made for the door, his flashlight moving wildly as he pulled through the water with his arms. He grabbed the handle of the door, tugging it open, quickly kicking up the stairs, swimming for his life, the tattooed man only fifteen feet back and gaining.

Suddenly, Dreyfus's mask was torn from his face, his regulator ripped from his mouth. He twisted around, unable to see. He dropped his light as he struggled to remain calm. Fighting for his precious air, he grabbed his regulator, slamming it in his mouth, breathing in deeply, only to inhale a mouthful of water. His air line had been sliced away at the tank. There was nothing he could do. He spun, trying to orient himself toward the air pocket, but he was lost. A shadow grabbed at his arm, yanking him. Dreyfus reactively gasped, breathing in water, then coughing, which only made him aspirate more water.

Dreyfus spun again in panic, his flashlight beam spinning as it drifted downward, briefly illuminating a glimpse of the large man in full SCUBA gear. Dreyfus briefly saw the man's hate-filled eyes before he disappeared into the shadows. Dreyfus began to convulse, nearing death, but the end came quicker than he expected as he felt a knife enter his back, then emerge from his chest.

Marcus swam through a second conference room, this one containing five suit-wearing people. They had come here to end violence and death in the world, only to meet it themselves.

Marcus cut back into the first conference room, past the dead body of the President and his aides, past the Secret Service agents, earpieces floating above their ears. He swam against the ceiling, lifting tiles here and there in search of a lifesaving air pocket, but found nothing.

Marcus had counted twenty-two dead so far. He couldn't imagine how they all had been shot, how all the guards had failed to protect their leaders. He wondered how many men it took to pull this off. When word got out, it would be cataclysmic. As bad as the broken dam and thousands of lives lost were, this was far worse. He looked at the three dead heads of state. They were world leaders whose countries were already at war. Marcus considered how the conflict would escalate as he swam out of the conference room and down the hall.

A red cloud caught Marcus's eye, distracting him from his thoughts, pulling him back into the moment. The blood hung and drifted in the water around him. And as he scanned it with his light, he caught sight of Dreyfus, floating motionless near the floor.

But before he could react, there was a man in front of him, holding a gun, aiming it straight at him. Marcus almost laughed: the gun wouldn't work down here.

Marcus never saw the spear leave the gun; it pierced the glass of his facemask, rammed through his eye, piercing his brain before exiting his skull.

Nick checked his air. He had fifteen minutes left in his tank, but that was not the time he was worried about. He knew he was nearing the top of the hour and he had yet to find Julia, to find any solution to what had happened here. The things he'd witnessed here—a trio of assassinations, including the U.S. president, the end to peace accords, the abrupt destruction of thousands of lives, with more to come—were not only mind-shattering: they were unprecedented in history.

Nick couldn't understand why Renzo had brought Julia here, but he suspected it had cost her her life. The agent had said he'd bring her someplace safe, guaranteeing her safety. Nick had tracked her phone here, he had seen her Audi; there was little doubt she was here, too. Nick had thought he was saving her, when he'd only been sending her to her death....

Stop, he told himself. *She could still be alive, couldn't she? Could—*

Nick's flashlight lit up a man dressed in SCUBA gear, bubbles rising from his regulator.

Nick recognized him. Not his face, but his tattoos; he could clearly make out a painted jaguar on his naked arm. Nick had first seen the man when he lay dead on the floor of the garage on Kavey Lane.

The man held a long dive knife, subtly waving the blade back and forth. Nick was unsure what to do. The man was bigger, deadlier. Nick slowly drifted toward him. Closer and closer. Ten feet, eight feet, five feet. Nick could see the tattoos running up his neck, his eyes unblinking as they stared back.

Nick's arm shot out, ripping the dive mask off the man's face, disorienting him. He kicked and pushed off of the larger body, swimming past him for the door. He dropped his flashlight as he dodged the blade, swimming furiously until he suddenly stopped and was dragged backward.

Nick frantically kicked and struggled—he needed to survive, not for himself but for Julia and Katy, for everyone who had died this hour, the thousands in the park, the dignitaries and staffers and soldiers.

Somehow, he burst free. He kicked harder than he had ever kicked in all of his years of swimming, in all of his years of triathlons. And as he drew a breath, water poured into his mouth. He quickly spit out the water and his regulator, realizing why his assailant had stopped his pursuit.

Nick's air tube was cut, bubbles erupting from the remnants of the hose leading from his tank, spinning about like a wild snake spewing gas. Nick grabbed at his reserve octopus, but it came away in his hand, also severed.

It was thirty yards back to the air pocket, but without his light, the watery world turned pure black. A green glow came from up ahead. One of his breadcrumb glow sticks. He swam hard but steadily, trying to conserve his last breath. He could hold his breath for at least a minute, two back when he'd been in top shape, but that was last year, not now.

He pulled himself through the doorway, his lungs on fire, and found himself in the large kitchen, bathed in an eerie green light. He had not been in here before; Dreyfus or Marcus must have come through. Vegetables, bread, and napkins hung in the watery space. A body floated by, startling him, its long blonde hair swirling about its face.

Nick forgot about his lungs and the pain in his muscles. He forgot about everyone who'd died in the flood, who'd been shot. All of it washed away as he looked at the woman, her eyes mercifully closed. No bullet wounds marred her face or body; she had somehow escaped one mass murder, only to be killed in another.

The last sight Nick caught before he blacked out and drowned was the woman he had loved since she was fourteen.

Nick had found Julia.

CHAPTER 6

11:00 AM

Nick gasped for air on his garage floor. Drenched in his wetsuit, he tried to stand, but his balance was thrown off by the tank on his back.

Julia was dead again. He couldn't help thinking that, no matter what happened, she would die, her fate real, inevitable...that no matter how many times he saved her, death would still find his wife.

He shook the thought from his head and stripped off the dive gear, leaving the tank, fins, and masks on the floor. He looked at his Jeep, which would be destroyed an hour from now in the dam break. But at 11:00 a.m., it was intact and ready for his use.

Nick now realized that the threat he faced was far greater than the lives lost in the dam break. He had witnessed a world-altering catastrophe that could escalate the Akbiquestan war to cataclysmic proportions. By this hour, the U.S. president was dead, as were the Russian president and the Prime Minister of Akbiquestan—all assassinated. When word got out, their successors would seek revenge and retribution.

And what of the destruction of the dam? Was that planned to cover the assassinations, or was it another piece in a grander scheme that Nick couldn't yet see? While he would again rally Marcus, Shannon, the FBI, the military, and everyone who'd already stopped the dam disaster to do it again now, that wouldn't stop the president and everyone else—including Julia—from being murdered in that bunker.

By imploring Renzo to protect Julia, to take her where she'd be safe, Nick had sent his wife to her death.

Despite this new knowledge, Nick had even more questions than before.

How had Secret Service and military personnel protecting the bunker been beaten? How did the killers get through the security of the bunker itself? And who exactly was the "who" in question? Zane? It couldn't be Zane alone. After all, Nick had been drowned by an Akbiquestani assassin *in the bunker.*

With a glance at the pocket watch, Nick took out his phone and started dialing.

Marcus and Dreyfus stared at Nick. Not a word said for three minutes as they stood in Nick's garage, re-watching the video. But this time it wasn't only the video from the future, their own deaths, or the impossibility of the pocket watch and its time-altering effects that shocked his friends to the core: it was the death of the heads of state and what would happen when the world found out.

"Are you shitting me?" Marcus whispered. "How the hell can the president be dead and the world isn't on fire about it?"

"Because no one even knows he's here," Nick said.

"How is that possible?"

"If you've been following the news, they've been saying that he's locked down at Camp David under a media blackout. The people who know he's here in Byram Hills are all dead down there with him. And they were dead before the flood hit, all shot," Nick said. "Who knows for how long...it could have been hours."

"Does that ever really happen?" asked Marcus. "Deceiving the public about where the president *is*?"

"Not often, but think about who else is down there," said Dreyfus. "I get it—heads of state wanting do their work without the world breathing down their necks."

"Well," Nick said, "their top-secret meeting got found out and they're all dead."

Dreyfus thought for a moment. "A few weeks back, Shamus had me walk a few people through the bunker. I didn't think much of it then, but now, there's no question they were Secret Service."

The room fell quiet as they tried to make sense of the senseless.

"Why did the dam blow up early?" Marcus asked. "Why at noon that time? The video showed six o'clock."

"Something Zane did?" Nick guessed.

"Or something you did," Dreyfus said. "You're changing so many things; you don't even realize it."

"You're screwing up time, Nick," Marcus added.

"No." Nick shook his head. "I haven't done that much."

"It may not take much," said Marcus. "Don't take this the wrong way, but you sent Julia into that bunker."

Nick nodded. It was weighing heavily on him. "But that's not why the dam blew."

"Probably true, but something you or Zane did made that happen—because from what you said, and from what the news story and the video show, the dam should have blown at six...not noon."

"Look," Nick said intensely, "we can debate and dissect how I've screwed things up, but we don't have the luxury of time."

"Fine. What do we do?" asked Marcus.

"The president was already dead when we got down there. We can't save a man who's already dead if we don't know the hour of his death."

"Or who's behind it," Dreyfus added.

"Zane is part of it," said Nick. "But he's a soldier on a mission. Taking orders. Not the planner." He shook his head and began pacing.

"He got at least four mercenaries into the bunker, but they shouldn't have gotten within a hundred yards of the place."

"And where would they be now?"

"Last time I saw them, later in the day, they were dead in a garage. But one of them was in the bunker, in full dive gear. He cut my airline." Nick pointed at the severed rubber hose leading from his air tank on the floor.

"Pretty safe bet at least one of them's alive now," Dreyfus said.

"With at least some of the answers we need," Marcus added.

"Yeah. Though they didn't strike me as the chatty type."

"I'm a pretty good conversationalist," Marcus said. "If we can find them."

"I need you to find Shannon," Nick told Dreyfus. "You have to convince him of what's about to happen."

"That's not going to save the president."

"But it will save thousands." Nick turned to Marcus. "I need you to pick up Katy early at daycare, take her to Winged Foot, away from this madness. I'll send Julia there."

"Seriously?' Marcus threw his hands up. "You want me to babysit?"

"Katy trusts you and I trust you. Call me after you drop her off with Julia."

"Where are you going?"

"Zane's still the key."

"How you going to find him?" Marcus shook his head as he looked at his watch. "You've got less than forty-five minutes."

"Listen up," said Nick. "I have a really bad idea."

The silver-haired man adjusted the curtains as he stared out the window at the sun- soaked mountains, longing to be outside and walking the trails, this entire day behind him.

He picked up the phone and dialed. Zane answered immediately.

"Have you found the location?"

"Working on it," Zane said

"Time is running out," the man said. "The woman knows. You're telling me you can't get her to talk? I know what you're capable of. Focus on her; use whatever means necessary, physical or mental torture, her husband or her kid, I don't care. Just get the location and find Colin Armor before it's too late."

The smell in the air was like freedom: no gunpowder, cordite, or death. The cool breeze carrying the smell of the pine-covered mountains into the Akbiquestan valley reminded Zane of the Berkshires in winter when he'd skied them as a child.

He walked the twenty-acre compound with Carter Bull, both men in fatigues and fatigued from the never-ending day.

"We're going to miss you," Carter said.

"Well..." Zane didn't know what to say.

"But I'm happy for you; if anyone deserves a pass out of hell, it's you."

Zane was finally going to leave the military and leave all the death behind. It had started with a joke...someone saying the only thing Zane could do with a book is shoot it. He hadn't read a book since he'd left school, his military reading limited to manuals, maps, and daily briefings.

With his combat record, he could work a high-level field position with the CIA, FBI, or Secret Service. He could become a consultant in the security business, work in the civilian side of the Pentagon, or be an advisor to a defense contractor. All of it represented hope in a world where he thought it had died.

Of course, it would be three months before he left, thanks to the snail's pace of military processing, but it was the proverbial light at the end of the tunnel. He had a future. He had possibilities. He had hope.

Zane had arrived back at the camp two nights earlier, his five bloodied and wounded men the only survivors of the mission. They had fought their way through Akbiquestan and Russian forces for eight days, slipping through mountain passes at night, hiding in caves during the day.

In all, twenty-two had been killed in the air disaster, including the twelve-man Special Forces team on the second plane, which Zane had been supporting on a mission to take out the central command and leadership of the Akbiquestan military and end the prolonged war.

Zane was to lead them through the mountains and into a vast cave structure, which intel had confirmed was the heart of the enemy. The mission was to be this war's turning point, its D-Day, Hiroshima, and Waterloo combined, albeit using only a handful of soldiers; such were the efficiencies of today's technological war machine. But with the complex technology, the room for error and disaster increased exponentially. These types of accidents hadn't been possible in wars of stones, swords, and horses.

All the planning had been for naught, the mission turning to an ordeal of survival for Nick and his small team after their planes were blown from the sky. Given the catastrophic loss, a full investigation had been launched, with Zane in charge.

Radar systems were checked and rechecked and survivors interviewed, but there was no indication of enemy fire. As for possible mechanical failure, maintenance logs were studied. Mechanics were not only questioned but interrogated in Zane's unorthodox ways, the conclusion being that perfectly tuned military aircraft don't just blow up.

As the possibility of mechanical failure faded, suspicion of sabotage grew: a traitor on the base. Everyone was interviewed by a military commission of three; when nothing was found, Zane interrogated everyone himself, from the lowest cook to the highest-ranking officers. Every weapon was inventoried, from bullet to bomb; every second of security video analyzed. A special panel was convened to review all the gathered evidence.

Two weeks later, in the middle of the night, MPs pulled Zane from his bed, threw him in the makeshift brig in the center of the compound, and charged him with treason, murder, and conspiracy.

Nick stuck his Sig Sauer in the waist of his jeans beneath his sport jacket—he was glad for dry clothes—put Theo in the mudroom, threw some food in his bowl, and hurried out to his Wrangler.

Nick needed to find Zane, who was not only the key to the dam's destruction but also the only lead he had for the bunker assassinations. He knew Zane had killers lying in wait, ready to kill Julia and him in the event of Zane's death. But no matter what Zane claimed, even if Zane lived to be a hundred, Nick knew the killers would never be called off. Once Zane had what he wanted, he would kill all witnesses. At some point, Nick would have to figure out how to end that threat, but first he needed to accomplish other things. The first thing was obvious: if Nick wanted to question Zane, he had to find him. But how?

As much as it scared him, Nick had one thing that Zane wanted.

Julia stood on the corner of Main Street and Bedford Road, in the middle of downtown Byram Hills. She had been locked out of a meeting with the president on what was to be the most historic day of the millennium because Nick had made her late, and now she was standing here, waiting for her husband for reasons unknown. If he hadn't pleaded so earnestly, she would have been back at her office finishing up arrangements for the fundraiser reception this afternoon while waiting hopefully for the call to be invited down into the bunker.

After all, she was the one who had arranged the location, procured it from Shamus, coordinated with the Secret Service, and ensured that everything was prepared for the delegation's arrival two nights ago.

As she watched the people walking on the sidewalks, the cars driving by, she smiled to herself. No one had any idea of what was truly happening in town right now; everyone was going about their day clueless to the history occurring in their midst. She'd smiled and waved to many fellow townspeople in the last few minutes. People jokingly referred to her as "the mayor," as she knew everyone from the residents to merchants, old, young, and middle-aged alike. And not only their names. She remembered everything about them: their kids' birthdays, their husbands' and wives' professions, their likes, dislikes, hopes, and dreams. This was why her name rarely landed on the tongues of town gossips. Julia sought to be honest and loving in a not-so-honest-and-loving world.

Of course, she *had* lied to Nick. If he found out what she was doing, after his anger wore off, he would understand, but she hated deceiving him, hated lying about where she had been all week, about Colin Armor and what was going on in Shamus's bunker.

Knowing everyone in town made it easy for her to spot the visitors—the strangers passing through. She had never seen so many tattoos on one body as that of the man across the street. He was large, steroids no doubt flowing through distended veins. His eyes were hardened, avoiding any and all contact with the world around him as he climbed into a white, windowless van. Not many things scared her, but that man did.

"Hey."

Julia jumped, startled by Nick, who had sneaked up behind her.

"Damn it, Nick."

He kissed her tenderly on the lips.

"What's *that* about?" she asked.

Nick stepped back and searched for words. No matter how much he wanted to, he couldn't express the overwhelming relief he felt at seeing his wife alive again. It wouldn't make sense; it would only startle her or make her suspicious.

"What's wrong, Nick?"

Too late.

The truth was, he feared what was coming next, and he hated that it would be of his own doing. If they survived this day, he could scarcely imagine the nightmares he'd endure for the rest of his life, having witnessed her death so many times and had his soul ripped in half repeatedly. His plan was dangerous, maybe reckless. But, given the threat, he couldn't see another way to ensure their survival.

"I just need a minute or two of your time," he began, instantly hating how false he sounded. He desperately needed to tell her what—and who—they were up against, but he couldn't do it here.

"You sound like a salesman," she said. "Why are you doing this to me? It's only the busiest day of my life."

Nick's eyes swept the street in both directions, looking for Zane. He knew he would be out there somewhere, perhaps nearby. First, he would go to her office looking for her, then check for her car at their house, then look around town, not stopping 'til he found her.

Nick hated using Julia as bait. After all, everything he'd done in today's future hours had been intended to keep her away from Zane. But this was the only way he could see to flush him out in the coming hour...and his only chance at getting Zane.

Like clockwork, Nick spotted him, sitting in his black car across the street. Staring straight at them. Nick felt the heft of the Sig Sauer tucked at the small of his back.

"What's the matter?" Julia asked. "What's so urgent?"

Nick saw a white van pull away abruptly; all he could make out of the driver was a tattooed left arm. Zane's car was parked in the shade of the trees by Broadway Pizza. Nick could easily go down the small alley and come through the pizza place behind Zane. The man's focus was Julia, after all.... He measured the plan out in his head, concluding that he could easily get the jump on Zane. Then—

"Hi, Julia." Renzo Cabral approached them on the sidewalk.

"Renzo?" said Julia, startled.

Nick kept his eye on Zane, giving only a glance to the Secret Service agent.

"Hey, Renzo," Nick said.

"You know each other?" Julia asked.

"No—" Renzo began.

"Yes," Nick said absently. "I mean, no. I mean—"

Julia and Renzo looked at him suspiciously.

"You said his name, I just—" Nick thrust out his hand. "Nick Quinn, Julia's husband."

"Renzo Cabral."

Nick kept his mouth shut, realizing he already stepped over the line of suspicion. Still, he had that same lingering sensation that he'd seen Renzo before—not later today, but at some other time over the past few days. It was hurting his brain.... Maybe it had happened in town ahead of the summit; after all, Renzo must have been around for some period, if only to inspect the bunker.

"Nick," Renzo said. "Can you excuse us?"

Nick looked between the two of them.

"Give me five minutes," Julia said. "I'll be right back."

Nick glanced back across the street, to the shaded parking spot, but Zane was gone.

Julia and Renzo walked around the corner, talking as they walked.

"I really didn't expect to be locked out."

"You never arrived," Renzo said. "We don't take chances and we can't wait for the tardy."

"I signed my life away. I've been running around for weeks deceiving my husband, my friends...only to be locked out?"

"I understand, but security takes precedence over feelings."

"It's not that." Julia didn't want to sound shallow.

"Do you want to follow me there?"

"I can get in now?"

"I'll get you in," Renzo said. "Meet me at the gate." They had arrived at his car. "Ten minutes."

Julia was giddy. She couldn't remember the last time she'd felt this way. She was on her way to be part of history, to see the president, to witness an historic moment. She knew Nick would be pissed that she'd stood him up, leaving him at the corner, but he would understand in the end.

One more reason that she loved him.

Heading up Route 22 in her Audi, she came to the stoplight in the middle of nowhere. She never understood why it had been put in, as there was rarely traffic on the intersecting road. It made no sense. She had—

Julia's head snapped back as her car jolted forward. Rear-ended.

"Unbelievable!" Julia yelled as she looked in the rearview mirror at the black car behind her. "What a frickin' day!"

She jumped out of her car.

"I'm so sorry," the man said on approach. "Are you okay?"

Julia nodded but couldn't help raging internally. An empty road, and he couldn't see her?

"I can't tell you how sorry I am. Are you sure you're all right?"

Julia reached back in her car for her purse. "I'm in a bit of hurry, if we could just exchange info...."

"Of course, Julia."

Julia tilted her head: she never forgot a face and yet she had no idea who this man was.

"My name is Janos Zane."

Nick was pissed, more at himself than Julia, as he drove out of town. How could he be so stupid to let her out of his sight? Her car was moving. He saw the blinking dot on his phone. She was heading up Route 22.

He realized where she was going and stomped on the gas. His wife had no idea what she was walking into.

Glancing at the tracker on his phone, he saw she had come to stop a mile ahead. A moment later, he spotted her Audi on the side of the road.

As he came upon it, he saw the damaged rear, the open door, her purse and phone on the front seat.

Julia was gone.

Marcus walked out the door of Flynn's Daycare, holding Katy's hand.

"Tank you," Katy said as she licked the lollipop.

"So, what's this?" Marcus asked as he looked at the drawing he'd brought along.

"Mommy, Daddy, me, and Theo." Katy smiled as she pointed at each of the stick figures. "Where are we going?"

Marcus picked her up and draped her atop his shoulders, where she sat high and tall.

"I can touch the clouds," Katy squealed as she raised her hands high.

"Grab me one that looks like a horse."

Marcus smiled as he walked to the car. He had always wanted children, though he'd questioned whether he would ever make a good father, given his penchants for drinking, fun, and fighting, but he suspected he could rise to the occasion. His relationship with Katy came so naturally. Her smile made him forget the stresses of life, her curiosity and pure love for everything around her reminded him that innocence, magic, and love could still be found in the world if one knew where to look.

His biggest impediment to having children was that he'd never stayed married long enough to become a father. He loved the chase, the courtship, the novelty of the new, but he never seemed to make the transition to normalcy after "I do." He was on marriage number four, and while he thought, hoped, and prayed this one would stick, he feared the reality of himself. Then again, Anissa had faith in him and truly loved him; he could feel it in her embrace, could see it in her eyes. She wasn't there for the money—she had her own career—and was far from materialistic, unlike his three exes.

Anissa had her own firm that specialized in mediation and coaching; she trained people before they testified in trials or negotiations, teaching them how to be convincing to judge and jury. She coached models and athletes to be media-savvy, how to handle questions, and how to appear natural on camera without falling into an *um*-filled stammer. Since the other aspect of her business was conflict resolution, she always listened to Marcus, and they rarely fought. Beyond brains and beauty, Anissa had something none of his other wives possessed: wisdom.

At thirty-five, she was well into her career. Now that her firm was well-established, she told Marcus that she looked forward to children with him in the next year.

"He wooks wike the man in my bad dreams," Katy said.

"What looks like what man in your dreams?" Marcus asked as he arrived at his car.

"The painted man." Katy pointed to a white van across the street.

"What do you mean?"

"He had scary things on his face and body. Monsters. He hurt Mommy and Daddy in my dreams."

Marcus looked across the street and saw a tattooed man in the driver's side on his phone. "Have you ever seen him before?"

"When Mommy dropped me off this morning, he was outside school."

Marcus hit speed dial on his phone.

Nick pushed the Jeep to eighty, hugging the turns, praying the top-heavy vehicle wouldn't tip.

There was no doubt in his mind what had happened.

And it was all confirmed when he saw the black Town Car a quarter mile ahead.

Nick pushed his Wrangler to catch up. He headed straight for the moving vehicle, never slowing, only accelerating, faster and faster until he rammed into the rear right quarter panel, sending the black car spinning, crashing into the guard rail and screeching to a halt as Nick spun to a halt on the shoulder.

Nick ripped open the door to find the airbags inflated, Zane unconscious against the wheel, and Julia dazed in her seat. Nick unlatched her seatbelt, grabbed her by the hand, and raced into the woods, helping her leap stone walls, dodge rocks and roots, tearing through underbrush and brambles as the terrain began to slope downward. Voices echoed in the distance as they raced down the wooded hillside.

A gunshot exploded behind, startling them. They both ducked reflexively.

"What's happening?" Julia panted.

A bullet ripped into the tree beside them, bark and splinters flying.

Nick pulled them behind another tree and to their knees. He drew his gun from his waist and fired six shots at the unseen Zane.

"Please, Nick," Julia whispered. "What's going on?"

Nick fired off three more shots, grabbed her hand again, and sprinted down the thickly forested hill.

And a hail of bullets followed from behind.

Anissa stepped out of her Mercedes, not a strand of her auburn hair out of place.

She leaned in and kissed Marcus, and, while he was happy to see her, his focus remained on Katy's scary man in the van across the street.

"Everything okay?"

"Yeah," Marcus said, though he wasn't sure. "You don't mind?"

"I would turn down a meeting with the queen to be with this one." Anissa reached in and picked Katy up while Marcus transferred the car seat to his wife's vehicle. "How about we go to Playland for a little while before going to see Mommy?"

"Yes!" Katy shouted with a big smile as Anissa buckled her in.

"Thanks," Marcus said as he grabbed Anissa's purse. "Hey, can I borrow something?"

"Of course." Anissa raised her eyebrows as Marcus dug through her purse. "Lipstick or eyeliner?"

Marcus pulled out a small metal canister of mace.

"What are you going to with that?"

"Just want to try something."

"You scare me sometimes," she said.

"I thought you liked that about me."

Anissa smiled as she shook her head. "Hey, don't be late to Julia's thing this evening. You know how she gets. And make sure Nick isn't late either."

Marcus nodded as Anissa got in her car and drove off.

The van still sat across the street. There wasn't a soul in sight as Marcus got out of his BMW and opened the trunk. He grabbed a roll of kitesurfing line, quickly cutting off several yards, and stuffed it in his pocket with the canister from Anissa's purse.

He got back in his car and slowly drove towards the tattooed man, pulling in front of him, blocking his way. Marcus got out of his car as the man threw his hands up in the air and emerged from the van.

He was bigger than expected, six-two, the girth of his arms bigger than many men's thighs. He was truly a "painted" man; elaborate tattoos overlapped, merged, and covered every inch of exposed flesh on his arms from wrist to shoulder; the artwork ran up his neck, with what looked like small Asian letters on his cheeks. Marcus noticed a hollow-eyed ghost on his left bicep, with the word Kasper written beneath it.

"You're blocking me," Kasper said in a thick accent.

"You got a thing for little kids?" Marcus whispered through gritted teeth. Without waiting for an answer, he hit him hard.

But Kasper saw it coming, blocked the punch and quickly countered with three quick blows to Marcus's body. Marcus darted away as best he could, bobbing and weaving like he had when he was younger, but these days, given his size and age, fighting wasn't as much about finesse as it was about brute strength.

Kasper hit him again and again—a relentless barrage of blows to the head and sides. Marcus was not only stunned, he was in pain. Of all the fights he had been in, he had never been hit so hard. The fourth and fifth blow shook his teeth and his confidence. He was losing and feared it was going to get worse. He reached for the left jacket pocket, but Kasper saw his move: hitting Marcus again, he tore at his jacket, tugging until it ripped away. He tossed it aside and attacked.

Marcus needed the man to take one step backwards, but that didn't seem like it would happen. The killer kept coming forward, driving Marcus back with each blow.

Marcus hit the ground hard, his head ringing with a concussion. Kasper was atop him, pummeling him like a cage fighter without mercy. As Marcus threw up his arms, protecting his head and face from the onslaught, he felt his focus slipping, his consciousness falling away.

Turning his face away from the blows, he saw his torn jacket on the ground.

His hand snapped out, scrabbling in his pocket, then finding Anissa's small device.

Marcus sprayed it in the thug's face, but the man kept coming, unfazed by the burning, his fists still hammering. Marcus drained the remainder of the mace into Kasper's eyes, blinding him. That was enough. Marcus scooted backwards, hopping to his feet, and went on the attack. He hit the thug again and again—now, without being blocked, without being hit back—knocking Kasper backward, then to the ground. Marcus grabbed for his torn jacket and pulled the rope from his pocket, looping it around the fallen Kasper's head.

The makeshift garrote reached Kasper's neck, tightening. The more the man struggled, the tighter the noose got. Marcus quickly worked one end of the line around the man's right wrist, pulling it behind him. Kasper kicked and struggled but it only pulled the noose tighter. Marcus now wrapped his other wrist into the knot, keeping the killer's arms trussed behind his back. He avoided the mercenary's kicking feet, waiting for the oxygen deprivation to take effect, finally hog-tying his legs with the line.

Marcus leaned down, staring into the man's beet-red face, his skin and veins distended around the thin kitesurfing line, his tattooed animals coming to life over throbbing arteries.

Finally, Kasper passed out. Marcus looked around, relieved to see no one on the street watching. The struggle had lasted less than a minute. Now, Marcus sized up his own car, wondering how he was going to squeeze the unconscious man in. No way he'd fit in the BMW's trunk. Hog-tied, he'd be too large for the confined space.

That's when Marcus remembered the white van.

Nick and Julia ran side by side, matching stride for stride, harder than they'd ever run before. Zane was only twenty yards behind, and Nick could feel the bullseyes on their backs.

They emerged into a crowd, thousands of people gathered for the day's festivities in Killian Park in the shadow of the dam. Nick pulled Julia through the crowds, past the baseball fields, the track, the three-legged race, past the carnival rides, game booths, and funnel-cake-covered picnic tables.

As they hurried, Nick and Julia wore false smiles, nodding to Mrs. Case, Mrs. Segatti, Mrs. Munoz, and Mona Spilo, moving too fast for conversation, struggling to stay ahead of unseen bullets. Hoping to lose Zane in the crowd, Nick could only pray he wouldn't shoot indiscriminately and kill the innocent townsfolk around them.

They needed a place to hide—to lie low and call in reinforcements.

Nick saw the podium ahead. Two of Senator Chase's aides were setting up the microphones while Officer John Goodheart stood atop the podium, staring out at the masses.

"Johnny!" Nick called out as he rushed to the stage.

"Hey, guy. Hey, Julia. Happy Fourth."

"I need a huge favor."

"Name it."

"Julia and I need a place to talk."

"Uh..." John couldn't hide his confusion.

Nick lifted up the red, white, and blue skirt surrounding the stage and Julia crawled under.

"A little kinky, but—"

"It's not what you think."

John shrugged. "All good with me."

"Can you make sure no one disturbs us?"

"Shit, didn't I do this for you back in high school? You guys had me guard the door to the locker room while you—"

"Yep." Nick crawled under, letting the skirt fall back in place.

The twenty-by-twenty-foot space was aglow in blue and red filtered sunshine.

"Oh my God," Julia said between breaths. "What the hell is going on? Who was that man?"

Nick put up a hand. "Who's Colin Armor?"

"Who?" Her lie was transparent.

"I know you know who I'm talking about...please don't play games. Our lives depend on it."

"Play games?" Julia acted offended.

"That man who's after you, his name is Janos Zane. He's after you to get to this guy Armor."

"I can't tell you who he is." Julia set her jaw stubbornly. "I signed a non-disclosure."

"Since when does an NDA come between marriage vows?"

"You don't understand."

"Then make me understand."

"I can't."

"What does he have to do with the president?"

Julia looked at him with surprise. "I can't say. Why do you think he has anything to do with the president?"

"This man who abducted you is after Colin Armor—he will torture you to get his whereabouts, and then he'll kill you."

Tears appeared in the corners of Julia's eyes. "He's the president," she blurted out. "Colin Armor's his current codename."

Nick nodded. He should have realized.

"They no longer use silly names like Eagle or Cowboy. People are smarter these days and radio chatter's easy to figure out. They change his name once a week," she continued. "This week he's Colin Armor."

Now Nick smiled.

"What?" Julia asked.

"That's your big secret?"

"What do you mean?"

"It's—" Nick didn't want to allude to the seeds planted in his mind by Zane. "You've been acting strange."

"It's been killing me," Julia said. "You have no idea what's it's like having to make up stories, having to lie to you about where I am, where I'm going. I'm sorry."

"You ever notice how a secret carries so much more weight before you learn it, but once you get the truth, it's always so mundane?"

"This is serious, Nick." Julia's fear was turning to anger. "That man's trying to find the president."

"More serious than you realize." Nick considered how far to go in the telling. "He wants to kill him and all the other heads of state."

Julia's eyes widened. "We need to warn the Secret Service."

"Not until I can be sure of your safety."

"What's going on, Nick? How are you involved in this?"

"Believe me, I'm just looking out for you."

"You need to trust me, Nick. You never trust me."

"I do," Nick said as he looked in her eyes. "But I don't think you'll ever trust me again if I tell you what's going on."

"Um, aren't we a little beyond that now?"

Nick nodded and held out his hand, the antique pocket watch in his palm.

"That's beautiful," Julia said as she picked it up. "Where did you get it?"

"Paul—but it actually belongs to Shamus."

"He has the most amazing things!" Julia examined the timepiece in her hand.

"Well, that's an understatement."

"What do you mean?"

"This is very hard to explain."

"Try me. You've explained your way out of some pretty crazy things in the past."

Nick thought for a moment. "This watch is special."

"In what way?"

"Shamus swore me to never tell anyone about it, and I haven't."

She cocked her head. "I broke an NDA for the president, which qualifies as treason. You'd better start talking."

"Okay, but just listen. Don't ask any questions, no matter how crazy it sounds...as scary as it *will* sound. It's the truth."

Julia handed him back the watch and nodded. "Tell me."

"Three years ago, there was a plane crash in Byram Hills."

"I don't remember that. A private plane?"

"A 737. One hundred and fifty-five people on board."

"Nick..." she chided. "I think I'd remember that."

"I'm the only one who does."

Julia stared at him, her analytical mind processing what he'd said. "I don't understand."

"You and Shamus's wife were on that plane."

"What? Are you dreaming?"

"I wish."

"You're not making sense. I think I'd remember being in a plane crash."

"Shamus gave me the watch, *this* watch, to save you. It has special properties.... Using it, I was able to step back in time and fix it. Fix everything. Afterward, Shamus took the watch back."

Julia's eyes widened. He saw the beginnings of a smile forming.

"It sounds impossible, I know," Nick said. "But this is no joke. And I'm not crazy."

Julia took a deep breath, trying to understand.

"Imagine knowing something incredible that no one else knows," Nick said. "You can't tell a soul or you'll be sent to the loony bin. There's no proof, but it's all real."

"Okay," she said. "I'm trying.... You said you gave the watch back to Shamus. Why do you have it now?"

"Paul Dreyfus brought it to me later today." He put up his hands. "I know. It sounds nuts, him giving me this in the future. But he did, and the watch sent me back in time. That's what it does, hour by hour. Every hour on the hour."

Julia shook her head as she tried to absorb what he was telling her.

"Look, you agree there's a threat against the president, right? The guy chasing us, Janos Zane? He needs you to get to him."

She gave a tentative nod.

"Well, I've watched that same man kill you. It happened three hours from now. I also watched him kill you four hours from now. All I'm trying to do is stop him from getting to you and the president."

Julia looked away, her gaze distant, in thought. Finally, she turned to him. "This is insane. What the fuck, Nick? How can you expect me to believe all of this?"

Nick pulled out his phone, debating whether to show her the video. It was so telling, so powerful. But seeing herself dead, seeing everyone dead.... Her first thought would be of Katy.... He tucked it back in his pocket.

"I can't, but know this: I watched you *die*. Imagine what that's like, how it crushed me. I would do—I *will* do—*anything* to save you. You have no idea what this has done to me. The agony, over and over, of watching you suffer and die."

"And yet here we are."

"And you don't believe me."

"I want to Nick, I do. I see the pain in your eyes, but you're asking me to believe in the impossible."

"There's something else I know. Another fact, but this one that's real and provable. And devastating."

"What?"

"Hadley's Woods."

Julia looked at him.

"I know all about Shamus's bunker and what's happening down there."

Now Julia looked alarmed. "*What*? What do you know?"

"Everyone down there is dead—the president, the Russians, everyone. Shot. Murdered...."

Julia's face went pale and her hands began to tremble. "How do you *know*?"

"Because, one hour from now, using this watch you don't believe in, Marcus, Paul, and I entered the bunker. I saw the president. I saw the Russian president, the prime minister of Akbiquestan, and thirty other people. All shot."

"That's impossible."

"Have you been able to get through to them? You're in that inner circle now. Call them."

Julia pulled out her phone and dialed. No answer. She dialed another number, no answer. "Renzo was going to meet there...."

"Why?"

"To be part of history."

"Why *now*?" Nick asked.

"They've been in lockdown since early this morning," Julia said. "I wasn't allowed in because I was late. But now you say they're... No, I don't believe it. The gathering was *above* top-secret. No one knew it was *happening*. They can't be dead."

Nick stared at her, unwilling to broach the destruction of the dam.

"We just saw Renzo," Julia said as if that would prove Nick wrong.

"He was topside, so he wasn't killed."

"That makes no sense."

"Trust me."

"How can you *know* this?" Julia begged.

"Because I saw it with my own eyes."

"Impossible," Julia snapped. "You could never get down there."

"But I did," Nick said softly. "With Paul's help. And believe me, I wish I hadn't...."

"What? Is there something else?"

"You want to know how I know your friend Renzo?" Nick asked.

"How?"

"I don't have time to explain it all, but at three minutes after twelve today, I had him pick you up at your office. He brought you to the bunker to hide you from the man who's hunting you—Zane. It's my fault you drowned down there. I sent you to your death." Nick could barely hold back tears.

"Drowned?" Tears appeared in Julia's eye, sympathetically matching Nick's grief as he broke down. "What do you mean I drowned?"

Nick tried to steady his voice. "Everything ties back to the man who's chasing us somewhere in the crowd." Nick lifted up the podium skirt and poked his head into the sunlight. He looked around but saw no sign of Zane.

"Nicky?"

Nick crept out and looked up at the podium, only to see Suzy McGloughlin staring down at him as she stood next to Johnny. "What the hell are you doing under there?"

Julia emerged.

Now Suzy smiled ear to ear. "You guys are so cute."

"Hey, Suze."

"You guys all right?" Suzy asked. "You look like you were run over by a tractor."

"Suzy," Nick said, "could I borrow your car?"

"Of course." She began digging through her purse. "Not much gas in it."

"Better yet," Nick reached in his pocket and pulled out his roll of cash, stuffing it in her hand, "can you drive Julia to Winged Foot in Mamaroneck instead?"

"What?" Julia shook her head. "Nick, no!"

"Just until seven o'clock."

"What about Katy?"

"Marcus is picking her up and will meet you there."

"I can't," Julia said. "What about the fundraiser? Senator Chase?"

Nick took Julia by the shoulders and looked into her eyes. "You have to do this." He turned to Suzy. "And promise me after you drop her off, you'll take the afternoon off, go home, have a beer, and take a nap. Stay away from town." Nick wanted her away from the dam in case all his efforts were for naught.

"I can't keep your money, Nick."

"Please." Nick held up his hands. "Just get Julia to Winged Foot as fast as you can. And, seriously, don't come back to town."

"What?" Julia asked, her expression matching Suzy's. "Nick, I'm so confused. Why—wait! Where are you going?"

"To stop this madness and save Colin Armor."

Nick drove his banged-up Jeep up the driveway to his home and hit the remote for the garage door. As the door rose, he was shocked to see the white van inside.

"You brought him *here*?" Nick said as he leapt from his Jeep. "What the hell, Marcus?"

The large mercenary was tied with kitesurfing line to a metal chair in the center of the garage; his wrists behind his back and a loop around his neck.

"Where was I supposed to go?"

"You were supposed to pick up Katy."

"I did, she's safe—she's with Anissa. They're heading to Playland and then she'll bring her to Winged Foot."

"What the hell happened to your face?" Nick stared at Marcus's swollen right eye and lip.

"My friend and I got into it."

"Jesus. What the hell are you *doing* here?"

"Getting answers from Kasper."

"His name is Kasper?"

By way of explanation, Marcus pointed at the guy's tattoos.

"You stole their van?" Nick asked. "Jesus, do you know what's *in* there?"

"Yeah."

"I don't think you do," Nick said. "Two hours from now, you and I—"

"Stop with that shit," Marcus said. "I hate that. I don't want to hear any more about the future unless you're giving me lottery numbers."

Nick shook his head. "Fine. What's your plan?"

"This is one of the guys that killed thousands, right? And we're trying to stop that from happening?"

Nick nodded.

"Well as you pointed out, we don't have much time, and he doesn't strike me as the chatty type."

Nick noticed jumper cables running along the floor, clamped to the legs of the metal chair, the other end lying next to the exposed wire of an extension cord.

"Dead men don't talk too well," Nick pointed out.

"Which is why I have this." Marcus held up a portable defibrillator. "Kickstart the sucker if he dies on me."

Marcus picked up a bucket of water and dumped it over Kasper, soaking him. He walked over and briefly touched the jumper cable to the extension cord.

Kasper's body jumped, muscles rigid, the thin lines that wrapped his limbs digging into his flesh as his body involuntarily flexed. Marcus released the jumper clamp and Kasper slumped, panting and twitching.

"The water really helps," Marcus said as he leaned over Kasper and lifted his head by the chin. "Now, what should we talk about?"

Kasper stared at Marcus and whispered.

"What's that?" Marcus leaned in to listen and Kasper head butted him in the nose. Marcus pulled back as the mercenary spit in his face.

In response, Marcus backhanded him in the mouth, blood exploding out of the thug's split lip. "You just made this so much easier."

He jolted Kasper again, this time for longer, watching the man shake violently as the current ran through his every nerve.

He stopped the electricity. "Who do you work for?"

Nick couldn't watch any longer. "I'll be back in a few." He walked through the garage door into his house.

Marcus circled around Kasper. "Well?"

Kasper tried to catch his breath.

"Janos Zane, is that his name?"

Kasper shook his head.

Marcus hit the current again. Kasper's eyes fluttered as his body shook.

"Where's the remote detonator?" Marcus held up the jumper cable and waved it in his face.

"Using timer," Kasper said in broken English. "In case detonator doesn't work."

"Who has the detonator? Zane? Does Zane have it?"

"I don't know Zane."

"Listen to my question," Marcus said as he held up the jumper cable. "Who has the detonator?"

"His name is Renzo."

A rusted Ford Bronco came to a stop on the street outside Nick's house. Three tattooed men pulled out their guns as they emerged from the 4x4, one of them looking at the blinking dot on his phone. The bald one pointed to the white house with the Jeep Wrangler in the driveway. They spread out and sprinted across the lawn, taking cover in the bushes.

Nick walked through the mudroom to find Theo asleep in his dog pen. *Some guard puppy*, he thought as he ran upstairs into his bathroom. He turned on the sink, splashing water on his face. He was physically, emotionally, and mentally spent; banged, bruised, and singed.

He walked back into his closet, reached into the back of his sock drawer, and pulled his emergency cash: three hundred dollars. He had given everything else he had to Suzy McGloughlin. He looked at the pocket watch: 12:55. He hoped Marcus got some information—he had no doubt that he would. Marcus didn't speak much about his time in the military; he said it gave him nightmares. Seeing his interrogation of Kasper, Nick understood why.

Theo's barking snapped his focus. It wasn't the usual bark...it was the angry bark, the warning bark, mixed with growling. The bark that sent a chill up Nick's spine.

Nick ran to the back stairs and down into the mudroom to find Theo jumping in his dog pen, going berserk.

"Hush," Nick scolded, but Theo didn't stop, his nervous whine doubling in volume. Nick opened the pen and released the dog. Theo leapt into his arms, licking his cheek nervously.

"Sh, sh, sh, Theo. Calm, boy."

Theo went silent, his ears perking up as the hair rose along his spine; he began to growl, low and fierce. You couldn't turn off an animal's instincts.

Suddenly, the dead silence felt anything but comforting.

He looked in the kitchen and realized the shutters were closed, as were the curtains in the hall, plunging the house into darkness.

Nick went back through the mudroom and slowly opened the garage door to find Marcus and Kasper gone. So were the chair and jumper cables.

A scream erupted somewhere in the house, the single light in the mudroom dimmed, flickering before getting brighter. As the scream stopped, it was replaced by the murmur of deep voices in a foreign tongue.

Nick quickly opened the breaker panel and flicked off the power, no doubt in his mind what was happening.

He opened the cabinet and grabbed a large bone, put it in the dog pen and tucked Theo in. "Stay."

Theo bit into the bone and all thought of fear, protection, and aggression disappeared from his young canine mind.

Nick looked around. He'd emptied his gun shooting at Zane. There was ammo in the safe, if he could get to it....

He slipped through the kitchen and into the hall, cursing the ticking grandfather clock that echoed in the foyer. He inched past the living room and edged toward his office, peering inside.

Marcus was in the same metal chair, the jumper cables affixed to the legs, soaking wet. He wasn't bound, his arms and legs free, but he was kept in place by the three mercenaries who stood around him, their guns aimed at his chest.

Nick could smell burnt hair and flesh as he looked at his large friend, weak and broken as he slumped in the chair.

"We torture back," growled Kasper. He grabbed Marcus by the left wrist, quickly twisting until it snapped. And he didn't stop there. He kept twisting, winding the broken wrist around, Marcus's flesh coiling up like a rubber band. Broken bone grinding against broken bone, flesh ripping as it stretched.

Marcus finally screamed.

Kasper released his arm and pulled out his pistol, then checked the magazine before slamming back in. He chambered a round. "I only have one bullet. Where would you like it?" Kasper said. "In the leg, the arm...in your balls?"

The three other mercs laughed.

Marcus struggled to his feet, defiant, angry, his left arm limp at his side. He stood six inches from Kasper, staring into his eyes. Faster than Kasper could react, Marcus's right arm darted, sending his fist into Kasper's jaw.

Kasper's head snapped back as two-hundred and thirty pounds traveled through Marcus's fist, catching him by surprise. Kasper dropped the gun as he stumbled backward, stunned. But he didn't go down.

Marcus crouched, snatching the gun from the floor, flicking it up, aiming straight at Kasper's eye.

The three mercs surrounding Marcus already had their pistols trained on Marcus's head.

"Only one bullet for the four of us." Kasper, crouched and bloody, pointed to his three compatriots. "Choose your victim wisely."

Marcus glanced across the room at Nick watching from the shadows. "Make this right, Nick," he said, looking straight at Kasper.

The four mercenaries looked at each other, confused.

Marcus rammed the gun under his own chin and pulled the trigger.

"No," Nick breathed in shock as Marcus collapsed dead on the floor. He slid back into the shadow of the hall, creeping toward the kitchen. He stayed low, out of the sunlight slipping through the drawn curtains, sidling into the kitchen, only to come face to face with Kasper, his gun inches from his head.

"Well, well," said the merc, his accent twisting his English. "Where is your wife?"

Nick was cornered, his back to the wall, nowhere to go.

The merc stepped back, his gun still trained on Nick.

"Where is your little girl?"

Theo growled, jumping up out of the shadows, his jaws clamping down on Kasper's gun wrist, his teeth puncturing flesh. Kasper spun in pain, flinging the dog across the room and into the wall. Theo yelped as he hit the ground. Kasper aimed his gun at the canine, rapid-firing, but Theo scurried away from the bullets, then came back at him.

Nick dived through the kitchen door, scooped up the dog, and raced around the corner, clutching him tight to his chest as gunfire peppered the walls behind. Nick raced through the living room door, only to find the three other mercs waiting, guns raised.

Nick was trapped ahead and behind, with nowhere to escape. Theo growled as he struggled to get at the men. Nick clutched him closer, holding tight as the first chime of the grandfather clock rang, startling the men, their heads snapping toward its source.

When they looked back at Nick, he was gone, vanished into thin air.

CHAPTER 5

10:00 AM

Nick stared up into big, happy eyes as his cheek was licked and slobbered upon. Theo was panting, his tail wagging double-time as Nick became fully awake.

Wait.... Theo? Here?

Nick had no intention of bringing the puppy back in time with him. A strange mixture of fear and curiosity ran through him as he picked Theo up and carried him to the mudroom, then slowly peered around the corner.

Have I broken one of the laws of God and nature?

But he smiled.

The dog pen was empty; there was no second Theo. *Thank god.* He wouldn't have known how to process that.

He put Theo in the pen with water and food and stepped into his home office as the front door shot open and Julia marched in.

"What are you doing home?" Nick asked as she charged through the foyer past him.

"I forgot a file." Julia ran up the stairs with Nick ten steps behind her.

"We need to talk." Nick followed her into their bedroom.

"We can talk tomorrow," she said as she opened the small drawer in the table beside the bed. "My day, as you know, is slightly overflowing."

Nick considered how to approach her this time. No way she'd willingly evacuate town, given her sense of urgency. How, then, to convince her of everything that was happening? Zane hunting her, the president dead?

He opted against trying. He'd seen how doubtful Julia acted an hour from now, how the only thing that had convinced her was being shot at. Actual, tangible danger worked, but no one was shooting at her now.

The truth wasn't going to save her.

He tried his best to erase what he had seen later in the day, but Julia's dead, milky eyes kept floating up, filling his mind and heart with anguish. She had drowned, been shot, burned, and every death had been his fault.

The closer Nick journeyed to 7:00 a.m., the more frightened he became. For he knew that after the final hour, any chance of saving Julia or anyone else would end, and the watch's ability would cease. Dead was dead, no re-dos, do-overs, or divine intervention. He needed to find a way to permanently keep Julia and Katy out of harm's way.

"Can we just sit for five minutes and talk?" Nick asked as she closed a drawer. "I need to discuss something important with you."

"I don't have time," she said as she charged for the door.

Nick reached out and gently held her arm, stopping her.

"Nick..."

"Please?"

"You have no idea how much stress I'm under," she said.

"I know," he said, nodding.

"No, you don't. Everything I have had to do for this fundraiser, everything at work, things you couldn't possibly understand."

Nick nodded again, releasing her arm.

"And I missed the most important meeting of my life this morning because of you." Julia's anger began to rise. "I worked and prepared for this for weeks."

"Okay," Nick whispered.

"We have problems, Nick. Do you not see them?"

"Yes, I see them" he said. "All we do is rush here, rush there. It's a side of you—a side of us—that was never there before."

"What the hell does that mean?"

"We make no time for us," Nick tried desperately. "We're chasing money, we're chasing careers, we're chasing meetings."

"You still find time to chase fun." She stared at him with accusing eyes.

"Sure, to blow off stress, we both go off and do our own things," Nick said calmly. "You go to spin class, I kitesurf. You work out, have lunch with friends; I play cards and jump out of planes."

"Stop right there and listen to yourself, will you? You're exactly right, and that adrenaline crap has to stop. It's like a death wish. We have a child, Nick—you need to grow up, be responsible." Julia looked away, her anger boiling over. "I remember when I was your excitement."

"You still are—"

"And I have to do *everything* for Katy!" Julia exploded. "I'm a full-time mom, a full-time attorney, and full-time stressed."

"That's true," he said. "I understand."

"And I have this terrible feeling." There were tears in Julia's eyes as she looked back at him. "I can't explain it, it's like a gnawing sense of dread, like something terrible is going to happen. Every noise I hear, every ring of the phone puts me on edge."

"It's okay."

"You don't understand. I'm looking over my shoulder as if shadows are following me. I think I'm losing it, Nick." Julia looked at her watch, defeat filling her face as she headed for the door. "I've got to go."

"You can't," Nick said as he quickly moved in her path.

"Get out of my way."

Nick stood his ground.

"I'm not going to ask again." She had never threatened Nick until now. "Go do your deals, play your games. I don't care anymore."

"What's that supposed to mean?"

"It means go off and do what you do best: think of Nick. Nick's got such a tough job. Nick needs time to work out, kitesurf, golf, clear his mind. You take no interest in anything of mine."

Nick tried and failed to temper his anger. "That's not true, and you know it."

"Do you know where I go while you play cards with your friends on Tuesday nights?"

Nick stared at her.

"Maybe I go find joy in the arms of another man." Julia stormed past Nick, down the stairs, and fast-stepped out of the house.

Senator Chase climbed into the back of his black Town Car, his phone pressed to his ear. He covered the mouthpiece, interrupting himself. "Floyd," Chase said to his driver without looking up. "Take me to Killian Park at the base of the dam."

As the car pulled out of his driveway, he uncovered the mouth-piece and continued. "I need to be dealt back in. Things wouldn't be happening without me." He listened a moment. "Fine. Call me back."

Chase quickly dialed again, barely taking a breath between con-versations. "Joel? Senator Chase." The senator listened. "Fine. I want to be sure I have those two Secret Service agents for my speech at the park, my book-signing, and the fundraiser this evening. I need to send a message. That was the deal. I lived up to my side of the bargain, now live up to yours."

Chase hung up and tucked his phone away. He pulled out a file and began reading as the car drove across town and up Route 22.

They weaved through a residential neighborhood of Colonial-style homes, into a driveway of a small, unkempt house, and into the open garage.

Chase finally looked up as the garage door closed behind them. "Where are we?"

"You don't recognize it?" The driver said as he got out of the car and stepped into the dark, one-car garage. He adjusted his baseball hat and left his sunglasses on, despite the darkness.

"No, actually." Chase said as his driver opened the door. He stepped out, squinting at his watch. "Where's Floyd?"

"Let's go inside," his driver said.

"I don't understand...*where* are we?"

They walked through a splintered door into a gloomy shag-carpeted foyer and then into a living room. It was shadowed, shafts of sunlight piercing the narrow opening of the drawn curtains. A single chair stood in the middle of the musty carpet.

"Please have a seat," the driver said, as he remained in the shadows.

Chase finally saw the gun pointed at him. "What the hell *is* this?"

"Sit down."

"I'm not sitting down."

Zane waved the gun. "Please."

Chase finally sat. "Where are we?"

"Bedford."

Chase looked around the dark room and his eyes widened in recognition. "Holy shit."

"You know where we are. Good." The driver nodded. "It means your memory is working."

"Who the fuck are you? When I don't show up to my meeting, the whole world'll come looking for me."

"I'll be quick," the driver said quietly. "I have somewhere to be at the top of the hour."

"I'm a U.S. senator, goddamn it!"

"So I've heard." The driver nodded without reaction as he dropped in his lap the picture of the senator with the Russian ambassador.

"What the hell is this?" Chase squinted at the picture, trying to see it in the dim light.

"Well, some might call it treason."

"Treason?"

"You played the sympathy card so well with your dead son...." the driver said quietly. "Did you think you could ride the wave of catastrophe to the White House?"

"What the hell are you talking about? I can barely see this."

Zane took off the baseball hat and sunglasses as he walked over and opened the curtains, washing the room in light. As Chase looked around, his eyes adjusting, he looked up into the staring eyes of his captor.

"Oh my God." Chase began to pant. "You died."

"You've got to be shitting me," Marcus said as he tried to come to grips with the crazy story Nick had told and shown him over the last five minutes. "What the hell do you mean, I killed myself?"

They were in Nick's Wrangler, racing across town. It fascinated Nick that every time he explained what was going on to Marcus, his reaction was different: sometimes scared, sometimes pissed, sometimes confused and fed up. It made him realize that reactions were not simply about the facts being faced; they were shaped by moods and moments. Marcus acted differently almost every time, but one thing remained consistent: his friend's first words were always the same.

"Did it ever occur to you that this is *wrong*?" Marcus shook his head. "That you shouldn't be playing around like this? We're not supposed to mess with time, mess with fate. You don't get a re-do."

"Sometimes, if we're lucky, we do."

"This is God stuff, Nick, it's crazy. And believe me, I know you, and you're not God."

"Believe what you want but convince me later. This isn't about me or some righteous crusade to change the world. This is about Julia. Her and Katy." Nick looked at the digital clock in the black dashboard of the Jeep. 11:19.

"I get that. I didn't say I wasn't going to help you." Marcus smiled. "If we're talking about breaking the laws of God and man, hell, you're talking to the biggest offender. My soul is toast. But maybe—after we save Julia and Katy—we can save yours."

"They ID'd your body," Senator Chase said, the photo on his lap forgotten. "What was left of it...."

"Is my being here inconvenient for you?" Zane asked.

"I just can't believe you're alive," Chase said.

"I wasn't alive to you when I *was* alive," Zane said. "None of us were—not Gerald, not Mom. The only time you showed up was when we died. I was a forgotten inconvenience until you found a way to make me an asset."

"That's not true." Chase hung his head, looking away.

"Don't worry," Zane said. "I don't harbor ill feelings against Daddy for walking out on us."

"Life is complicated," Chase said by way of explanation.

"It's what you did for yourself, the people you stepped on, and what you did to your country that brought me to you." Zane raised his gun. "Why did you meet with the Russians?"

"To set up a very important meeting with the president," Chase answered quickly.

"And these?" Zane pointed at the architectural drawings of the dam.

"What the hell are *they*?" Chase looked in confusion at the drawings.

"Tell me the truth." Zane walked over and held the gun to his head.

"I am." Chase's eyes were wide with fear. "There's a peace meeting happening at this very moment between Akbiquestan, Russia, and the US. I helped bring that meeting together."

"Why were these plans in your safe?"

"What safe?" Chase's tone grew angry.

"The safe in your library." Zane pressed the gun to his head.

"I don't own a safe, goddamn it!" Chase barked. "If you're going to kill me, then just kill me."

Zane stared at his father, suddenly confused. He had seen the safe during his first time through the eleven o'clock hour, when he unsuccessfully tried to open it. Nick, who somehow cracked it, had brought him its contents. "I saw the safe."

"Where?"

"Behind your desk in your library."

"You broke into my house? Well, that's no surprise." Chase shook his head as he regained a bit of confidence. "I've had the same small fridge behind my desk for years, filled with beer...German beer. And last I checked, you just pull the handle to open it. None of this bullshit was in my fridge—just beer. Now, what the hell are you talking about?"

Zane stepped back and looked out the window.

"What *are* you?" Chase asked. "What happened to you after they declared you dead? If you're not here to kill me...."

"I never said that." Zane didn't turn around.

"Tell me what's going on...maybe I can help."

Zane looked at the small lawn he played on when he was little. The house of cards was falling...all around him.

"Jason, please tell me what's happening."

Zane didn't respond as he walked toward the door.

"Hey!" Chase called out. "I was a shit father. I screwed everybody up. I'm sorry. Okay? But I'm glad you're alive. I'm truly glad you're alive."

Without a look or a word, Zane walked out.

Dreyfus closed his eyes and digested everything Nick had showed and told him about the coming hours. In his analytical mind, he pieced together each hour in the day, everything Nick had discovered about Zane, what they had found when they dived into the flooded bunker, and how Renzo had tried to protect Julia.

"You said the president and everyone was dead *before* the flood," Dreyfus said. "If they were already dead, why would Renzo have to go back down? Why bring Julia down there?"

"Maybe he didn't know they were dead," Marcus said.

"Head of the president's Secret Service detail?" Dreyfus shook his head. "Not a chance."

"What are you thinking?" Nick asked.

"Renzo needs Julia—she's critical to whatever he's doing."

"Why?" Marcus asked

"When I asked Renzo to protect Julia," Nick said, "he told me he had been looking for her for a few hours."

"Did he say why?" Marcus asked.

"No, but he called the house a bunch of times today and hung up on me when I answered."

"When did he call?"

Nick thought a moment, trying to keep the flow of time straight. "Long after the president was dead."

Everyone fell to silence, thinking.

"He's not bringing her down there to protect her," Dreyfus said.

"To kill her, then?"

"He could do that anywhere," Dreyfus said. "Sorry, Nick. I don't mean to sound cold."

"He seemed anxious to protect her." Nick thought a moment. "That's just great. I pushed Julia from the threat of death into certain death."

"Don't start thinking that way," Marcus said before turning to Dreyfus. "Something else is down there: any idea what it might be?"

Dreyfus looked at Nick, but his gaze appeared distant for a long moment. Then his eyes filled with recognition. "My God..."

"What else is in Shamus's bunker, Paul?" Nick asked.

"A vault."

"What kind of vault?"

"A huge one. It's actually more like a steel storage room."

"Filled with what? Money?" Marcus guessed.

"A little, but that's not what they'd be after," Dreyfus said.

"What then? Art, jewelry, and antiques?"

"Shamus sold off most of his art." Dreyfus shook his head. "He never told me what was in there specifically, though he said it was personal stuff."

"But what does that have to do with Julia?" Marcus asked.

"Because," Dreyfus said, "Julia is the only one Shamus trusts. She's also the only one who can open the vault."

"So, now I need to protect her from Zane *and* Renzo?" Nick asked. "An assassin and a Secret Service agent? Are they working together?"

"Both seem to want the president dead," Dreyfus said. "Though that doesn't mean they aren't working at cross purposes."

"We could kill them both," Marcus said, half in jest.

"No," Dreyfus said. "Even if we did, they'd both be alive an hour earlier with the same goal in mind. The original Zane wouldn't remember anything about the future, about chasing my ass and killing Julia, or anything about his backwards journey because to him it never happened. But he'd still be after the president. They'd both still be after the president."

"Now that we know what's going on, what do we do?" Marcus asked.

"This amount of death isn't about a robbery...it's far more than that," Dreyfus said. "And it isn't just about killing the president or blowing up Killian Dam."

"What do you think it is, then?" asked Marcus.

Dreyfus shrugged, frustrated. "I don't think we have any idea what's going on."

As Zane cut through town, his mind was spinning. Someone was onto him. The items in the safe had created a road map of blame that led to the senator. There was no question in Zane's mind that it was false, carefully crafted to paint a picture of guilt, then wrapped in a triggering blanket of photos that would serve only to enrage Zane and blind him with hate toward the father who had walked out on his family so long ago. It was a false narrative designed to convince Zane to turn his father over to the authorities. Or, more conveniently, murder the senator to slake his anger and resentment.

But who'd had time to place a safe in Chase's office? Who knew the senator was his father?

All things being equal, Zane hated the man for what he had done to his mother, how his selfishness and callous disregard had shattered his and his brother's childhood. But he didn't dwell on it then and he wouldn't dwell on it now. That was life. Cold and cruel. It hadn't shaped Zane's psyche and it wasn't the motivation for any of his actions. In fact, he hadn't thought about the man for years, despite the fact that he was a senator positioning himself as the heir-apparent to the Commander-in-Chief.

Zane thought he'd figured this whole thing out. Get the pocket watch, complete the mission. Of course, there would be people standing in his way. Nick was an impediment, but hardly a threat. Zane had dealt with true threats, dispatching them quickly and without difficulty. But it was the unseen threat, coming from an unknown direction, that was his real problem....

"Why?" Colonel Carter Bull asked as he stared through the metal bars of Harris Marine Base's brig in the foothills of Akbiquestan.

The colonel had been not only Zane's commanding officer for four years, but also his close friend.

"You really think I did this?" Zane shot back from the small bench that was his bed.

"I go by the evidence, JC. And it's not so much what I think, but what everyone else thinks and what the military tribunal thinks. The evidence is troubling. Overwhelming, actually."

"What evidence?"

Bull counted it out on his fingers. "One: video of a shadowy figure slipping a grenade-sized explosive into the right-wing fuel tank. Two: the weapons inventory doctored under your log-in. Three: video analysis matching the unidentified perpetrator's size and gait to yours."

"That's the evidence, but what do *you* think?" Zane asked.

"I think you're very good at killing, the best. Maybe you don't want the war to end, because when it ends, you'll lose your purpose."

"I hate war. I hate it so much that I was leaving...or did you forget that?"

"Most soldiers hate war, JC, but there are some who—"

"I was going *home*," Zane interrupted. "You know that. I chose to go home. You think I don't want this war to end? Why would I have put in my papers?"

"Don't take this the wrong way," Carter said, "but no one's better at deception than you."

"If you respect my ability at deception, why would I log in as myself to change the log?" Zane moved within an inch of the bars. "You don't think I could alter or erase my image from the video?"

Bull shrugged. "It's what the evidence is saying. And that's all we got."

In the following weeks, things got worse: the Akbiquestan base within the cave was abandoned and the enemy relocated, hiding themselves even better than before. The war, the battles, and US casualties escalated precipitously. And it was all blamed on Zane.

He was kept in the small, makeshift prison for a month while senior brass decided how to approach the case. It was a political problem, among other things. *Stressed Soldier Snaps, Kills Own Men.* How would that affect support for the war back home?

It was decided a secret military tribunal would hear the case.

In cuffs, leg irons, and hooded mask, he was escorted out of his cell and into the back of truck, his chains locked to the floor. He was to be driven fifteen minutes across a mountain and flown to Germany for his court martial, thus avoiding any record of aircraft leaving the base with personnel.

Zane sat on the metal bench, jolted again and again as they navigated the dirt road—a road he knew well, and from which he'd conducted more than a few raids in order to secure it for the United States.

He hadn't felt such emptiness since his brother died. He knew the rules of war; he knew that the world would never learn the truth, that he'd be found guilty and executed without anyone the wiser...not that there was anyone left who'd care.

And the truth was, Zane *was* a monster. There'd be no redemption, no great beyond for his soul. He had accomplished nothing but fighting on behalf of others. Nothing to show for his efforts, no one to go home to, no one to mourn when he died. He'd fought for his country, but now...his country wasn't about to fight for him. He was done, spent like a shell casing. Empty and useless.

He realized now that he'd fought for a myth, for a greater good that was anything but. And he'd bought the whole story, sucked in by the DoD's ad line: *Sacrifice for America.* He'd convinced himself he was a patriot because patriots fought and died for their country, but what did that really mean? Did God judge according to that standard? Could any death wrought in the name of peace really be for the greater good?

It was fitting, Zane supposed, that he now questioned everything he'd done, everything he'd stood for. His country was turning its back on him. There would be no redemption, in this life or the next.

An explosion hit the truck, flipping it on its side, then slowly rolling it over onto its roof. Zane's ears rang with a high-pitch echo as he hung upside down by his chained legs. He shook his head, using gravity to slip off the hood. Clouds of dust filled the small space, followed by the smell of fire, smoke seeping in.

He wouldn't be tried after all, he realized. He was being executed, and this was it.

He would burn to death.

He didn't fear dying, though he feared burning almost as much as drowning. He had seen those touched by flame, their disfigured, contorted bodies becoming open nerves in constant agony.

The rear door opened, sunlight cutting through the clouds of smoke. Upside down, he couldn't make out the figure who charged in with the bolt cutters. To his surprise, his wrists were cut free first, enabling him to break his fall as his leg chains released. A hand reached out to help him to his feet.

Standing in the sun was Renzo Cabral.

"What's going on?" Zane asked as they hurried away from the burning vehicle through the bright sun to where a Humvee waited.

Ten minutes later, Zane sat in the kitchen of a small mountain house across from Colonel Carter Bull. Renzo remained outside standing guard.

"You're dead," Bull said.

Zane stared at him.

"You'll be buried with full honors in two days."

"What?"

"It was the only way to wash away the charges against you. Missile strike. *Poof.* Dead."

"So, you..."

Bull shook his head. "Don't get it twisted: some still believe beyond a shadow of a doubt that you blew up the plane. Those good men are all dead. Be thankful I was able to manipulate the political machine."

"Political machine? Is this to protect my dad and his precious reputation?"

"No, he has no idea. Though the embarrassment he'd endure if your survival became public would end his career."

A short man in a lab coat walked in and pointed at Zane. "Is this him?"

"Give us five minutes," Carter said.

The man nodded and left.

"What's this really about?" Zane glared at Carter. "You could be brought up on—"

"Dr. Cossette will be performing several procedures. He will be permanently removing your fingerprints and all of your teeth, replacing them with artificial ones. Your teeth will be used in helping to ID your remains. He'll tweak your nose and chin, slightly alter your angry face."

"And then what? What the hell am I supposed to do?"

"You're going to be working for me," Carter said. "Special projects, off the books, full deniability. You will no longer be known as Jason Chase. From now on, you're Janos Cristiano Zane. As far as the world is concerned, Jason Chase is dead."

Bull dropped two passports, U.S. and Cayman Islands, in his lap; two credit cards; a New York driver's license; and two stacks of cash. "Your dreams of working for the FBI or Secret Service are obviously over, though this role will be far better suited to you and your talents."

"So, I'm dead."

"Yes. But your crimes will be swept away with no charges. In fact, we're going to rewrite the facts and make you a hero. And we're going to get you a posthumous Medal of Honor for saving your men and saving Renzo."

"But I did nothing wrong." He tilted his head, trying to catch Carter's gaze. "You really think I'd kill our own men?"

"Life isn't fair," Carter said. "The fact of the matter is, you were legitimately on your way to being found guilty and put to death."

"Did it ever occur to you that there's still a saboteur on the base? *Someone* blew up that plane."

"Renzo and I will continue the investigation."

"Is he the new me?" Zane asked.

"So to speak. He's very good, but unlike you, he has that Boy Scout eagerness to please me, to do things right. He's not ruthless like you."

Zane laughed bitterly at that.

"Hey," Carter said. "I'm the one person in this world that believes in you, so be careful."

"What about my life? Where will I live?"

"I'll take care of it."

Zane knew that line...Bull would take care of it until he no longer wanted to.

The four men sat in the garage at a makeshift table beside the white van.

"What are we waiting for? It's after eleven." Erik, the shorter man, spoke in accented English. His hair was pulled back in a severe ponytail that fell down his wide back. He stood and walked about the room, his hands slapping his thighs, burning nervous energy.

"When he gets here, he gets here," Kasper said. "Sit down."

Erik ignored him as he continued to circle the van.

A noise startled them all into drawing their guns, aiming them at the door as it creaked open.

Renzo stepped in.

"Are they dead?" asked Erik, impatiently.

"Of course they're dead." Renzo didn't even look at him.

"Then why are we still here?" Kasper asked. "Why haven't we blown the dam?"

"You know why." Renzo pulled his phone from his black suit jacket.

"Where's the trigger?"

"I'll find it," Renzo said.

"Your uncle—"

"That's right, my uncle. He found you, paid you, got you all out of prison. Gave you purpose."

"And kept the trigger to himself."

"Which is why the Semtex is also on a timer," Renzo said. "Worst-case scenario, it'll blow tonight."

"Not if anyone figures out what happened down in that bunker," Erik said.

"No one will make the connection or even suspect what we've set up. Not until the military check-in at seven; for now, I'm the sole point of communication and protection for everyone down there."

"If you think you can keep that secret for nine hours, you're dreaming," Kasper argued.

"We each have a job; stick to yours." Renzo looked into each man's eyes, inviting them to argue. They did not. "I'll find the bag and the trigger, but before we leave, I need to get into the old man's vault."

"Screw the vault," Kasper said. "This was never about the vault. It was about the right thing. Revenge. Winning. Conquering. It was never about vaults. It was about wiping out presidents and prime ministers, showing them how the world really works."

"This world isn't controlled by presidents or prime ministers," Renzo countered. "It's controlled by invisible kings and queens, people with immense power who lurk in the shadows and control the politicians. The elected officials cry and moan about the most recent flu outbreak, the latest insurance debacle or bedroom scandal, but that only distracts the public from what's *really* going on: the powerful taking more power, more control, and more wealth."

The men stared at Renzo. He wondered if they understood. "This peace summit? The signing of whatever accords? It didn't come together because enemies came to their senses; it happened because *real* men of power pulled the strings."

"And who are they?"

"Shamus Hennicot made the summit happen," Renzo said.

"Why do they listen to him?" Kasper said. "Who is he? Why be afraid of him?"

"His wealth and his secrets...which are down in his bunker vault."

"Fuck the money—"

"It's not money that's in that vault—it's something greater."

"So, open the safe and let's get out of here," Erik said.

Renzo stared at him.

"You can't open it?"

"The woman who *could* open it didn't come to the bunker this morning."

"Where is she?"

"I've been looking for her. I'll find her and get her to open it."

"What's in the vault, then?" asked Erik, a greedy glint in his eyes.

Renzo didn't answer.

"What?"

"Secrets that will afford us far more than we have today. Secrets that will not only make us powerful," Renzo said, "they'll make us gods."

"What do we do while you're gone? Sitting here is a waste of fucking time," Erik said.

Renzo sighed. He intended to shoot them all, but that could wait until later. "I need you to go find someone for me. Take the Bronco."

"Who?"

"A little girl...let's see if you can handle that."

"What? Since when did we become kid-snatchers?"

"We're about to wipe out a town and you're worried about one kid?" Renzo shook his head. "The kid is leverage I might need."

"I'll find her," Kasper said, "but you need to answer a question for me."

"Maybe," Renzo said.

"Who pulls *your* strings?"

"What do you mean?"

"You're a smart man, smarter than me," Kasper said. "But you're not smart enough to think of all this." He spread his arms expansively. "To pull all this off."

Renzo stared at him. "What's your point?"

"Everything has come together perfect, yes? It was all planned... by someone smarter than you. But now you want into this vault. Which," Kasper raised a hand, "was not part of the plan."

Renzo considered killing him now instead of later.

"Greed got us into this war," Kasper glared at Renzo. "Be careful... or your greed will destroy you."

Renzo's grandfather came from Akbiquestan. He had whisked Renzo's father out of the country at age sixteen, settling in Greece with new names and papers purchased with all the money the family possessed.

All his life, his grandfather sent money from Greece back to his brothers, his friends and neighbors, doing everything he could to help those left behind. Renzo's father, Papito, was devastated at leaving the only world he knew, leaving behind his friends and his girlfriend, Sonya, in a country with a bleak future and an intolerable regime.

One night, Papito, with the help of his older brother Tuslav, sailed from Greece and hiked over the mountains back into Akbiquestan. It was a two-week journey through the blazing heat of day and frigid desert temperatures at night. They slipped through fences and past guards posted to keep people from leaving; the guards never suspected that any person would want to sneak *into* the country.

Papito found Sonya in the dirt-floor house where she had always lived and spirited her out of town. She never got to say goodbye to her parents or sisters.

As they approached the border, shots rang out, lights blazed, and trucks raced towards them. Tuslav told them to run for freedom as he charged the trucks, sacrificing himself. The last thing Papito saw before crossing the border was his brother being thrown in the back of a truck as the butt of a gun smashed his head.

Papito married Sonya and emigrated to the US, settling in New Jersey and working as a handyman during the day and toll-taker on the Turnpike at night, finally becoming a US citizen at the age of twenty-eight, a year before Renzo's birth. Back then, life was simple for Renzo and his parents. Sonya doted on him and Papito pushed him, encouraging his son to seek a better life. They never spoke of what they had gone through to make it to this country, never spoke of Tuslav, who remained imprisoned in Akbiquestan.

Renzo excelled in sports and academics, was popular, and wore a perpetual smile. His proud parents watched him graduate from West Point and deploy to Iraq. But when war broke out with Akbiquestan and he was sent into the heart of battle, his family nearly crumbled.

He was at war with his relatives, killing the sons of their friends, murdering his cousins—people he had never known. His mother pleaded with him, his father refused to speak to him, but as a military officer, Renzo could only see the people of Akbiquestan as the enemy, much as German-Americans had willingly fought the Nazis.

Two months later, everything changed. Renzo was captured during a failed raid and held in a mountainside prison.

For three weeks, Renzo was shown what his country and Russia had done to his parents' homeland. He was reminded how war was never fought in the U.S., how no drone strikes plagued Washington or Chicago. Yet the United States targeted cities, civilians, and innocents around the world.

And he was tortured.

Barbarous techniques brought him to the edge of passing out, to the edge of death, but his mind and will refused to break. He knew he was on the side of right; that the United States' ideals, morals, and values were correct and should be embraced by the enemy.

When word of his capture leaked into the Akbiquestan ranks, generals came calling with his father's brother, Tuslav, in tow, along with his two adult children, Jenna and Erik.

Erik was a soldier, scarred and battered, but proud. Twenty-two-year-old Jenna had suffered far worse in the war. She had lost not only her left arm and leg in a missile strike but also her two-year-old son Milo. She told Renzo about Milo's smile and bright blue eyes, about their bombed-out home far from the battle lines, and how she'd been kept from crawling into the rubble simply to hold his burned and bloody body.

Renzo's mind filled with shame, pity, and conflict, Jenna's words and appearance far more convincing than any of the torture or propaganda.

When at last Renzo escaped into the desert, he was broken, starving, and infused by a new ideology. Recovered by American forces after a week, he was quickly nursed back to health and returned to war, battling "the enemy." In a grand gesture, Carter Bull ordered a missile strike that destroyed the mountainside prison and base that had held him.

In his remaining years of his service, Renzo passed intel to the enemy: planned troop movements, advance word of ambushes, internal weaknesses to be exploited, and more. He undermined his outfit, his commanding officer, and his country. But in the eyes of his superiors, he played the game of war better than any soldier since Janos Zane. He returned to the U.S. as a decorated war hero.

When he arrived home, he thought there to be no better way to serve his father's country than in the service of the leader of their enemy. Working his way up through the Secret Service, he was finally posted to the president's side. In that post, he knew where the president would be at all times. And when the opportunity presented itself, if it ever did, he intended to avenge and save the home of his ancestors.

"Nick," Shamus said, his eyes lighting up. "Come in, come in."

Nick stepped into the elegant entry hall, glad to see the man smiling and alive. He was dressed in a freshly pressed suit with sharp creases and pinstripes, his tie perfect, his polished cane steady in his hand. Monday through Friday, Shamus Hennicot wore a suit—working or not.

"How's Julia?" Shamus said as he led Nick into his library. "Frantic, I'm sure, as only she can be."

Nick laughed. "You know her well."

"Sometimes better than I think I know myself." Shamus went to the oak bar and put up two glasses. "What can I get you? Orange juice? Virgin Mary?"

"I'm good, thank you." Nick picked a book up off the bar and frowned as he read the cover.

"Senator Byron Chase's book," Shamus said. "Julia had him autograph it for me. I didn't have the heart to tell her he already sent me an autographed copy after my contribution to his campaign."

"Hmm..." Nick thumbed the pages to the pictures in the center. "Not a fan."

"I know."

Nick looked at the pictures of Chase with his wealthy wife, pulling a voting lever, giving a speech. Other photos were pre-politics, showing Chase back when he was Coach Carl: photos of him with his two boys and his first wife, and several pictures of Jason Chase in full-dress uniform, the son who had died in Akbiquestan, killed saving the lives of eight of his men, for which he had been awarded a posthumous Medal of Honor. Nick took a breath, holding back his rage as he stared at Jason.

"I see anger in your eyes," Shamus said. "Don't let it consume you."

"I'll try." Nick shook his head, thinking he recognized Chase's son and not sure if he was feeling clarity or confusion. He closed the book and put it back on the bar.

"What brings you here? I see no wine or gifts in hand, so this must not be a social visit."

Nick reached in his pocket, pulled out the antique pocket watch, and laid it on the bar before Shamus.

"Oh dear," the old man said as he took a deep breath, his hand unconsciously reaching up to the key hanging from his neck, beneath his shirt. "Whatever happened must be worse than awful. Did I pull you into this again?"

Nick wasn't sure how to answer, but he was talking to the one man who knew the watch better than anyone.

"I thought Dreyfus was supposed to destroy the watch three years ago. Now there are *two* watches?"

"Well..." Shamus took a moment before answering. "Yes, there are two watches. Dreyfus and Zachariah were to have dropped both of them in the Marianas Trench. But Dreyfus wouldn't go through with it; he said that as evil the purposes were that the watch could be used for, there might come a time that it would correct a horrific wrong, a world-shattering disaster. We agreed that each of us would keep one of three keys required to open the box, in case such a horrifying occasion presented itself."

"When I used the watch last time, you said it only worked for twelve hours," Nick said, "but clearly it can be used again."

"The twelve hours is true. But there is a reset."

"I don't want to know."

"It has failsafes," said Shamus. "You can't *keep* going back in time. You can't move beyond the twelve hours in your immediate past. You can't go back and rewrite history."

He turned around and pulled out a bottle of Macallan Scotch from the shelf behind the bar, poured it, and took a sip. "I usually wait till noon. I'd offer you the bottle, but I know your predilection for the non-alcoholic sweet stuff."

"Things are worse this time, Shamus...worse than awful."

"Tell me everything."

Nick hesitated.

"Start with what's holding you back," Shamus said, patting Nick on the shoulder. "And work your way from there."

"Okay." Nick took a breath and looked at Shamus. "You die."

"I figured." Shamus nodded. "Julia?"

"Yes."

"How about Katherine?"

Nick nodded glumly.

"Zachariah?"

Again, Nick nodded. "They killed you to get the keys to steal the watch, or as I recently learned, the two watches. I ended up with one."

"Both watches are in play?" Shamus winced. "Then I imagine the twin to that watch is not walking the moral high ground."

"Most definitely not, but as bad as things are...there are worse things. The president and everyone in the bunker were killed."

Shamus closed his eyes.

"And then they destroyed the Killian Dam, wiping out most of Byram Hills and killing thousands."

Shamus moved to a chair and sat heavily as Nick explained how he'd gotten the watch from Dreyfus; how Julia was killed over and over; how the dam was destroyed twice; how he was trapped in a cat-and-mouse pursuit with Zane, who possessed the second pocket watch; and how he was not only trying to save Julia, but also to figure out how to prevent the president from being killed.

"To kill everyone down there..." Shamus began, then paused. "To shoot them all would require a traitor...multiple traitors. Tell me about the man behind it."

"We believe there are at least two. The head of the president's Secret Service detail."

"Renzo Cabral?"

"You know him?"

"Met him on a few occasions. Who're the others?"

"Janos Zane. He's an assassin, ex-military—ruthless. He's not only trying to ensure the president's death...he's investigating something."

"What?"

"He had me break into Senator Chase's home and into his safe. There were things concerning the Russians, plans of the Killian Dam, and a fake passport in there."

"Chase is a man with high aspirations," Shamus said. "Arrogant, can be smart when it comes to advancing himself, but I don't see him being a traitor. He wants the oval office; he won't risk screwing that up. Someone else is working with your friend Zane."

"Well, I have no idea who, and I only have a few hours left to put things together and stop it all from falling apart."

"How can I help?" Shamus said as he rose to pour himself another Scotch.

"Is there something else down in the bunker? Something of value worth killing the president for?"

"How do you mean?"

"Julia was taken down there by Renzo *after* the president was dead."

Shamus watched Nick trying to keep events straight in his head. "It's confusing thinking of the future as the past."

Nick nodded. "She was brought down there after everyone was dead, which doesn't make sense unless there's something that only she can do down there to help them."

"Two things. One, there's a safe room. Perhaps someone escaped the carnage and is locked inside. She couldn't open the door from the outside, but she might be able to talk to whoever is in there and help them release the door themselves."

"That makes sense. What's the other thing?"

"A vault. And if they access it, it will be worse than Byram Hills being destroyed, worse than the assassination of the president or the continuation of the war."

Nick felt fear trickle through his veins. "How so?"

"There are things in there that I have hidden from the world for decades. Some of the secrets are centuries old. Things my forebears collected, secrets gathered through the ages that are unfit to be shared. If whoever killed the president gets that vault open and gets hold of those things, the modern world will be thrown off its axis and into hell."

Shamus Hennicot was a man of wealth and secrets. Inheriting a family fortune amassed over three generations, his worth now measured in the billions. His grandfather, Caleb, started out as a gambler—cards and horseracing with a string of luck that enabled him to enter the financial markets of 1860s London. Caleb was known as "The Soothsayer" by virtue of his uncanny foresight of the daily market trends, windfalls, and catastrophes, until the day he was shot in the middle of Trafalgar Square by Honest John McCarthy, a local dandy and mobster. Some say Honest John was hired by a conglomerate of businessmen who feared Caleb Hennicot would one day bet against them and drive them to ruin.

Hollis Hennicot, Caleb's only son, seemed to possess a similar gene for forecasting, though he expanded the family talent into real estate, manufacturing, and antiquities, growing the Hennicot wealth to truly royal proportions.

On his bed, succumbing to a sudden illness—which many said was poison—Hollis spoke to his eighteen-year-old son Shamus, giving him a small box.

Shamus never felt gifted, never felt that he inherited any genius from his father; in fact, he feared that the family talent would disappear with his father's passing. There was no soothsaying, no genius or brilliance, no ability to read tea leaves in his inherited genes. Inside the box from his father was a note, handwritten and detailed. It revealed that his family inheritance had nothing to with genetics.

It directed Shamus to a brick warehouse in Halsey. When he arrived, he found two armed guards at the windowless structure. Neither they nor anyone had ever seen the inside, the two guards having no idea what they were guarding. They were paid a three-times-scale rate to ensure no one but the most senior living Hennicot entered.

Shamus was surprised that, after all those years, no one's curiosity had been piqued as to what they were protecting. What, after all, was so important that they'd receive such a high salary for such menial work?

But when Shamus opened the door, he understood. They must have peeked inside and seen what he saw: nothing. A vacant, fifty-square-meter cement floor with wooden stairs leading to an equally vacant second level.

It was only the directions in the note—bring a pickax and three lanterns—that told him things aren't always what they seem.

Shamus paced off the dimensions exactly as instructed in his father's note, outlining a large square in chalk. He pulled out the pick and began breaking concrete. For hours, he pounded away until his shoulders and arms were nearly useless.

Under ten inches of concrete, the steel door was revealed. Shamus brushed away the dust and debris and pulled open the door to reveal a set of stairs.

He lit one of the lanterns and descended.

In the center of a large stone room was a table upon which sat a mahogany box. Shamus opened the box to find a single gold-and-silver watch and another note. He read the accompanying instructions.

He lifted the crown, twisted it twice counter-clockwise as outlined, pressed the crown post back down, then rode back through his day, amazed, confounded, confused, and ultimately angry. He understood now how his family had played God, had manipulated others and time for their own gain. He vowed to never follow in their path, never succumb to the greed, the narcissism, the temptation of playing with the divine.

As Shamus looked around the vast subterranean space carved from the London earth decades before, his mind was overwhelmed. As magical and mysterious as the watch was, it paled compared to what he saw now.

Shamus singlehandedly boxed and crated everything; it took him four fifteen-hour days. He hired a team of armed men to help him load it out and onto steamships and accompany him and his inherited cache to America.

He settled in Byram Hills, building a life of redemption for the sins of the father and the fathers before him, the contents of the English warehouse finding a new home in Washington House, his large colonial home on Bedford Road. Certain crates were sent to his home on the water in Massachusetts. Others, he discarded: some hidden away forever and others destroyed.

As he looked into Nick's desperate eyes now, Shamus wished he had destroyed everything.

"You said the bunker was flooded...that they were all shot, but it was also flooded?"

"Yeah," said Nick. "That came after the murders. We had to dive in. The whole place was underwater."

"If the bunker was flooded, someone opened the fresh-air intake."

Nick nodded. "Dreyfus figured the same."

"There's a large air intake a half-mile from the bunker that runs underground to the mechanical room. For the bunker to flood, someone had to have opened that room from the inside. Renzo must have had others on the inside to pull it off." The old man took a sip of Scotch and sighed. "It seems you've been playing catch-up, trying to put things Renzo and Zane are destroying back together again. Maybe you should wreck *their* world, put them on their heels, stop them from achieving *their* goals. The best thing would be to take and destroy his watch. Then you could simply go back an hour and fix it all without interference from Zane. I know that's a long shot.... It sounds like both men would kill you before they'd let that happen."

"That's an understatement."

"It seems Zane's leveraging you by manipulating your emotions— by using and threatening Julia."

Nick nodded.

"Then figure out what he's after, what he needs or cares about. That's your leverage. Take it from him, dangle it before his eyes, then make him beg for it and do your bidding instead of you doing his."

"Thank you," Nick said.

"If you can," Shamus said as he walked Nick to the door, "please save Katherine. But if you can't, then let me go, too."

Nick and Marcus made their way across the park below the dam, heading for the podium at the other end of the grassy expanse. Even at this early hour, the sea of celebrants was already pouring onto the green, friends and families gathering for the big event.

And all to be washed away two hours from now.

As Nick and Marcus weaved through the crowd, Nick silently digested Shamus's words about the watch, about warnings and strategies and leverage, he realized the man had never answered his question—never mentioned *what* was worse than dead presidents, shattered dams, thousands dead, or war. Clearly, that was what Renzo sought. Yet Shamus never specified what terrible things he'd hidden away in his vault.

"What does Janos Zane want?" Marcus asked as he walked alongside Nick.

"The satchel."

"Okay, well, where is it?"

"In the future."

"That does us no good."

"Nope, it doesn't, but there's something more valuable than the satchel."

"What's that?" Marcus asked.

Nick made his way around the blankets and sunbathers and walked along the gravel track to the corner of the park, where Senator Chase stood on a podium, giving a speech. There were two Secret Service agents conspicuously planted in the crowd before him. Nick couldn't help but wonder if they were merely actors hired by the egotistical senator to make him appear more important than he was in his own mind.

As the senator finished, he walked down the back of the podium and ran headlong into Nick.

"Nick," Senator Chase said with a practiced smile. "So great to see you."

"Coach Carl," Nick said as he reached out and shook his hand, enjoying the annoyance on the senator's face. "It's great to see you."

"Thanks so much for coming down. Where's Julia?" he said as he looked around. "She always was your better, classier half."

Nick forced a smile.

"Senator," Marcus thrust out his hand. "Marcus Bennett."

"Nice to meet you, Marcus. Thanks for your support." He turned back to Nick. "I'm kind of surprised to see you down here."

"I was hoping I could get you for about fifteen minutes," Nick said. "We need to chat about something."

"Sorry, but duty calls. Full schedule right through ten tonight. But I'll see you at the gala."

"It's not a gala, just a reception," Nick pointed out. "And this chat is kind of important. If you could—"

"Thanks for stopping by." Chase's attention had already moved on, dismissing Nick without another thought.

"I need to talk to you about your son," Nick said, his words halting the turning senator.

"Thank you for your sympathies, Nick." Chase nodded. "Julia was very kind with her note and flowers when he was killed."

"Of course." Nick walked along with the senator and leaned to his ear, causing the Secret Service agents to take note.

"It's okay." Chase waved the men off.

Nick whispered, "I know he's alive."

Chase's eyes narrowed.

"And while that could have an impact on your career, I'm sure you'll spin his miraculous resurrection into the second coming, making you the father of God and getting yourself elected president."

"Is this blackmail?" Chase whispered, smiling for the people around them. "You always were a little shit."

"No." Nick matched his fake smile. "It's worse than blackmail."

"My men could take you down right now."

"Yes, they could, but when it's discovered that your son's behind an imminent terrorist plot and you may be complicit in it...." Nick let it hang.

Chase nodded and smiled.

"Why don't we take a ride?" Nick pointed to his Wrangler.

"That won't sit well with my keepers." Chase pointed at his security detail.

"I'm not giving you a choice, Carl. But they can follow us. Actually, I insist upon it." Nick led the way to his vehicle as the senator assured his security detail that all was fine and they should follow along.

As Chase got in the Wrangler, Nick pulled his phone out and dialed.

"Nick?" Zane said.

"I have something I think you might be interested in."

Zane pulled up a block away from the house with peeling paint on Kavey Lane, affording him a clean view of the driveway. He turned off the car, settled back in his seat, and waited for Nick.

Zane had actually stolen the satchel from this very location at 11:05 today on his way forward through the day, before he had the pocket watch, before he started playing with time. It occurred to him now that, since there were two of Julia Quinn's phones as a result of one being brought back from the future, the same should hold true for the satchel. He had gone in at three o'clock on his second time through the hour, seen the bodies and equipment, but hadn't found the satchel. Keeping the back and forward motions in time straight in his mind grew increasingly difficult. But it seemed to make sense: while the satchel hadn't been there *then*, it could show up in an earlier hour. In fact, it *would*. But he had no idea at what time, exactly. Events were not playing out the way they had originally...things changed, so many things, and he didn't know how far the changes went, and he wondered whether Nick had figured it out.

Nick drove up Route 22 toward downtown Byram Hills with Chase riding shotgun in his blue pinstripe suit and Marcus in the back; two Secret Service agents followed close behind in a black Suburban.

"How do you know my son's alive?" Chase asked as he held tight to the rollbar.

"Two things," Nick said. "One, he's been trying to kill Julia all day, so we've gotten to know each other."

"Julia?" Shock shone in Chase's eyes. "Why would he try to kill her?"

"We'll get there. And second, I saw pictures, starting with a photo album that I stole from a safe in your house."

"You broke into my house too?"

"Yep, broke into that safe. Nice house, by the way." Nick looked at him. "Didn't think much of it when I saw the pictures of your young boys until I looked through a copy of your new book. It had lots of pictures of Jason, his military heroics. His nose was slightly different then, as was his jaw, but those eyes... That's when the pieces came together."

There was panic in Chase's eyes.

"Nice how you didn't hesitate to stand on your son's dead body to further your career. Even though he wasn't."

"I *thought* he was dead," Chase said. "You have no idea how it feels to lose someone you care about."

"You're wrong about that," Nick said with a glance at Marcus in the rearview mirror. "Anyway," he said as he turned onto Wago Avenue, "the safe also had some interesting pictures of you and what I believe was the Russian president. Not exactly the thing you'd want on a campaign button or front page."

"You don't understand what's going on," Chase said. "This is way above your simple mind."

Nick chuckled. "You can take the coach out of the pool, but you can't take the asshole out of the coach. I honestly don't care how simple or complicated things are, but your bullshit agenda has put my family and friends in grave danger. I don't think you realize what you've unleashed, but you're about to find out."

"Where are we going?" Chase asked as they drove up Kavey Lane, the Secret Service still close behind.

Nick passed a car on the side of the road, the driver behind the wheel watching them pull into the driveway of the grey house a block later.

Chase and Nick got out of the car.

"Whose house is this?" Chase looked at the uncut lawn and several days of newspapers.

"It's for rent," Nick said as he leaned into his Wrangler. "You stay here," he told Marcus.

"You sure?" Marcus asked. "This house looks a little creepy on the outside."

"You should see the inside."

"I have a bad a feeling, Nick...like we've been here before."

Nick nodded. "I get that. Do me a favor—things may get a little crazy in a few minutes. Get in the driver's seat in case we need to make a quick exit."

Nick walked with the senator over to the BMW at the end of the driveway and felt the hood; it was cool. He did the same to a rusted Ford Bronco beside it and found it also cool. He turned to see if anyone had taken note of their presence but saw no one except the Secret Service detail still in their vehicle.

"Are you going to tell me what's going on?" asked Chase.

Nick turned to be sure the man in the black Town Car a block away could see them both. He watched as the window of the car slowly rolled down. Nick subtly waved, wondering what was going through Janos Zane's head right as he watched Nick and his father walk toward the house.

As Chase and Nick moved closer to the garage, the two agents exited their Suburban and followed.

"You need to tell us what's going on," the first agent called to them. "Whose house is this?"

Nick lifted the garage door to find the white van parked facing them.

"What's this?" Chase asked as he followed Nick around the van.

"Let me show you." Nick flung open the back doors, relieved to see everything inside.

Chase looked in, as did the Secret Service agents, who grabbed the senator's arm as they drew their guns.

"What *is* this?" Chase said as he took in the rack of rifles and handguns, dive gear, and Semtex.

"We need to get you out of here, Senator." The two agents were now on high alert, glancing outside as they pulled Chase away from the van.

Chase held his ground. "My son...?"

Nick could see the pain in the man's eyes. An unexpected jolt of regret filled Nick as he realized what he was doing: playing the pawns on the board in much the same way Zane had done with him.

Sudden gunfire erupted, shredding the wall behind them. Two shooters, outside. The Secret Service agents returned fire, taking cover behind the van as they alternated shooting at the invisible assailants.

Nick pushed Chase into the back of the van and pulled the door closed behind them.

"Who's shooting at us?"

Nick saw the mixture of fear and confusion in the senator; he worried he had pushed things too far but shook off the emotion. If he were to defeat Zane, he would have to play by his rules: lack of emotion and malevolent tenacity.

Nick jumped in the front seat, finding the keys exactly where he saw them a few hours from now, jammed them in the ignition, started the engine, and hit the gas.

"Stay down!" Nick shouted as he blindly peeled out of the driveway, his head beneath the level of the dashboard, bullets peppering the side of the van as they raced into the street.

Nick popped up to see Kasper and a tattooed partner reloading their guns and running for their rusted Ford Bronco.

"Holy shit!" Chase yelled from behind Nick. "Stop the van!"

Moving down the street, Nick glanced in the rearview mirror to see not only Marcus behind him in the Wrangler, but also Zane following in his Town Car.

"Get in front and put your seatbelt on!" Nick shouted over the roar of the engine.

Chase didn't argue as he crawled from the back into the passenger seat and strapped himself in.

Nick again looked in the mirror, seeing that the old Ford Bronco had also taken up the chase, with the Secret Service agents racing after them in their Suburban. "If you haven't noticed, we're being pursued."

"By my security detail."

"And the mercenaries who want to kill us," Nick said. "Oh, and also by your son."

"My son?" Chase looked back to see the string of cars racing behind them.

Nick's phone rang. He lifted it to his ear.

"What the hell are you doing?" Marcus said from the Wrangler, two cars back. "This is nuts. You're going to get yourself and all of us killed."

"I'm not going to die."

"Die?" Chase yelled as he braced himself in the passenger seat.

"I don't give a shit about your life expectancy," Marcus shouted through the phone. "I'm far more concerned about mine."

"Just try to run interference as best you can," Nick said and tucked the phone back in his pocket. In the rearview mirror, Nick looked at the box with two blocks of Semtex in the back of the van. The way Marcus had described it, it could rip the face off of Mother Nature; not a good thing to have in car when you're being pursued, though without a fuse, the plastic explosives would remain inert. But it wasn't the Semtex Nick was worried about. He already knew from experience that there was a block affixed to the underside of the van, fused and armed to detonate.

Nick cut into town, hung a left onto Maple, avoiding the construction zone on Main Street, and swung back toward Bedford Road. He raced around two cars at a stop sign, cutting off approaching vehicles that braked frantically to avoid him, their blaring horns quickly silenced as gunfire erupted from the rusted Bronco in pursuit.

"Keep your head down!" Nick shouted as bullets pinged off the back doors.

He looked in the rearview mirror to see Marcus ram the rusted Bronco, sending it into a skid, but it quickly regained traction, continuing the chase. A tattooed mercenary leaned out the passenger window and aimed. He got off one shot before Marcus rear-ended them, causing the merc to drop his gun and nearly fall out of the car.

Nick hit the gas, going sixty in a thirty.

"You're going to get us killed!" cried Chase.

As Nick sped around the corner of Bedford Road, the van nearly tipped before he was cut off by a line of cars at a stop light, forcing him to swerve back onto Main Street. He had avoided the construction site all day, detoured around it constantly, but now he had no choice: he was heading directly into it. There were no roads, driveways, or alleys to divert onto. Soon he'd run out of road.

"Shit."

The Suburban came out of nowhere, its engine roaring as the Secret Service raced past the Bronco and Jeep, came up alongside the van, and slammed into Nick's side, trying to slow them.

"Jesus!" Chase yelled, holding on for his life.

Nick never slowed as he looked at the sidewalks, at the people staring in fear, some starting to run out of the way. There was nowhere to drive but straight ahead.

"I have an idea."

With no alternative, he crashed through the wooden construction barrier. Debris flew, the blue tarps wrapped about the van, scooped from their stanchions as it raced through the construction zone, covering the windshield.

The Bronco spun around and raced away as Zane fishtailed onto Main, fifty yards back, then halted.

Looking ahead, Marcus also screeched to a stop in the middle of the street, watching the disaster unfold. The blue-tarped van ran between two concrete barriers, over the metal plates, and barely missed plunging into the open dig. It continued forward, but there was nowhere else to go, no room to stop—

The van smashed into a backhoe and crumpled like tinfoil. A half second later, the explosion shattered the day. Shop windows blew out, people dived for cover, everyone assuming they were under attack as the giant fireball rolled into the sky, the massive heat peeling the paint from the buildings alongside the road. A second explosion shook the earth, and as the smoke cleared, there was nothing left of the van but the blackened frame of the chassis, everything inside it vaporized and charred.

Marcus jumped out of the Wrangler as Chase's men ran toward the wreckage, then retreated, forced back by the heat.

Zane got out of his car and stared in disbelief at the fiery blast zone.

Townspeople murmured and cried, the fire whistle sounded, sirens approached, but there was nothing anyone could do.

Zane pulled out and looked at his watch—11:59—shocked that Nick had killed not only his father, but himself.

CHAPTER 4

9:00 AM

Nick was very much alive, though a bit more of his hair was burned, now. His clothes were torn and muddy, which was to be expected after crawling through a newly dug sewer trench.

He had unbuckled Chase's seatbelt and dragged the senator with him, jumping as the van raced through the cordoned-off construction zone, the pair disappearing into the open pit that had gaped in the street all week. As the van exploded on the street above, he pulled Chase into the new concrete pipe that had been laid ten feet beneath the road. The detonation shook the subterranean tunnel, dust and debris falling around Nick and the senator as the glow of the fireball lit up the hole behind him.

And then the pocket watch had hit the top of the hour and he'd arrived here: at his dining room table. Papers spread the length of the polished oak surface in the same way they had when he'd worked here during his first pass through the nine o'clock hour.

Nick tried to imagine the look on Chase's face when he'd disappeared before the senator's eyes. But he had an even greater sense of satisfaction: as far as Janos Zane knew, Nick was now dead. He'd played Zane's own trick back on him, seeming to die while freeing himself from what had held him back. Free to figure out a way to save Julia, once and for all.

Nick shook off the adrenaline from the car chase and explosion and ran upstairs, stripped off his clothes, and headed into the bathroom. He wiped down his body with a wet washcloth, bandaging some of his deepest cuts and abrasions, then quickly dried himself. He left the sink running as he changed into fresh clothes, returning to brush his teeth.

The front door slammed. Nick heard Julia's heels marching hard through the foyer and up the stairs. He knew why she was mad—he'd heard it a few times already. She didn't get to go down and play with the president. Well, the president was dead and she would be too if she hadn't taken Katy to daycare in Nick's absence.

Normally we never know which of life's detours keep us out of harm's way.

Nick knew. Julia did not.

She poked her head in the bathroom, an accusatory finger pointing at him. "This is your fault."

"Sorry," Nick said.

"You don't even know what you're sorry about."

"You missed your meeting with the president."

"You think you're so smart—What?" Julia paused, her anger morphing from shock, to surprise, to fear. "How do you know that?"

"Sit down." Nick motioned her toward the bed.

"How do you know that?" Julia asked again. "Have you been going through my things? *No one* knows—"

"I know," Nick cut her off softly. "Please, sit down."

"Nick?"

"Peace accords...Shamus's bunker in Hadley's Woods."

"Oh my God...you didn't tell anyone, did you? You didn't tell Marcus? If Marcus.... Do I smell burnt hair?" Julia walked into the closet and saw the muddy clothes on the ground, next to Nick's pile of clothes from after the accident. "Is all this from the car accident?"

"No, actually."

"How did you get *all* these clothes so dirty?" Julia looked at him more closely, took in the bandages and his hair. "Did you get burned?"

"Let me explain."

"Actually, I don't have time," Julia said as she grabbed a briefcase and headed for the door.

"Can we just sit for five minutes and talk?" Nick called, following as she neared the stairs. "I need to discuss something important with you."

Nick felt a déjà vu moment, impossible because the original moment still lay in the future. It occurred to him that maybe déjà vu could happen in reverse, originating from events still to come.

"I really, *really* don't have time," she said as she moved for the stairs.

Nick gently reached out and grabbed her arm, stopping her.

"Nick..."

"Please?"

"You have no idea how much stress I'm under."

"I know."

"No, you don't. Everything I've had to do for tonight's fundraiser, work, things you couldn't possibly understand."

Nick nodded at the familiar litany.

"And I missed the most important meeting of my life this morning because of you." Her anger began to rise.

"I know how hard you worked and prepared for that," Nick said calmly. "It took weeks. On top of everything you've done for me and Katy. You're a full-time mom, a full-time attorney, and full-time stressed. I take you for granted, and I'm sorry."

"We have problems, Nick."

"I know," Nick said, remembering the words she already uttered to him an hour from now. "And it's my fault. I'm always rushing off to work or play, forgetting about us. I'm sorry."

Julia was listening now, confused but also calmer.

"I'm going to stop chasing money, chasing meetings, and chasing fun. No more trying to keep up with Marcus."

Julia's eyes softened. "Maybe less skydiving...?"

"No more skydiving," Nick said. "You're my excitement. You're all the adrenaline I need."

Julia looked up. There was no anger left, though her eyes had begun to mist.

"It's okay." Nick reached out, taking her hand.

"I've had this terrible feeling all day." Tears flowed freely as she looked at him. "I can't explain it; it's like a gnawing sense of dread, like something terrible is going to happen. Every noise I hear, every ring of the phone scares me, like I'm about to learn someone died."

"It's okay," Nick soothed.

"You don't understand. I'm looking over my shoulder like shadows are following me. I think I'm losing it."

Nick took her in his arms. "It's going to be all right. I've got you."

They held each other, enjoying the moment, lingering....

"I have a confession to make," Julia said as she stepped back.

"Julia," Nick said. "You don't have to—"

"I do. The guilt is killing me."

"It's okay."

"It's not okay," she said. "There are things I didn't tell you, couldn't tell you. I signed this NDA. I never thought how awful it would be. I was working with Shamus and President McManus."

"Working with the president," Nick smiled. "That's amazing."

"But I lied to you...deceived you so much."

"For a good reason, I'm sure," Nick said. "I get it."

Julia hugged him, her whole body relaxing, free of its burden.

"Shhh, it's okay."

"And there's something else."

Nick released her and saw new concern in her eyes.

"Tuesday night, when you go play cards...." Julia gave him that get-out-of-trouble smirk that she'd used so effectively since they were teenagers.

"Yeah?"

"When you leave to go play cards, as soon as you're gone, Bonnie comes over to stay with Katy and I go out."

Nick raised his eyebrows but managed to keep his mouth shut.

"I go down to this studio on the second floor of the Legend building across from Valhalla."

"Paulie B's restaurant?"

"Yeah." Julia nodded. "I go there and I dance. Just me and the owner Maurice. I dance for two hours."

Nick nodded.

"And we just dance...that's it...but I'm in the arms of another man." Julia couldn't hide the panic in her eyes. "It's just dance moves, I promise: rumba, salsa, tango. There's no feeling there."

"Except joy," Nick said softly.

"From the dancing, not from—"

"Hey, I get it. You lose yourself in the moment—it's where you find happiness. It's been part of you since before there was an 'us.'"

Julia nodded as a tear rolled down her cheek.

"And you gave it all up when life got crazy."

Julia nodded. "But that was my choice."

Nick smiled, seeing how hard it was for her to confess. "I have a confession to make too."

Julia looked up from her tears.

"You have to promise me you won't get mad."

"Nick...?" Julia said, not knowing where this was going.

"Okay, you *can* get mad, but don't get too mad. Tuesday night, when I leave, I don't go play cards with Marcus and the guys."

"Where do you go?" Julia asked, genuinely confused.

"I go to the same place every week. The second floor of Valhalla. I order the same thing each time: a Coke, French onion soup, steak, and fries."

Julia was afraid to ask the question, but did. "Who do you meet?"

Nick paused before answering. "I eat alone."

"I don't understand."

"I eat alone and I stare out the window." Nick took a breath. "It was purely by accident. A couple of months ago, I did go and play cards with Marcus and Dreyfus. Paulie B was there, which is to be expected, as we were at his restaurant. Marcus was the one who saw it first and pointed it out to me."

"Pointed what out?"

"Something that he saw out the window. At first, I was a bit shocked, hurt.... But then Marcus punched me in the arm and told me I was an idiot for even thinking suspicious thoughts."

Julia still wasn't following Nick's story.

"Every Tuesday night," Nick continued, "I go to Valhalla. Paulie B reserves me the same second-floor table, the one by the window. He brings me my food, I stare across the street through the large picture window in the Legend building, and I watch. I watch you dance."

"You've been watching me...?" Julia face was a mixture of anger and embarrassment.

"Not like a voyeur," Nick said. "Never suspicious, never ever suspicious or jealous. A man who loves his wife and knows she loves him is never jealous. You know I've always loved to watch you dance, and I know it makes you uncomfortable for me to watch. I'm sorry, but it's one of my greatest loves...to see you indulging your passion."

She began to speak, but Nick held up a hand.

"When I see you across the street and watch you get lost in the moment, it's beautiful. *You're* beautiful. I get to be alone with you for two hours, watching you do what you love, all the while thinking how lucky I am, how blessed I am to have you."

Julia stared at Nick. He wasn't sure if he had gone too far, if some things were best left unsaid. But then Julia leaned forward and kissed him.

"You watch me...?"

Nick nodded. "You dance?"

"I guess we both have secrets." At last, Julia smiled. But then she looked at her watch, defeat filling her face as reality came rushing back. "I have to go."

Nick stood in front of her. He reached down, taking her wrist, releasing the clasp, and removing the watch from her wrist.

"What are you doing?"

He laid the watch on the side table and took her in his arms.

"I don't have time."

Nick ignored her, holding her face gently between his hands and pulling her into a soft kiss. Her lips were stiff, resistant, but he didn't stop. Wrapping a hand behind her head and running it through her hair, he kissed her again, pulling her in.

"Nick..."

"Shhh..." He kissed along her neck, behind her ear, inhaling her scent, the unique flavor behind her earlobe, softly exhaling on her skin.

He ran his hands up her back, gently massaging as his fingers danced over her flesh, stripping away her stress, wiping away her anger until she slowly began to kiss him back: strong, passionate, wet, and full. Her arms wrapped about his shoulders as their souls entwined, washing time away, the moment dragging them into a world where only they existed.

She tore at his shirt, ripping the buttons. Nick dragged down the zipper of her dress, slipping it from her shoulders and watching it pool on the floor. He lifted her, carrying her to the bed.

They made love for the first time in forever, slow at first, arms and legs entangled, awkward yet smooth as if they were sixteen, not as if for the thousandth time, knowing each other's hearts, knowing how to pleasure one another.

It was heated and wet, their minds wrapped with lust, with love, all their troubles falling away, seeking to give pleasure as much as take it. Nothing mattered but each other, nothing existed except their fragile souls as they reached for release.

As their racing hearts calmed, and they slowly caught their breath, Nick lay atop her, smiling down as she smiled back.

"This is crazy," Julia whispered. "I've got so much—"

"This is right," Nick said. "This is us."

"What time is it?"

"Whatever time it is, we have five more minutes." Nick kissed her softly as he rolled off of her and snuggled close.

"Thank you," Julia said, though he knew she meant, "I love you."

Perched on his side, Nick rubbed her shoulders and kissed her forehead as their breathing fell in sync.

"Did you ever check on the guy you saved earlier this morning?" Julia asked. "I heard they can't ID him...that he's still unconscious."

"What about his family?"

"Who knows if he even has any? They say he's a foreigner."

Nick looked at her. "How do you know that?"

"When I saw Donna getting coffee earlier. She said all the other nurses were talking about how heroic you were. Said the poor guy had no ID. He mumbled in some language the nurses never had heard. Said all he had was a satchel filled with architectural plans, a car key, but no ID."

Nick sat up. "What kind of satchel?"

Carter Bull had been in the military all of his life—the son of a colonel and grandson of a general, his destiny a forgone conclusion.

Childhood was spent on the move, nine bases over thirteen years. He went to the Fork Union Military Academy at fourteen, West Point at eighteen, Vietnam at twenty-one. He was a career officer who spent wartime in the midst of conflicts. In times of peace, he hung his hat in the Pentagon. He was a brilliant strategist who created victory from no-win scenarios, a master tactician, and an expert at chess and all games of strategy, which made him the ideal officer in wartime.

He was equally as skilled in management and finance, ensuring that his soldiers were never lacking in the tools, weapons, or supplies required for success. He understood the machinations of politicians, cajoling where necessary, manipulating when needed: whatever it took to keep the war machine oiled, maintained, and humming.

He had nearly ended the Akbiquestan war by dispatching an 18-man assault on the heart of the enemy's mountain stronghold, its base of operation and brain trust, but the mission had been undermined from within.

When considered for head of the Joint Chiefs, Bull instead requested and was granted the role of "special advisor," a far more powerful position, as he could speak with brutal honesty away from the crippling spotlights of the Cabinet and Congress.

When the peace-accord initiative was begun by Shamus Hennicot and President McManus, his strategic mind was brought to bear, playing out solutions, detecting pitfalls, and avoiding unintended consequences. Bull's forty-year friendship with Shamus and the trust of the president brought him a central role in the peace-summit talks, as evidenced by the nearly 25 percent of the peace-agreement language that consisted of his exact words.

He abhorred the loss of his men—of any American. No one hated war more than the solider. He was one of a dying breed: he bled red, white, and blue, and would stand against anyone who didn't.

As he stared at his window's view of the Rocky Mountains, he longed for this whole ordeal to be over. No one had any idea what was happening in Shamus's bunker. Everything had spun out of control. If Zane didn't succeed....

Carter turned back to his desk, picked up the phone, and dialed.

"What?" Zane said.

"It's been almost two hours," Carter said as he looked at his watch. "Where do you stand?"

"You need to stop calling me," Zane snapped. "I'm running out of time."

"What the hell are you talking about?" Carter asked, confused. "This is the first time I've called since earlier this morning."

The elevator door opened and Nick hopped out, hurrying down the white linoleum hall. Not much activity for a holiday Friday, but he supposed that was a good thing for a hospital. He slowed his pace as he approached the nurse's station of the ICU. Two women were lost in files as Donna Shreyer rose from her desk and headed in the opposite direction.

Like so many people in Byram Hills, Donna was friends with Julia and, by proxy, Nick. She had assisted with Katy's birth and saving Julia on that day of joy, fear, and relief.

Nick slipped unseen into the ICU room of the man he had saved earlier this morning (or two hours from now, depending on how he wanted to confuse himself). He quickly opened the small closet and found the satchel, peeking only briefly inside it to confirm everything was there.

Nick stepped over to the tubed and wired comatose patient and stared down at the man's gauze-covered face, the right side burned and bruised. *This* was the man behind the plan? How could someone have such disregard for life—such hate in their heart? Nick wanted to reach down and choke him; instead, he asked himself what might have happened if he hadn't saved the man two hours earlier, if he had simply let him fry—let the bag, its contents, and this man burn to ash.

In that moment, it finally hit Nick. Now he remembered where he'd seen Renzo Cabral before. It had been this morning at the accident. Nick had glimpsed him out of the corner of his eye, running toward him as he dragged this man out of the Mercedes as Marcus fought the flames. Renzo had only been on-scene for the briefest time before stepping back and disappearing. All of it forgotten in the intensity of the moment.

"You're a hero, Nick."

Nick dropped the bag to the floor as he turned and smiled at Donna, who entered the room behind him.

"Do you know who he is?" she asked.

"No idea," Nick lied. "Just someone driving through town."

"It's so nice of you to come and check on him."

"Well, it's no big deal. Just concerned." Nick kicked the bag under the bed.

"How's Julia? Bet she's overwhelmed prepping for that party this evening."

"You know Julia." Nick smiled. "You'll be there, I hope."

"Wouldn't miss it," Donna said, as she turned toward the door. "Can I get you anything?"

Nick shook his head and turned his gaze back on the man. Time was running out; his greatest worry now was that Zane would arrive any minute to steal the satchel. He waited until Donna was out of sight, then reached down, grabbed the satchel, and exited the hospital.

Nick threw the bag on the seat of the Wrangler and drove out of the parking lot. He saw Zane coming up the far side of the hospital entrance and hit the gas, hoping he wouldn't be seen. With any luck, his fellow time-jumper assumed Nick had died in the van crash.

Nick was unsure when Zane had grabbed the satchel on his first time through the day—whether it was from here at the hospital or at some later hour. He only knew that Dreyfus stole it from Zane's hands much later in the day, before slipping it around Nick's neck moments before he died, before the dam blew for the first time, beginning this whole backward nightmare. None of that confusion mattered now; he'd beaten Zane here by five minutes.

Everything today seemed to come down to a matter of minutes.

Nick raced down Byram Road, his eyes darting to the rearview but seeing nothing except vacant road behind him.

It was all about playing offense now.

Donna walked back into ICU, three coffees in hand when she glimpsed a shadow in the comatose patient's room.

"Excuse me," Donna said as she walked in. "May I help you?"

The man had torn everything out of the closet, tossing it onto the floor.

"There was a bag...this man had a bag."

"And who are you?"

The man held up his ID. "Secret Service."

"I don't care if you're the president, this man is in critical condition." Donna looked at his ID and face. "What kind of bag, Mr. Cabral?"

"Has anyone been in here?" Renzo asked.

Bells and whistles went off in Donna's head; she didn't know why, but her gut was screaming a warning.

"No." She knew the bag the man was looking for. She had looked through it in hopes of finding some identification for the injured man. Now she knew, even without looking, that Nick had left with the satchel. She had known Nick for years; he was a good man, not known for trouble, and until she got more answers, she wouldn't be throwing him under the bus.

"Are you sure?" the man demanded.

Hearing the commotion, another nurse came in.

"Has anyone else been in here?" Renzo repeated his question to the younger nurse.

She looked to Donna. "Wasn't Nick Quinn in here five minutes ago?"

As Nick glanced again at the mirror, he saw a car nearly a mile back, racing closer to him. He pushed the paranoia from his mind. Hundreds of cars traveled this road every hour. He couldn't discern the make or model. Nonetheless, he hit the gas.

When it came within a half-mile, he recognized the vehicle.

Nick grabbed his cell phone and dialed, but the phone went straight to voicemail.

"It's Shannon," Shannon's voice answered. "Leave a message."

"It's me! I'm in trouble. Big trouble. Heading for the Lumber Yard."

Zane was a hundred yards back and closing.

Nick tore into town, hitting the brakes as he came upon several slow-moving cars. He glanced up at the mirror.

Zane was no longer behind him. Nick slowed, turning left on Maple Avenue, avoiding the construction in Main Street, and again checking his mirror. Then, when he looked in front of him, he saw Zane coming at him from ahead.

Nick cut through the Decicco's Supermarket parking lot, praying no one got in his way, and exited onto Bedford Road, quickly turning right. But somehow Zane had made it around the block and was, once again, heading straight for him. Nick spun a 180, wheels spinning and smoking, peeling off in the other direction.

It felt as if Zane were herding him, knowing his every move ahead of time. Nick continued at sixty down Bedford Road.

Zane kept coming, and there was nowhere else to go. Nick raced to the terminus of the street, the Lumber Yard that was closed tight for the holiday.

Zane skidded up behind him, swinging his car into a skid, blocking the road and sealing Nick's only exit.

Zane leapt from his car. "Give me the bag, Nick."

"Not a chance," Nick shouted through his window.

Zane held up his gun, walking toward him. "I don't know how you survived, but I'm too close to fail now."

"You can't possibly think that I'll hand it over."

Three police cars screeched to a stop behind them, blocking Zane's exit, jumping from their cars, guns raised.

"Drop it!" John Goodheart shouted as he ran up on Zane.

Zane glared at Nick, finally putting his hands in the air.

Goodheart snatched his gun away as he pressed his gun into the back of Zane's head, forcing him to the ground.

Shannon got out of his car, shaking his head on approach. "I can't wait to hear this story."

"Believe me, it's a good one," Nick said.

Goodheart looked at Shannon and the third armed officer. "And I thought it was going to be a boring day."

A hundred yards back, Renzo slowed as he saw the flashing lights ahead. He watched as they cuffed a man, throwing him on the hood of their car, frisking him and clearing his pockets.

And then he saw it: a civilian handed it to one of the officers. It was his uncle's satchel. Everything was in there: the detonator, the blueprints and memory stick, evidence that would end his plan before it began. He thought of approaching, identifying himself, and taking the satchel, but a chill ran through him as he recognized the man in cuffs, the man he'd saved from a burning military truck and helped disappear from the face of the earth.

"What is this?" Shannon said as he took the satchel from Nick.

"Do me a favor and lock it up."

"Why was he chasing you?" Shannon asked as he looked inside to see papers, a memory stick, a smart key.

Nick pointed at the bag.

"Is it his?"

"No, but he's after it." Nick didn't know how far to go with his explanation.

"Why?" Shannon pressed. "Nick, what's going on?"

"Don't let that bag out of your sight. I'll meet you at the station in few minutes to explain everything." Nick pointed at Zane. "And lock him up."

"On what charge?"

"Murder."

Nick tucked his gun back into the safe in his home office and headed to the kitchen. Zane was in lock-up; the satchel was out of everyone's reach. Now he only needed to make it to the top of the hour to put these things behind him and—

"Hi," Julia said from the kitchen counter, a plate of bagels and juice on the counter before her.

"You're home?"

Julia smiled and nodded. "I can't get into the bunker to see the president, and the reception's pretty much set. I just need to stop stressing about it. I figured we could spend the morning together. No work, Katy's in daycare—just a simple breakfast date. Maybe continue what we started earlier?"

"So, who are you?" Shannon said. "You've really screwed up my holiday. I have to do paperwork now and call the DA."

They sat across from one another at a table in a small interrogation room. Zane's hands were cuffed, a chain affixing his ankles to the floor. Before him were his personal effects: gun, wallet, phone, and the pocket watch.

"Do you want to tell me why you were chasing my friend? Why you were pointing a gun at him?"

Zane said nothing.

"So, what's up with the bag? He said he's going to tell me all about it, and you, but let me hear what you have to say."

Zane looked at his watch on the other side of the table; he had never been in greater danger of failing his mission than in this moment. Without the watch, he'd be stuck in the regular flow of life with no way back. It was 9:20. He had a half-hour to retrieve his watch before everything fell apart. He pulled against the cuffs and kicked his legs against the chain.

"Don't bother—they're secure." Shannon smiled and pulled out a fingerprint card that looked like a mess of black blotches. "What is it with no fingerprints today?" Shannon shook his head. "The guy in the hospital has none...you've got none. That's quite the disturbing trend."

Zane looked at Shannon, finally speaking softly. "You need to let me go."

"I don't need to do anything." Shannon said. "See, it's a holiday, and I'm not happy to be working. I've got a senator in town, you with your guns, another mystery man in a coma. I don't believe in coincidence. So, until I understand what's going on, letting you go is the farthest thing from my mind."

"Good morning," Martha said from behind the bulletproof glass in the reception area of the Byram Hills police station. "How may I help you?"

"Good morning. Renzo Cabral, U.S. Secret Service." The tall man laid his ID on the counter, sliding it through the small slot in the glass. "I'd like to speak to the duty officer."

"This is turning into one interesting day," Martha muttered as she turned around. "Shannon? The Feds are here."

"And why was he arrested?" Renzo asked. He sat in Bill Shannon's office, which was small and decorated with award plaques, softball trophies, and brass boxing gloves.

"A whole host of reasons," Shannon said from behind his desk. "Resisting arrest—"

"For?" Renzo interrupted.

Shannon stared at him, not liking this man very much. "Speeding, harassment, weapons charges, attempted robbery—"

"Attempting to steal what?"

Shannon leaned forward. "What exactly is your interest in this man?"

"He stole a satchel from us that belongs to a terrorist."

"Well," Shannon nodded, "we have that satchel. It's in the evidence cage."

"Well, I need it."

"Well, in case you didn't hear me, it's in the evidence cage."

"I hate to pull rank...."

"Then don't." Shannon leaned back. "Because in this building, I rank."

"Okay." Renzo looked around. "I'm sorry. I got us started on the wrong foot."

"You think?" Shannon said, tempering his anger.

"I'm the head of the president's Secret Service detail. The man you're holding is helping a terrorist. In his bag is a memory stick, plans to blow up the dam on the other side of town, and a smart key. I need the smart key."

"Thank you," Renzo said as he signed eight documents, each in triplicate.

"What do you mean...blow up the dam?" Shannon handed him the satchel.

"Just a plot, not a reality." Renzo threw the satchel over his shoulder.

"You're sure about that?"

"Do you know how many plots are uncovered daily? There's nothing to worry about. This satchel and that man you're holding are the extent of the insanity."

"Is there anything else I can do?" Shannon asked, more as a perfunctory question than meaning it.

"Well," Renzo said, "since you asked, yes, there is."

"This is a surprise," Renzo said as he sat directly across from Zane.

Zane's feet were still cuffed by a long chain to a hook in the floor, his wrists in handcuffs.

"How are you, JC?" Renzo asked. "I always thought you were one of the good guys."

"And has your conclusion changed?" Zane asked.

"Last time I saw, you were in cuffs on the way to being court-martialed and probably executed," Renzo said. "And I saved you."

Zane simply stared at him.

"Should I do it again?" Renzo grabbed and jingled his leg irons. "Should I set you free?"

"We both know that's not going to happen," Zane said.

"Why?"

"Because those who appear perfect never really are."

Renzo pondered his words and finally smiled. "My parents thought I was the golden child, my commanding officers loved me, as do my current employers. But not you? Do you really think they could all be so wrong?"

Zane nodded.

"Wow, you surprise me."

"Get used to it."

"Who do you work for?" Renzo leaned in.

"Carter Bull, but I imagine you already know that."

"You still work for Carter?"

"Surprise." Zane met his gaze. "How about you, Renzo? Who do you work for?"

"I'm head of the president's Secret Service detail."

"Not doing a very good job at that."

"How do you mean?"

"Seeing that he and everyone else is dead—"

"What are you talking about?" Renzo couldn't hide his shock.

It was Zane's turn to smile. "As head of his detail, shouldn't you know that? I mean, they were killed about two hours ago. How do you think that happened?"

Renzo went silent; Zane could see his confusion and worry. "But that's par for the course for you. Everyone dies under your watch. You're just real good at covering it up." Zane leaned back in his chair. "Me and my new friends are about to have a conversation about you and what's happening in the woods of their quiet, little hamlet."

"Well...." Renzo paused, thinking. "Here's something to choke on in whatever hole you end up in. It was me: I blew up that plane, killed all those men, slipped a small air-pressure bomb in the fuel tank of the right wing. I planted the evidence and doctored the video. I set you up...and the irony is, you saved me. Plucked me out of the sky. I would have died that night if you hadn't saved me."

"We all make mistakes." Zane held his rage in check.

"True," Renzo held up the smart key, "but I'll be the one smiling in the end."

"Maybe. But once I explain about you, and the president, and the dam—"

Renzo reached for the gun in his shoulder holster.

Zane shook his head. "Shoot me. Go ahead. They'll lock you in here."

Renzo stared at him a moment before he stood from his chair, walked to the door, and knocked. "You're always right."

A moment later the door opened and Renzo walked out.

Zane knew what was about to happen. He'd thought not having the watch was bad, but this was worse.

A minute later, gunfire erupted. The small window of the interrogation room shattered as bullets peppered the space. Constrained as he was by his shackles and cuffs, Zane could scarcely duck.

Moments later the door burst open. Goodheart ran in and slammed the door closed.

"Are you hit?" Goodheart asked, as he stayed low. "I'm going to take you to the holding area. I can seal you inside."

"He's going to kill me." Zane held up his cuffs and leg chains. "I'm a sitting duck in these chains."

Goodheart pulled out his key and released him from his shackles.

Zane grabbed the chain and whipped it around Goodheart's throat; he pulled it tight, and in with a violent tug, snapped his neck. In a flash, Zane had the officer's cuff keys; quickly freeing his hands, he took Goodheart's gun and bolted out the door.

Racing down the hall, he looked through chicken wire into the evidence pen. He tried the ring of keys, hitting success on the third. He saw his personal effects in a clear bag on the table. He ripped it open, tucking away his own gun, wallet, phone, and, most importantly, the pocket watch.

Peering out into the bullpen, Zane saw the detective who'd arrested him along with two other cops dead on the floor, along with a lifeless, blood-drenched woman in the corner.

No sign of Renzo.

Holding a pistol in each hand, Zane counted to three, then charged into the bullpen.

Nick and Julia sat on the slate terrace off their kitchen, Nick eating a peanut butter and bacon sandwich (to Julia's disgust) while she finished her bowl of berries.

"So, after tonight," Nick sipped his Coke, "we each take the week off, take Katy up to Cape Cod, turn off our phones, and get buried in the sand."

"Something like that." Julia smiled.

"And no more talking about what we're going to do in the future. We do it now before time gets away from us. Focus on experiences instead of things."

"Agreed." Julia hoisted her glass of orange juice, clinking Nick's can of Coke. "As long as those experiences are on terra firma and relatively safe—like riding bikes and climbing mountains, instead of jumping off them."

Nick tilted his head. "I still get to kitesurf."

"That's fair, but no stupid tricks." Julia smiled as she stood. "I need to make a few calls, but I'll do it from here, if that works for you."

"Works for me," Nick said as he picked up their plates and followed Julia through the kitchen door. He set the plates in the sink as Julia—

The front door crashed in. Renzo and three tattooed mercenaries burst into the house, guns held high as they spread out.

Nick ran for his office, hoping to reach his gun, but Kasper was already in the room. He tackled Nick face-first into the floor while Renzo grabbed Julia.

"Renzo?" Julia screamed as she recognized him. "What are you doing?"

Julia kicked and punched at him, stronger than most men imagined, but Renzo quickly pulled her into an arm-bar chokehold, cutting off the flow of blood until she passed out.

"You son of a bitch." Nick struggled against the weight of Kasper upon him, trying to get up, to break free. "I'll kill you."

Renzo tucked the still-unconscious Julia into the front seat of his car, wrapping the seat belt around her.

"Where are you going?" Kasper asked as he walked out into the driveway.

"Back into the bunker," Renzo said as he stepped around the car and opened the driver's side door.

"Are you insane?" Kasper said. "You got the smart key. Why take the chance? What the hell do you need down there?"

"Trust me. I wouldn't risk it all on something foolish."

"Yes, but that is exactly what you're doing." Kasper stepped into Renzo's space. "Give me the smart key in case something happens."

"I don't feel like drowning today." Renzo climbed into the car.

"What are we supposed to do?" Kasper shouted.

"Wait here, put the van in the garage."

"Kill the guy?" Kasper pointed toward the house.

"No, not yet. I may need the husband to make the wife a bit more compliant."

Nick sat bound to the chair in the center of his garage. His head snapped back as Popov's punch crunched into the side of his head. Blood already poured from his lip and nose, his eye beginning to swell as he gasped for breath.

"Renzo said to leave him alive," Kasper said as he looked out the window.

"He's still alive," Popov grabbed him by the hair, lifting his head up and looking in his good eye.

"Where did Renzo go?" Erik asked.

"There's something in the bunker."

"Besides the dead?"

"He's losing focus." Kasper looked at his watch. "Whatever is down there, he thinks it's more important than blowing up the dam."

"So, we blow it without him," said Popov. "Let him die—drown with everyone else."

"He's no idiot. That's why he has the trigger."

"And this guy." Popov slapped the back of Nick's head.

"His wife is helping Renzo. Once he's done with her, he'll kill her, and then you can kill him."

Popov smiled.

The bullet hit Popov in the left temple, exiting the right side of his skull in an explosion of bone and tissue that coated the side of Erik's face. Erik spun toward the shooter but never saw him as the second bullet caught him in the left eye.

Kasper dived left, behind the wall, below the window the bullets had come through, gun drawn.

Nick didn't know who the shooter was. Marcus and Dreyfus were living out their daily routines at this hour, unaware of the watch, the future, or the danger. He guessed it must be Shannon outside.

Nick watched as Kasper crawled along the garage floor below the windows and toward the open door to the mudroom. Out of his range of sight, Kasper pulled out his phone and dialed.

"We need—"

A gunshot from the mudroom doorway echoed in the garage, startling Nick. It was a moment until he heard the footsteps behind him, someone approaching. He turned his head to see Kasper's twitching leg in the corner of the garage.

Nick waited until his savior came around and crouched in front of him.

"Hey, Nick," Zane said.

Nick rubbed his freed wrists, blotted the blood from his nose and swollen lip, and glared at Zane with his good eye. "What are you doing?"

Zane looked out the garage window before turning to him. "As we've moved back in time, it seems our goals have converged."

"I doubt that," Nick said as he rose to his feet.

"I help you save Julia and you help me save the president."

"So now you're going to *save* the president?"

"My job was always to save him."

"That's rich," Nick said. "You've killed how many today?"

"And how many of them are still dead?"

"That's not the point." Though, this early in the day, they *were* all still alive.

"My only job is to save the president."

"Without regard for who dies?"

"Like I said, everyone I killed is alive."

Nick shook his head, wondering how that was supposed to comfort him.

"Your wife is alive," Zane pointed out.

"And how many times did you make her suffer? Who's to say you won't kill us all in the end?"

"I need to stop the murder of the president. It's why I was called; it's why I stole the watch from your friend Dreyfus; it's why I needed to know where the president was; and it's why I need you to help me get in where they are now."

"He's dead...they're all dead."

"I know. I need to get down there to figure out when and how Renzo killed him. If I can reach a time *before* they pull the trigger, it'll be stopped. You know how this game is played. Only you and I remember the future. Renzo won't see me coming."

Nick thought on his words, knew them to be true.

"And I'll stop Renzo from blowing the dam," Zane added.

"Bullshit. That was you."

"Never was. Think about it."

"The first thing you wanted from me, the thing you put me through hell over, was the satchel."

"Correct, because it was Renzo's and the smart key was in it."

Nick looked at him, confused.

"See, the smart key's actually the detonator for the bomb. The bag also contained info on Renzo and his team. I was trying to stop everything he was doing."

"Your methods suck. Why didn't you just tell me?"

"Because I trust no one but myself. Dreyfus gave you the satchel he took from me. I didn't know you, and I didn't have time to screw around. I get one chance at this—one chance at saving the president."

"And the people in this town?"

"President comes first, dam comes second. But they're one and the same now."

Nick tried to digest the words of the man he'd thought of as nothing but evil.

"Look, Nick, I still don't know who's behind today's attacks. It's not just Renzo. I'm turning to you and your friends because I have nowhere else to turn and time is running out."

"Assuming I help you, and assuming we succeed...then what?"

"You go on with your life, I go on with mine."

"That's it?"

"What else is there?" Zane asked. "I'll have saved the president and everyone else."

"But no one will know."

"I'll know, you'll know. Does it really matter what the public knows? I'll have done something that changes the course of history."

"But at what cost?"

"What do you mean?"

Nick shook his head. "How can you be so cold?"

"Let me ask you a question," Zane said. "How far would you go to save Katy?"

"She's my daughter."

"Is her life worth more than a thousand lives?"

Nick shook his head at the impossible question. "She's my daughter," he repeated.

"Exactly. You'd do anything. The value of a life is relative to how much we care for them, how much they mean to us. In my work, no one means more than the president."

"But you're not in the Secret Service."

"I was a soldier. A good one. And I guess I still am."

Nick tilted his head, thinking. "And then you died...and your father made sure the world knew that. It got him elected."

"Good for you," Zane with a hint of admiration. "You figured out who my father is."

"He's not my favorite person."

"Well, that's something else we have in common. As dislikable as the man is, he didn't know I was still alive. He and the world were made to think I was dead. Renzo was a soldier under my command in Akbiquestan. He killed twenty-two men and set me up to take the blame. I was charged in secret with murder and treason and was about to be court-martialed."

"So you faked your own death?"

"Someone did it for me. Gave me a new identity, made me a soldier again. I still believed in our country, even if it no longer believed in me. So I went to work for that someone, doing the things no one else would do."

"Killing people..."

"And much worse."

"You killed Shamus, his wife, and his friend." Nick shook his head in disgust. "You killed a ninety-three-year-old man."

"No." Zane shook his head. "He was barely alive when I got there. His wife and friend had already passed. Shamus told me it was Renzo. Said he demanded a vault be opened. Shamus died protecting whatever was in his vault."

"But you still stole the key from around his neck."

"I did. That's why I went there."

"So, you would have killed him anyway?"

"Only if I had to. Shamus gave me his key and told me to stop the madness. I took the other from the neck of his assistant. He told me the third one was with your friend Dreyfus. He was not an easy man to find."

Nick began to pace. "So what's really going on? Renzo kills the president, kills everyone down there, to break into a *vault*?"

"Shamus's secret vault, yes. Whatever's in there, that's why he took your wife."

Nick tried to accept everything Zane was telling him, but he kept returning to the same indisputable fact: "You killed my wife."

"I'm sorry, Nick, but I'd do it again to save the president. And don't forget, I just saved you."

As crazy as it felt, Nick understood the man. He didn't agree with him, but he understood him.

"You help me get into the bunker," Zane said, "and I'll help you save your wife."

Nick Quinn and Janos Zane stood in Dreyfus's kitchen as Dreyfus pushed his half-eaten breakfast away, transfixed by the video Nick was showing.

"Everyone dead?" Dreyfus asked.

Nick nodded. He had explained it all, showed him the footage. And while it had been relatively easy to convince him the other times, this time was different. Dreyfus was a true skeptic. Nick wasn't sure if that was a function of the earlier hour, the day, the moment....

"How did you get the watch?" Dreyfus asked Zane.

"I stole it from you."

"What?" Dreyfus turned to Nick. "What else happened?"

"It's probably best you don't know. But the Killian Dam was blown, a lot of people were killed, and it's about to happen again."

"I need you to get me into the bunker," Zane said to Dreyfus.

"Impossible."

"Everyone down there is dead already. I need to figure out exactly what happened so I can go back an hour and stop it all. And you're going to help me."

"Go to hell," Dreyfus said.

"Okay, okay, back to your corners," Nick said, throwing up his hands. "You can get us down there."

"And how do we get past the guards?"

"Shamus said there was an airshaft," Nick said. "So did you."

Dreyfus stared at him. "I never said that."

"Yes, you did. A few hours from now."

"Do you have any idea how crazy that sounds?"

Nick nodded. "I do. It's the watch. Remember what it does."

Dreyfus closed his eyes, thinking.

"The air shaft was left open," Nick told him. "That's how the flood-waters got in. Shamus said it's on the other side of Hadley's Woods."

"It's a half mile long. It's a crawl. And there are multiple security protocols."

"Can you disable them?" Zane asked.

"Only if I'm there."

"Good, then you can lead the way."

Julia dreamt. She dreamt of Nick and Katy and summers in Cape Cod, taking Katy to the beach for the first time, her fascination with the sand, grabbing it in handfuls, the grains slipping through her small fingers, tasting it, trying to spit out.

As joyous as the dream was, Julia couldn't shake the sense of dread in the ether. It had permeated her day, her vision, and now her sleep: death was all around her.

As her eyes opened, Julia's head throbbed worse than any migraine she'd had. Confused at her surroundings, she tried to get her bearings before her eyes finally fell on Renzo.

He leaned in close. "If a smile isn't painted on your face in the next ten seconds, you're dead. Act different, signal anyone, and I will not only kill you...I'll kill your husband."

Julia struggled awake in the front seat of Renzo's Suburban and she realized they were driving into Hadley's Woods. Renzo stopped at the gate and waved. The three guards smiled, nodded to him and Julia, and opened the barrier.

Arriving in the main drive, they got out of the car and hustled into the small house, nodding to Sergeant Walker and four Marines who stood guard.

They headed through the entrance and straight to the two marines at the security checkpoint.

"Morning, Ms. Quinn," Private Michael Lowery greeted her.

"Morning, Mike," Julia said, forcing a smile. "Happy Fourth."

"That it is." He turned to the other marine and nodded. "You're both good to go."

The other marine waved them through, and they climbed into the elevator.

With the door fully closed, Julia turned to Renzo, her fear turning to anger. "What's going on?"

Renzo didn't say a word as they descended.

Dreyfus led the way through the woods, leaping over rocks, ducking under tree branches, with Nick and Zane right behind him. Each had a small bag on their back and a gun at their waist.

Dreyfus halted at a stand of rocks on a small hill, crouched down, crawled, and disappeared. Zane and Nick followed him through a narrow entrance into a small cave, his flashlight illuminating a large circular grate in the wall in front of them. He pulled an electric screwdriver from his bag and removed the grate. Before entering the three-foot circular shaft, he pulled out a device.

Crawling into the shaft's tight confines, he stopped at a small red light and slid the device halfway past the glowing LED, its screen coming to life with a yellow sensor. Dreyfus pulled out a small right-angle screwdriver, slipped it into an unseen hole, and quickly spun it while watching the readout on the screen. Six turns and the readout flashed green.

Without a word, he turned off his flashlight and continued forward through the metal tube, awkwardly belly-crawling into the pitch black.

The elevator door opened. Renzo pushed Julia out and opened the first security door of the airlock. They stepped in, the door closing behind them, and Renzo quickly released the next door.

Walking into the vestibule lounge, Julia saw a near-empty tray of donuts, water, and coffee, surprised that no one was there. "Where's Charlie?"

As Renzo opened the large white door into the facility, Julia saw the body. She had never seen anyone dead except her parents at their wake as they lay in their coffins. This was different. This man had been murdered—she could see the bullet hole on the right side of his forehead. She fought back a gag reflex, but that sensation quickly dissipated to grief as she realized who it was. "Oh, my God."

Charlie, his broad shoulders bursting his suit. Always so kind—

Renzo grabbed her by the arm and stepped over the body. Two more lay by the entrance, Kylie and Janice, the president's legal advisors.

As Julia was dragged deeper into the complex, they passed the main conference room, its door ajar and two Secret Service agents lying atop each other, shot in the head. And then she saw the sight that completed the nightmare: President McManus, slumped back in his chair, half of his head missing. The ten people in the room were all frozen in horrid positions of death, contorted, mangled, and covered in glistening scarlet.

Julia tried to cry out but couldn't make a sound. A moment later, her knees gave out and she collapsed.

"How about a little light?" Zane whispered.

Dreyfus didn't answer. A hundred yards in, a red glow illuminated the shaft ahead of them. A second LED cast eerie shadows upon their approach.

To create a bunker for survival in the event of catastrophic event, an event where outsiders would grow desperate, where people would turn on one another, Dreyfus had needed to include extreme protocols. In fact, he had insisted upon them for Shamus, knowing the tenacity and desperation of those seeking to survive.

If violated, the tunnel would not only close and lock the gate within the bunker, but it would also send an electric current through the shaft, shocking any man, animal, or beast that dared enter.

"Any way to move a little faster? We're on the clock," Zane said from the darkness.

"We screw it up and we're stuck crawling a half-mile for nothing... and believe me, you won't like the intruder countermeasures."

"And if we don't get there in time, you'll have the death of thousands on your conscience."

Slipping the angled screwdriver in the hole, Dreyfus made quick work of the second shut-off switch and continued ahead.

Knees and elbows aching, they wiggled through the cold, metallic tunnel. Dreyfus didn't tell Zane that six more red LEDs remained, each requiring almost a minute to disable.

Renzo dragged Julia down the stairs to the lower level, through the halls, and past three more bodies before coming to a halt.

"Open it."

She turned to see Renzo pointing at the smooth, seamless, safe room door.

"I think I'm going to be sick," she said.

"Please open it." He pointed at the large red plunger-button beside the door and pressed it with his palm, but nothing happened.

"They're all dead...." Julia's words seemed to be an effort to convince herself. She had never been more scared, more confused. "Everyone's dead. What happened?"

"I can't explain it. I need you to open the safe room." Renzo slammed the large button three times in anger.

"I can't," she said, her mind starting to come to grips with the horror around her. "It can only be opened from the inside."

She looked up at the green light above the door. "Who's in there? Survivors? How many people survived?"

Renzo checked his watch.

Julia's mind was spinning, piecing things together, finally becoming focused again.

"Open it," Renzo demanded. "*Now.*"

"It's a *safe room*. It can only be opened from the inside." Julia's voice quavered as tears filled her eyes.

"Don't tell me that!"

Julia shook her head, unsure how to react. "I..."

"Open this fucking door!" Renzo screamed. He pounded on the door, kicked it over and over again. He looked up at the camera and lost it. "I'm going to kill you!" he told whoever was inside. "Do you understand that? You betrayed me, you set me up. I'm going to kill you all!"

Renzo spun and grabbed Julia by the arm, then marched off, dragging her behind him. He rounded the corner and came to the large vault door.

"This I know you can open."

"It needs Shamus's handprint and pass code in addition to mine."

"Bullshit, you opened it for me for my security inspection. Open it."

Julia looked at the door, at the keypad and palm reader. She placed her hand in the reader and punched in a series of numbers. A red light flashed with a shrill beep. She took a breath and punched the numbers in again. The light flashed again along with the beep. Julia looked down, tears flowing down her cheeks, afraid to look at Renzo, and punched the numbers once more, without success.

Renzo's anger and frustration mounted with each failure. He pulled his gun and placed it to her head. "You have three minutes to get it open. Call Shamus, call God, I don't care, but if it's not open in three minutes, you're dead."

Defeating the last sensor, Dreyfus caught sight of a white glow ahead.

He pulled out several more tools and made quick work of the screws and wires of the large valve-like structure in the floor at the end of the shaft and pulled off the grate.

Lowering himself down from the opening, Dreyfus hit the floor of the mechanical room. He drew his gun and scanned the room.

"Where are we and where might they be?" Zane said as he joined him.

"Mechanical room, sublevel, of two levels. The vault's on the other side of this level. Out the door to the right, then left one hundred feet."

Zane pulled his gun, checked the hall, and walked out to his left. Fifty feet down the hall, he stopped and looked at the safe room door: no doorknob, no hinges, all mechanical parts safely ensconced within the steel shell. Only a red plunger button. He saw no way to penetrate it. He looked at the green light above.

"Who do you think is in there?" Nick asked as he checked the time on the pocket watch.

"No idea," Dreyfus said. "Either a staff member or the people who helped Renzo kill everyone. They could burst out and kill us all."

"Not if they don't know we're here," Nick said.

"They know." Dreyfus pointed up at the camera above the door. "They have monitors in there—they see everything. Make no mistake, we're being watched."

"Worry about that later," Nick said as he headed down the hall. "We're here for Julia."

Nick rounded the corner to see Julia's right hand on a print reader while her left punched numbers into a keypad. Tears poured down her face as she desperately hit the keypad.

"Julia!"

Renzo grabbed Julia and pulled her into a chokehold, gun up in front of her. "Back up!"

Nick and Dreyfus both raised their guns as Renzo shrank behind his human shield.

"Nick!" Julia cried out.

"Let her go." Nick took a step forward.

"You killed the president," Dreyfus said. "You and your friends killed everyone down here."

"No," Renzo said. "It was the man locked in the safe room. He killed them."

"Let her go," Nick said evenly. "Or I'll shoot you where you stand."

"And risk hitting your wife?" Renzo jerked Julia's head closer to his. "I don't think so. In fact, you'll both put your guns down now."

"Nick, do what he says," said Dreyfus.

"No."

Renzo wrapped his arms tighter around Julia's neck. She began to twist and kick, struggling to breathe.

"Let her go." Zane stepped from behind Dreyfus and Nick, gun held high in both hands.

"JC?" Renzo said in shock. "Wow, how the hell...."

"Renzo." That's all Zane said as he pulled the trigger.

"You don't unders—" The bullet sailed in, marksman perfect, an inch above Julia's head catching Renzo in the forehead, the bullet entering and spinning through his skull, smashing him back against the wall, where he crumpled dead on the ground.

Nick caught Julia in his arms and carried her across the hall to an empty lounge, where he laid her on a couch.

Zane walked alone back down the hall. Rounding the corner, he passed the mechanical room and came to a halt outside the safe room. He looked up at the green light and the camera that pointed down at him.

He gathered his thoughts as he looked at the large smooth steel barrier. He reached into his pocket and pulled out the watch. He stared at it a moment, then held it up to the camera as if it were some sort of identification. He stood there waiting, time ticking by. Ten seconds, thirty seconds. He turned to leave when a heavy thud came from the walls; he turned back and watched as the door slowly slid open.

Nick handed Julia a bottle of water. She took a sip and closed her eyes. "Everybody's dead: both presidents, the prime minister, everyone...." She opened her eyes and looked at Nick. "Charlie."

"I know," Nick said. "Just drink that down."

"Charlie has small children.... A daughter Katy's age." Julia wiped tears away from her face, then looked to Nick. "What do we do?"

"Zane's handling it. The world will be down here in a few minutes."

"So much death." Julia could barely speak. "How could Renzo do this? How could this happen?"

Nick took her in his arms.

Zane stood with his pistol aimed, watching as the safe room door slid fully open. A moment later, a man was revealed.

Zane hadn't seen him in six months.

"Are you hurt?" he asked, gun still up.

"No," the man said.

Zane approached him but remained vigilant, keeping his weapon trained on him. "What the hell happened?"

"Renzo began shooting," Carter Bull said.

"He couldn't have done this alone."

"No. There was at least one other person. I managed to get in here."

"Not very heroic." Zane stepped in the room and looked at the desk, the security monitors, and the TV on mute. He looked at the large, curtained window, seeing the swaying trees and snowcapped Rocky Mountains, quickly realizing he was looking at a digital display of the landscape. "This is where you called me from?"

Carter nodded. "I only called you an hour ago."

Zane didn't mention their conversations throughout the future day: neither his forward march to get the watch nor his hourly steps back to this moment.

"You can lower the gun, for Christ's sake," Carter said.

Zane took a breath and holstered his weapon.

"Well," Carter said. "You got it. I can't believe you got it."

Zane nodded.

"And it obviously works."

Zane pulled out a bottle of water and drank it as he sat on the floor, leaning back against the wall, his body finally relaxing after nearly twenty-four hours of stress. He nodded again.

"I never doubted you," Carter said with pride. "So, you've been to the future?"

"Ten hours into the future and then back. I killed a lot of people to get here."

"And soon you'll save the president. Save everyone and prevent a tragedy like no other."

Zane peered out the door at the body at the end of the hall, a reminder of how much death he'd wrought, how many commandments he'd broken. Today, it felt nothing like the killing he'd done in the past. Today had changed him. The watch had changed him, made him realize that the choices we make not only transform our own destiny, but that of so many around us.

"Renzo?" Carter asked.

"Dead. Down the hall, if you care to see him." Zane sat up straight and looked at Carter. "How could he be in a position like that? How the hell could someone like *him* be in charge of protecting the president?"

"A highly decorated soldier," Carter said as he ran his hand across his silver, bristly hair. "A hero, West Point, no indication of a troubled background. It's not the first time bad men have gotten into government."

"*Hero*? He set me up. He was the one who blew up the plane in Akbiquestan. He killed those men, not me, and my life was destroyed over it."

"How do you know that?"

"He told me."

"Really?" Carter took that in. "Well, he's dead."

"This isn't over yet. He'll still be alive an hour earlier. And my life is still ruined."

"But you'll save the president—not many people can say that."

"I'll never be able to say it either. An hour from now, this'll have never happened." Zane climbed to his feet and walked to the door. "As soon as I step back an hour, I'll stop Renzo, have him arrested for treason, and, if need be, killed. The president will be out of danger."

Zane fell silent, the moment hung in the air.

"What was it like?" Carter asked, unable to hide his excitement. "Moving backwards through time?"

"Like dying, every time. Like dying and being pulled back. Cold, dark." He turned to Carter. "It was death, over and over again."

Carter nodded, his expression serious.

Zane refocused. "How did you know about the watch?"

"In 1981," Carter said, "I was a captain pushing Pentagon papers between the president and the head of the Joint Chiefs. I was at the

Washington Hilton Hotel with a close friend of my father's. Shamus was a bit older than Dad and had been a great mentor. We grew close after my father's passing....

"It was the day President Reagan was shot. Shamus said something that seemed impossible. If the president died from his wounds, he said, there was still a way to save him, but he'd have only twelve hours. I didn't get it. It made no sense, even in this illogical world. Shamus said there was no guarantee it would work. If he went back in time, he'd have to know every detail of what had occurred: who was involved, details on the assassin, the doctors, time of death, everything.

"I still couldn't believe him. The sanest man I knew was telling me to believe something *crazy*. Shamus assured me it was true but said it could only be done by him. No guns or violence. All he needed were the exact names and details of the shooting...and his pocket watch.

"That threw me, but what he said next was equally crazy. He told me if he did do the impossible, no one would ever know. The president being killed would never have happened, and he and I would never have had the conversation.

"I'd seen Shamus's watch. He always carried it back then, constantly checked the time. I held it once, years earlier: gold and silver, Latin engravings, master craftsmanship from a forgotten age.

"I have to admit, I completely dismissed what Shamus was claiming. I figured it was senility. Either that or my dad's old friend was flat-out crazy. Instead, I focused on the reality of the doctors trying to save Reagan. Of course, the president survived via modern medicine instead of ancient watches, and Shamus's crazy story faded from my mind.

"When the world fell apart, when President McManus was shot, that memory became crystal-clear. But to achieve the impossible, I needed someone who'd achieved the impossible for me time and time again. I needed you."

"Colonel Carter Bull," Zane said, introducing the tall, sil-ver-haired man.

"Nice to meet you," Nick said, shaking his hand.

They were in the hall, Renzo's body lying twenty feet away, Zane having asked Nick to come out from the lounge.

"He's the one that sent me on this chase," Zane said. "He was in the safe room."

Nick stared at him, unsure what to say.

"I know about the watch," Carter said. "Shamus is a friend. But Zane is a hero."

"It's a bit uncomfortable out here," Nick said looking at Renzo's and the other bodies down the hall. "I need to get back to Julia."

"Of course," Carter said. "I just wanted to say thank you."

Nick looked at the bodies and nodded; there was nothing to be thankful for. He walked back into the conference room and closed the door. Before he could speak to Julia, the door opened and Zane poked his head in the room.

"Do you have second?" He motioned for Nick to join him out-side again.

Nick nodded. He turned and whispered something to Julia, who sat on the couch sipping water, before following Zane out the door again.

"Thank you," Zane said.

Nick nodded. Carter Bull was nowhere to be seen.

"In five minutes, this'll be over." Zane said as he looked at the pocket watch. "Go back to your life, enjoy your wife. The president, everyone down here will be alive. Renzo and his men will be arrested at thirty seconds after the hour begins. I promise you."

"They should be killed," Nick said.

"I'm sure the courts will agree with you."

"What about your assassins—the people you said would hunt my wife and me down if anything happened to you?"

"Don't worry," Zane said. "There never were any. I just needed you to think there were. I needed your fear, Nick." He raised his hands to stop Nick from responding. "Always remember: in battle, we'll do anything to win. It's not the power of the bomb but the fear of it. You may not hold all the cards—I didn't—but if the enemy believes you do, you can win without firing a shot. Don't you use those tactics in business? Sun Tzu, *The Art of War*?"

"Not in *my* business," Nick said. "How will I know that Renzo's been dealt with? It's not that I don't trust you, but...I don't trust you."

Zane smiled. "I'll call you. Give you the all-clear."

"You're a sick man, but thank you...I think," Nick said. "Remind me to never be on your bad side again."

Zane nodded. A moment later, he looked up at Nick. "Do you think our sins are washed away once everyone's alive again?"

Nick remained silent, unsure of the answer.

"I don't either." Zane reached out and shook Nick's hand. "I'm sorry for what I put you through."

"I'm sorry for you too."

Zane walked down the hall. He stopped and looked back with a smile. "And Nick? For the next two hours, don't change a thing."

"He's been through a lot," Zane said as he sat down in the safe room.

"Tough times call for tough people," Carter said.

"They aren't soldiers, though. They haven't been to war, seen death like this. Most *soldiers* haven't seen carnage like this. Nick Quinn's been through hell."

"I understand, but there are bigger things than Nick Quinn."

"Maybe life isn't always about the bigger things," Zane said. "Maybe we're missing the point."

"Don't feed me that new-age bullshit. This was bigger than one man and his family. This was about saving the president in a highly unorthodox way. You're saving the president, JC."

"Am I saving him, or was this about saving you?"

"You should know me better than that," Carter said. "You're not only saving the president but possibly preventing World War Three."

"I agree." Zane nodded. "It was about more than saving the president."

"What do you mean?"

"Renzo."

"What about him?"

"All those men, the spec-ops teams...I had friends in those planes, the pilots, radio men. Brothers, really. They're all dead, and I was blamed for it."

"So said the evidence," Carter said. "I did the best I could. I made you a hero."

"In death, postmortem," Zane said. "The only person to benefit from that was my father."

"You know," Carter pointed out, "if you went to trial, they'd have executed you."

"Not if they knew the truth."

"Meaning what? That Renzo did it?"

Zane nodded.

"Well, if we knew that," Carter said, "he wouldn't have been the hero, and he damn sure wouldn't have been on the president's Secret Service team. None of this would have happened."

"I didn't realize there was more to the story," Zane added.

"About Renzo?"

"About you. You covered it all up, made him a hero, and saw your opportunity."

"For what?"

"To get me to work for you in your special programs. A dead man has little choice but to agree."

Carter stared at Zane and finally nodded. "Yeah, I saw the opportunity. That's what I do—I see things. I saw you facing a court-martial and death and I couldn't let that happen. So, yeah, you didn't have much choice, but it was a better choice than death."

"Quinn and his wife didn't have much choice."

"Why are we still talking about him?"

"You're missing my point," Zane said as he leaned forward, looking at Carter. "He has a watch too."

"*What*?"

Zane allowed Carter to digest his words. "I killed his wife in the future. I chased him and he chased me every hour until now, until I could finally tell him what I was doing. He could have killed me and we wouldn't be sitting here, but he didn't. He's a good man. Better than us."

"There are *two* watches?" Carter asked.

"Yes."

"So, he knows everything that's happened?"

"Painfully so."

"Can he be trusted?"

"To do what?"

"Keep his mouth shut?"

"Who would believe a story like this? There's no proof. Technically, it never happened. He'll be haunted the rest of his days by this nightmare and there's not a soul who would believe him if he told the story."

"I can't imagine...." Carter thought for a moment. "Maybe you're right—maybe we should do something for him."

"I think if we left him alone, that'd be enough."

"May I see it?" Carter asked.

Zane reached in his pocket and pulled out the watch, placing it in Carter's palm. Carter rolled it about, looking carefully at the etchings. He pressed the crown, opening the cover, and looked at the watch face. Two minutes to 10 a.m.

"That thing is as dangerous as anything," Zane said.

"But also a miracle." Carter studied it, fascinated. "Think of the possibilities...."

"I don't know where it originally came from, but once I go back an hour from now and the president's alive and Renzo's in prison, it should be destroyed."

"I agree." Carter looked closer at the detail. "How does it work?"

"No idea. It just works. I kept it with me and it works."

"It's incredible...this thing's saved not only the president, but thousands of lives."

Zane looked up at Carter. "You said thousands?"

"Yeah," Carter said. "The blowing of the dam."

"The dam bombing happened twice—at six o'clock this evening and at noon. Both in the future, and you haven't been there."

Carter looked up from the watch. "What's your point?"

"How did you know?"

"Oh, JC..." Carter clutched the watch in his left fist while his right arm snapped up, pistol in hand. And shot Zane in the head.

CHAPTER 3

8:00 AM

"Holy shit!" Marcus shouted. "Look out!"

Nick heard the blaring horn before he saw the car heading straight for him. He swerved the Jeep back into his lane, barely missing the rusted Ford Bronco and the man giving him the finger.

"You okay?" Marcus held tight to the roll bar. "This is not a good day to die. We *save* people from accidents, not get into them."

Nick turned to Marcus, confused and shaken as he gripped the wheel of his Jeep, trying to regain his bearings.

"You look like you saw a ghost." Marcus opened a bottle of water and chugged it. "Maybe I should drive."

"I'm okay," Nick said, though he wasn't. The pocket watch had never transported him into a moving vehicle. He focused on the road, and his thoughts cleared as he calmed his heart.

"And what the hell happened to your face? You look like shit."

Nick glanced in the rearview mirror and got a look at himself. Bruised, scraped, and singed from the day's events. He did look like shit.

"All that happened back at the accident?"

Nick nodded, not in the frame of mind to explain everything again. Yet.

"Okay." Marcus stared at him with a mix of confusion and sympathy. "A bit of water and wind'll make you feel better."

Nick looked in the rearview mirror at the Jet Ski they were towing, at the kitesurfing gear in the back seat.

"I need to go home." Nick hit the brakes and pulled a 180 in the middle of the street.

"Um, okay." Marcus grabbed the roll bar again. "I'm so confused right now."

"Good morning," President McManus said. "This is figuratively and literally the dawn of a new day, a day for peace, a day when we all agree that it is time to begin a new era."

President McManus sat at the center of a long conference table; to his left sat President Maximov Egorenko of Russia, a heavyset man with tired eyes and a quick smile, who nodded in assent, then repeated the same phrase in Russian. "*Dos veida cnost.*"

"*Zha rvost kqei,*" Akbiquestani Prime Minister Zulich Kharda said in his native tongue as he took his seat to the right of the other two heads of state. His close-cropped beard flecked with gray gave him an older appearance than his thirty-seven years.

All three spoke before a young woman in a pinstriped pantsuit who focused her camera phone, recording video. "Thank you. Now just a couple of photos."

Everyone smiled as she took three pictures and left.

"So much easier than having the bloody media watch our every move," McManus said. "How did you sleep?"

"Very well," Egorenko said. "This is exhausting."

"It's kind of you to accommodate our time difference with early start," Kharda said in significantly rougher English.

"I'm up at six every day," McManus said. "The earlier the better for me."

The room grew more relaxed, everyone taking off their suit jackets, leaning back in their chairs, and sipping their coffee and tea.

"The three of us got more done in the past three days than our dozens of negotiators could do in two years," McManus noted.

"That's because there were no attorneys and no soldiers." Kharda smiled. "People forget, we all love our children."

Three aides walked in and sat across from their respective leaders.

Nick dropped Marcus off and drove the hundred yards to his own house. He pulled into the driveway, pulled out his phone, and dialed.

"Hello?" Zane answered.

"Hey," Nick said. "Are we good?"

"Nick?"

"Yeah."

"We're all good," Zane said.

"You're sure?" Nick held his breath. "Everyone is safe? The president is safe?"

"Positive. Everyone's been rounded up," Zane said. "I'm here with Carter—he said you can rest easy. He told me to thank you. Where are you?"

"Thank God." Nick sighed. "I'm home. But I gotta go. I'll call you later."

Nick leapt from the Jeep and ran in the house.

"Julia," he called out as he ran up the stairs.

"Hi, Daddy," Katy said as she poked her head out of her room.

"Hey, pumpkin." He kissed her on the head as he ran by.

"Nick?" Julia emerged from her closet. "You okay?"

"I'll take Katy to daycare," he said. "You go to your meeting."

"What about kitesurfing?" She looked him over. "Are you okay? Did you get hurt helping those people in the accident and you're not telling me?"

Nick took her by the shoulders and stared into her eyes. "Go to your meeting."

"Oh my God, Nick. What happened to your face?" Julia touched his swollen lip, his swollen eye from where Kasper had beaten him an hour from now. "You did get hurt. How the hell did this happen?"

She ran in the bathroom, emerging with a wet washcloth and applying it to his eye.

"Damn it, Nick—"

"I'm fine." Nick took the washcloth. "You need to go. I don't want you to be late for your meeting."

Julia stared back, trying to grasp what Nick was saying.

"Go, it's important. You can still make it."

"How do you know about my meeting?"

"The president is waiting."

Julia stared at Nick, shocked and confused. "How the hell do you know about that?"

Nick put a finger to his lips.

"No one knows about this meeting. How could *you* know?" Julia began to panic. "You can't tell a soul! This is national security, Nick. I could get in a lot of trouble—"

"Shhh, it's okay. My swollen lips are sealed. If you're late, they won't let you in."

Julia reached in her closet, grabbed her shoes, and ran out of the room, kissing Nick's cheek as she passed him by. "Love you."

"Daddy's taking you to daycare, honey," she said as she patted Katy on the head on her way out.

Nick watched her hustle down the stairs, loving the energy that poured out of her, always so confident and sexy. He couldn't bear to live without her.

A sudden thought hit him. He chased behind her, taking the stairs two at a time. "Wait!"

She didn't hear him as she ran out the front door.

Nick burst out the front door. Julia halted, getting in her car and turning around with concern in her eyes.

Nick ran up to her and kissed her on the lips. "I just wanted to say good luck and I love you."

Nick crouched, kissed Katy on the cheek, then her other cheek, her forehead, then her nose. Katy wrapped her arms around his neck and squeezed tight. Then he opened the daycare facility's main door and followed her in. "You be a good girl and we'll pick you up later."

"Are you going to take me every day, Daddy?" Katy walked like she owned the place.

"Would you like that?"

Katy nodded as she ate the last bit of her toaster strudel. "I like your breakfast better than Mommy's."

"Well, whatever you do, don't tell Mommy that. She's still upset about the whole cake-for-breakfast thing last weekend."

"Our secret." Katy put her finger against her lips.

"Good morning, Nick," Sara Bitton greeted them, Nick's face causing her to do a subtle double-take. "This is a surprise."

"Or the beginning of a new routine," Nick said. "Thanks for everything."

"Bye, Daddy," Katy said.

"Bye, pumpkin."

Nick walked out, got back into his Jeep, and smiled.

"Thanks, Jimmy." Julia nodded at the guard as he lifted the gate and she drove into Hadley's Woods. She rode up the dirt road and parked across from a Humvee.

"Good morning, Sergeant."

Sergeant Walker nodded. "Nice to see you again, Ms. Quinn."

"Nice to be early," she said as she handed him a tray of coffee.

"Thank you, ma'am."

Julia walked in the small white house and nodded to Private Lowery, the guard standing beside the elevator.

"Morning, Ms. Quinn." Lowery's pressed camouflage uniform looked sharp, as always.

"Morning, Mike. Another beautiful day."

"That it is." He turned to the other marine and nodded. "You're good to go."

She rode down the elevator, stepped into the small vestibule, placed her hand in the palm reader, and proceeded through each of the airlock's security doors.

"Good morning, Charlie." Julia smiled, finding him standing inside the small reception lounge.

"Good morning, Ms. Quinn. How are you today?"

"I'm well. Did you speak to your daughter last night?"

"She passed. Thank God she got her mother's brains for fourth-grade math."

"I fear math."

"New math, old math, it's all hard math to me."

Julia laughed as she continued through the white door and down the hall.

After dropping off Katy, Nick returned home to find Zane's black Lincoln Town Car parked in his driveway, Zane leaning against it.

"Hey," Nick said as he got out of his car.

Zane nodded and smiled at Nick as Carter Bull emerged from the rear of the car.

"For the record," Nick said, "that's the first time I got Katy to day-care on time ever."

"Mr. Quinn." Carter offered his hand. "Carter Bull."

Nick shook his hand. "Nice to meet you."

The man was far more polished than when Nick had seen him last: suit pressed, his silver, buzz-cut hair clean. A man oblivious to what had happened to him the first time he rode through this hour.

"You helped save the day." Carter held the door open for Nick. "We'd like to include you in the day's events."

"I don't understand," Nick lied, looking back and forth between Carter and Zane.

"We thought you might enjoy being with your wife and the president of the United States in what is surely to be a historic moment."

"The president?" Nick feigned surprise as he glanced at Zane.

"That's right," Carter said. "We'll fill you in on the way. Zane said you're worth the extra trouble, though he's tightlipped as to why. "

"I would love that," Nick said. "Can I just grab a suit?"

"Beautiful home," Carter called out as he looked around the foyer. He closely examined the grandfather clock. "You both must work hard."

"We try," Nick said, as he came down the stairs in a blue Ralph Lauren pinstripe suit. "Always working."

"Not much time for sleep," Carter said.

"Julia goes to bed early. I'm more of a night owl."

"I'm an up-at-dawn kind of guy," Carter said. "It's a military thing."

"Not me." Nick finished looping his tie. "I'm not up till after 7:00—I need an alarm clock every day. Didn't hit the pillow till 3:00 last night."

"Playing?"

"Working," Nick said as he shut the front door behind them. "I set my alarm for 7:15, gave myself fifteen whole extra minutes. Felt like I was dead when it rang.... I *so* wanted to throw it out the window."

Carter smiled as Nick followed him into the rear of the Town Car and Zane drove them away.

"You have a terrific wife," Carter said. "She organized much of today on behalf of Shamus Hennicot and the president."

"Do you know Shamus?"

"A very close friend." Carter nodded. "Not many men more powerful than him. He trusts only a few and no one more than your wife."

Zane turned into Hadley's Woods. They bumped and jostled over the dirt road, finally coming to the security gate.

"Can I have your ID?" Carter held out his hand.

Nick passed him his license and the older man got out and began a dialogue with the three men at the gate.

"What the hell is going on?" Nick whispered as he leaned over the front seat to Zane. "Everything's so formal with him."

"We're bringing you to see your wife." There was an unexpected coldness to Zane's response.

"How did it go with Renzo this morning?"

Zane slowly turned to Nick, a sudden fire in his eyes. "Renzo?"

Carter got back in the car. "We're good to go."

Zane put the car in drive as the gate was lifted. They drove the quarter mile into the woods until they came to the small contingent of Marines.

Zane's eyes kept darting into the rearview mirror, looking at Nick.

A sudden blast of fear hit Nick as he realized that Zane had no idea who he was. This was all a charade.

Both rear doors were quickly opened by two young marines. Nick got out and turned, seeing all the men salute Carter, who returned the gesture with sharp formality.

"Good to see you again, Colonel," Sergeant Walker said.

Four young soldiers escorted Bull and Nick toward the small white house, while Zane remained in the car. When Nick looked, he caught Zane staring at him. In that glimpse, he recognized the Zane he'd first met—a man filled with anger, a deadly soldier on a mission, a stranger who'd kill anyone who got in his way.

The marines opened the door to the house and led them into the kitchen and the security checkpoint.

"Please empty your pockets," Private Lowery said, the pistol and the rifle slung over his shoulder leaving no room for argument. "How are you this morning, Colonel?"

"I'm fine, son." Carter smiled as he reached out and shook Lowery's hand. "Thank you for your hard work and service, both overseas and here."

Nick was filled with dread as he emptied his pockets into the small white bowl. He concealed his watch beneath his keys, phone, pocketknife, and billfold, which passed through a small scanner as he walked through the large one. With the colonel still engaged with Lowery, he quickly gathered up his things and tucked them all back in his pocket.

Carter followed suit, placing his gun, wallet and the watch in the white bowl and headed through the scanner.

"That's a beautiful pocket watch, colonel," Lowery said.

Carter picked up his watch and held it out. "Thank you, son."

He tucked it in his pocket, holstered his gun, and held the elevator door open for Nick, guiding him in.

"Keep up the good work, gentlemen," Carter said as the doors closed.

"What have you done?" Nick said, once they were alone and the elevator began its descent.

"Stepping back in time is something else, isn't it?" said Carter. "I thought I was going to die when it happened. It's...incredible."

"You have Zane's watch?"

"Yes, I do," Carter nodded. "You're the only other person in this world who knows what's happened today. Zane got me what I wanted. Now it's just a matter of erasing the evidence."

"You killed the president just to get the watch?" Nick realized it as he said it, his eyes widening with the epiphany. "To make Zane desperate to reverse the president's death, to force him to find the watch, to bring it all the way back here for you. It was all a ruse.... Shamus would have never given it up except in the most desperate of circumstances."

"Like the president," Carter said, "you're a bright man."

"You engineered all of this." Nick slammed him up against the elevator wall.

"Nick, so you know, everyone down here knows and trusts me. To them, I'm a hero and you're a stranger, a visitor...and right now, you're a threat."

The elevator door opened into a small vestibule.

Standing there was Renzo Cabral.

Carter's leap back in time had been disorienting at first.

The top-of-the-hour transition had caught him off-guard. There'd been no sound, no flash of light, no fanfare. He'd simply gasped, unable to catch his breath like a child who'd had the wind knocked out of them, but much worse. He found himself suffering full-body spasms on the floor of a small office in Shamus's bunker, stars dancing in his eyes as his head pounded, his body shivering from the cold, heart thundering on the verge of seizure. He hadn't been prepared for the side effects; he'd assumed it would be a quick shift with no physical consequences. His first clear thought was fear of failure: all his planning, all his strategy, might've been in vain as he prepared to meet death.

And then the air poured in, filling his lungs, breathing life into him. He lay there, panting like a dog, drinking in renewed hope that he'd survive.

He struggled to his feet and sat in a chair, clearing his mind.

He had his doubts, severe doubts that filled him with moments of regret for his treason, for the inhuman acts he'd so carefully planned out.Acts that had, beyond doubt, happened in the near future, for without them, Janos Zane would not have obtained the watch.

Carter looked in his hand and realized he possessed a miracle; he was now capable of the impossible. He could rewrite mistakes, win wars through a prism of intelligence beyond anyone's imagination. He could win any bet he placed, profit from the stock market without risk. He could experience the future and rewrite it to his liking.

And it had all been done without a single death. The president was alive, as were the Russian president and the Akbiquestani prime minister. They may have died in the future, but that was all wiped away now.

He'd regretted killing Zane an hour from now. The young man was a superb soldier. But now Zane lived in the present, unharmed, never to be aware of what he'd done hours from now. No memory of stealing the watch, of all the killing he'd carried out.

But what truly shocked Carter was there was *another* watch. He had never imagined that. Shamus had never mentioned it. *Two watches.* If he could accomplish so much with one, imagine what he could do with a pair....

"Who's this?" Renzo asked Carter Bull, nodding at Nick, who walked between.

"Julia Quinn's husband."

Nick gave Renzo a long, steady look but said nothing.

"And why is Julia Quinn's husband here?" Renzo whispered as they moved past the president's conference room flanked by two Secret Service agents, passing staff aides and agents along the way.

"You need her to open the vault," Carter said softly, then indicated Nick with a tilt of his head. "People do what you want when you dangle a loved one in front of them."

"How do you know about the vault?" Renzo asked.

"We both know there are things of great value in there. Don't worry, though, you can take whatever you want. I already have what I need." Carter paused in the hall. "Where is she?"

Nick looked around at the all the faces he had seen only in death, murdered by these two men who'd been sworn to protect them.

"She's tucked in the back," Renzo said as he led him down the stairs to the lower level.

"Why?" Carter asked as they arrived in the sub-level.

"Don't want her caught in the crossfire."

"You're still going to kill everyone?" Nick asked in shock as they walked to the rear of the lower level. "Hey!" Nick yelled to a Secret Service agent that stood at the end of the hall.

The wide-shouldered man looked their way. "Problem, sir?"

"No, Phil," Renzo told him. "Just giving a VIP tour."

"No one down here's taking orders from a stranger," Carter whispered.

"You're being set up," Nick told Renzo.

"What's he talking about?" asked Renzo.

"Desperation," Carter said.

"If your wife agreed to open that," Renzo pointed at a large steel vault door as they walked by, "maybe we wouldn't go through with it."

They arrived at a door marked *Mechanical.* Renzo unlocked the door, pushed Nick inside, and locked it behind him.

Renzo checked his watch. "At exactly 8:40, we start," he told Carter. "We'll have two minutes while the radio headsets are disabled before someone figures out what's going on. I start with the president and his guests and move outward. You start down here, moving upward."

Renzo handed Carter a sheathed military knife. "Use blades where possible. Every agent's in their assigned location. Take them first. The unknowns are the staff personnel. They move around at random. Count your kills. Separate counts for agents and the others. Understood?"

"It's not my first war," Carter said.

"No," Renzo agreed, "but it's your first assassination."

"Nick?" A mixture of shock, fear, and relief filled Julia's eyes. She was in the corner beside the large air vent, next to the electrical panels and water tanks.

"Are you okay?" Nick hugged her close.

"What's going on?" she asked. "I'm talking to Renzo and, next thing I know, he pushes me in here and locks the door. Why are you here?"

"They're killing everybody," Nick said softly.

"Oh my God." Julia jumped, her body in full panic. "Why? I mean, what do we do?"

"There's nothing we can do."

Nick was so angry at himself. He'd known that the conspiracy went above Renzo, but he'd failed to consider an insider like Carter Bull. It was all an inside job. He understood that now. But it was a little late for that realization.

At the end of the prior hour, Carter Bull had clearly killed Zane and taken his pocket watch. Meaning, Carter Bull—not Zane—had leapt back to now. Renzo and Bull were wise to what was about to happen in the bunker, but this version of Janos Zane was not.

Now that Carter had the pocket watch, he was free to wreak all the havoc he wished.

Nick tucked his hand in his pocket, grasping his own watch.... He would have one last hour to make things right. No more chances after that. He sat on a box and gestured for Julia to sit beside him.

"We need to do something," Julia pleaded. "We need to warn them."

"Believe me, there are far better people at doing things like that, and they're being beat right now."

"Don't say *that*. How can you be so calm?"

"I'm not. I'm trying to figure this thing out." He patted the box next to him. "Please, sit."

"How could this happen?" Julia finally collapsed next to him.

"What's in the vault?" Nick asked.

"The vault here in the bunker?"

"Yeah. What's in there?"

"Shamus's personal things—things from Washington House: records, files, lots of files. A few antiques and a bit of cash. Mostly things that are important only to him."

"Like what, Julia? Think."

"Lots of boxes, crates with artwork, but nothing of real value... nothing to kill the leaders of the world over."

Renzo stood in the conference room behind President McManus. Freshly printed copies of the peace accords had been stacked before McManus, Egorenko, and Kharda. Each had an aide to walk them through every line of the legalese.

In two corners stood the bodyguards of each foreign dignitary. The U.S. President's men, Herb Wells and Ed Mitchell, Renzo's best agents, flanked the door. Renzo had worked with them for three years and trusted them implicitly. He looked at his watch: 8:39, the second-hand riding toward twelve and the appointed moment.

Renzo's gun rose suddenly and both foreign bodyguards died before they knew what was happening. He spun, his silenced gun spitting bullets into Agents Wells and Mitchell, both caught halfway through their draws.

As if in a first-person shooter game, Renzo worked his way down the table, six shots, each to the head, the final bullet catching the president between his shock-filled eyes.

Though silenced, Renzo's weapon still made noise. As had a couple of his victims before dying. Predictably, the room's door burst open and two agents crouched and entered. Both died before they took another step.

Carter walked calmly along the lower-level corridor. He passed Phil, the agent Nick had shouted to.

"Historic day."

"That it is, sir. Happy Fourth."

"You too," Carter said. "And thank you for your service."

As Carter passed him, he drew the blade and slit Phil's throat, silencing him before he could cry out, the agent's lifeblood pumping out of him in seconds. Carter shot the two other agents on the lower lever and stabbed the pair of White House lawyers in the middle of their hallway conversation. Working his way upstairs, he went to the lounge and shot six exhausted aides dead at the breakfast table.

He ejected his clip and slammed home another as two women emerged from their quarters, falling before they could scream.

Carter continued down to the main hall toward the elevator vestibule, spied an agent taking aim at Renzo's back, and shot him in the head.

Renzo spun around. "Count?"

"Eight agents, seven civilians," Carter responded.

"Nine agents. Ten civilians. Missing two. Shit. You stay at the elevator."

Renzo checked his watch, then worked his way through the bunker, room by room, confirming the dead, seeking the two survivors. He came to the kitchen, spying the reflection of two people crouched behind the stainless-steel stove.

He could see the young, tear-streaked, blonde bleeding through her grey jacket. She trembled behind an agent who had his gun drawn, protecting her. It was Charlie. Renzo felt a moment of regret but knew there was no room for that. This was just the beginning—Carter had no idea. Once he got Shamus Hennicot's vault open, Renzo would kill Carter Bull, Julia Quinn, and her husband, exit the facility, and blow the dam. He would be out of the United States before anyone had any idea what happened and welcomed by his true homeland as a hero who'd struck a devastating blow to their enemy.

Renzo took a knee, grabbed a glass from the counter, and hurled it against the wall. Charlie popped out, gun ready.

Renzo took the shot.

The bullet hit Charlie in the neck, knocking him down. Renzo sighted in on the cowering woman and fired.

He turned back to Charlie, who was scuttling down the hall toward the elevators when a bullet knocked him flat. Carter stood over Charlie as Renzo approached.

Charlie looked up at Renzo, confusion and fear contorting his face. "Why?"

Renzo shot him in the head.

The mechanical room door jiggled and opened. Renzo stood there, gun pointed at Nick and Julia, motioning them out. He pointed the way down the hall and around the corner.

"Where's Carter?" Nick asked.

"Open the vault," Renzo told them, ignoring Nick's question. They arrived at the large brushed-steel door and he pointed at the handprint and keypad.

"I can't," Julia said.

"Open it!" Renzo shouted.

"But you don't understand. I can only open it with Shamus."

Renzo placed the gun against Nick's head and looked at Julia. "I saw you open it before; you opened it for me."

"Only so you could inspect it. Once the agreement was reached to use the facility, Shamus activated his protocols to protect his personal effects. His rules, not mine."

"Bullshit." Renzo wrapped his finger around the trigger, pressing the barrel harder against Nick's head.

Nick knew Shamus's safe room was only twenty-five feet around the corner—a haven, a place to hide where no one could get to them. But with a gun to his head, it might as well have been in England.

"Open it, right now," Renzo said through clenched teeth. "Call him if you have to."

"Forget the vault, Renzo," Carter said as he came down the hall.

"Forget the vault?" Renzo sounded as if he were being asked to kill himself. "That wasn't part of the deal. We'll be the most hunted men on the planet for the rest of our lives. I want what's in there. I *deserve* what's in there."

"Do you even *know* what's in there?" Carter asked.

"Open it!" Renzo shouted at Julia, pressing the gun harder into Nick's temple.

"Enough," Carter said as he drew his pistol.

"What the hell?" Renzo trained his gun on Carter, and Nick and Julia slipped to the sides as the pair faced off.

"You wouldn't dare—"

Carter shot Renzo in the center of the forehead, dodging left as he did so to avoid Renzo's simultaneous gunshot.

As the shots echoed, Nick grabbed Julia and they raced down the hall for the safe room. Julia smashed the large red button on the wall, and the stainless-steel door slipped open. Diving inside with Nick, Julia hit a large black button on the interior wall; the metal door slammed shut behind them, its multiple locks engaging with a multitude of clicks.

"He can't get in here," she told Nick, her breath coming in great gasps. "Dreyfus built it."

Nick nodded as he looked at the video monitors. Charlie lay dead by the elevator vestibule door, blood pooling beneath him. He turned to Julia and saw tears filling her eyes at the sight of her friend.

The rest of the closed-circuit monitors showed the same carnage: puddles of blood on the floor, red mist on the white walls, bodies in contorted positions of death.

Julia gasped as she looked at the screen showing the conference room. The president was slumped back in his chair, half his head missing; everyone in the room, every dignitary and aide, had been slaughtered in cold blood.

Nick pointed to the single monitor showing Carter standing outside the safe room. He was yelling and kicking the metal door.

Nick turned up the volume.

"Open the door!" Carter pounded. "I know you can hear me."

"Don't worry, we're safe in here," Julia whispered to Nick.

"I know."

"Give me your watch!" Carter yelled as rage filled his eyes.

"What's he talking about?"

"Give me the fucking watch, Nick!"

Carter walked away, out of the camera's scope, but quickly returned with a piece of paper and a roll of tape. He began scribbling, his back obscuring his writing. He taped the note to the wall, turned, smiled at the camera, and walked away.

Nick watched on the next monitor as Carter came to the end of a hall, then disappeared. Nick searched the other screens, ignoring the dead bodies, until he caught sight of Carter on the upper level, walking down the hall, heading through the open airlock, and entering the elevator.

"Where the hell is he going?"

"Oh my God," Julia breathed as she stared at a different video monitor.

Nick leaned in and saw Carter's one-word note on the sheet of paper taped to the wall:

Katy

Above ground, Nick and Julia ran out of the elevator, nearly tripping over the two bodies at the security checkpoint. Both marines' throats had been slashed. Outside the cottage, they saw Sergeant Walker and four of his men on the other side of the lot.

"Carter Bull?" Nick called out.

"His driver drove him out of here two minutes ago," Walker said.

Seeing the panic in Nick and Julia, they all reacted at the same time, drawing their weapons.

"What's wrong?" Walker asked as they scanned the house behind them.

"Everyone's dead," said Julia, her voice cracking. "Renzo and Carter Bull killed them all, including the president."

Panic overtook the marines.

"On the ground," one of them yelled, aiming his weapon, ready to shoot.

Nick and Julia fell to their knees.

"You don't understand," Julia pleaded to Walker. "Carter Bull's going to kill my daughter."

"I'm sorry, Miss Quinn." Walker pulled out his radio. "Code Blue."

"Can we just—"

"How many are alive down there?" Walker interrupted. "Any other shooters?"

"We told you, they're all dead," Nick said, with heat. "Bull *was* the shooter!"

"Steve, please." Julia couldn't hold back her tears any longer. "You know me. It's my daughter. He's going to kill her."

Zane stopped the car in the driveway of the daycare facility and turned to Carter. "That guy Quinn mentioned Renzo Cabral...what's that about?"

"Oh, well..."

"Are you working with him, too?" Zane stared at Carter. "Is he here?"

"Oh, JC...." Carter said. "Renzo's dead."

"When?"

"About five minutes before you." Carter pulled his gun and shot Zane in the head.

Nick drove Sergeant Walker's Humvee down the dirt road, not a word spoken between Julia and him as they raced out of Hadley's Woods and through Byram Hills.

Nick tore across town, skidding around corners, blowing through red lights to the scream of car horns and squealing brakes. Julia held tight to the roll bar, watching for stray pedestrians and cars, silently urging their vehicle toward the daycare center.

Finally, they screeched into the driveway of Flynn's Daycare.

Nick and Julia leapt from the Humvee and ran across the parking lot. Nick stopped at Zane's Town Car, peered inside, and ripped open the door to see Zane's form slumped in the driver's seat, a bullet hole in the side of his head.

"Oh, God," Julia whispered.

Nick reached in Zane's back pocket and took his cell phone, quickly thumbed the camera, took a picture of Zane's body, and tucked the phone in his own jacket.

He ran for the building, Julia a half step behind, and burst inside to find a group of young teachers standing outside a door. They all turned and looked at the couple, fear and desperation in their eyes.

"In there," Sara Bitton said through her tears. "He came in and grabbed her. He told everyone else to leave."

Nick put a hand on her shoulder. "Take everyone outside," he said quietly.

Without a word, Sara led the others down the hall and out the front door.

"What are we going to do?" Julia said as she looked through the small window into the classroom.

Katy sat at a small desk, two dolls in her hands. Carter sat across from her, the small chair barely holding his large frame.

Nick pulled out the pocket watch: 8:56. "We need to—"

Julia burst through the door.

"Mommy." Katy jumped up—

But Carter grabbed Katy's hand.

Confusion spread across Katy's face, slowly morphing to fear. "Mommy?"

"It's okay. I'm here." Julia smiled at her daughter before turning to the military man with a hate-filled smile. "She and I need to leave."

"And you can," Carter said. "As soon as your husband gives me what is rightfully mine."

"Yours?" Nick said as he walked in the classroom.

"Give me the watch, Nick."

"Nick?" Julia said. "What's he talking about?"

"That watch belongs to me." Carter picked Katy up in his left arm; she couldn't see the gun in his right.

"Mommy?" Katy whimpered.

"It's Shamus's watch, just like the one in your pocket," Nick told Bull. "You had it stolen after you had him killed."

"He's very much alive," Carter said. "You should know that."

"You're insane," Nick said.

"Maybe, but sane enough to pull the trigger one more time."

A cacophony of sirens filled the air, quickly growing closer.

"Please," Julia said calmly. "Don't do this. Just let me have my daughter."

"Once the police are here, you can't get away," Nick said.

"Give me the watch, Nick. It's the only way you all live. If you don't..."

"Give him the watch," Julia said as she kept eye contact with Katy, smiling at her. "It's okay, baby, Mommy's here."

Carter nodded. "Listen to her, Nick."

Nick looked from Julia to Katy, his heart breaking, his mind on fire. He knew what would happen if he gave Carter the watch. He'd slip back in time, kill Nick in his sleep, and there'd be no way to stop him; no one would ever know Carter possessed both watches or posed any kind of threat. A man like Carter Bull in possession of two watches was world-endingly dangerous. The colonel hadn't hesitated to kill the president, Zane, and Renzo—all close confidants. Nick could scarcely imagine what he'd do to the future.

"Put my daughter down," Nick said.

"I own the moment. You have no way to stop me. Are you willing to trade your daughter's life for the watch?"

"Just give him the watch, Nick!"

"You don't understand."

"Are you crazy? It's Katy!" Julia turned to Carter. "Please, it's my daughter."

"The last time I'll ask..." Carter whispered.

Nick stared at Carter, Zane's words running through his head: *Is her life worth more than a thousand lives?*

The simple answer to Nick was yes. He couldn't let her suffer. He moved toward Carter.

"No, no, no." Carter sidestepped and moved toward the doorway, still holding Katy. "You don't want to make that mistake."

"Give me my daughter."

"Daddy...?" Katy cried out. "What's happening?"

"It's okay, pumpkin."

"No." Carter waggled the gun in his right hand. "It's not okay, pumpkin. Give me the watch or this ends now."

Nick gave him nothing.

Without another word, Carter slipped out through the classroom door, pulling it closed behind him.

"Katy!" Julia screamed as she sprinted across the room.

Nick pulled open the door—

The gunshot was like thunder, echoing down the hall.

"No!" Nick cried, envisioning the unthinkable.

Julia bolted past him into the darkened hall as Carter Bull strode away.

Nick caught up and grabbed him, slamming him against the wall. "I'll kill you—"

Carter didn't react, didn't resist. "You all could have lived."

"She was innocent!" Nick screamed.

"I have to go." Carter raised his pistol and placed the barrel against Nick's head, forcing him back. With his free hand, he pulled out the pocket watch and looked at the time. "Give me your watch."

Nick shook his head as the sirens grew louder.

"I can shoot you and take it."

"You clearly don't understand how it works. You don't know the consequences of carrying two of these watches at the same time." Nick's eyes never betrayed his bluff.

Carter hesitated, pressing the gun harder into Nick's brow.

"The police are here," Nick said. "They'll catch you, they'll take your watch, and you'll hang for this, for everything."

His confidence broken, Carter lowered his gun and ran for the rear exit. Before exiting, he turned back. "You think you'll go back and stop me, but you forget…. Your alarm doesn't go off until 7:15. You told me all about it. I'll be coming for you, Nick. I'll kill you in your sleep and take the watch from your dead hand."

Julia sat in the dark, cradling Katy in her arms, tears falling from her face onto her daughter's as she hugged her close, a mother's mind snapped with grief.

Nick looked at his watch: thirty seconds till the top of the hour.

Carter was right—he was smarter.

Nick's mind spun.

He needed help.

He needed someone as desperate as he was and driven by the most powerful, most fundamental emotion.

He couldn't remember where Julia had been an hour earlier— working out? Shopping? Getting coffee and the paper? All things she routinely did before he awoke. He prayed she hadn't been behind the wheel at 7:00. Would she even get home before his alarm at 7:15— before Carter arrived to kill him?

He had no time to explain to his wife what was about to happen. He remembered his first leap and how disorienting it was, how nauseated it left him, and the five minutes it took to shake it off.

Even if Julia arrived safely an hour ago *with* Nick, what would go through her mind? Would she even be able to function? Would she be crippled by grief? She had just held her murdered daughter. Nick felt all of her pain, all the anguish that came with seeing one's innocence stolen.

While the emotional agony crushed him, he held hope in his pocket; he knew there was one last chance to put everything right. This was it...there would be no more resets, no more second chances. Everything came down to the final hour.

Everything came down to now.

Nick reached down and took Katy from Julia's arms, laying his daughter's body gently on the floor, his heart breaking as he looked upon his dead child.

"What are you doing?" Julia sobbed.

Crying with her, Nick put his arms around Julia and held her tightly, the pocket watch in his hand clutched firmly against her back.

"Let me go," she said through her tears.

"I need you to trust me," Nick said.

"Let me go!" she screamed, trying to pull away. "I can't leave my baby!"

"Julia," Nick whispered, still holding her tight. This was madness.... He had no idea if it would work. It was by accident before with their puppy, Theo, but this was something entirely different. "Trust me."

CHAPTER 2

7:00 AM

Carter Bull gasped, writhing on the ground beside his car, trying to catch his breath. It was even worse the second time, as if someone had ripped out his lungs; his head felt on the verge of exploding and his pounding heart seemed about to burst. Shivering, strangling, he began to pray, certain death was imminent—

When a sip of air slipped down his throat, he gulped it, then gulped greedily again as more oxygen entered his bloodstream and his body began to inch back toward life.

He lay in the grass beside his car in the motel parking lot on the edge of Byram Hills for precious minutes before finally struggling to his feet and climbing into the driver's seat.

He had his doubts, despite his first leap, about how time would be affected, beyond everyone being alive again. He thought for a moment that it might all be a dream, briefly questioning his own sanity.

Quickly, he realized that he needed to conduct a test: drastically affect the present, then step back an hour to erase it.

What better way than to carry out the assassinations again?

He'd managed to carry out the killings the first time. It was sloppy and barely succeeded, ending with him being chased into the safe room by a Secret Service agent, then locking himself in to watch Renzo finish killing everyone.

He had quickly called Zane at 8:42, told him what he had to do to save the president and where to find Shamus, despite Zane's severe doubts as to what the watch was capable of, he didn't question his orders. Just over an hour later, at 9:45, Zane was there in the bunker with the watch.

The second time, he and Renzo had carried out the assassinations easily, despite having to deal with Nick Quinn.

Carter felt like a child who had just taken the training wheels off his bike: he still wasn't sure how the pocket watch worked. Which meant he had no idea what would have happened if he shot Quinn at the daycare center and traveled back with both pocket watches in hand. Quinn's warning had shaken him. He wasn't about to risk success by taking unnecessary chances.

It had pained Carter to kill the child, but he told himself it was no different than in war: another life sacrificed for the greater good.

Nick Quinn was the only one who knew the truth, and the new world Carter lived in had no room for those truths.

He pulled out his phone and dialed.

"Yes?" Zane answered.

"How are you?"

"Good, sir."

"Where have you been?"

"Here in my mother's empty house, waiting for your call."

While knowing that was true, Carter knew it wasn't, but that was in another reality.... "Did you pick up the two people I asked you to?"

"Yes," Zane said. "Four hours ago. They're secure in the house you designated, restrained and unconscious."

"Good. Have you ever heard the name Nick Quinn?"

"No, sir. Should I have?"

This confirmed what Carter hoped, that—although Zane knew exactly who Nick Quinn was two hours from now, and despite having spent hours in the future seeking the watch, then bringing it back to Carter—the soldier knew none of that now. Whatever had changed

Zane's mind, whatever had caused him to turn on Carter, it no longer existed in the young man's mind. It had never happened. Zane remained the soldier he had been, the killer Carter had created.

Carter continued the conversation with Zane for two minutes before ending the call.

He dialed his phone once more.

Janos Zane opened the garage door and got in the black Town Car Carter had provided. He'd arrived at his nearly-empty childhood home two days earlier and hadn't left it since, except to kidnap two people. He had been told to expect a call at precisely 8:40.

He had spent those two days studying the dossier on Shamus Hennicot and a map of the town of Byram Hills, which he'd now memorized as if it were a war zone. His only point of contact was to be Carter Bull, one of the few men in the world he trusted. There were no other details to his mission, other than he would be protecting the president and the nation.

At 1:30 this morning, he'd picked up the man and woman, snatching them from their beds, binding them in plasticuffs, driving them the three hours to Byram Hills, and locking them in the basement of the colonial house on Harper Road. Zane had no idea who they were or what purpose their captivity served.

He reached over to the side table and picked up the small family bible. He hadn't read a passage or adhered to any of its tenets in years. In truth, it had served a far different purpose. It had been his mother's and her mother's before her, dating back to 1880 and inscribed with each birth, death, and sacrament of everyone in his lineage, filled with handwritten notes about his maternal ancestors' lives right up to his brother's and mother's deaths.

Zane felt tired and lost. He had no family, no friends. He no longer even had his name; as far as the world was concerned, he was dead. There would be no more updates to the family bible, no births, no marriages. The only remaining death would be his, and there'd be no one to write about it.

The only thing Zane truly loved anymore was his country, but it hadn't loved him back. He'd been a pawn in the ever-shifting chessboard of alliances, wars, and aggression. Despite it all, though, his loyalty had never wavered. He would kill to protect his president and country, regardless of what was offered in return.

Zane's phone rang. He looked at his watch: 7:04—more than an hour and a half before he'd expected the call.

"Yes?" Zane answered.

"How are you?"

"Good, sir."

Zane listened to Carter Bull's directions for two minutes, then hung up.

Having committed the name and address to memory, he checked and rechecked his gun, tucking it in his shoulder holster and headed out to the car.

His mission would begin with the assassination of a man named Nicholas Quinn.

Julia awoke from a nightmare, her head swirling, her gut twisting to send coffee back up her throat. Her mind was nothing but a jumble of confusion, a host of images, darkness, and unnerving cold.

She lay on the bathroom floor, the tile chilling her through her clothes.

And then it hit her. Katy was dead. It hadn't been a dream. In fact, it felt more real than anything she had ever experienced. She didn't know how she'd ended up back here in her bathroom, how she'd made it across town without being aware, but she had no doubt: the bond that connects the souls of mother and child had been severed. Never again would she sense her daughter's pain, her need, from miles away. Katy was dead, killed in front of Julia by an insane man spouting nonsense about a watch. None of it made sense; none of it even mattered because Katy was dead.

Julia screamed from the depths of her soul, unhinged by grief.

Nick's eyes opened, the scream tearing him from his nightmare, ripping his soul like nothing he'd heard before.

Nick leapt from bed and raced to the bathroom to find Julia on the floor, her eyes filled with tears as she moaned. Nick knelt and held her tight.

"Shhh, it's okay."

"She's *dead.*" The words fell from her lips, barely audible. "He killed her."

Nick's mind fought to clear itself, to shake off sleep, confusion, and the cold...and then he remembered.

"No," he told her. "It's not what you think."

A bitter light entered her eyes. "*You...* You let it happen."

Julia pushed back from Nick, climbing to her feet. "You let her die. You could have stopped him!"

Julia slapped Nick across the face. It was the first time she'd ever struck him, and she kept hitting him, her fists pounding his chest.

"You didn't save her! You let her die!"

Nick allowed her rage to pour out; he knew there were no words that would quell her anger and desolation. He finally caught her flailing arms, gently held them, and pulled her toward him.

"No! Don't *touch* me! You let her *die!*"

"Just come with me," Nick whispered. "I need to show you something." If he could only get her to Katy's bedroom....

He took her hand and began to pull her.

"No!" Julia screamed again, pain and anger that had welled within her released upon him.

"Mommy?" The small voice was drowned out by Julia's cries. Then it came again, louder. "Mommy?"

Julia looked down to see Katy standing in the doorway of the bathroom, her tiny fists wiping the sleep from her eyes.

"Why are you crying?" Katy asked, tears beginning to drip down her own cheeks as her emotions aligned with her mother's fear and confusion. "Daddy, what's the matter?"

"It's okay." Nick knelt, picking her up, then stood, giving her a kiss on the cheek. "Mommy needs you."

Julia looked on in confusion, panting as she tried to catch her breath, her body shaking from her adrenaline-fueled attack on Nick.

Nick moved to his wife, holding Katy close between them.

"It's okay, Mommy." Katy reached out her hand and ran it softly down her mother's cheek. "Don't cry."

Julia's eyes were vacant, as if drugged or still entwined in a dream. She stared into her daughter's eyes, finally reaching up and taking her hand as it swept along her cheek. And with that touch, she returned to the land of the living.

"Katy?" she whispered.

"Mommy." Katy reached out as Nick placed her into her mother's arms. "Pease don't cry...pease?"

"Honey," Nick said as he looked at the clock beside their bed, "we need to go. Now."

Nick held Julia's hand as she carried Katy. They raced across the long grassy expanse between their home and Marcus's to see him in his driveway pulling the Jet Ski on its trailer out of his garage.

"Marcus—"

"Don't even think of canceling," Marcus growled.

"Listen—"

"Save it for the drive. We're missing good wind and you're the one who said we needed to be back by ten—"

"We're not going kitesurfing."

"What the hell?" Marcus sighed. "This'd better be the world's greatest excuse."

Zane entered through the back of the house on Townsend Court. He was walking through the kitchen when a large puppy erupted into frenzied barking. Zane pulled back into a corner, waiting for someone to emerge to hush the pet. He held tight to his Sig Sauer, lying in wait.

But no one came.

He swung out into the front hall, an incessant ticking from a large grandfather clock echoing in the foyer. He swept his gun through the paneled office, the living room, the dining room, but found no one. He opted for the back stairs and crept to the second floor. Three rooms, empty, as was a stuffed-animal-filled child's room. He peered into the master bedroom and found the bed unmade. He felt the pillow and beneath the sheets detected a hint of warmth. He crouched low and checked the bathroom.

No one here. No one anywhere.

The alarm clock blared, startling him.

He checked his watch: 7:15.

They knew I was coming.

"I'll be back before the hour's over," Nick said as he turned on the small TV and placed Katy's plush giraffe on the table beside the cot.

Paul Dreyfus's personal safe room was twelve by twelve and overflowing with stuff, both practical and undefinable.

The gun safe's door hung open as Dreyfus handed Nick and Marcus each a gun.

"Two guns?" Marcus said. "What about you?"

"I use my brains more than bullets." Dreyfus gave each of them a spare clip.

Nick closed the safe and spun the wheel. He took Julia's hand. "It's hard to explain right now, but everything'll be fine."

Julia nodded uncertainly.

On the drive over, Nick had tried to explain the watch, his day of desperation, and how what had started out as saving her and Katy over and over from death had become something even more earth-shattering. Julia had just stared at him, listening to him without question. She didn't need to believe his words—she had already seen and experienced the impossible.

"You can see every room and even outside on these." Dreyfus tapped the six monitors, their images cycling through various views of his home.

"Don't open the door for anyone but us," Marcus said as he kissed Katy on the head.

"Can I come?" Katy smiled.

"Next time," said Marcus.

Nick leaned in and kissed Julia gently on the lips. Not a word was said; it didn't need to be.

Next, he kissed Katy, then followed his friends past the thick steel door, closing it behind them.

"This is it," Dreyfus said. "No more re-dos. The watch can't help you anymore."

"Nope," Nick said as they walked through Dreyfus's workshop and into the hall. "Only help I'm getting is from you guys."

Marcus looked up at Nick as he clicked off the video on his phone. "Don't say it," Nick said.

"I don't need to," Marcus said. "But you've *got* to be shitting me."

Carter raced across town, one hand on the wheel, the other pulling out his phone, dialing, and holding it to his ear. Now that he had the pocket watch and understood how it worked—he'd killed and seen the resurrected; he'd erased the actions of everyone—the president didn't need to die again. None of them did, and none of them would. He'd done it—literally pulled off the perfect crime. He'd reached into the future, stolen the watch, and brought it back in time. Now, all the violence, all the crimes of the future, would be erased with a simple call.

"Cabral," Renzo answered.

"Abort."

"Why?"

"No *why*, just *do it*. Abort and remain silent, or I will turn over evidence implicating you in a conspiracy to kill the president."

Renzo stared at Shamus Hennicot's vault door as déjà vu washed over him. Here he stood, on the verge of stealing the vault's contents, but now...he'd never get in, never know what Hennicot was hiding, treasures more valuable than money, than life. Things that could change the world.

He continued on, checking each of the doors in the lower level, the billiard room, the theater, the lounge. He entered the mechanical room, looked at the hot-water heaters, the vast size of the water tanks. He examined the generators and fuse boxes, inspected the air handlers and cooling units. He pulled out a key and inserted it into a wall lock where he punched in the code that Julia had given him during orientation. He heard several clicks, and, in response, he pulled the heavy, red lever, opening the valve of the fresh-air intake. He could smell the morning on the air as it poured through the large ducts connected to the surface.

Renzo locked the room and walked through the lower level of the bunker, up to the main floor, past clusters of diplomats in deep discussion, and around the trays of breakfast food prepared for the president and his foreign guests. Renzo nodded to each of his agents along the way, finally arriving at the airlock by the elevator.

"Charlie," Renzo said to the agent who stood at the elevator, "take point for fifteen minutes. I need to go topside."

"Yes, sir," Charlie said and headed down the hall.

Renzo stepped in the elevator and rode up. There was no question that Carter was nervous, probably realizing too late how foolish and impossible his plan was. Renzo took Carter's phoned threat seriously. In fact, he assumed it would happen no matter what he did next. Whatever panic Carter was suffering, whatever entanglements or second thoughts he was having, he'd lay the blame at Renzo's feet. Treason. The death penalty. Awful things, but nothing remotely as horrific as failure.

"Sergeant," Renzo said as he greeted Walker outside.

"Sir, good morning," Sergeant Walker said. "Heading out?"

"Back in ten, just running an errand."

Renzo pulled out his phone and dialed as he jumped in a black Suburban. "Where are you?"

"Almost to town," the accented voice answered. "The team is behind me."

"We need to move it all up and do this in the next fifteen."

"Praise be our cause," his uncle said.

"Where should I meet you?" Renzo asked.

"Round Hill Road. Get one last look at the town."

"Good. See you in five."

A white panel van cut through the town of Byram Hills, closely following a grey Mercedes and a black Suburban. They passed the early risers clutching coffee cups as they engaged in small talk before heading back to their comfortable homes, never knowing what was about to happen.

Kasper and his team had worked underwater through the last two nights, inserting the charges in the dam, twenty-six points at the base and mid-point with five linked detonators, precisely as directed by Tuslav, who had smuggled them to the U.S. from their war-torn country to exact their nation's revenge and strike at the heart of evil.

The plan was to detonate the charges at 8:55 a.m. It was already confirmed that all three countries' leaders were in the underground facility.

They had considered waiting until later that morning, when more Americans would stand in the wake of the dam, but they feared the peace negotiations might end early, costing them their opportunity. It was ultimately Tuslav's call. His plan, his design.

With two of his team, Popov and Fetizos, in the back, Kasper drove the van, following Tuslav in his Mercedes. Kasper would film Tuslav as he pressed the button on the detonator, the first moment of the dam's destruction to be broadcast for all the world to see.

No one saw the landscaping truck as it veered over the double yellow line, drifting into Tuslav's lane.

The impact was deafening.

Rob Risken hit the brakes, squealing to a stop in front of a three-car accident with head-on damage. There was a landscaping truck, a Toyota, and a Mercedes on its side. He could see gasoline trickling along the ground, pooling into an ever-growing, flammable lake.

Risken stepped out and approached the accident as a dark-haired man leapt from a Suburban, ran to the smoking Mercedes, and ripped open the door. Risken could see him reach in and fumble about with the unconscious driver. As Risken moved closer, he saw the man rifling through the driver's pockets, pulling things out and stuffing them into his own pockets.

"Hey!" Risken shouted. "What are you doing?"

Two more men emerged from their cars and raced for the burning Mercedes.

The dark-haired man looked up as he pulled a satchel from the car and took off in a sprint, jumping into a white van. Risken couldn't believe his eyes. How could someone rob an injured motorist?

Risken approached the vehicle. He could see flames licking out of the hood. Not much time before it all went up.

"We need help here!" Risken shouted as the others charged toward the wreck.

Risken reached in the car to find a bloodied man slumped against the wheel. And that's when he saw it in the man's lap. It took Risken's mind a moment to register that there was no pin in the grenade.

Risken turned as the two other men arrived at his side.

"Run!" he cried.

They only took a single step before the grenade exploded, tearing the car, Risken, and the two other men to pieces. The pool of fuel erupted into a wall of fire, engulfing the surrounding vehicles as a succession of explosions shattered the morning.

Renzo jumped into the van as Kasper hit the gas.

"Your uncle?"

Renzo shook his head without emotion as he dug through the satchel, through the plans and files, until he found the BMW smart key.

"What about your SUV?" Kasper said.

"Forget it. We'll be gone within a half-hour." Renzo looked at the two others in the van. "Where's Erik?"

"Not sure," Kasper said. "He didn't show."

"That makes no sense." Renzo turned. "He wouldn't bail on us. Do you think someone caught him?"

"Not Erik. He can take care of himself. He'll catch up," Kasper said.

Renzo looked at the BMW smart key, which his uncle had adapted into a remote detonator. Everything was in place: he had opened the air intake vents; breakfast was underway; President McManus, President Egorenko, and Prime Minister Kharda were all early risers, looking to get everything signed by noon and off to their respective homes by nightfall.

No one outside of a select few knew where the three heads of state were. The press pool was 250 miles away, outside Camp David, in the proverbial dark, crying into their cameras and microphones about radio silence and White House secrecy on the Fourth of July.

Renzo's entire existence came down to the next half-hour. West Point, war, working his way up within the Secret Service.... It all culminated in this singular moment of revenge for his family, for his Uncle Tuslav, and for his true country of origin.

It would be an assassination like no other. No knives, no bullets. It did not matter how many Secret Service agents surrounded the President—they couldn't prevent his drowning. And given the secrecy of their location, it would be hours before the world realized that it had been transformed.

It had all started with Carter and his plan to shoot the three world leaders, their staff, and their protection. Foolish, dangerous, and impossible, though Carter thought it could be done. Renzo and Carter were to carry it out together; only two men, reducing any chance of discovery.

They had planned it meticulously. Renzo was to start within the conference room, taking out the three leaders and their aides with a silenced weapon. Carter would be in the lower level, working his way up, a trusted military hero betraying everyone.

It was from that origin that Renzo's plan had blossomed. He had gone to his Uncle Tuslav, his father's brother, the man no background check ever discovered due to his father's name changes and falsified heritage, presented the opportunity, and asked for his help. Few knew his uncle was the leader of an underground network of Akbiquestani rebels.

The dam had been Renzo's idea, not only to kill the world leaders, but also to leave a mark on the country for years to come. It was a plan whose execution not only created death and mayhem, but also washed away the evidence at the same time.

Renzo had never questioned his former commander and had remained a loyal "soldier," a clandestine voice relaying the top-secret inner dealings of the president and his staff to Carter when possible. But Renzo was shocked at the assassination request and had vehemently pressed him, asking why he wanted to kill his own president after following the chief executives' orders for decades. After all, Renzo was the head of the president's detail; it was his job to protect him with his life, to ensure that his team protected the head of the United States with their own lives. If Renzo went along with Carter's plan too easily, it would have raised his old boss's suspicions. If Carter were laying a trap for Renzo, he'd be caught instantly.

Carter explained that humankind was far more successful when at war than at peace—a typical military answer. But Renzo suspected there was more. Carter had always been a selfish man; winning battles glorified his ego, not his country. There was something Renzo wasn't seeing.

Still, Renzo had played Carter's game, had gone as far as constructing a duplicate model of Hennicot's bunker in a warehouse, where he and Carter practiced the assassination op in the same way they'd rehearsed military raids overseas. They'd worked the scenario dozens of times, moving room to room with live rounds, taking out dummies, planning for contingencies, planning for disaster. They had worked it to the point where the entire op would take less than three minutes.

But none of that would happen, now; he'd be skipping the bullets and Carter's plan.

Water would be the death of all of them.

Marcus drove his BMW through town, Nick riding shotgun, Dreyfus in the back.

"How are we going to find Carter?" Marcus asked.

"I imagine he's looking for me and my watch."

"So, you're the bait?" Marcus shrugged. "Better you than me."

"I may be bait, but I'm not foolish," Nick said as he dialed his phone.

"Shannon," the detective answered.

"Hey, it's Nick."

"Gotta call you back. Dealing with some insanity."

Nick heard the sirens in the background, then realized what he'd forgotten. ""Car accident? On Round Hill Road?"

"How the hell did you know that?"

Nick had been there, had pulled that mysterious man—who was no longer mysterious in the least—from the car while Marcus doused the flaming vehicle with his fire extinguisher. Nick wondered if the man had died this time.

"Anyway," Shannon went on, "huge explosion, at least five dead, and on a day when every cop is on vacation. And would you believe it? Witnesses saw someone reach into a wrecked vehicle and rob the driver? Why do I think the day's only gonna get worse?"

Shannon ended the call without another word.

Nick turned to Marcus. "There were only two dead before."

"What?"

"Holy shit...."

"Stop that!" Marcus snapped. "What the hell's going on?"

He and Marcus had been driving a few cars behind the Mercedes on Round Hill Road and witnessed the whole thing, pulling the older man from the car and preventing an explosion. But now, since Nick and Marcus weren't there, there was no one to stop Renzo from getting hold of the bag—no one to stop him from getting the smart-key-turned-detonator and blowing the dam.

The simple act that Nick and Marcus had performed during Nick's first time through the morning had delayed the destruction of the dam. Now, despite every effort to prevent it while reliving multiple hours of the day, it was still going to happen. And soon.

"They've got the detonator," Nick said.

"So, where are we going?"

"The Killian Dam."

"We're going to the place that's going to blow up?" Marcus sighed and stepped on the gas. "All right, let's go have some fun."

Katy sat on the small cot in Dreyfus's safe room, watching TV while Julia watched the security monitors and checked through the boxes of food, water, and other supplies. As she looked harder, she realized that what had started as a safe room was slowly becoming a storage room in the same way that closets become the overflowing repository for half-used Christmas paper, throw-away coats, broken umbrellas, and cheap wine. Dreyfus's shelves were filled with spare electronic parts, spools of wire, power tools, a large mahogany box, a couple of packages of Twinkies, and various household supplies.

The room was a smaller—much smaller—version of the one in Shamus's bunker, which made perfect sense, as Dreyfus had built both.

Julia remained in a form of shock after what she had seen...what she had experienced. The memory was real, worse than a nightmare, a pain she would never escape—yet Katy sat before her, not a scratch on her. Because it had never happened.

Julia had always been practical, logical, and a nonbeliever in magic...yet she had to face facts: she'd stepped back in time. She'd witnessed how life could be changed through a single action in an earlier timeline.

She wondered what she would do with Shamus's watch if given the chance.

"Mommy," Katy said, "I'm hungry."

"Well, let's see what Uncle Paul has." Julia opened the safe room's freezer and smiled. "How about ice-cream?"

Katy's eyes lit up. "For breakfast?"

"Absolutely." After this morning, all rules went out the window.

As she scooped the vanilla ice cream into two bowls, she caught a movement in one of the monitors. A rusty Ford Bronco was in the driveway. She flipped the switch and saw a large, tattooed man carrying something, though she couldn't make it out. He disappeared from the monitor.

She heard noise outside the safe room's door. She checked the monitor that showed the workshop outside the safe room. It was dark, shadowed, quiet, until a bright light ignited, the video image turning to pure white. A steady sound like running water filled the air.

"Mommy, what's that noise?"

As Julia watched the safe room's steel door began to shimmer. She could feel heat emanating from it.

Julia spun around to the gun safe. Locked. She pulled hard on the handle. It wouldn't budge. She frantically looked around, tearing through the drawers, through cabinets, the boxes on the shelves. She pushed aside power tools and wires, the mahogany box, the small containers—

Sparks began to pour in, the door bubbling, molten steel beginning to drip.

Katy noticed and looked at her mom with a smile: "Pwetty."

Julia pushed Katy behind her.

"Mommy, what's that?"

"It's okay, baby. Mommy will protect you."

The hole started small and quickly grew, the hissing growing louder as the smell of burnt metal and smoke filled the air. Suddenly, the noise stopped.

A thickly muscled, tattooed arm reached through the hole and opened the door.

"Where are you?" Carter said into his phone. "Why aren't you with the president?"

"I had to step out," Renzo said.

"If you're trying to play games...."

"Play games? You threatened me with treason." Renzo expelled air in a hiss of disapproval. "Always the one pushing the buttons, but your ego blinded you. The irony is, it will all be blamed on you—everyone's death, the president's, everyone. Your infamy will be unparalleled. The evidence I've planted will implicate you and the senator beyond denial. We can both play games, Carter."

"What the hell are you talking about?"

"You have no loyalty to anything but yourself. You're gonna die along with everyone else."

"Is that what you think?"

"Goodbye, sir."

"Renzo, there's something you don't understand," Carter said.

"I fully understand," Renzo said.

"No, you don't. Have you spoken with your parents today?"

The phone rang for the sixth time. No answer. It wasn't like his parents not to pick up their only phone. They liked their single, wall-mounted, kitchen phone with the long cord that could extend all the way to the living room. His parents still couldn't understand why people needed cell phones. The world had existed without them for nearly a century; now everyone could be called twenty-four hours a day, no matter where they were, no matter for what nonsense. It wasn't for them.

Renzo knew their routines well enough that he normally reached them without fail. It didn't matter if he was serving on the other side of the world or in the White House; apart from Saturday night between six and eight, when they would go out for dinner, and on Sunday morning, when they attended church, his parents always picked up. One of them was always around—gardening, cooking, doing jigsaw puzzles, reading.

In all of his years they'd always picked up, except now, at 7:25 on a Friday morning....

"What's wrong?" Kasper asked from the van's driver's seat.

"Nothing." Renzo's facial expression matched his words.

"Are we a go?"

Renzo ran Carter's words through his head. The man was a brilliant strategist, always planning for contingencies. Could he have known what Renzo was up to? Could he have anticipated this far ahead?

Where were his parents?

Nick looked at his ringing phone, seeing Julia's number come up.

"Hey, babe, what's up?"

"Hey, babe," Carter Bull said mockingly. "Big, impenetrable, steel door in your friend's house isn't so impenetrable."

"You son—"

"Just listen," Carter said. "If you show up with anyone else, I'll kill your wife in front of your daughter. And if you don't bring me the watch, I'll kill her too."

Nick struggled to contain his rage. "Where are you?"

"Be at the corner of Bedford and Maple in three minutes." Carter hung up.

"What's up?" Marcus said as drove up Route 22.

"We need to split up," Nick said. "You need to drop me in town."

"Really?" Marcus asked. "Why?"

"He's got Julia and Katy."

"How the hell did they get through the door?" Dreyfus asked.

"Screw the dam," Marcus said, his anger boiling over. "We'll go with you."

"If I'm not alone, he'll kill her. You guys need to stop Renzo from blowing the dam."

"How the hell are we gonna do that?"

"He's got the detonator; you'll have to figure it out on the fly."

"And you? You can't go after Carter alone."

"No do-overs this time," said Dreyfus.

"Thanks for the reminder."

The Town Car stopped at the corner of Maple and Bedford Road. Zane got out and motioned Nick to turn and put his hands on the roof. Zane frisked him and took his gun.

Nick turned and stared at him.

"Do you have the watch?" Zane asked, once again unaware of the recent past they'd shared.

Nick held it up as he opened the door and climbed in the back.

Zane got behind the wheel and pulled away from the curb without a word as Nick tucked the watch in his pocket.

"You have no idea who I am, do you?"

Zane looked at him in the rearview mirror and shook his head.

Nick reminded himself that Janos Zane had been used. Used in war, used in life, used by Carter Bull to do his bidding, set up to steal a watch and bring it back through time to Carter, only to be murdered for his success.

And now, here they sat as strangers. Nick knew the man's deadly potential well. Intimately, even. He knew that, as dangerous and cruel as Zane was, he was also a man of principle. Zane was far from a good man, but he had a code—his own morality and rules.

"Where are we going?"

Zane didn't answer.

"How long till we get there?"

"Five minutes."

Five minutes. He had less than that to convince a trained killer to become his ally.

"Tell me something," Nick began. "Do you believe in magic?"

"This needs to go in Senator Chase's home, behind his desk." Carter patted the three-foot safe that sat in the back of the garage on Kavey Lane.

"What's in it?" Erik asked as he picked up the hundred-and-fifty-pound safe and tucked it in the back of the Bronco, his tattooed muscles straining with the effort.

"Evidence."

"Against me?"

"No. Just Renzo and the senator. No sense in letting a good plan go completely to waste."

Senator Chase was on a trajectory to the White House. While he was not a fan of the military and would, if elected, seek cuts in funding, that wasn't the reason Carter chose to tie him to Renzo.

Chase was an opportunist. Carter had gone to the senator when Janos was first accused of killing his own men. Chase's reaction had not been one of concern. He'd never asked if his son were guilty or innocent...he only wanted to know if the info could be classified and made to go away.

When the story of Jason Chase's heroic death surfaced and the world mourned, it was the only time Carter saw the senator claim the soldier as his son. He wrote a book, cried for him on TV, prayed for his sacrifice at his campaign rallies: an anti-war politician using the war to advance his career.

Erik thought about it for a moment and nodded.

"Hope to never see you again." Carter handed him a thick envelope.

"Likewise." Erik got in the Bronco and drove away.

Carter turned around and opened his car door to reveal Katy sitting on Julia's lap.

"Let's take a walk."

Dreyfus cringed at the melted door to his safe room, then tore through his electronic gear, grabbed a box, and raced back outside, jumping into Marcus's BMW.

Marcus white-knuckled the wheel, speeding through early-morning streets.

Dreyfus began calibrating some sort of electronic gadget.

"What's that gonna do?" Marcus asked.

"The bomb trigger is a BMW smart key."

"Like this?" Marcus held up his own smart key.

"Yep."

"Fancy terrorist assholes," Marcus said, as he tucked his key back in his pocket. "Why put it in a smart key?"

"Inconspicuous," Dreyfus said. "And it already has a radio-pulse generator."

"Meaning?"

"You can remotely open a door or, in this case, set off a bomb."

"Great." Marcus pulled off Route 22 and raced down a side road that quickly changed from pavement to dirt.

"But the signal won't carry below water," Dreyfus said. "There has to be an antenna, a relay above the surface—something near the dam with a hard-wired repeater that extends the signal from the water's edge down to the explosives in the dam. Now, the range of a smart key is next to nothing. You need to be within fifty yards of the receiver for it to work unless the smart key has a radio boost, which I doubt theirs has. That means both the repeater and the antenna will have to be very near the dam."

"So, we're looking for an antenna? That shouldn't be too hard," Marcus said.

"A little better than a needle in a haystack. Odds are it's this side of the reservoir, maybe under the cover of the forest, but somewhere within a couple hundred yards of the water's edge and the dam." Dreyfus held up a black box with a glowing meter. "This will help us pinpoint it. If we can do that, we can delay their plan for hours."

Marcus nodded.

"Here," said Dreyfus suddenly.

Marcus hit the brakes, pulling to the side of the road and parking the car beside a stone wall. "What the hell am I supposed to do?"

They both exited the car and entered the woods.

"I'll check the trees for the antenna. You run along the water's edge, look for a thick wire running into the reservoir."

"That's it?" Marcus asked as he cut through the thicket toward the water.

"And kill anyone who tries to stop us."

"That I can do."

"I'd like to show you a trick that's not a trick," Nick said.

Zane stared at the road as he drove, ignoring Nick.

"You have your phone," Nick said. "Correct?"

Zane said nothing.

"I'm going to make your phone jump into my pocket." Nick waved his hand, reached into his breast pocket, and pulled out an iPhone in a slim black case. "Look familiar?"

Zane stared at the phone in Nick's hand. "How the hell...?"

Zane reached in his own pocket and pulled out his phone, identical to the one in Nick's hand. "What are you trying to prove?"

"Press your thumb." Nick held the iPhone out, the thumbprint scanner facing Zane.

"Why?"

"Just do it. I promise, it's no game."

Zane swiped his thumb over the button and the phone unlocked. He looked from Nick to the perfectly matching phones.

"Now, look at your phone," Nick said. "Open it."

With eyes darting back and forth between the road and his phone, Zane pressed his thumb and opened the screen on his own copy of the phone, seeing the exact same screen. "This is mine."

"As is this one."

"You cloned my phone?"

"And yet we've never met." Nick smiled. "And, no, I didn't clone your phone."

"Who the hell *are* you?"

Nick handed Zane the copy of his phone. "Check something personal, something that no one else would know about...something that would convince you that this other phone is not a fake."

Zane quickly opened an app in the shape of a safe and punched in a code, opening up a new screen with his Last Will and Testament. "How did you do this?"

"It's easier if I show you. You may want to pull over for this."

Zane hesitated a minute, then skidded onto the shoulder of the road and stopped.

"Look at the photos on the cloned phone from today. Do you remember taking them? Look at when the pictures were taken."

Zane looked at the date and time stamp. "Today."

"And the time?"

Zane's eyes widened. "An hour from now.... How is this possible?"

"I'll explain that in a moment. But first you need to understand something: Renzo and Carter framed you. They set you up in Akbiquestan."

Zane absorbed Nick's words for a moment. "How do you know about that?"

"You told me," Nick said softly. "An hour from now."

"What are you talking about?"

"It was Renzo who blew up the plane in Akbiquestan, killed the Special Forces team, and made it seem like you." Nick held up a hand to stop Zane from protesting. "And he did it on the orders of Carter Bull. Carter needed you—couldn't afford to lose you. So, he hit you and hit you hard, broke you, made you desperate, on the verge of a court-martial and execution for treason. He saved you from a bleak future that *he* caused."

Zane seemed to be listening, but his face betrayed nothing.

"Look at the last picture taken on that phone."

Zane looked at the final image, which depicted his own death: the lifeless eyes, the blood pouring from the fresh wound in his temple.

"What kind of mindfuck *is* this?"

"It's no trick. Carter killed you."

"This is impossible."

"Look at the time stamp."

Zane read the date and time on the photo. "That's..."

"An hour from now."

"It makes no sense. You're talking about..." Zane stopped, at a loss.

"I know, but it's true." Nick pulled out Shamus's pocket watch. "And this is what makes it true."

"Bullshit." Before Nick could react, Zane had his gun trained on Nick's forehead.

"I know you can kill me right now, but even if you do, the truth doesn't change. There are things in life that can't be explained. This is one of them."

"Why?"

"This." Nick held out the pocket watch. "There are two of them. Carter has a duplicate."

"Valuable?"

"Beyond value. And Carter won't stop until he has them both. Please help me save my wife and daughter," he pleaded. "Please help me stop Renzo."

"Where *is* Renzo?" Zane whispered.

"On his way to blow up the Killian Dam and drown the president," Nick said. "If you don't believe me, call him. Here's his card."

Nick dropped the card Renzo gave him on the car seat. "He has a detonator that looks like a smart key for a BMW."

Nick pulled up the video of the dam's destruction on his phone, quickly texting it to Zane's.

"What the hell *is* this?" Zane said as he held up his phone, the video showing in his text-message inbox.

"Just look at it."

Zane opened the video and watched for ten seconds, images of the shattered dam, of the raging waters. He looked up at Nick before slipping the phone back in his pocket.

"Please," Nick said.

"Bullshit." Zane stomped on the gas and peeled back onto the road.

They drove in silence for three minutes. Zane was the one person on earth who could help him, but Nick didn't blame him for his disbelief: his story was crazy, the only thing crazier being the full story.

Zane screeched to a halt in front of Byram Castle. "Get out."

"No armed escort?"

"I was supposed to bring you to Carter, shoot you, and take that watch. He said something about being his protector, about changing time. But I'm done. They took my life, my identity. I'm not about to allow them to take my sanity. Get out."

"Why would Carter come here?" Nick said as he got out of the car.

"Not here," Zane said as he pointed up. "Up there."

Nick looked 250 feet up to the top of the dam.

"He's expecting us to arrive from the opposite side, the west side."

Nick looked up and saw movement, a woman. No mistaking, it was Julia.

Zane put the car in drive.

"Where are you going?" Nick asked.

"To kill Renzo before he kills the president."

Zane stood on the side of the road beside his car. He looked at the duplicate of his phone, still unable to grasp how it could've been created. He looked again at the video, stunned at what he watched: the shattered dam, the flooded valley, the vast destruction. It wasn't so much the death that shocked him—he had seen too much of that already in his life—but the fact that it appeared so *real*, despite the dam standing in front of him, fully intact.

He looked at the business card and dialed Renzo's number.

"Cabral," the voice answered.

"You destroyed my life," Zane said evenly.

"Who is this?"

"You blew up the plane, you killed all those men, and pinned it on me."

The line went dead. Zane redialed, but Renzo didn't pick up. No surprise that Renzo wouldn't answer the phone again, but he realized he had an easy way to get him to talk.

He typed in a text message and hit send. Within seconds, Zane's phone rang.

"Where are they?" Renzo yelled.

"Mom and Dad?" Zane asked. "Right where I left them a few hours ago."

"You son of bitch, I'll rip your lungs—"

"Believe me, I'm going to give you the chance, but don't you want to know where they are first?"

"Where?"

"Carter's a smart fucker, always three steps ahead of everyone."

"What do you mean?"

"They're in a house in the dam's floodplain. If you blow the dam and kill the president, you kill your folks. Let's see how much you believe in your cause now."

Silence.

"Oh, and don't bother running...you know I can find anyone anywhere, and I'm coming for you."

"Where are my parents?" Renzo said into his phone.

"You don't think I'd be foolish enough to trust you, do you?" Carter said. "I don't trust anyone, which is why I always give myself a little insurance. Money has a way of buying a loyalty that's only second to blood and sometimes even stronger than blood, in the case of your tattooed cousin, Erik. You didn't think I knew what you were doing: you, Kasper, Tuslav, Popov, and Fetizos?"

Renzo didn't reply.

"I've known your plan for weeks. I've been monitoring Tuslav and your tattooed friends." Carter paused. "Careful who you trust."

"You son of a—"

"Shhh," Carter interrupted, "seems you have a problem. Mom and Dad will get washed away with everyone else."

Nick ran to the door of Byram Castle. Locked. He turned and ran around the structure, through the gardens and down the steep hill, to the base of the stone building. He remembered the balcony door, the one he'd emerged from twelve hours from now. He pulled it open and ran through the dark, up the granite stairs to the first sub-level. He ran in the kitchen, tearing open drawers, searching shelves, rummaging through bags of tools, looking for a weapon, something that could at least give him a chance to kill Carter before he killed his family. He grabbed a pair of vice-grip pliers, tucking them in his pocket, but found no knives or make-shift weapons.

Julia and Katy were on the dam, out in the open, held by Carter Bull, a man who hadn't hesitated to kill his daughter once already.

Nick needed to get close, needed an element of surprise, but more than that, he needed a weapon.

And time was running out.

Renzo stood on the westerly hill, looking down at the dam a quarter mile away as he clicked off the call. He pulled out the smart key, turned, and looked at his men.

"What are you waiting for?" Kasper said. "Do it."

Renzo looked at the open land in front of the dam, the valley filled with homes directly in the floodplain. If his parents were down there, the house would be destroyed; everything would be fifty feet underwater. He had no way to find them, no time to search every residence.

"Not yet," Renzo said.

Kasper snatched the smart key out of Renzo's hand and pushed the center button three times.

"No!" Renzo shouted.

But nothing happened.

"What the hell?" growled Kasper.

"You guys must have screwed it up." Renzo heard the relief in his own voice.

"No." Kasper shook his head, looking at the key. "The antenna may be broken, but if anyone tries to rip the relay out of the ground or pull any of the leads, the dam blows. We just need to get closer to the relay."

"How close?" asked Renzo

"We need to be within fifty yards of the dam."

Renzo turned to Kasper, snatched the smart key back, and tucked it in his jacket pocket. "Do that again and I'll kill you."

Marcus ran along the shoreline, his heart pounding in his ears as he scanned the ground looking for the relay cable. He had no idea what it looked like. He feared it had been camouflaged or buried. In which case, they were screwed. He glanced at his watch. He had never felt the weight of time upon his shoulders more than he did now.

Dreyfus climbed down from the tree, the four-foot antenna in his hand. He traced the antenna wire down, running along the lake's edge, through the trees and brush. The relay box had to be on land. It had to be small, containing the feed from the antenna and the relay to the dam explosives embedded deep below the surface of the reservoir.

Dreyfus traced the antenna wire until it led to a small, blue metal box. A rubber-coated wire ran from the box into the reservoir, snaking down to the dam's underwater base and the explosives.

He pulled out and quickly dialed his phone. "Marcus?"

"Yep."

"I've got it. I'm a quarter mile north of the dam. Hurry."

Dreyfus stuffed his phone in his pocket and leaned over the blue box. He peered around it, looking for triggers, booby traps, deadman's switches that would set off the explosives instead of disabling them. Pulling out his screwdriver, he carefully loosened the four top screws and lifted the cover to find a spaghetti-like mess of wires, diodes, and resistors. He shined his flashlight inside but had no idea how the contraption was wired.

Dreyfus didn't hear Popov come up behind him until he was two feet away. He quickly rolled as the man lunged with a large knife. Dreyfus leapt to his feet as Popov jabbed and swiped, his blade glinting in the rays of the morning sunlight.

Dreyfus grabbed a thick branch from the ground, swinging at Popov, hitting him in the head and stunning him. He swung again, shattering the terrorist's nose and crushing his eye socket. Popov pulled away, then lunged, this time plunging the blade into Dreyfus's chest. Dreyfus tried to ignore the pain as he smashed the limb into Popov's temple again and again until the terrorist fell to the forest floor.

Dreyfus sagged to the ground, looking at the box only a few feet away. He struggled to crawl, clawing at the ground, pulling himself forward as the blood pumped from his wounds, his strength ebbing with every beat of his heart.

The two-foot distance felt like miles as he belly-crawled, his hand finally touching the box. He dug his hand inside, grasping the wires... but it was too late. His eyes shut as he rolled over and died.

Zane marched a limping Renzo down the path, six feet ahead of him, gun at his head. They came to the roadway that led to the spillway on the eastern side of the dam. Zane shoved Renzo out onto a narrow metal walkway that jutted fifty feet out over the water, until they came to a locked gate ten feet above the water's edge. Zane placed his gun on the metal decking fifteen feet behind him, then returned to Renzo.

"JC...." Renzo said. "What the hell—"

But he never finished his sentence as Zane hit him hard in the jaw. Renzo immediately hit back, harder, although he was no match with his injured leg. Zane was also bigger, faster, and stronger. But what gave Zane the critical advantage was his hate for the man who'd destroyed his life. Zane hit Renzo again and again, passing and penetrating his blocks and parries. He threw him against the gate, elbowing his skull, then kicking him hard in the chest, once, and again, driving all of his power into the man until the fencing bent and two hinges snapped, nearly pouring Renzo into the reservoir below. Renzo drew back his fist, but it was a mistake. He'd left himself open, and Zane sent a blow to the sweet spot by his ear. Renzo was out cold before he hit the ground.

Zane grabbed the gate and pulled it from its hinges.

Two minutes later, Renzo was lashed to the chain-link gate with cords made from his belt and clothing; his arms and legs splayed on his makeshift crucifix, propped upright against the fence, teetering on the walkway's edge above the reservoir. Zane slapped him hard across the face. Renzo's eyelids parted slightly as his eyes tried to focus.

"You set me up," Zane said from inches away. "You ruined my life."

Realization washed through Renzo, his arms tensing, fighting his bonds, struggling like a chained animal as he came to.

He spoke slowly and deliberately: "I did what I did at Carter's direction. He used you, and he used me."

"You were going to kill the president—"

"Carter's plan was to shoot him, shoot them all."

"Don't hide behind him," Zane said. "You were going to commit an atrocity."

"You don't understand—"

"You were not only going to drown the president, the man you swore to protect with your life, but thousands more." Zane rifled through Renzo's pockets. "If I could go back in time, I'd let your ass fall out of the sky, and smile as you hit the ground." He found a wallet, some receipts, and nothing else. "Where is it?"

"What?"

"The detonator?"

Fear blossomed in Renzo's eyes.

"Let me show you something." Zane twisted Renzo's head, pointing it toward a line of houses. "Back there behind the stand of pines. There's a house right in the path of the floodwaters."

Renzo looked from the houses to Zane, blinking, waiting.

"That's where I tucked your mother and father. They're alive, but—"

Renzo cut him off. "Then we all die for the greater good."

"Fine," Zane said. "You first."

He kicked the detached gate, letting it tumble backward until it and Renzo hit the water with resounding slap.

Renzo struggled to free himself from the heavy gate, but quickly sunk, pulled to the depths. His mind was a jumble of panic. He had never imagined failure, never imagined dying. Despite all of the death he had delivered in war, all of his fellow soldiers he had placed in the crosshairs, he never thought *he* would be the victim, never believed himself anything but invincible. He frantically pulled at his bonds, but the effort was futile as the gate dragged him down. At thirty feet, his ears throbbed from the pressure. At fifty feet the pain became excruciating, as if his lungs were on fire. At ninety feet, his eardrums imploded. He struggled to not breathe as white blotches danced before his eyes.

At three hundred feet, his lungs gave out, water pouring in as he sank to a cold, dark hell.

Kasper watched from the van as Renzo was kicked into the lake. His only regret that he hadn't done it himself. He'd feared that Renzo would find a conscience and abandon their plan.

He held the smart key in his hand, having snatched it from Renzo's jacket pocket when he was pulling him behind the rock in the parking lot. He considered pressing it now, but he had to wait.

He didn't give a shit about Renzo, Renzo's parents, or anyone else. But brothers were brothers. Most of the freedom fighters were family or the remnants of families that had been killed, shattered by war. If you let your brothers die, then what were you fighting for?

He would wait for Popov to check the antenna and get clear of the dam, and then he'd unleash hell.

Marcus ran through the woods, under brush, leaping fallen trees and rocks as he searched the water's edge until he saw it up ahead: a body, motionless by the shoreline.

"No!" Marcus shouted as the realization hit him.

He raced to Dreyfus's side, leaned over him, checking his wounds, listening for a pulse, shook him, gave him two mouth-to-mouth breaths, and began CPR, rhythmically pumping. At thirty seconds, he gave him another breath and began more chest compressions.

"Come on buddy, don't do this to me...."

He continued, focusing, praying with each pump on Dreyfus's chest, but there was no reaction. His friend was dead.

The snap of a branch brought Marcus to his feet. He heard the movement of uneven steps through the woods and raced toward it, deeper into the thicket.

Ahead, Marcus spied Popov, bloody and limping, stumbling up the hill.

He drew his gun and charged.

Nick ran atop the easterly side of the dam, a two-lane road running the course of the half-mile structure but closed to vehicles since 9/11.

A hundred yards ahead, he saw Katy in Julia's lap, sitting near the edge of the dam, the four-hundred-foot drop to the plaza only a few feet away. His eyes sought Carter, then spied him fifty yards beyond his family.

Nick sprinted to their side. Julia looked up at Nick without a word.

Nick pulled out his pocket knife.

"Daddy...?"

"Hi, honey."

"Nick," Julia said as she looked up into his eyes. "If we die—"

"You're not going to die." Nick quickly cut her free, then helped her to her feet, looked her in the eyes, and said, "Run."

"It's a beautiful morning, isn't it Nick?" Carter said as he walked along the top of the dam, his gun on display as he came to a stop beside them.

"Let them go."

"Where's Zane?" Carter asked. "I know you didn't kill him. I don't think he's killable."

"He had a change of heart," Nick said.

"Really?" A hint of concern creased the corners of the older soldier's eyes.

"Let them go." Nick lifted up the pocket watch, held in the jaws of the vice-grip pliers. "Or I crush it."

Carter lifted his gun. "I could just shoot you now, step back an hour, and take it from your sleeping self."

Nick didn't flinch.

"You and your wife will both be in dreamland. I'll kill you all with no one to stop me. And I'll have both watches."

"You don't get it, do you?" Nick smiled. "Our run's over. Time's up—that's it. *This* is it. This is reality. Death's permanent now."

"For you, yes," Carter said. "But I'll figure out the reset. I know there's a reset. Shamus Hennicot will tell me. Bigger picture, Nick. The bigger picture is always more important."

"No. You'll let the two of them go," Nick said evenly. "Let them walk away."

"Or what?"

Nick held up the watch with the vice-grips. "I'll crush it, render it beyond use...beyond even telling time."

Carter looked at Julia and Katy, then back to Nick. "How do I know you won't crush it after I let them go?"

"You have my word."

Carter thought for a moment. "They've got two minutes to get away."

Nick turned to Julia, pulling her close with his free hand, and kissed her on the lips as if it were the first time. He looked into her teary eyes; he didn't need to say it, she knew.

"Go," he said.

"No, I'm not leaving you."

"Take Katy and go, *now!*" He knew she'd understand. It was about saving Katy now.

Reluctantly, Julia turned and walked quickly for the west end side of the dam, leading Katy by the hand.

"Hand it over," Carter said.

"Not until they're at the end of the dam, out of range."

"You think I'd shoot a woman and child in the back?"

Nick held up the watch in the vice-grips.

"Fine," Carter said. "We'll wait."

Marcus emerged from the woods and spied the white van by the entrance to the top of the dam. As he got closer, he saw Kasper looking out over the valley, the smart key in his hand.

"He cried just before he died." Marcus held up Popov's ripped Metallica t-shirt, covered in blood, while aiming his gun with the other.

Kasper stared at Marcus, clearly realizing what the shirt meant. Instead of speaking or running for the van, he charged Marcus.

Marcus calmly aimed the gun.

With the crack of the bullet, Kasper dodged right, and the bullet hit him in his left shoulder. He continued charging, bull-rushing Marcus, his fist crunching the side of Marcus's head as his other hand snatched the red-hot barrel and flung the pistol away.

Unarmed, Marcus unleashed a flurry of blows, punch after punch to the thick man's ribs, their cracking met with a howling cry from Kasper. But the killer never let up. He matched punch for punch, each strike going for the kill, targeting Marcus's throat, temples, and chest.

Instead of acknowledging the pain, Marcus looked for opportunity and finally he found it, connecting a fist squarely to the side of Kasper's jaw. The behemoth of a man went down instantly, hitting the ground hard. Marcus dived atop him, but Kasper threw a handful of dirt in Marcus's face, blinding him momentarily.

Kasper rolled out from under Marcus and leapt up, wrapping his arm around Marcus's neck, spinning him into a headlock and cutting off his air supply. His powerful tattooed arms throbbed with effort as he crushed the life out of his opponent.

Marcus's hand swept back, grabbing at arms, uselessly slapping at his hips, trying to get a hold of anything. He grabbed at Kasper's waist, hoping for a knife, then Kasper's pockets, praying for anything.

Nothing.

Desperation filled Marcus as he tried in vain to pull Kasper's arm from his throat. It was useless: he had no leverage against the man's power; the effort only wasted his last bit of oxygen, his last trace of strength.

Marcus thrust his hands into his own pockets, seeking a weapon but only finding his lucky poker chip, which wasn't bringing him any luck; his wallet; and the smart key for his car. If only it were like his old car keys, serving as a stabbing instrument in a pinch.

As the stars whirled in his vision, darkness creeping at the periphery, Marcus fell to instinct and panic. His hands shot up and back like a wild animal in the throes of death, grabbing at anything. His thumb stabbed at Kasper's eye, fingers dug into his captor's nostrils and pulled, tearing the flesh from flesh, ripping his nose wide open.

Kasper screamed and his grip loosened. Marcus slipped out of the hold and scrambled along the ground, gasping for air, his only thought to fill his burning lungs.

As he turned back to defend himself, a bullet hit him in the knee, and he collapsed to the ground. He stared at Kasper's torn, bloody face as he stood beside his van, Marcus's gun in his left hand, the smart key detonator held high in his right.

He pushed the button.

Julia ran as fast as she could, Katy in her arms now, doing her best not to stumble and fall as she felt a bullseye on her back.

She made it to the western edge of the dam, out of breath, filled with fear, not for herself, but for Nick, who was still on the dam with Carter.

Nick watched Julia make it off the dam. Without a word, he squeezed and crushed the watch with the vice-grips.

Carter tensed, raising his gun at Nick. "I had a feeling you were going to do that."

"Then why didn't you just shoot me?"

"As much I'd like to have two watches," Carter said, "it's more important that you *not* have it."

"Why?"

"Well, your death would be a bonus, given what you know. Maybe more valuable than having two watches. And with no second watch, no one can chase me through time like you did with Zane. No one can stop me."

"Stop you from doing what?"

"I could go back a year and—"

"No." Nick shook his head.

"What do you mean, no?"

"I told you. Each use is for twelve hours, no more. It's a built-in failsafe, and there are more like it. You only get one reset every twenty-four hours, which means you can't go back weeks, months, or years, and rewrite history."

"I don't need to rewrite history, Nick. I just need to control it. Manipulating twelve hours is plenty. Think of the implications for battle, for war; being able to correct mistakes, defeating your enemy by knowing their every move before they make it. Knowing the decisions people make, then going back an hour to capitalize on them. There's no one we can't defeat with this."

"You make it sound like you're doing your country a favor."

Carter squinted in the morning light, a smile spreading across his face. "Okay, then. How about manipulating markets for easy windfalls? How do you think the Hennicots amassed all their power and money? Only the person who controls the watch will know of what could have been, what was, and what will never be. And what happens here on this dam will never have occurred."

"Yes, it will," Nick said. "What happens now can't be undone. The twelve hours on that watch are up. That's it."

Carter thought a moment. "Unless I reset it."

"You have no idea how it works," Nick said.

"Shamus will tell me."

"He'd die before telling you a thing." Nick looked at the lip of the dam, ten feet away. He thought of pushing Carter but knew a bullet would stop his effort before it came to pass.

"You know how to do it, don't you?"

"Do what?"

"Reset it."

"It can't be reset that easily—"

"Yet it *can* be reset." Carter aimed his gun at Nick. "Show me or die."

Nick turned and looked at Julia in the distance. He couldn't leave her alone with Katy. But he also couldn't let Carter keep Shamus's watch.

He couldn't stop thinking of Katy, of her smile, her laugh, her innocence, and how none of this had anything to do with her. She had died once when Nick had failed to stop Carter. He wouldn't let that happen again.

"And after I kill you, I'll kill Julia and your daughter." Carter pointed in their direction. "If you do show me how to reset the watch...well, I'll let 'em live. I'll go back before all this happened and let all of you live. She'll forget it all just like Zane did. You will too. You can live happily ever after, never knowing any of this happened. Your friends'll be alive, you'll be alive. Or..." Carter placed the gun to Nick's head as he held out the watch. "Show me."

Nick considered Carter's offer: Forget this...none of it will ever have happened. No nightmares for Julia or him. No trauma for Katy....

Nick closed his eyes and took the watch.

Kasper pushed the button on the remote again, three times, and waited, anticipating the heavy thud, the shaking of the ground. But it never came.

Kasper hit the button again. And this time he heard it. In the distance; a beeping; a car horn beeping. He looked back at Marcus bleeding upon the ground, smiling a shit-eating grin as he held up a smart key.

"Oops," Marcus smiled. "Look what I found in your pocket when I was looking for a weapon. If only you weren't so busy trying to choke the life out of me.... You can have *my* key if you'd like."

And without another word, Marcus cocked back his arm and threw the smart key, sending it through the air until it landed with a splash in the reservoir.

Kasper raised his gun, walked over to Marcus, and aimed. Marcus bowed his head and said a silent prayer—

Kasper's head snapped to the right, gore splattering the ground next to him, his body following it to the dirt.

Ten feet behind him, Zane lowered his gun.

Nick took the pocket watch from Carter and pressed the crown, opening the lid and looking down at the dial that he'd seen for the first time three years ago. Dreyfus's words of warning echoed in his head while Marcus's voice cautioned him about playing God. Nick's own conscience screamed at him.

He turned around toward the sun, allowing its glow to reflect off the silver-and-gold case, the reflection dancing upon the road beneath them. He let the sun warm his cheeks, feeling the rays paint his skin as it had when he was child....

Nick dropped the watch, the heel of his booted foot crunching down, the pressure shattering the glass, the case, and the watch to pieces.

"No!" Carter cried at the destruction of his dreams.

"This is the power of God," Nick said. "And you're no God."

Carter closed his eyes, taking a deep breath. "And neither are you." He raised his gun and pulled the trigger.

The small, one-inch bullet was like a two-ton truck, hitting Nick in the chest, the force knocking him off his feet. He could barely breath, his chest on fire, spreading up his neck and down into his legs. He hit the ground, blood blossoming from his torso, a chill running through his veins as the broken watches lay on the ground beside him.

"No..." Carter moaned again as he looked at the shattered watch on the roadway. He spun and aimed the gun at Nick's head.

Nick closed his eyes. He knew he would die; he had known it when he kissed Julia goodbye. He'd known when he seduced Carter with his exaggerated story of resetting the watch. Now, his mind held tight to the image of Katy and all that was pure about his daughter....

The gunshot echoed across the reservoir as the bullet pierced Carter's hand, shredding it, his gun falling to the ground with bits of his fingers. As he sank to his knees in agony, Carter looked up to see Zane marching toward him, smoking gun at his side.

Zane walked straight up to Carter and kicked his former commanding officer in the chest, sending him sprawling toward the edge of the dam.

"No," Carter pleaded as he tried to stand, his bloodied hand clutched to his chest. "Please—"

Zane kicked again, this time catching Carter in the head. He reeled back to the edge of the precipice and tumbled over the lip of Killian Dam.

As he fell, Carter caught the edge with his good hand. His legs kicked air, trying to gain a foothold, as his feet scraped the stone blocks, seeking purchase four hundred feet above the concrete plaza.

"JC!" Carter screamed. "You can't do this!"

Zane had formulated a speech, the words he would say to the man who had made him, who'd betrayed, and used him in the worst of ways—ways he couldn't even remember.

Zane stepped on his former superior's hand, crushing the small bones as he aimed his gun at Carter's head.

A moment later, Zane lowered his pistol and tucked it in his shoulder holster.

He stared into Carter's desperate eyes....

And lifted his foot.

With no grip left, Carter fell. He plummeted nearly a hundred feet before his foot hit the face of dam, spinning him like a top, end over end, for three hundred feet more. He was fully alive as his cartwheeling body slammed over and over again against the blocks, shredding his skin to the bone; his neck finally snapped as his fall ended four hundred feet below.

Julia ran back across the top of the top of dam faster than she had ever run. She fell at Nick's side, out of breath, tears pouring down her face. She saw air bubbles speckling the blood pouring from the hole in his chest and put her hand atop it, pressing as hard as she could.

"No...please don't leave me," she cried. "I can't survive without you."

"It's okay," Nick whispered. "I'll never leave you. I promise. I'll always be in your heart." He struggled for breath. "Tell Katy to be good. Tell her to always smile." Blood trickled from the corner of his mouth. "Tell her Daddy loves her.... And tell her I'm sorry."

"You can't die!" Julia said through sobs. "Please..."

"It's okay. You'll be fine.... It will all be fine...."

As the silence slowly fell around them, Nick died in her arms.

Julia looked from Nick's now-peaceful face to the antique pocket watch beside him. The crushed device was still working, its hands still moving, the second hand sweeping to the top of the hour. She stared at it as it ticked toward eight o'clock.

As the second hand swept over the twelve, continuing its journey around the watch face, nothing happened, nothing changed. The world irreversibly marched forward, around and beyond Nick's death, while Julia's heart broke.

CHAPTER 1

8 AM, AGAIN

Julia sat on the dam road, cradling Nick's head in her lap. In an ambulance at the entrance to the top of the dam, Katy sat on a gurney, using an iPad given to her by an EMT to distract her. The rest of the paramedics stood to the side. It was already too late to save Nick; they wouldn't interrupt Julia's mourning.

Marcus approached her, a single crutch helping him walk along the top of the dam, his leg heavily bandaged. He collapsed awkwardly beside her and brushed tear-soaked hair from her cheeks.

Without a word, he gently lifted Nick's head from her lap and lowered it to the concrete roadway.

"I can't leave him," Julia said between sobs.

"You won't," Marcus said. "They just need to do a few things."

He rose with his crutch and gave Julia a long, one-handed embrace while she wept, her soul dying with each breath.

He finally guided her toward the ambulance where Katy waited.

"Where's Daddy?" Katy asked as she reached up and took her mother's hand. "When can we go home? I want to go home."

Julia had no idea how to explain it to Katy—how to tell her that Daddy would never be coming home again.

Behind the ambulance, hundreds of police, emergency, and military vehicles lined the narrow road. News trucks filled the parking lot of Byram Castle below; Julia had never seen so much attention paid to her town.

The area below the dam teemed with FBI, police, and military personnel; divers had already dropped into the reservoir. A small team of law-enforcement officers—Julia didn't catch their names— approached her at the ambulance and questioned her, but her answers were few, a mix of true and feigned confusion.

At 8:30, they finally allowed her to go.

Marcus played with Katy, lifting her up and down as she clung to his crutch, still asking for Daddy but still unaware what had happened.

A long black limo forced its way around the official vehicles, a Byram Hills Police escort clearing the way. It pulled up beside Julia, the door opened, and Shamus Hennicot stepped out.

The elevator descended into the earth, the fifteen-second ride seeming to take hours.

According to Shamus, the authorities were still piecing together what had happened. Navy divers had removed the detonators from the Semtex charges buried in the dam. Renzo's body had been recovered and was en route to the morgue, along with Carter Bull's broken corpse and the bodies of the three terrorists. At the moment, beyond the deaths on and near the dam, the media were in the dark, unaware not only of what had *almost* happened, but also that the president and his Russian and Akbiquestani counterparts were actually in Byram Hills and on the verge of signing peace accords. It would take days of piecing together the terrorist plot and how close the world came to the edge of disaster before the full story was known.

As the doors slid open, Charlie stood there at attention, greeting Shamus and Julia with a bow of his head, his eyes conveying his sorrow. He ushered them through the airlock, lounge, and into the hallway. Shamus remained at Julia's side as she walked past a line of agents, each lowering their head in respect as Charlie had.

President McManus emerged from the conference room and greeted her with outstretched hands.

"My deepest condolences, Ms. Quinn." He took her hand. "On behalf of not only everyone here, but the entire country, we honor your husband's sacrifice and are heartbroken by your loss."

Julia could barely contain her tears. She struggled to respond.

"Ms. Quinn," President Egorenko said, taking her other hand. "Your husband saved all of us. Russia is eternally grateful for his and your sacrifice."

Finally, she accepted the condolences of Akbiquestani Prime Minster Kharda, who spoke in his native tongue through his translator.

"On behalf of my country and the world, thank you," the translator said, as the prime minister bowed his head. "His sacrifice allowed us to achieve peace."

Julia nodded to each of them and continued down the hall with Shamus, Charlie three steps behind.

They descended to the lower level, walked down the hall, and arrived at Shamus's vault. "Please be sure we're not disturbed and that no one else enters," Shamus told Charlie.

"Of course, sir." Charlie nodded and stepped back.

"My dear," Shamus said when they were alone, "my heart breaks for you. To see you in such pain crushes my soul."

Julia reached in her purse and pulled out the pair of shattered watches, handing them to Shamus. "My understanding of what happened today is...confused at best." She paused. "I experienced the death of my daughter, Shamus.... I mean, it happened, but she was alive again this morning. And..."

"Nick," Shamus said.

Julia nodded stifled a sob. "How's a person to know what's real and what's...potential? In the past? The future?"

"I know." He looked at the pocket watches. "It's not a rational tool. And it's so utterly corruptible. It's my fault," he said. "I not only used it, I kept it. I let it *exist*. Even knowing that those with the purest intentions can bring about the worst consequences."

Julia placed her hand in the vault's palm-reader while she punched in a series of numbers before stepping aside. Shamus pocketed the watches and repeated her actions, hand on the reader while he typed in a second set of numbers. A thunk sounded from within and the large metal door creaked open. Julia opened it wide enough for Shamus and her to step inside.

Bright fluorescent lights flickered on, illuminating a large room nearly forty feet square, filled with rows of metal shelves. Dozens of filing cabinets lined the four walls and a large table stood in the center of the room.

Julia walked down the main aisle to the table, where she saw that all the shelves in the middle of the room that faced the table were filled with mahogany boxes like the one in Dreyfus's saferoom, hundreds of them, all identical and cramming the shelves, each indistinguishable from the next.

Julia turned to Shamus with a questioning look.

"Welcome to the room of my greatest fears," Shamus said.

"Why? What are those?" she asked, taking in the sheer quantity of mahogany boxes.

"It's not easy to explain."

"Try me."

"All right. Bear with me." Shamus took a long breath. "You enter a room to find a mahogany box. You open it to discover a single, elegant pocket watch and remove it. You activate the watch and it carries you back two hours to the same place you were those two hours before. You now enter that same room, where the same mahogany box lies before you.

"Every time the watch is used," Shamus explained slowly, "and goes backward in time with you—now listen very carefully—in whatever hour you have leapt back to, the same watch that's in your hand remains in that same mahogany box from which you took it." He smiled and waited as Julia let it sink in. "Confusing, I know. The watch in your hand is the same watch as the one in the box because two hours earlier you had not yet taken it out.

"Here's the really strange part: When the watch finishes its twelve-hour journey back, you become part of forward-moving time and reality, just like everyone else, right?"

Julia nodded uncertainly.

"When you arrive back to that hour that you first took the watch from the box, you find there are now *two* watches: the one in your hand and the one in the box. Perfect clones of one another."

Julia squinted, trying to understand.

"Put simply," said Shamus, "every time a watch is used, it duplicates itself."

Julia nodded more certainly now, looking to the shelves. "That's a lot of boxes."

"Yes," Shamus said. "It's a lot of boxes."

Julia took in the vast collection of identical boxes. "Do they all work?"

"Every single one. After a watch is used, it resets itself but can't be used again until twenty-four hours have passed. It's a built-in failsafe. That means there are only so many mistakes that can be corrected. You can't go back in time and back and back. You can't go to the last century, last week, or even two days ago. Only twelve hours."

"If you fear them so much, why keep them? Why not destroy them?"

Shamus indicated the crushed watches. "Even broken, they're dangerous. I don't profess to know how they work, but if someone were to reverse-engineer them and figure it out...."

"My god," she said. "There are so many of them...."

Shamus nodded. "Now, as far as Nick, Zachariah, and Paul knew, there were only the two watches. So, to the rest of the world, there are *none* left, since these two were broken. Only you and I know the truth."

Julia looked at the hundreds of mahogany cases. "You've used the watch so many times...."

"Yes."

"For dire reasons, I'm sure."

"You have no idea the horrible things I've seen and managed to erase from time: deaths, tragedies, disasters...mistakes. Thirty years ago, I stopped. I realized that the disasters I erased could, in fact, be compounded by my actions. Save an innocent child, kill an entire city. It wasn't my place to play God."

"And the files?" Julia pointed at the surrounding cabinets.

"History that never happened." Shamus paused. "I documented it all, every time: terrible things, lessons learned, worlds saved, people who died."

"Why?"

"So I wouldn't forget. So I could pass on wisdom gleaned from awful errors that need never occur again. We learn from our mistakes, Julia, not our successes."

"No one will ever know what Nick did today," she said.

"He lived nightmares that we can't imagine. And it's not the first time. Three years ago, he went through hell to save you, my dear," Shamus told her. "But that's a story for another day. Now, it's your turn. Any one you wish," he said, gesturing to the multitude of mahogany boxes.

"I don't understand."

Shamus lifted a box at random from a shelf and placed it on the table. He pulled two keys from his pocket, each oddly shaped, exquisitely crafted, and passed them to Julia.

She inserted the first key into the brass slot on the left and the second into the steel slot in the middle. Shamus loosened his tie, reached into his shirt, and pulled the third key from around his neck. He inserted it into the silver slot on the right.

"Ready?"

Julia nodded.

They turned all three keys at the same time. The box creaked as its internal tumblers turned and fell into place.

"As you said," Shamus told her, "we can scarcely imagine how Nick suffered—three years ago *and* today. He deserves to live. And you and Katy have gone through too much not to have him at your side."

Julia reached over and slowly raised the lid and stared at the beautiful gold-and-silver pocket watch that lay inside.

CHAPTER 13

6:00 PM

The bells chimed their melody, then tolled the hour six times—the familiar sounds of the grandfather clock echoing through the stony halls. Nick and Marcus had carried the huge clock out of Nick's foyer, tucked it in a truck, and placed it by the door in the lobby of Byram Castle as a donation to the town.

Nick'd had more than his fill of timepieces.

The party was in full swing. Byram Castle overflowed with guests, the celebratory mood not only for the Fourth of July, but the signing of the accords ushering in world peace.

There was no mention in the news of the terrorists picked up in a three-a.m. raid earlier in the day, nor the arrest of Colonel Carter Bull on the charge of treason. Both incidents had occurred during the abrupt replacement of Renzo Cabral as the head of the president's Secret Service detail. Nor would the public know about the SEAL team that had been working underwater all day, rendering the explosive charges at the base of the dam inert.

Senator Chase walked along a line of well-wishers, nodding with a strained smile as he angled for the door, trying to escape after two hours of glad-handing, too much wine, and not enough recognition for his role in achieving world peace.

Chase came to the final man, who extended his hand. As they shook, Chase's eyes were on the door, his perfunctory words spoken in haste. "Thank you for your support."

As he turned to exit, the man didn't release his hand. The senator's Secret Service escorts saw it happen and moved. Chase turned back in annoyance and looked his constituent in the eye.

His heart nearly exploded, emotion washing through him as he saw the man he'd thought dead, the son he believed he'd lost.

"Hello, Dad," Zane said.

As Nick surveyed the festivities, he smiled; things could not have gone better. He'd only had to fake a smile twice tonight, both times in deference to Coach Chase. He'd found more than enough mini-hot dogs and Coke. And Julia had not been this relaxed and joyous in months.

Everyone Nick cared about was there: Martin and Yolanda, Kirstin and Rocco, John and Anita, Chris Knudsen, Sue and Brent, Marcus and Anissa, Shamus and Katherine, Paul and Sandy Dreyfus, Bill and Sheila Shannon. These were not only his friends, they were his family, the people he trusted and loved.

"How was kitesurfing this morning?" asked Dreyfus as he approached Nick and Marcus.

"Amazing," Marcus said. "I jumped thirty-one feet today. Nick's still trying to bust through thirty."

"Don't listen to him," Nick said. "I always jump higher."

Julia walked over, pulled Nick aside and kissed him, long and deep. "I love you," she said.

Nick pulled back, smiling. "I love you."

"Thank you."

"For?"

Julia smiled. "For all the things I've never thanked you for. For the things you do for me every day, for the things you do for me in my dreams."

Nick took her hand, their fingers entwining—

"Mommy!" Katy dashed through the crowd and wrapped herself in her parents' legs.

Nick picked her up. "How about we go get you a Shirley Temple with extra cherries?"

"Yes, pease." Katy looked adorable in her blue princess dress.

"I need another Coke." Nick looked at Julia. "Another Malbec?"

"Perfect."

She walked over to Shamus, who was heading for the door. She kissed him on the cheek while surreptitiously slipping the pocket watch into his palm. "Thank you."

"You're welcome, my dear," Shamus said. "It looks like we did well."

She looked around the room, nodding. "Yes. I'm so grateful for the second chance."

"As am I, though I am a bit tired."

"Thanks for leading the way."

"It had been a while, but...." The nonagenarian smiled wearily and gave a small shrug.

For twelve upside-down hours, Julia had experienced but a fraction of what Nick had gone through. It remained beyond her imagining: the struggle and sacrifice her husband had endured for her, the pain he had suffered at seeing Katy's and her deaths, at seeing the death of his friends, the president, and thousands of innocents.

She couldn't conceive of the nightmares he faced. Her journey had been more straightforward, stepping back in time along with Shamus and using every ounce of their hard-won reputations, credibility, and social and political capital to convince the authorities of the threats and to right the wrongs of Renzo and Carter Bull before they happened. Saving her husband and countless others was obviously the critical part, but the fact that Nick's memory of the trauma he'd seen and suffered no longer existed gave her the greatest peace. He had gone to hell and back and given his life for Katy and her.

Nick walked over and handed Julia a glass of wine. "You look exhausted."

She looked at him, their eyes locking, sharing the feeling that warmed them, a love that neither could live without. She clinked her glass against his. "Always my hero."

"I don't know why," Nick said, "but it feels like it's been a really long day."

"Yeah," Julia nodded. "A really, *really* long day...but worth every second."

The End

ACKNOWLEDGMENTS

Life is far more enjoyable when you work with people you like and respect. I would personally like to thank:

Heather King and everyone at Post Hill Press and Permuted Press.

Ed Stackler for keeping it all in tune with that amazing ability to understand what I'm trying to say.

Steve Fischer at APA for untangling the insanity and reorganizing it into success.

All the great people at Sony Television.

And head and shoulders above all, Cynthia Manson. First and foremost for your continued friendship—it is something I truly treasure. Thank you for your innovative thinking, your continued faith in the face of adversity, and unlimited tenacity. Your inspiration, guidance, and business acumen is exceeded by no one.

Thank you to my family:

To my children, you are the best part of my life. Richard, you are my mind, your brilliance and creativity knows no bounds; Marguerite, you are my heart, constantly reminding me of what is important in life—your style, grace under pressure, and sense of humor is an example to all. Isabelle, you are my soul, your laughter and inquisitive mind keeps my eyes open to the magic of this world we live in.

Most importantly, thank you, Virginia. Even in the craziest moments, you fill my heart with hope, opening my eyes to the joys of life that can become so obscured by the trials, tribulations, and tragedies in this journey.

I love that you greet every day with a smile and end every night with a kiss; that you walk through life with such beauty, grace, and passion; I love your never-say-die, hate-to-lose competitive spirit, and how it infects all around you. I love your heart, your warmth, your beauty, and your dark eyes that reflect your soul; I love the way you put everyone else first and then revel in their success; I love the way you fill a room with laughter and smiles when you enter and how the party is always over when you leave.

Thank you for being you, for being mine, for being everything that's good in my life, I love you with all my heart.

Finally, thank you to you, the reader, for taking the time to read my stories, for reaching out through your notes, tweets, letters, and emails. Your kind words inspire and fill me with the responsibility to never let you down.

—Richard

Thank you to you, the reader who has never heard of me but took a chance and purchased *The 13th Hour: Chaos*. And to those who took a chance in buying one of my prior novels, thanks for coming back for more.